D0948691

THE
Head
OF
Dionysos

THE
Head
OF
Dionysos

Anne Redmon

SINCLAIR-STEVENSON

First published in Great Britain in 1997
by Sinclair-Stevenson
an imprint of Reed International Books Ltd
Michelin House, 81 Fulham Road, London SW3 6RB
and Auckland, Melbourne, Singapore and Toronto

A CIP catalogue record for this book
is available at the British Library

ISBN 1 85619 677 1

Phototypeset in 11 on 13.25 point Ehrhardt
by Intype London Ltd
Printed and bound in Great Britain
by Clays Ltd, St Ives PLC

For Benedict, Zoë
and Ann Shearer

The characters in
The Head of Dionysos
are fictional and the situations
are purely imaginary.

Acknowledgements

THE MAIN action of *The Head of Dionysos* takes place in Salonika, the second most important city in Greece and the capital of Macedonia. I have called it Thessaloniki throughout the novel, for this is its Greek name and the major characters think of it in this way. I am indebted to the Society of Authors for an Authors Foundation Grant which enabled me to travel there and do the large amount of research I needed to complete the novel, the last in my *Byzantine Trilogy*.

Thessaloniki is a fascinating city built up in successive layers from its foundation in 316 BC. It is not, however, easy to discover without help. I am most particularly grateful to Vassilis Papadimitriou, Press Officer with the Greek Embassy in London, for providing introductions to eminent residents of the city, who were both hospitable and informative to me and my husband on our visit; we were also privileged to talk in depth to a number of archaeologists, who gave generously of their time and helped me to construct the conundrum surrounding the discovery of the Classical head of the title. Most of all, I would like to thank Dr Vassilis Gounaris, Curator of the Museum of Macedonian Struggle. Although this unusual collection is mentioned in a pejorative way by a disreputable character in the novel, it is essential for scholars of modern Greek history. And in equal measure I would like to thank Professor Dimitris Pantermalis, chief archaeologist of Pella, the ancient site near Thessaloniki, for the great pains he took to reveal to us the rich treasures of the ruined city.

Closer to home, I am indebted to Father Anthony Meredith SJ for his patient answers to numerous questions about the religious theme of the book, and to Clare Banyard. I would also like to thank Dr Hamish McMichen for medical information, Professor Jocelyn Hillgarth, the distinguished medieval historian, David Burton and especially Ann Shearer, to whom this book is partly dedicated, for steering me towards helpful reading matter on Dionysos.

Any inaccuracies are entirely my own.

Among histories and studies too numerous to mention, I have drawn most particularly on *Dionysus: Myth and Cult* by Walter F. Otto, translated by Robert B. Palmer (Indiana University Press, Bloomington and Indianapolis, 1965). In a more popular vein, those who might be interested in the ancient history of the area would be rewarded in reading *The Alexander Trilogy* (Penguin) by Mary Renault and *Thessaloniki: Old Town* by Agis I. Anastasiadis, in the Greek Traditional Architecture Series. 'Melissa' Publishing House has been very helpful, as has *Living in Turkey*, by Yerasimos, Guler and Rifat, Thames and Hudson, 1992.

Cast of Characters

The Head of Dionysos stands independently from *The Genius of the Sea* and *The Judgement of Solomon* in the *Byzantine Trilogy*. While some characters have their origins in the earlier books, it is not necessary to have read the first two novels to understand this one. I have compiled a cast list, mostly observing family affinities. This should serve to remind those who have already read the other novels in the trilogy of the characters who have gone before, and to introduce new readers to the pattern of relationships in a logical way.

Catherine Phocas – *a chief protagonist of* The Head of Dionysos. *She also played a large role in* The Judgement of Solomon.
Theologos Phocas (known as **Theo**) – *a shipowner and estranged husband of Catherine, a major character in* The Judgement of Solomon.
Xenia Phocas – *Theo's daughter and Catherine's adopted daughter, subject of* The Judgement of Solomon, *who also appears in* The Head of Dionysos.
Missy Kavanagh – *former mistress of Theo and biological mother to Xenia. Her story was told in* The Judgement of Solomon *but she is referred to in* The Head of Dionysos.

Isabelle, Lady Simon – *Catherine's mother, also a character in* The Judgement of Solomon.
Mother Mary of the Assumption (also known as **Beatrice**) – *Catherine's sister and Prioress of a Carmelite Monastery.*
Theresa Simon – *Catherine's sister, a farmer.*
Charles and Rosamund Simon – *Catherine's brother, a well-known publisher, and his American wife, whose story was told in* The Judgement of Solomon.

Marina Mason – *an expatriate American, Catherine's best friend and widow of*
Arthur Holt – *a famous poet. Their story was told in* The Genius of the Sea, *in which Marina was a chief protagonist.*
Paul Mason – *Marina's present husband and a doctor, also a major character in* The Genius of the Sea.

Maureen Doyle – *Marina's birth mother, who was discovered at the end of* The Genius of the Sea.

Maddy Horner – *Marina's adoptive mother and New York socialite, discussed in* The Genius of the Sea.

Gregory Lipitsin – *a dealer in antiquities, a character in* The Genius of the Sea.

The following group appear only in *The Head of Dionysos:*

Father Edward Knight – *an old Catholic priest, once adviser to*

Susannah Vaughan – *although dead when the* The Head of Dionysos *opens, she is one of its chief protagonists. She is also Catherine's first cousin.*

James Vaughan – *an elderly archaeologist who lives in Thessaloniki. He is Catherine's uncle and Lady Simon's brother.*

Nancy Vaughan (née Schuyler) – *Susannah's mother, also dead, from a rich American family.*

Phil Deals – *James Vaughan's eccentric companion, an American and Susannah's other first cousin through Nancy Schuyler.*

Leila Deals – *Nancy's sister and mother of Phil Deals.*

Geoffrey and Sandra Deals – *Phil's brother and sister-in-law.*

Dr Passides – *a distinguished Greek archaeologist.*

I

ALTHOUGH CATHERINE PHOCAS was anxious not to miss Father Knight's arrival, she had obscured herself at a small table behind a pillar in Zonar's Dionysos Restaurant so that she had to crane her neck to see the door. She had chosen this meeting place because it was central and respectable. Now she regretted her decision, for she had forgotten how easily she could still be recognized in Athens, where she had come resolved to break her ties with Greece altogether.

This stately café stands on unchanging principle near the Grande Bretagne Hotel, right on Venizelou, the broad boulevard which leads northwards from Sindagmatos Square to the less salubrious Omonia Square. However long ago it was established as a watering hole for Athenian gentry, its owners seem to have decided that its recipe for success needs no addition or correction. The walls are of an eternal ochre, the cakes and pastries stand rigidly expectant in the refrigerated display case, as if always ready to be of service to the discerning wives of politicians and shipowners who throughout the day and evening trickle in, with friends or husbands, to while away a fattening hour or two. The distinguished husbands, more interested in sugar futures than in cake, eke out ouzo or coffee while they discuss the market. The suggestion of Dionysiac revels built into the restaurant's name seems to be misconceived; even the thought of orgiastic abandon at one of the deeply polished little tables might draw a look of censure from the solemn waiters in green livery.

One such delivered a tall, cold *frappé* to Catherine, for which she thanked him in Greek; he raised his eyebrows in approval. She was not dressed like a tourist, but her elongated bone structure and fair complexion had always made her look suspect and foreign until she spoke. In fact, although Catherine now lived permanently in London, she had spent half her life in Greece. Her estranged husband Theo, himself a shipowner, had sometimes brought her and their daughter Xenia here for cakes and coffee on their visits to Athens from Chios, where they owned a large house. The memory of that time seemed to Catherine like a bizarre sequence from a nearly irretrievable dream. She even found herself fumbling now for Greek words; she had once been completely fluent.

It was early evening and the tables were filling up. Athenians trickled in, riding the tide of well-heeled tourists, and Catherine realized that she recognized many of the clientele by sight, if not by name. The recollection of these familiar faces and their thickening figures encased in the deadening respectability of formal jackets, skirts and blazers gave her the shudder of *déjà vu*. After a drink or a coffee, they would all move elsewhere for a late, substantial meal. It upset Catherine's stomach just to think of it.

Father Knight had never been to Athens before, and she wondered why she had assumed he could find his way here. What was more, although she had corresponded with him Catherine had never met the man, and had only the sketchiest idea of what he looked like. It was her sister Beatrice, now Prioress of the Carmelite Monastery near East Grinstead, who had set the whole thing up after their mother's funeral. Catherine was very nervous about meeting him.

She peered discreetly from behind the pillar to see if any new and lost-looking arrival might be scanning the now busy restaurant, and then glanced at her watch. It was 7 p.m. Although she had fixed the rendezvous for 6.30, she had meant to get away early in order to give Father Knight an hospitable surprise at the airport. Such a welcome would have shown her as willing . . . a dutiful if not zealous daughter of the Church. It was an ironic coincidence, she thought, that she had not been able to extricate herself in time from her lawyers, with whom she had spent an enervating afternoon. After four years of tranquillity without Theo, she had more or less made up her mind to divorce him.

Catherine sipped at her iced coffee without tasting it. Why had she not seen how upsetting the whole thing would be? She had travelled to Athens knowing that Theo was a comfortable distance away on business in New York, but, now her legal advisers had got the ball rolling, the speed and ruthlessness of its sudden momentum appalled her. Large sums of money were involved and large financial shifts. Any decision to divorce, it seemed, might mean selling the Chios house . . . That afternoon, she had spoken to Theo over the telephone, and now all her foregone conclusions seemed oddly superficial. The conversation had been more disturbing than she had imagined it would be . . . far more.

Feeling sick, she put down her glass. The very thought of a Catholic priest breathing down her neck for the next few weeks now struck her with the full horror of all that it implied. Divorce was no sin, she knew he would think, only remarriage, which she certainly did not contemplate. Even so, she had no wish to discuss her situation with such a person or even to argue it out in her mind in his presence. How could she have agreed to the mad scheme her sister Beatrice had proposed to her at the funeral?

Catherine had spent the last four years of her separation from Theo assessing the damage she had done to herself by disregarding her own feelings, and here she was, doing it again. How had she thought it possible to act as a guide to this elderly cleric at a time when so many familiar landmarks on her own inner map had been so recently demolished? She needed guidance herself, but not, she was certain, from the likes of him.

On the telephone, Theo had been kind, even tender to her about the recent death of her mother, and this had thrown her. Indeed, although he had accepted her decision as a consequence of the wrongs he had done her in the past, he had asked her to think it through. This was not at all what she had expected him to say; nor had she been prepared for the flat defeat in his voice. Was she sure, he had added, that she wasn't behaving rashly in the upsetting aftermath of her mother's funeral?

Catherine was not sure.

She jiggled the straw in her coffee and sighed. Perhaps she had agreed to conduct Father Knight to Thessaloniki as a means of expressing that very unsureness. His business there was unusual, to say the least, and he really did need a member of the family to pave the way. Who better than Catherine to get him an introduction to her awful uncle James Vaughan? She knew Greece, she spoke Greek and, apart from that, according to Beatrice, the old priest was very nearly blind. Catherine felt another twinge of guilt. Perhaps he was late because of this disability. She should have gone to meet him. He was late because he was lost, or, worse still, he might have met with an accident. She had been selfish, uncaring, inhospitable. Whatever moral ground he occupied, he was a stranger and she had not made him welcome.

She looked up again from the shelter of her pillar and iced coffee, and there, it seemed, he was. Standing in the doorway, dressed in black suit and Roman collar, was a man of indeterminate age. She had expected someone more decrepit. He stood quite straight and his hair was the sort of biscuit colour that goes with any age. She was surprised, too, she had to admit, to notice the amiable expression on his face. He looked a little lost, as well he might, but in a mild and bookish way. He could not be quite so blind as Beatrice had painted him, for he stood and scanned the rows of tables, a suitcase at his feet and a black mackintosh draped over his arm, obviously looking for someone of her description. The only sign that might indicate defective vision was a pair of horn-rimmed spectacles with frames heavy enough to support thick lenses.

Catherine took pity on him and rose. He could not see her. For a fifty-year-old woman, she was well-preserved; in her youth, she had been beautiful, an accident of nature, she had always thought, which had deterred people from liking her for herself alone. Other women had envied her and men were forever putting on some sort of display. As for Theo . . . well, the broken marriage was a painful demonstration that she had never been adequate to the pedestal he had erected for her. On the whole, Catherine welcomed middle age.

As she approached, the priest blinked owlishly at her and looked down shyly as if he had noticed her pleasing appearance.

'Father Knight?' she inquired.

He nodded. 'Yes. You must be Catherine Phocas.' He looked straight at her now, blinking once more, his face happy. 'Goodness, I thought I was going to miss you. You must forgive me. I came straight here with my luggage. The aeroplane was late.'

'It is I who am sorry,' she said, liking him more than she had expected. 'This is a stupid place to meet. I forgot how crowded it becomes this time of the evening. I should have met you at the airport, but my business took longer than even I had thought it would.'

He took off his glasses and wiped his face with his large, white pocket handkerchief. His eyes, normally magnified by the heavy lenses, looked vulnerable without the protective frames. They were a faded blue. 'Warm,' he said, gesturing somewhat helplessly as if he were at fault for insularity, for not knowing Athens was bound to be warm in late April.

'Not always this time of year,' said Catherine. 'But you must be longing for a drink. Something.'

He looked only too grateful for this suggestion, and together they cut a path to her table through the busy restaurant. Suddenly, Catherine spied Varvara Bean, a rich Athenian, whose dour Yankee husband wearily subsidized the artistic salon she liked to entertain. What on earth was she doing at Zonar's? It was a little low-powered for her. She was usually draped in a caftan at home, 'receiving'. Now, however, she was talking earnestly to a female friend whom Catherine did not know. Catherine ducked. 'Oh dear,' she said.

Father Knight inquired mildly with his eyes as they sat and she summoned the waiter.

'An acquaintance from the past,' Catherine said. Firmly, she added, 'From the time I lived with my husband. You did know, didn't you, that I was . . . no longer . . . in fact, today I started divorce proceedings.' Catherine was appalled by herself. Why on earth had she not inquired instead into the pleasantness or unpleasantness of his journey?

4

'Mother Mary – that is, your sister Beatrice – did mention . . . I'm so sorry . . .'

She had not expected the commonplace of sympathy from him, but condemnation. 'It's been a ghastly day!' she found herself saying, and then realized that before this outburst of intimacy she had exchanged only a few sentences with this man whom she had never met before.

'Would you like to go somewhere else?' he asked. 'I can wait for my drink . . . at least for another few moments. In any case, I shouldn't mind checking in at my hotel.' He waved his hand again at the encumbering case. 'And changing my shirt, too.'

Catherine was vastly relieved. She paid the waiter for her half-finished *frappé*, and offered her guest the water which had come with it. 'If you're thirsty, then this will help until we can get something stronger, Father Knight,' she said.

He hesitated.

'The water is quite all right,' she added, smiling.

'Oh, I'm sure . . . It's Edward. Please.' He drank gratefully, indeed greedily, her untouched glass of water.

'Father Edward.'

He nodded shyly, seeming happy enough to settle on this.

'Catherine,' said Catherine.

They walked out into the Athenian dusk, having avoided Varvara by the judicious use of a side exit. Huge chocolate Easter eggs bound up in bright ribbon stood like a guard of honour to marshal their escape through the adjoining shop. 'It's nearly Ascension Day in England,' he said, looking at the confectionery with perhaps a professional eye.

'Not here. Actually, not even for the Greek Catholics. Recently, they have been going along with the Orthodox calendar,' she told him, wanting to make the point that she had remained in the fold. She waved a hand down Venizelou in the direction of the Catholic Cathedral.

'Confusing when we get to Thessaloniki,' he said. 'I shan't know which schedule to go by, but I suppose "When in Greece . . ."' He smiled at his clumsy little joke.

'Well, you might want two Easters, but surely you don't want two Lents,' she said sharply.

With his case, they blundered across the road, avoiding death by a whisker. He was staying in Apollonou, he told her. 'At the Hotel Aphroditi, of all places,' he added gloomily.

'I know it,' she said. Athens was coming back to Catherine just when she wanted most to forget it. Although the house in Chios would be a dreadful sacrifice, she told herself that she never wanted to live in Greece again. And as for forgiving Theo for what had happened in the past, she found she was unable. It simply wasn't in her. What was more, she was not even sure she should. Theo's infidelities had done much more than simply humiliate her. His liaison with the American tart Missy Kavanagh had nearly resulted in Xenia's suicide. The stones of Athens proclaimed this monstrous time to her; mutely, they spoke of ruin. With the owlish priest in tow, bumping along behind her with his case down the narrow pavements, past shops which sold fur coats only to visiting Japanese and Russians now, she wondered how shocked he would be at a confession of her radical new love of freedom. She shocked herself at how angry she had become and how much she almost gloried in the rage. She hoped Father Whatever – Edward, he wanted to be called – would not subtly moralize all the way to Thessaloniki on the train the next day.

As they walked, she noticed that he gazed about himself in wonder, probably at being in Athens at all. Well, she would give him a good meal, maybe at Xenou, which was atmospheric and in the Plaka, and probably exercise him around the base of the Acropolis for a postprandial stroll. Out of the corner of her eye, Catherine assessed Father Knight. Given his apparent interest in the Vaughans, he was probably just a little eccentric, but he looked harmless enough. She hoped that he was more robust than he seemed, for they were in for a thick time of it with Uncle James, who was not going to be in sympathy, she felt certain, with the nature of their search, and who most certainly would not wish to be reminded, for any reason at all, of his daughter Susannah's terrible death.

It was at her mother's funeral not two months ago that Catherine had first heard the curious story of her cousin Susannah Vaughan. At the time, she had no way of knowing that becoming implicated in the quest for information about Susannah might land her with the task of shunting an unknown Catholic priest around Greece. The truth was that Catherine and her mother Lady Simon had never been close, and this had made her death more difficult to sustain than if they had been friends. The High Requiem in the Abbey Church, which should have united them in the faith they somewhat variously held, had left her feeling more than ever before the grandeur of the distance that had been between them. The cold eloquence of the Latin (permitted in the case of her ancient, pious mother) had seemed to express only an eternal sadness of failure on both sides, and the structured formality of a merely dutiful history.

Lady Simon had lived in Gloucestershire with Catherine's unmarried sister Theresa, who had a farm and ran it, guns blazing, as a going concern. Theresa thought the rest of the family spoiled and effete. She wore trousers, smoked cheroots, and propped up the bar in The Bull, where she could and often did drink any man under the table. Locally, she had respect as old-fashioned gentry, for despite her ham-fisted eccentricity she had an exact sense of class. Atheist and lapsed Catholic though she was, she did the flowers for the parish church; she was a fair-minded employer and she visited benefits on her tenants with unabashed condescension.

In contrast, Lady Simon had been elegant and frail, her coffin tiny like a child's; the tendrils of freesias had quivered on the lid as if they mourned the passing of the grace which had eluded Theresa so utterly. It was perhaps because Theresa knew better that the funeral feast she had provided seemed so slapdash, incongruous not only with the dead woman herself, but with the Mass that had preceded it. Mozart had been sung, and plainsong. Catherine supposed that her sister needn't really fuss over family and the few surviving friends, who had made their way down the dirt track to The Gables, but she could not help shudder slightly at the ham sandwiches and very unpretentious sherry which Theresa had heaved upon an old oak dining table that was usually employed (a strong impression this) to doctor sick animals. After all, their brother Charles, with Rosamund and the children, had come all the way down from London, as she had herself, and pressed against the wall with faintly malodorous thimblefuls of supermarket Oloroso had stood a black flock of Benedictine monks from the Abbey, who had benefited not only from Lady Simon's devotion to them in life, but from a generous bequest. They, in turn, seemed somewhat cowed by Beatrice who, under the title of Prioress, now outranked all of them but the Abbot himself, who had been unable to attend.

Catherine had not seen Beatrice for many years, partly because Catherine herself had lived abroad in the purdah of her marriage, and partly because her sister had led a strictly enclosed life. In fact, it seemed mildly astonishing that Beatrice had allowed herself the luxury of the funeral at all. She was the eldest of the Simon clan and, even in childhood, Catherine had been in awe of her. Theresa, a law unto herself, had never been in awe of anyone. Their brother Charles, a publisher, who had been the baby and the boy to boot, had had his own mysterious separate status in the family, but the three girls had been as different as it was possible to be. Each had gone her own way without the heat of rivalry fuelling her decisions, but a certain warmth between them was lacking too. Catherine was surprised, therefore, when Beatrice, or Mother Mary of the Assumption

7

as she was called 'in religion', had lit the gloomy scene in the dining room with a delighted smile when Catherine had entered with the tray of limp, shop-bought quiche that she had been detailed by Theresa to pass amongst the guests. 'Cat!' she had cried, detaching herself from the phalanx of monks. 'Dear Catherine,' she had added, amending the childhood name. Beatrice was nearly sixty. Unlike most modern-day nuns, she wore the full rig, a white wimple draped in a black veil, a brown habit.

Catherine greeted her sister with a kiss, embracing starchy folds that rustled. 'Isn't this frightful?' she found herself saying.

Beatrice had fine skin, almost as pale as the wimple, and her face was patterned with wrinkles like lace, in a pleasant way, as if she often laughed and smiled. She drew her brows together, however, at Catherine's remark. 'You mean Mummy?'

Catherine made a wordless complaint at all of it. Their brother Charles was being harangued by Agnes Gerard, who had been Lady Simon's best friend. Rosamund, their sister-in-law, was doing her best with the small flock of local gentry who had assembled, and the grown-up children stood in a sombre group by the bay window, chatting amongst themselves, ceremonious in unaccustomed hats and smart haircuts. They seemed to illuminate the room more than the actual source of light, a dreary February sun that hovered dankly on the horizon beyond them. Only Theresa gave energy to the scene, as she hectically served her guests with the horrid fare she had prepared for them.

'She's still angry with Mummy,' Beatrice observed, 'and no wonder, poor Tess . . . Are *you*? I think I may be, although I have never really discovered quite why.'

Catherine was astonished and mildly riveted by this honesty. In the past, her sister had abounded in pious euphemisms. 'I thought you had won the rosette, Beatrice,' she said, 'after Charles, that is. Either Tess came in last or I did. It shifted.'

'I like the idea of a rosette,' Beatrice said, putting her head to one side so that the starch creaked. 'To feel one had to win some sort of prize was perhaps the source of pain.'

As one, they regarded their sister Theresa with her heavy head and raw hands: she was done up in her Gor-ray skirt and dark silk blouse, and they hung loosely on her spare, hard-working frame. The get-up looked as if it had died in the mothballs of which it faintly smelt.

Catherine was not sure what to say next. Her mind flashed back to the open grave they had just left. She had seen her mother only recently, the presiding dowager poised in a seemingly deathless rigour at Charles's

8

dinner table. Their conversation, as always, had been consciously shallow. It had never struck Catherine that Lady Simon could die, and she still did not believe that it had happened.

'She was a cold woman,' Beatrice said, 'yet it was not her fault. Perhaps it was ours, more, for expecting her to be otherwise. It has taken me literally years in religion to realize that one does not get very far by varnishing the truth. It is easier to forgive once the offence has been acknowledged. Otherwise, the enemy worms away from within and grows stronger. Tell me, has anyone heard yet from Uncle James?'

Catherine edgily wondered if being cloistered drove people to speak as if they were reading aloud. Running counter to her stiff speech, there was something almost too powerful about Beatrice with her magnetic, candid eyes. Catherine wanted to break loose and talk with someone else. She was glad her sister had changed the subject and shifted away from their mother. 'Well, Charles told me he had tracked him down through the British Council – an inspiration, I thought. Can you imagine, he's still living in that house in Thessaloniki! Charles sent several messages, but they've been completely ignored. Poor Mummy, her only brother!'

'I knew where he was living, but I was hoping he would be here,' Beatrice said, looking around her as if he might have arrived on the scene while they were talking.

'I suppose we all thought he might have made the effort, but there weren't even any flowers.'

'Oh, don't be indignant, Cat! It probably frightens him that Mummy's dead. In any case, if she was cold, she was really only the tip of the iceberg. Those Vaughans were simply Arctic. I am sure you don't remember Grandmama, because you were too young, but I certainly do, and Uncle James.' Beatrice laughed at the family foible of coldness, reducing the idea of its frigid wastes to something that might interest the more adventurous kind of tourist. 'What really interested me in seeing him again was the hope that I could talk with him about Susannah.'

In the bay window, Catherine saw Xenia throwing back her head in laughter at one of the cousins' joke. She looked fine, even pretty now, and had gained some weight. The warmth of gratitude for this surged through her. Xenia was growing up, having a nice time at last, even at a funeral. 'Susannah?'

'Oh, let's sit down, Cat. I'm shattered by all of this and I'm sure you are too. I have quite a story about her and, now I think about it, you can be some help.'

Beatrice moved in her medieval garments through the small throng of mourners, who had now picked up some steam from the continually replenished sherry. Together, the sisters crossed the hall, where Rosamund now bustled with teacups from the kitchen, and made their way into the sitting room with its stuffed, chintz-covered chairs. There were comfy old relics from their childhood, a painting once attributed (wrongly) to Landseer, and a rickety Early Victorian table upon which Lady Simon's work basket had always rested. An old Labrador, banished from the dining room, thumped his tail in greeting, then went back to snooze in front of the fire. Despite this homely scene, the room had a forlorn air. Beatrice sank into a sofa and closed her eyes. She really is in pain, Catherine thought; she really is upset about Mummy. Then realized that she herself was upset, far more upset than she had thought. She sat on an old chair that had once been in their nursery and, trying not to cry, stared into the oddly unfriendly fire. 'Tell me about Susannah,' she said.

Beatrice opened her eyes. Her garb all at once seemed more than ordinarily outlandish, for her expression suddenly suggested large areas of herself that had little to do with her being a nun, areas of childhood and the strictly personal. Suddenly, Catherine saw her as she had been long ago, her much older sister, always an ally of the adult world, and no less mysterious for that than she was now in her habit. She had been Head Prefect at St Winifred's when Catherine had been in the Junior School. She remembered Beatrice seeking her out in the little girls' dorm, asking her if she was all right with that pained conscientiousness which had always characterized her. She had not wanted to show favour to a sister. Even at the time, Catherine had oddly understood. The shining cloud of Beatrice's holy destiny had always enveloped her.

Beatrice sighed. 'Well,' she began, 'I wonder how you will react when I tell you that there are those who think Susannah was – *is*, I suppose I should say – a saint.'

'Susannah? A saint?'

Beatrice extended her palms upwards and made a comic little face. 'I know it sounds a bit absurd, but there it is. According to my sources (and, as you may imagine, they are of the best), there is a little cultus that has grown up around her. What is more, the chief devotees are trying to start a Cause – you know, get the Holy Office to look into it and all that, prove miracles, establish evidence that she led a holy life, that kind of thing.'

'Goodness!' said Catherine. 'How extraordinary!' She gave the fire a prod and put on a few lumps of coal. 'I remember when she died. There was a terrible outcry, a diplomatic incident, wasn't there? I can't say I remember it very well, because even though she died in Greece I was miles away. In more ways than one,' she added wryly. 'But Charles was talking about it just the other day. He was interviewed on the telly about it at the time – trust Charles! That's why he couldn't fathom how Uncle James could still live in the place where his daughter was murdered.'

'Or martyred. That's the point her new clients are trying to make.'

'I don't believe it,' Catherine snorted. 'I remember her, of course, but she was more your age. I expect I was usually at school when she was about. Wasn't she keen on horses? A saintly aura was not the first thing you noticed about her. You were always the one for *goodness*, Beattie. I mean holiness, that kind of thing.'

She saw she had hurt her sister's feelings. Maybe there was a sort of professional jealousy in the religious life.

'The rosette,' Beatrice replied dryly, 'is still there. I can't tell you how grateful I am for that remark.' She paused, then continued. 'Susannah was not *un*holy. She was odd.' Beatrice frowned swiftly in self-correction. 'Maybe that's why she caught God's eye.'

'Wasn't she at Roedean?' Catherine asked, steering out of deep waters.

'Yes, indeed. So she was quite nearby and Mummy made rather a fuss of her. You remember, her mother was dead and Uncle James was always bound up in his archaeological digs. I was always supposed to be nice to Susannah, you know.'

'Kiss of death,' said Catherine.

Beatrice ignored this self-evident truth and plunged on. 'She spent the long holidays in America with her mother's family, so I can't say we were close, but you're quite right, she did like to ride. I was hopeless, of course. She used to lend a hand with exercising the Bucktons' horses – you remember the Bucktons – and her idea of heaven was to gallop across the Downs.'

'She was very self-absorbed,' Catherine said, identifying this quality.

'I know what you mean,' Beatrice said carefully. 'But now I realize that she was quite "interior", as we say. I remember she enticed me out on one of those terrifying rides once. On a horse, she was completely different. She seemed reckless, but in reality she was completely unselfconscious – a thing I can't be and never could. She gave herself over to the animal.'

Beatrice seemed to weigh something in her mind. 'I run my monastery now very efficiently, but it is only the side effect of having been brought up by Mummy to take it for granted that, if things were to be run, we Simons ran them. I can see Susannah abandoning herself to God.'

It had been a generous thing to say. They paused for a moment and looked at a blue flare spurting from a coal. Catherine was suddenly charmed by Beatrice, warmed by her. 'Beattie, I think you're being hard on yourself. But then you always were.' It subtly delighted Catherine to swap adult observations with the hitherto unreachable Beatrice. She had taken her solemn vows at twenty-two, when Catherine had been only thirteen.

'Think why!' Beatrice said sharply. 'Not that it's done me too much harm in my profession. In the long run, it really is what I wanted to do, Cat. I'm very happy.'

At this apparent *non sequitur*, the two sisters exchanged a look, too poignant for both of them. 'Susannah!' Catherine said abruptly, but she laughed.

'Ah, Susannah. Now I shall come to the point, having rediscovered you.' Beatrice resumed something of her conventual posture. She sat straight in the sofa, her eyes once more in her custody. 'I suppose you didn't know that she became close to Mummy after we had both grown up and gone our separate ways?' She paused long enough for the self-negating statement to sink in.

A sharp memory of their childhood home in Sussex came back to Catherine. Like her mother, the house had seemed eternal and she had been unconscionably upset when it had been sold. It had had a gloomy prospect of the sea. Despite their grand connections, the Simons had eked out their existence close to the wind that came off the Channel, disdaining their more affluent neighbours, partly out of a necessary thrift. Lady Simon, however, had been determined that the girls should 'come out'. Ironically, the only sister who had been persuaded to do the Season had been Theresa, who saw even less point in balls and flirtations than did Beatrice.

Lady Simon had not been deterred from putting her painfully religious daughter in the firing line. Beatrice must have found it agonizing to go to those county parties, Catherine now thought, and all at once she remembered the two cousins, Beatrice and Susannah, standing at the front door one winter evening waiting to be delivered into the cold in their circumspect taffeta frocks. She had been about nine at the time, ready for bed and crouching by the banisters in the upstairs hall, her dolly clutched to her. Her mother had been prinking the two young ladies, checking stocking seams and knifing kirby grips into unstable hairdos. The two girls had looked utterly miserable, like circus animals in clothes. And yet their misery had not united them. They had stood oddly apart.

'I suppose it isn't strange that Mummy never mentioned her to me,' Catherine said. 'She was, if anything, reticent. All the same, if Susannah was as religious as you say she became, she'd have talked about her. She would have liked a holy niece and would have made a good example of her.'

Beatrice frowned again, somewhat inscrutably, Catherine thought, then seemed to change the subject on her mind. 'I'm not sure Mummy would have perceived Susannah as holy. Mummy was very devout, of course, but Susannah turned out to be a bit unconventional.' At this, Beatrice spoke with sudden tears behind her voice. A terrible regret seemed to surface, one that Catherine understood but could not define closely. 'It was Mummy who was doing Susannah good, you see, and it's to her credit that she did not draw attention to it.'

The two women sat in silence for a moment, letting this effort of praise for the dead stand as a decency they were determined to maintain for their mother.

'In any case,' Catherine said, suddenly craving the sound of words, 'it was my impression that Susannah was not even a Catholic. Don't you remember? Wasn't there some sort of resentment that Uncle James had not had her baptized? I forget about her mother, except that she was rich, American, Protestant and dead.'

'Well, that's the point, you see. Susannah did not become a Catholic until some time in her twenties,' Beatrice said. 'Mummy was her god-mother.'

'So, as it is a contradiction in terms for a Vaughan not to be a Catholic, Mummy triumphed.'

Beatrice smiled a little too thinly for charity. 'Well, be that as it may, Susannah wrote letters to Mummy, pious reflections – *pensées* . . . an odd and rather nineteenth-century thing to do, don't you think?'

It amused Catherine that Beatrice could think anyone else old-fashioned, but she said, 'I'm surprised she didn't write to you.' She thought about her mother receiving letters from a putative saint. Somehow, it was not so incongruous as it seemed. The very inflexibility of Lady Simon might have appealed to someone with a single mind.

'I think she took the term "godmother" quite literally,' said Beatrice. 'In any case, shortly before Mummy died she sent me a packet containing these letters, and also a small journal. In a way, it was her legacy to me, and this is why I feel something must be done. In fact, having read through it all, I do think there is some point in pursuing the matter. There is something extreme about Susannah. Perhaps she overvalued her mystical experiences, but at the same time she writes about them with that immense care for detail that typifies real visionaries. When you add to all of this the little band of enthusiasts who have grown up independently from the writings, it does seem to make a *prima facie* case for investigation.'

Catherine looked at her sister, whose eyes were trained on the fire. For a moment, it was almost possible to see her in her cloister, recollected to a fine point of concentration. This was her subject, after all, her expertise, and she spoke about it with the same tranquillity and interest as a don might speak of the doubtful exegesis of a poem.

'It seems a bit strange that Mummy did not give them to you before. Did she know about this "cultus", as you call it?'

There was a sharp hesitancy which made Catherine aware that her sister habitually spoke to outsiders, even family, from behind a grille.

'Whether she knew or not, there may have been other reasons,' Beatrice said obscurely, then softened. 'Let me put it this way: I do not think it wise to discuss Susannah's writings with anyone at all until I find out more about her. The theological content of her journals is unexceptionable, but there are various loose ends in the biographical sphere and they need tying in before her case is taken to the Bishop in the diocese where she lived before her death.'

'What is it that you want me to do?' Catherine asked.

'Your familiarity with Greece would help enormously. It struck me when I saw you today in the Abbey Church. Most of all, I would like you to persuade Uncle James to help with the inquiry,' Beatrice said, 'and I have no illusions that it will be an easy task . . . You don't have to answer me right away.'

The two sisters said nothing for a long time. It was almost as if the drawn-out afternoon had finally sealed them with its solemnity, caught up with them, exhausted them, as if they, like their mother, had also run out of time. They sat together, the fragile threads of an attenuated kinship finally reconnected.

Catherine studied the meditative face of Beatrice, illumined in the dying light of the fire. She had no sense that her sister had missed her calling; her vocation was no martyrdom. All the same, as Catherine remained sitting with her she found herself resonating to an almost inaudible chord of long-sustained sadness, until the snoring dog woke and padded out of the room, and their brisk sister-in-law Rosamund entered to disrupt their silent colloquy with offers of more drink.

The abrupt, well-meaning intervention of Charles's wife had jarred Catherine into fumbling for concealment. She had unclasped the handbag on her lap, reached into it and withdrawn her handkerchief. To her great surprise, she had found she wanted it. Little rivulets of tears had stained her cheeks and she had no idea how long she had been crying.

'Will you do what I ask?' Beatrice had said.

II

FATHER EDWARD peered at Catherine Phocas as she settled herself in the seat opposite him. She had insisted on buying his ticket to Thessaloniki, and now she firmly planted herself in the shabby first-class carriage, her back to the engine. He had tried to resist her on both points, but she seemed determined to treat him like visiting royalty – and without any kind of display.

He hesitated to gauge anyone's character on such a short acquaint-ance, but he sensed her to be one of those genuinely unselfish people who have no idea that they are behaving generously. It was true that her manner was a little stiff, but he put this down to shyness. The night before, she had given him a splendid meal and had gone out of her way to show him the sights, making sure she explained in the most tactful way what she thought he could not see. She was far too modest about her abilities as a guide, for she had been a mine of information about the Parthenon. Even though it had been closed, she had taken him round the base of the Acropolis and had wonderfully evoked the illuminated ruins perched on its crags. He could almost see the lost, glistening Athene by Phidias in his mind's eye. This morning, she had wanted him to have the best view from the train. Not that there was much of a view: the windows were filmy with grime, and even with his spectacles his vision was impaired.

Especially given the purpose of his journey, Edward had not expected to take such childlike delight in Greece. In fact, under the circumstances, he thought it incongruous to feel so suddenly buoyed up out of the sombre frame of mind in which he had come. Perhaps, he thought, it was the delayed effect of his classical education which had hit him along with the heat, making him feel just a little drunk with the spirit of odyssey. In fact, the night before, he had actually been a little drunk, having polished off rather a lot of wine with Mme Phocas – Catherine – and even the sense of guilt which might have accompanied such an indulgence had burnt off in the morning sun, leaving him once more with the effervescent consciousness of being on hallowed ground. Whether in the raising of his blurred eyes up to the lighted Parthenon or in imagining St Paul's foot-prints below him in the dark Agora the night before, Greece seemed to him bound up with aspects of the soul.

Edward had assumed the task of sifting through the details of Susannah Vaughan's biography with the greatest reluctance. It was, he
thought, like being forced to look through the cupboards of a loved but
awful relative after the funeral. He did not want to let anyone down, least of
all Susannah, but if her violent death had to be inspected for evidence
of her sanctity he did not want to be the one to see the anomalies he was
afraid he might find.

It had been almost fourteen years ago, in 1979, when he had picked
up the copy of *The Times* which reported her death. It had already
been thumbed by the two other priests with whom he had then shared a
presbytery, and had lain crumpled on the breakfast table. Edward had had
no difficulty in seeing then: Susannah's face, posed in an out-of-date
photographic portrait, had stared up at him prim and bland. Underneath
it, the disjunctive copy had announced her gruesome murder abroad. He
knew how he had felt, but it was still hard to say what he thought about it.
Although they had rather lost touch, he had once known her well and for a
while the news had knocked him senseless. How could it have happened?
Who could do such a thing?

For a while, he supposed, he had toyed with the idea that her death
had been some kind of martyrdom, but there had been no evidence to
suggest it. What was more, Susannah had for a long time worked in a risky
business. She had started a controversial community for violent ex-mental
patients, the result, he had always thought, of an inner recklessness he
found hard to pinpoint or describe. This did not diminish his respect for
her, nor had it eased his own sorrow at losing a somewhat itinerant friend.
She had been a mass of contradictions, almost stupidly orthodox in some
religious matters, eclectic on others. Above all, her character had been shot
through with the unconventional streak of something like genius. With
its attendant dark side, this quality made her very difficult to classify. If
she had sought out the lost, she had found them by lightning flashes
of intuition, which corresponded to a kind of pathology she had always
acknowledged in her own soul; and while this had taught her humility, it
had not stopped her from being erratic . . . Not that he knew.

However, when it came, as it now did, to associating her with Saints
Lucy, Agnes, Cecilia, Felicity, Perpetua et al, Father Edward could not
quite rise to the occasion. He still prayed for her soul and, though he
thought of her as better than himself, he could not quite imagine a situation where she might pray for him. In fact, when Mother Mary of the
Assumption had summoned him to East Grinstead, it had never crossed
his mind that Susannah was at issue. He had had no idea why the Prioress

wanted to see him. He had not been overjoyed when he found out, and he still felt a residual guilt about this. He should want Susannah to be canonized. Well, he did, didn't he?

In the first place, because he liked to think of himself as having a cautiously modern outlook, the whole canonization process seemed to creak with arduous legalism. Edward was a loyal sort and when he could not agree with the Curia he kept silent. Still, he privately thought that the issues governing sanctity were too bound up in Vatican politics. He was not sure that Susannah, for all her faith, had much of a chance against a conservative Papacy, and, even if she did, he somehow felt she might have abhorred the fuss.

Thinking of this now, he glanced a little nervously through his befogged eyes at Catherine Phocas as she sat looking out of the window, waiting for the train to leave the platform. He was relieved that she was not as forbidding as her cloistered sister. Still, he was not sure what attitude to expect of someone whose first cousin might become a saint.

Although she seemed to make her marital status something of an issue, religiously speaking, Catherine came from a formidable family, and not one to jettison the bastion of past practice for Folk Masses and ecumenism. Susannah had found all that sort of thing quite jolly, but then she had always been tone deaf to ritual. The Prioress, however, was strictly Old Guard. Her Carmel had reminded him of the days when holiness had seemed inevitably combined with the smell of oil and wax. The lay sister who had let him into the enclosed monastery, keys jangling, had put him in mind of female officers in prisons he had visited. When at length Reverend Mother had entered the parlour and seated herself behind the thick iron grille, he had felt oddly as if he were about to be questioned about a crime he had not committed. He had been astonished enough to hear she was initiating preliminary inquiries into a Cause but, when she told him that she had discovered his name from entries in Susannah's spiritual journals, he had been seized by an unwarranted sense of guilt, as if surprised in a forbidden pleasure long concealed.

Throughout their conversation, the grille had made her almost invisible to him. It had been as unnerving as it might have been to consult an ancient Sybil crouching in the shadows. He was, she told him, Susannah's only surviving confessor, even though he had been her first. When she had suggested he might shed light upon Susannah's spiritual disposition at death, he had had the impulse to quit the parlour and stumble into the sunlight of the twentieth century.

Edward did not know why he had been so resistant to the nun. He had known a number of Carmelites over the years; although he had a contemplative streak himself and understood the necessary rigours of the cloister, her veiled presence made him feel lax. Still, this was not the reason he was unwilling to look into Susannah's death. He had stammered out objections: it was difficult for him to travel, and so on. In the end, he had agreed. As redoubtable as the Prioress was, he became oddly sympathetic to her as their hour together went by. Father Edward had some reputation as a perceptive confessor. Obscurely, her barely visible movements behind the iron screen had brought him to the strange conviction that she herself needed to know if Susannah was a saint or not, and that the evidence she had so far was in some personal way disturbing to her.

As Susannah had been to him.

Now that he was in Greece and he had had some time to think about it, it struck him that Susannah might do better in the diffuse and venerable light of classical mythology than she would fare in the Roman market of heroic virtue. Indeed, her pious legend so far would have to be weighed against an impressive catalogue of women who had been crushed, tortured, burned and mutilated for the Faith. Not that it was entirely necessary for her to be a martyr. A few miracles had already been attributed to her, and if they held water a holy death was quite enough to prove. Still, even that begged a question for Edward. In one way, Susannah seemed too fragile for such heavy honour, and at the same time too fluid and intense to be made something so fixed and sedate as a saint. She would be a better Antigone or Alceste, perhaps even Electra, a tragic heroine of pagan tradition of which her father was such a distinguished scholar. The sheer starkness of Susannah's consciousness came back to him and made him shudder a little.

Edward forbade himself the luxury of wallowing in this idea, and he was also a little ashamed of himself for thinking less of Susannah than others more detached did. Whatever the truth, he must pray to find it and hope to see it dispassionately.

As he settled himself in the carriage for the long journey to Salonika, he was seized, as he had been the night before, with an inexplicable sense of peace and liberty. Could this be a sign that he had made the right choice after all in coming? It had been a hard decision. Edward always measured God by His goodness. A strong sign of His presence in any given situation was joy.

Early that morning, Catherine had fetched him from his modest hotel in a taxi and as they had made their way to Larissa Station through the sheer jammed clutter of Athens, he had eyed her nervously, hoping that he had not talked too much the night before at dinner, for by nature and training he was a listener. The taverna where they ate had a rustic, jolly atmosphere, and yet there had been a guardedness about her that had made him want to offer himself as a human being against what she possibly saw in him as a priest. He had found himself rambling on in order to ease the situation and, at last, he had been rewarded by a quickening in the rhythm of their conversation. By the time they had strolled up to the Acropolis he felt they had reached the happy plateau of a *modus vivendi* which he hoped would carry them through their journey. Maybe he could do her some good on the way. Although she was not exactly forthcoming, she had blurted out enough during the evening to make him see she had been through a rough time. Perhaps, he thought now, it had been Catherine and not he who had said too much the night before. Perhaps she thought it was she who had gone too far.

Edward was only too at home with emotional reserve and he was sympathetic when he saw it in others. It was not that he was incapable of spontaneity, it was more that it so often seemed incompatible with the expectations people had of him, people he felt bound not to disappoint. He had been a posthumous child, the only boy in a family of four. For this reason, he took women to be the mainstream rather than the second sex, and if he had fled their too large influence into a male preserve he had found the inflections of their moods, the importance they assigned to feeling, and the general drift of their aspirations, like a second language learned in childhood. This had come in handy both as an access to under-standing the dilemmas of the women he encountered and as a defence against them. As for Catherine Phocas, he was not entirely sure what to think. For a woman who was supposed to be so rich, he found her incon-gruously simple and direct. He supposed his inner portrait of her had included a kind of gloss and vanity that often flourishes with wealth, but so far she had given no evidence of it. In fact, she was without subterfuge to the point of being rather charmless. He had discovered that he wanted her to like him. He wondered if he had been ingratiating last evening and if she had found him over-familiar, or even a bit silly.

Certainly she gave no impression of this, but she did have again, that morning, the blankness of Englishwomen who come from a certain background, a coolness, a control that left whatever she was thinking to the imagination. He had been surprised to find her formally dressed in a light navy suit, all crisp with a white blouse and amber beads so that she slightly resembled a schoolmistress going to a conference. She greeted him in a friendly enough manner, but he began to wonder, as the taxi made its way past the solid, ochre, Athenian houses cool with drawn shutters and heavy with old vines, if the little symposium of the night before had been a test in which he had not gained top marks. When they reached the station, however, and he offered her a cup of coffee, she accepted it with alacrity, and they sat in the cafeteria under slow fans and soaring flies in a cordial silence while she jolted herself awake with the strong brew. Greek dolls were for sale at the counter and an old woman in peasant costume, looking for all the world like a sample of the wares in the display case, stared an unblinking disapproval at the world in general. She was accompanied by a man, evidently her son, who wore knife-creased trousers and who bore all the trappings of a successful businessman.

'By her dress, I can tell you that the old lady comes from Epirus,' Catherine had said *sotto voce* to Edward, registering his surprise at someone who seemed to have stepped out of an operetta. 'I should think she would be travelling to Ioanina . . . and I expect he's not too displeased to see the back of her.' Although Catherine had spoken very softly, the Greek mother and son looked with faint hostility in their direction. 'Ah,' she said, noticing this too, 'politics. The British are in bad odour at the moment. I must warn you that we'll be in Macedonia, although you are probably aware of it. We are a bit *non grata* at the moment and it is best to carry one's Englishness with an attitude of diplomacy in mind.'

Edward was suddenly aware of the shut faces of the other travellers who were assembling for the Thessaloniki train. Indeed, he had earlier descried an elegantly produced sign with a gold sunburst emblazoned on it, proclaiming the message 'Macedonia is Greek' rather like a polite public-health warning. Edward listened to the world service news every night, and had followed the crisis with interest. 'I must say, the whole thing does seem a storm in a teacup to me,' he replied.

'It isn't,' Catherine said shortly, and he was worried that he had offended her.

'I am sorry.'

She made a wide gesture just short of a shrug. 'It's not my problem,' she said, 'but it is *a* problem, and not so trivial as it seems. If Skopje has hijacked the name of Macedonia, it might have further plans. On the other hand, it is a secular state and stands inconveniently between Serbia and Greece. People shouldn't play with matches in the Balkans.'

'Do you know, I've been thinking,' he said with that reflex for concili-ation he had, 'that it does seem an awful nuisance for you to take me such a long way by train – or at all, though now is hardly the time to mention it. If I had only thought about it, I could have flown directly to Salonika, but I did not really clock on to that until I got to Heathrow yesterday.'

'What! And face out Uncle James cold? Father Edward!' She laughed in a dull way. 'Throwing Christians to the lions is not my thing, as it were, and that is why I decided on this arrangement. I had to be in Athens anyway. We are going to have to rehearse each other, you see, all the way up.'

'You make him sound a monster!'

She accumulated her luggage and gestured to him to assemble his. Movement stirred amongst the small crowd that had collected during their conversation: the train was coming. 'Well, I haven't any particulars on his monstrosity,' she said, smiling her deft, remote smile. 'It is only a general view of him. He's "a wicked uncle", you know.'

'A black sheep? That is interesting in respect of Susannah.' Edward bumbled his case forward and attempted to help her with hers. A little tremor of excitement passed through him. A huge diesel engine, the like of which he had not seen since childhood, ground its way into the station and stood majestic and panting while whistles blew. Old-fashioned steps descended from the carriages and relatives kissed goodbye and friends waved and parcels were pressed into hands of travellers bound for the north.

'Not so much a black sheep as a mystery,' she said. 'He cut himself off from the family, though no one knows exactly why. But he's awfully distinguished. I have no foundation for this whatever, but I always think of him as being a bit like Anthony Blunt.'

'Does he know we are coming?'

They clambered up into the train. When Catherine had told him they were travelling first class, he had imagined the luxury of brass fittings, velour and mahogany, and perhaps even the pressed glass that would go with the entire sensation he had of being returned to the fifties. The idea of Balkan conflict, the odd formality of dress he had observed in middle-class Greeks, the sense of leisure generated by their unhurried, protracted conversations mooted past times when a certain courtliness could be entertained. In Edward's childhood, his mother had thought it a great treat to have tea at Debenham's whenever they trekked up to London to top up his school uniform at Gorringe's. Thus, he was surprised not to find the first-class carriage equipped with potted ferns and a liveried staff. The compartments were dowdy, worn with age, and clean only through successful if half-hearted attempts to swab down when the impulse occurred. Edward loved it.

'He knows that *I* am coming. You, however, are to be a small surprise – if, of course, I can get him to meet you.'

She smiled and settled herself. She was carrying, he noticed, a thing he had not seen in years, a tapestry work basket with carved handles. The moment she was seated, she took out a complicated piece of needlepoint and started to stitch. He peered across at it, hoping to distinguish what the pattern was, and she obliged him by passing the canvas to him. Edward flushed. He had not been meaning to pry. 'Pretty,' he murmured, and it was. She was working on a patch of blue delphiniums, but there were wild roses, peonies, myrtle and eglantine already nimbly completed in rich and subtle wools. The picture was the essence of an English garden, its flowers freshly cut and arranged by a delicate hand. Catherine's hand was delicate, and she wore half-moon spectacles perched upon her nose. He might have been sitting in her drawing room at home. 'I hope you don't mind my occupying myself in this way,' she said.

He could not imagine why anyone might think it was bad manners to sew. 'It's lovely,' he said. 'Is it for anything in particular?'

'I design patterns,' she replied. 'Knitting, patchwork, crewel work, for a company I've started since my husband and I separated. My daughter was very ill a few years ago and it kept me sane. An American friend of mine suggested that I start a business with my husband's generous guilt money. It's been the salvation of me,' she said, snipping a thread.

Edward wondered if priests were the only category of people to receive angled remarks baited with language symbolic of their profession. Perhaps doctors were treated to disease imagery and soldiers to metaphors for combat. He was aware that Catherine's speech, when flavoured (as it often seemed to be) with little religious referents such as 'guilt' or 'salvation', tended towards a muted truculence. 'I think that's a wonderful thing to do,' he said gently, 'and your design is so beautiful that I can imagine it's all a great success.'

The train had got underway almost without his noticing, and they glided northwards through the Athenian suburbs. It was terribly hot, and miles of jerry-built apartment blocks and shops flashed past in the harsh sunlight like cars in a slow-moving jam on an August Bank Holiday at home. He would have loved to have removed his jacket, but Catherine sat there darkly suited, perhaps in deference to the recent death of her mother. She was cool, immobile except for the lightly stitching hands, and he decided to continue wilting with a good grace.

Edward's heavy spectacles were slippery on his nose; he removed them and wiped his face. He had initially slid into the priesthood rather as an egg to be poached finds itself in a pan of simmering water. He had never been particularly ambitious, and although he was genuinely religious he had never had to take the Kingdom by force. His vocation had been more an osmosis than a crucial decision to turn his back on the world. Because of his cleverness and the creditable first he had attained in Classics at Cambridge, he had been pulled in the direction of scholarship and, having taken a second degree, he had discovered that he wanted to teach. It was when he was on the verge of writing his *magnum opus* on the Jansenist heresy that his eyesight began to fail. He could still see enough to get by, but not to sustain long hours of reading original source material. He had inherited a degenerative eye condition from the father he had never met and, though he had successfully battled against total blindness, there was no cure.

As Edward saw things now, the catastrophe was manageable. If he wasn't to write his great *oeuvre*, then he wasn't. At the time, however, he had become quietly and politely unhinged. He had never been a clubbable, drinking priest, one who might have found solace in parish social life. Although he had a lively charity towards the needy, he had not been one to plunge himself into causes. His one cause had been the task of unsnarling the reasons for the seventeenth-century heresy which divided body and soul, one he believed still persisted in Catholic thinking. And when this unexceptionable and meritorious goal had been taken from him, he had had the sensation of falling through space.

If Edward's fault at the time had been a slight tendency towards muzziness it had been quickly burnt off in the painful coming to terms with his disability. He still lectured from time to time, and he had become a favourite with students in the university chaplaincy where he was of great use. Perhaps his suffering or his blindness had put him in touch with tones, movements, the timbre of voices. He seemed to elicit from his penitents their genuine state of mind. Awkward cases seemed to come his way, from unexpected people, who were stranded and in trouble.

He thought again now of the Mother Prioress, Catherine's sister, Susannah's cousin, and of how she had entered her parlour on light and smothered footsteps, the tallow smell of polish rising, the stiff scent of starch exuding. She had sat back in her section of the room behind the screen of bars, a powerful but oddly helpless presence. After a clumsy beginning, she had told him that a letter, which had been posted to Lady Simon a few days before Susannah's death, had contained a shocking revelation which made necessary the most delicate kind of investigation into the circumstances of James Vaughan's household. Mother Mary of the Assumption was not at liberty to say what it was, but she could see why her mother had concealed the letter. Susannah had not actually been at fault, she felt sure, but if aspects of the situation were to come out later in a full investigation of her Cause, then the devil's advocate might make something of them and it was better to clear them up from the outset. She felt sure he understood. Edward had not understood, but in the eclipsed woman behind the grille he had sensed a muffled crisis. And, much as the enterprise was distasteful to him, her urgency had been something he could not ignore.

Edward opened his eyes to a white sheen of mist, then put his spectacles on. Slowly, he adjusted to the shadow of Catherine Phocas in the corner of the swaying carriage. He hoped she was not in the category of awkwardness, but he supposed she might be. Over the years, he had discovered strange pleasures in semi-blindness. Sometimes there would be a moment of snow that preceded vision, almost as if a distinct aura accompanied certain times. As he slowly focused on her, the movements in her fingers in the nimbus that surrounded her suggested some kinetic abstract of a woman sewing. It was as if a living fresco emerged from behind a coat of whitewash: perhaps a lost Fra Angelico. His fleeting impression of the state Catherine's soul was not religious confusion at all, but innocence.

'Tell me about Susannah's "miracles",' she said abruptly.

Edward started at the sound of her voice. He realized she probably thought he had been staring at her. 'Ah,' he said.

'I'm not mad keen on that sort of thing, if you don't mind my saying so,' she continued. 'I think it's best to get that established before we even begin.' She paused and held her work out at arm's length, inspecting it through her half-moon glasses. 'It's not that I don't believe, it's simply . . .' She looked up at him and her shoulders collapsed in an attitude of sudden meekness.

He laughed. 'You relieve me!' The train had picked up speed and was chugging through Boeotia. 'I didn't know what you thought, except I suppose I imagined that most people would probably like to have a saint in the family.'

'Well, it's not like Beatrice to go in for any kind of hysteria on religious matters,' she said in apparent contradiction.

'Quite!' he said, a little falsely.

'Have you read these famous diaries?'

He had been denied a request to see them. 'I don't need to for the moment,' he said. 'You see, I knew Susannah – quite well, as it happens.'

'Good Lord!' Catherine said. 'I had the impression you had never met her.'

'I instructed her; she was my convert, if you like.'

24

'Well, she was obviously a good study!' Catherine laughed.

He thought for a moment about that remark. 'Not really,' he said. 'In fact, quite the opposite. She was not the easiest woman to get on with.' He smiled to himself at the understatement and a quick shaft of memory illuminated Susannah slamming his study door against some small point of doctrine he could not now remember, then phoning, full of contrition, the following day. 'But I suppose you could say,' he added, 'that the whole thing mattered to her a lot. She never took anything for granted just because I said it was true.'

Catherine put down her work and laid it to one side. The bright flowers she had embroidered seemed to spill out of the crushed cambric as if they fell out of some rococo trug. 'Well, what do they *say* about her? I mean, has she cured cancer or something like that?'

He squirmed a little. 'Demons,' he said at last. 'It seems she casts them out . . . or, to be more up-to-date, she has been appealed to in cases of intractable mental illness.'

'Oh,' said Catherine.

'Well, it seems to work,' he said, surprised to be on the defensive. 'And, after all, she did have a lot to do with the mentally ill. On the other hand, you do see what a problem it poses, to prove that kind of thing.'

Catherine scrabbled around in her work basket and retrieved a skein of green silk. 'You didn't like her, did you?'

This seemed an odd thing to say and would have been presumptuous if she had not been so direct. Edward had the urge to stand up and pace about the carriage, but the train moved dreamily on, slowly rocking and lulling him. 'On the contrary,' he said at length. '*Liking*, however, was something a little sub-Susannah. She always asked and often got more from people.'

Catherine's glance shifted to the side, but she calmly threaded her needle, and at once he felt safe in her company. It had all been so long ago and he was innocent. 'At one time, she was very troubled,' he found himself saying instead. He remembered Susannah crying, awful tears which only a beast would have used to his advantage.

Catherine picked up her work and filtered in the curl of a jagged leaf. 'How did she die?' she asked very gently, as if she had heard the faint reverberation of his memory. 'You see, because I was living in Chios at the time, I only heard the story after the fuss had died down.'

Edward's enthusiasm for Mme Phocas suddenly knew no bounds. Hers seemed a family of tough-minded women who concealed a deeper vein of sensitivity. 'It's a horrid story,' he said.

'Well, we're soon approaching Thebes,' she replied. 'And so you might as well . . . that is, unless you find it too upsetting.'

'*The* Thebes?'

'The same! I don't imagine what happened to Susannah can be worse than putting one's own eyes out or being buried alive in one's brother's tomb,' said Catherine. 'The family version is that she was stabbed to death when she surprised some art thieves making away with Uncle James's precious Dionysos.'

Edward blinked and looked out of the window at the wide plain that stretched to shadowed mountains in the distance. He had the impression that women were harvesting wheat sheaves in the fields, gathering and binding them up, until he realized that it was only April and he could actually see little but the outline of the landscape. 'She was stabbed rather a lot,' he said shortly. 'Forty times. It was butchery. She was massacred, like a village.' His hands started to tremble, so he linked his fingers firmly around his knee.

'How ghastly! I had no idea it was so . . . well, gory. Would mere burglars do such a thing?'

'Some of the papers said the murderers mistook her for someone else; others implied that the Greeks covered up the crime because there was some political motive behind it. Yet again, although I am sure it is slander and quite untrue, others hinted at a domestic quarrel. It was burglars or Turks or Albanians or Bulgarians . . .'

'Or Uncle James?'

'Well, I hardly think so.' It seemed, after all, that the shivering had not diminished. He thought he had recovered from the attacks, which during the year after her death had actually made his teeth chatter.

He was startled, therefore, to hear Catherine's odd and inconsistent laughter. It came to him as if there was something troubled, *wrong*, about it, as if she had a hidden brutality that manifested itself when she was too much tempted or off her guard. He imagined she was angry, like many women, in an unfocused way at compound targets.

'Quite honestly, I can't see him summoning the energy,' she said. 'Not that I remember him terribly well.'

He tried to retrieve the tone of intellectual inquiry. 'Of course, her adherents claim that she died shielding her father. He was reported to have said this to the police directly after the murder, but somehow this did not find its way into the English press, so presumably he changed his story. Whoever it was that killed her, they got what they wanted.'

'The Head?'

The head of Susannah Vaughan had nearly been severed. For years, any detail concerning the murder had set him off afresh with the unbidden images of it. He blinked at Catherine and then realized what she had meant. 'The Head of Dionysos? Yes, they got that . . . what they were after. The Greeks seemed to take that more seriously than . . . poor Susannah. An artefact of such incalculable value being in the hands of an Englishman.'

He dimly saw that her brow was contracted and she gave a sudden tremor. 'Ugh!' she said, adding it not so much as an afterthought but as something she had caught up with. 'So I suppose what you're really trying to find out is why, how, for what cause she died.'

'Exactly so.'

'And if she measures up?'

He did not like her question, one he had repeatedly asked himself. 'For wings, you mean? I'm not some spiritual tailor!'

'I'm sorry.'

'No, I am.' Edward really was, for he had snapped at her. 'It's all right. It's your shock. You knew her as a child.' They briefly recovered their comportment in a moment's silence. 'I suppose, to be really precise about it, I have to discover whether her life was simply taken from her or if she gave it. That seems to me the critical difference. And once I've worked it out, if that's possible, I can put it into other hands than mine . . . thankfully, gratefully!'

'Shall I give you my own hunch?' Catherine asked, deftly biting off the green silk.

'Go on.'

'I've been thinking a lot about her, of course. Susannah had poor health as a child. I can't remember exactly what was wrong with her, but I used to think she was a bit of a fake. It just shows how heartless children can be. You see, she was a fanatical horsewoman, and she was always well enough to ride. She took risks. I do remember my mother worrying about that. And it did seem odd for someone who managed to get beef tea in bed rather a lot.

'Actually, I think I resented her, and I know Beatrice did. She seemed to wobble between desperation and collapse. But that's probably because her mother died when she was young. Will you forgive me for saying that I think she was one of these self-punishing women? We lived in a house that overlooked the sea, and it was just the other day that I remembered her standing on the chalk cliff which fronted the house. I was only about ten, I suppose. We had a lot of evergreens, rhododendron, yews – things like that

27

– because of the soil; all quite dreary. I remember having the distinct impression that she was going to jump, but she sensed me behind her and looked round, then walked slowly, deliberately, away.'

'You mean to say you think she was a suicide?' For good reason, he found himself desperately wishing her to deny this.

'Oh, nothing as clear-cut as that. I don't know why I think so, it's intuition. She seemed needy somehow. But that does not preclude her *giving* her life. In fact, I'm almost sure she did. I can almost see her doing it with my very own eyes.'

'What do you mean?' he asked, startled by her perspicacity.

'I'm not sure!' she said, more sharply than perhaps she had intended, then firmly recollected herself. 'Look,' she said, 'we really *are* at Thebes now.' And the train drew into a neat suburban station, garnished with geraniums in pots and window boxes. A glaring, modern Orthodox Church seemed the only notable landmark along the dismal thoroughfare of cinder-block houses. 'And you see? If this is what the birthplace of tragedy looks like nowadays, maybe saints are in for a hard time too.'

III

Now SHE had heard the nauseating details of Susannah's murder, Catherine could see why her uncle had become a recluse. Still, when she inquired for messages at the reception desk of the Electra Palace, the hotel where she was staying in Thessaloniki, she was irrationally annoyed that he had not even sent word welcoming her, or at least confirming that he was expecting her to call on him that morning.

She had never been one to exact tribute from people, but now she was back in Greece she found herself slipping into slowly acquired custom. A Greek – Theo, for instance – would have sent a car or appeared in person for a niece or even a cousin, and would certainly have invited her to stay no matter what the family circumstances. Of course, it was silly to expect such behaviour from an Englishman, and a very old one at that. Why was she so quick to resent little things these days? Was it a sign that she was becoming *une femme d'un certain âge*? Perhaps.

According to her brother Charles, their uncle had once cut quite a figure in Thessaloniki: he had restored the house of a Turkish pasha and even after the murder, had held his ground, occupying it in Ottoman grandeur. Charles, in trying to locate their uncle before their mother's funeral, had discovered that the old man had long been the subject of local fascination and gossip. Apart from the scandal surrounding Susannah's death, it seemed he had always been embroiled in one archaeological wrangle or another. Apparently, he had even done battle with the Orthodox Church over consecrated sites shared with pagan ruins; this was a fruitless exercise, as Catherine knew, and one which did not bode well for Father Edward's inquiries about Susannah. If now her Uncle James held himself aloof, it seemed to be in consequence of a struggle to be vindicated over the loss of the notorious Head of Dionysos, which he claimed dated from the fifth century BC, and which he said had been stolen from his house the night of Susannah's murder. Enfeebled though he was, he still lived, Catherine had been told, as if he were maintaining an outpost of the British Raj, a posture ridiculous in its own way and, as Catherine knew, thoroughly reprehensible in Greek eyes.

All of this Catherine had learned from Charles during a snatched lunch at a bistro in Pimlico shortly before her departure for Greece. Either

Charles had been preoccupied with his work, or he had been secretly convinced that her quest was barmy, but he had hardly encouraged her. He hadn't had anything to contribute about the divorce either; he had saved his own marriage to Rosamund, and did not feel qualified to judge anyone else's, he said.

It astonished Catherine now as she prepared herself for the ordeal ahead of her that no one, not Charles nor Beatrice, had bothered to tell her how savage the murder of Susannah had been. It was true that as a child she had been squeamish about blood, and maybe that was why they had spared her the details. (But there she was, at it again, resenting people for no real reason.) Presumably they all thought she knew the story. Still, the faint subtext common to so much ill feeling in families was in her case the accepted truth that she was somehow too much of a story-book princess to cope with reality as stark as this. If that was so, how had she weathered the storm over Xenia?

It was perhaps for this reason that she was so irritated that Uncle James had not acknowledged her arrival. Here she was, about to become a company director, and he was dismissing her visit in some way, just as if she were a tiresome child. Catherine liked to think she was not over-sensitive, but this was a situation in which she had found herself before, most eminently in her married life. Theo had swaddled her from any unpleasant truth, even the most vital to her, that of the true parentage of her adopted daughter Xenia. It was the story of her life, this finding herself to be sheltered or disregarded, and there was nothing she disliked quite so much. She told herself, however, that it was in Uncle James's capacity as the only surviving relation of her mother's generation that he failed her as a host. Surely he could have had the sensitivity to see she might still be feeling very raw and might need special courtesy after so recent a bereavement.

For all this, Catherine had early learned not to make a fuss about herself. It was antithetical to the regime of fresh air and self-sacrifice upon which she had been raised to elevate her own sense of loss and deprivation to the level of suffering. In the past few months, however, she often woke drenched in sweat, unable to fight off the arid moment of realization that a cold childhood had laid the foundations for a cold marriage and both were at an end. Even her daughter had grown up, and she was now left with nothing but the hope of making her new business succeed.

Of course there was more to her life than that. Since she had left Theo, Charles and his family had been punctilious about her. She had never really warmed to Rosamund, but she supposed they got on all right.

She had, it was true, seen something of Theresa, but theirs was a loose connection, based on an ancient childhood allegiance which had never matured. To be sure, Catherine was enormously proud of Xenia, thankful for her progress. It seemed almost too wonderful to believe that the girl who had been so crushed and ill was now a confident young woman, committed to her studies at the Royal College of Music and doing well. After all their struggles, they now lived in pleasant tandem in the vast Bayswater flat that Theo (a gentleman in this and much besides, she had to admit) had left at their disposal, at least until something was settled. But now she had started divorce proceedings, she had come to see that the flat would have to go. Xenia would need her own place soon and was already mildly suggesting it.

What, she often wondered, was she now to do for human warmth? It had come as a shock that she actually needed love and it upset her to think that she had recognized this need too late. For the past four years she had poured all her energy into Xenia's recovery and this had successfully muted her own cravings. Catherine had never been an extravert, not even as a girl, and had found herself a bit of a fish out of water back in an England which had changed for the worse, in her view, since she had left it.

Before her mother's death, she had given no thought to altering her situation. Lady Simon had disapproved of divorce as intensely as she had disliked Theo, and so it was easier for Catherine to shelter in the Bayswater flat, keeping the marriage on hold. She was barely conscious of how much she dreaded the old woman's opprobrium – or worse, her condescension. 'Poor darling Catherine,' she had known her mother would say, 'I always knew Theo would never really work out.' Yet, now that she no longer had to conceal the estrangement from her mother, it left Catherine with nothing to do but act. And if she were to divorce Theo, where was she to go?

Since her return to England, Catherine had made one real friend, and secretly she hugged to herself the delight of being able to ring up and chat with Marina, go shopping with her, confide. It charmed them both to be 'best friends' as at school. At the back of it all, Catherine had the bleak realization that the time was past when being merely chums would do. She craved genuine, deep-rooted affection, and she hung on to Marina and her husband Paul Mason with a pitiable gratitude she never let show. In fact, Marina had suggested that Catherine move to Oxford so that she could live nearby. This made sense because together they were forming a company, but Catherine was wary of depending too much on anyone ever again.

Charles and Rosamund had accidentally brought the friendship about. With an unflinching determination to take an interest in Catherine after the separation, they had invited her to everything indiscriminately – drinks, launches, lunches, dinners. After their own reconciliation, they had taken to entertaining on a large scale, and it gave them an opportunity to do the decent thing without having to get too involved in Catherine's marital catastrophe, which was, she thought, a little too close to their own turmoil for comfort. To buck her up, they hurled her into the deep end of their literary pond. The exercise in survival, she supposed, was bracing.

Rosamund, having done a Pru Leith course, cooked up a storm these days. Catherine swam through shoals of literati in order to keep from drowning in loneliness. She hated the parties but she went in an effort to show she was determined to try. When she had disappeared into the Balkans in the sixties, marriage itself had seemed an achievement; on her return, she felt like Rip van Winkle waking from a long slumber. No one censured her for being a detached woman; that she had been kept and pampered, however, seemed to exude from her like cheap scent. Faced with Charles's famous friends, she became mute, humiliated by her own obscurity and angry with the unspoken expectation that she should be more interesting.

She met Marina Mason on one such occasion, a huge thrash celebrating the poet Arthur Holt whose biography Charles had published to large acclaim. Holt had died in relative anonymity, but the book had caused his reputation to be reassessed and Charles had brought out his back list in triumph. Catherine had never heard of him, but Charles was very proud of the *coup* and Rosamund had made it seem beastly somehow not to be on tap to cheer the resurrection of Holt as a misunderstood genius.

Catherine was bewildered by the heady din of the party, the girl editors who looked like starlets as they dashed to and fro with red and white plonk. She was literally backed against a wall and would have fled in panic if she had been able to move. It was like being stuck in the tube, only less agreeable because she was supposed to be having a good time. Squeezed next to her was a woman whose striking good looks were undermined by a slightly desperate air; she grinned sheepishly, waving a helpless hand at the fray. She was about Catherine's age, but she had a look of youthful surprise, an ingenuousness which jarred with the tone of the party. They exchanged a glance – the sort, Catherine thought, that might have been exchanged by crated calves bound for France.

'Are you an author?' the woman asked, a little wildly.

'No, I'm Charles's sister. Are you?'

She shook her head, looking relieved. 'I'm trying to catch my husband's eye. He seems to have become ensnared – possibly by a hypochondriac. He's a doctor. People tell him their symptoms.'

'Tiresome,' Catherine said, trying to sound languid; somehow she wanted to create a good impression. The woman was an American, she could tell by the voice, but although these days any American put Catherine in mind of Missy, there was something unusual, sympathetic, about her fellow wallflower.

'Maybe not. He's a psychiatrist!' she said with an engaging giggle. 'Mental illness is one disease people do not like to talk about socially.' She cleared her throat nervously. 'We have to get back to Oxford tonight. I'm driving,' she said, lifting a glass of water for Catherine's inspection. 'I was determined to get through this cold sober – not that I normally drink a lot . . . oh dear.'

Catherine smiled. It had the effect of illuminating her usually impassive face and deepening its beauty. 'Don't worry about my being related to Charles,' she said. 'I'm being *included*. I recently separated from my husband, you see. I hate the party quite as much as you do.'

The woman made a rueful grimace. 'I'm not so sure about that. You see, I am Marina . . . Mason now, but I was Arthur Holt's second wife. You know, the bimbo.' She raked twitchy fingers through her wiry flaxen hair, which was propped up by a set of pretty combs, and glanced in the direction of her present husband. Catherine spotted him. He was a tall, thin man who wore a conscientious frown. 'I only hope they're not taking it out on him.'

'I don't know whether you're a bimbo or not,' said Catherine. 'I don't know what a bimbo is.' This was not true. She spoke gently, however, because she knew a rabbit in the headlamps when she saw one.

'Oh, it's a sort of mindless hussy,' said Marina. 'Surely you read Arthur's biography? I thought the whole world had.'

'I haven't, actually. *Are* you a mindless hussy?'

'I don't think so.'

'Well, then.'

'I suppose you wonder why I am at the party at all,' Marina said. 'It would seem to draw attention to myself, I know. Sort of as if I were cashing in on Arthur.'

'I wonder why I'm here, I know that.' Catherine rolled her eyes. 'I used to enjoy books, but obviously there's an exam I haven't taken and I don't know where it sits.'

Marina laughed aloud, an infectious gurgle. 'I was married to that concept for twenty years.' More seriously, she said, 'I came because I had to face it out and because it seems sort of a last rite for Arthur. He would have loved it so much. Also, your brother has been very kind. He stopped all sorts of horrible things that my stepchildren wanted to say in the biography. I thought it would be letting him down not to come tonight.'

Catherine was suddenly and privately furious at Charles. Like herself, Marina was decorative, but unlike her, prey to the gossip columnist who would lure her into a situation where she would be discussed and sell copies. Charles had probably not even been aware that he was doing it. 'Kind!' she growled.

'Well, he is, I think,' Marina said helplessly, but a covert look established a bond between them.

At the end, they had exchanged addresses, and to Catherine's surprise she herself made the first move and asked Marina up to lunch. In no time at all they had become fast friends, and when Catherine had come to know Paul he had shone more than a little light through some of her fogs and confusions. Catherine had 'clicked' with both of them and she was as proud as a child that she had managed to do this all on her own.

It had been Beatrice who had named the Arctic Circle as the family's second and spiritual home, and Catherine had been taken with the idea. Had it not been for Marina, Catherine doubted she would have been able to survive the separation from Theo; the warmth of her new friend had been a private fire against the desolation. Yet, to carry the image to extremes, there was really just so much comradeship could achieve at the foot of Mount Erebus, and the darkness of her mother's death had brought the temperature down even farther, invading her with the penetrating authority of absolute winter.

It had been absurd – pathetic, really – to expect some thawing sign of welcome from her uncle, but she realized, as she stepped out that morning into the strong, hot sunlight of the Plataea Aristotelous, Thessaloniki's modern plaza near the harbour, that she had dreamed it might happen in the alchemy of kinship. Perhaps it was a measure of her desperation that she did. She looked down the stiff and serried arches of the square that reached down to the Thermaic Gulf, the sea. Father Edward had managed to commandeer a flat from the Catholic Church in Frangon Street, borrowed from a priest on a visit to Rome. She had left him there the night before, and she now wondered how he had got on. Although they had not discussed it, she sensed he was determinedly independent about his impaired vision, but it had worried her a little to leave him on his own blundering about with strange electricity and water taps. In fact, the thought of him cheered her. She had become so self-absorbed after her own unsettled night that she had quite forgotten him.

Although Catherine had been exhausted by the journey, she had not slept for the intensity of her fatigue. She had expected to collapse into oblivion, only to find herself staring into sudden, thorough recollections of her uncle from childhood. Having been unable to give anything but a blurred account of him to Father Edward, one which had been made up from the composite picture she had gleaned from her siblings, she had the night before suddenly recalled what must have been her own last meeting with him. Out of a whirl of thoughts and impressions gathered in the day, he materialized with startling vividness – a tall column of a man.

There he was, dandified and lordly, escorting her mother, Charles and her own seven-year-old self around the British Museum. He had neither stooped nor pandered; his every move had articulated authority. The moment she remembered the day, she realized that she had always, indeed, associated Uncle James with the British Museum, not because he had taken her there, nor because he had made contributions to its collections, nor because he had books and monographs preserved in its library, but because he had looked like it. He was lofty, an unassailable repository of the precious and the curious, things somewhat arcane and having to do with remote antiquity. Why had she failed to retrieve this memory until now?

She propped herself up against the headboard of her bed in the dark hotel room, anxious to uncover more. Had Susannah been with them that day? Surely if her cousin had been there she would have remembered it. It struck her now even more forcefully than it had done on the train journey that Susannah had been a sickly child, and it came back to her that she had been in hospital that day. What had been her problem? Some lingering complaint, Catherine felt sure, like asthma or eczema. Yes, it had been one of those nervous things, and Uncle James had seemed obscurely irritated by it. Visiting hours then had been draconian, so they had not gone to see her because they had simply been up in London for the day and had had to get back to Sussex. Uncle James had personally taken them round the statues – not that he had been a curator or anything like that – and Charles, the baby of the family, a rather aggressive, precocious little boy of six, had insisted (no, wanted, for the Simon children never *insisted*) on seeing the mummies instead. Unexpectedly, Uncle James had seemed to take an interest in her younger, bright brother, and in the end his grisly wish had been granted.

Catherine had taken it for granted since his birth that she would play second fiddle to Charles, the long-awaited boy and scion, so she had

naturally assumed that the museum trip was his treat and for his edifi-
cation. But she herself had been given that day a new pair of strappy shoes
– Clarks – with buttons, and this had slaked and absorbed her, for they had
been the right sort, at long last, and *de rigueur* at school. That was it! They
had come up to London to shop for school, and Uncle James had also
given them lunch at Simpson's-in-the-Strand, where there had been un-
imaginable roast beef with Yorkshire pudding. Because of the war, its
aftermath, this was so rarely seen that only millionaires had it, they
thought.

It was understood that her uncle had been a great success. He had
found something, sold something, a Getty had been involved? Ah, no,
as she and Beatrice had discussed, he had married money, hadn't he?
Susannah's mother had been a (dead) American heiress – van
Something . . . a Dutch name anyway, from New York. Whatever the cause
of his being so flush, the treat of beef had been seen as easily afforded. He
looked as comfortable with the surroundings of Simpson's as if he had
been giving them all a fish supper on Brighton pier, but not so jolly. In fact,
he had been very thin and had worn a well-cut suit and a foulard tie,
spectacularly sumptuous, and a silk handkerchief to match it in his breast
pocket. Catherine had been terrified of him.

No one had had to remind her of her manners. She had been as
conscious of them as if Nanny had been *right there*. She had heard Nanny's
locutions as if by spiritual means. By the time pudding (treacle tart)
arrived, these locutions had become so internalized (as the saying went
these days) that Catherine had sat bold upright, thanking and pleasing and
putting her cutlery together as if born knowing. She had had little praise
from her mother, who expected this kind of behaviour always as the very
least her children could do – that and not to get in the way.

At any rate, they had later glided in their sated state into the icy halls
of the British Museum, past vast granite tombs and daunting Pharaonic
heads . . . winged lions from the palace of Assurbanipal, from Babylon.
Her mother and her uncle had sidled off together and seemed to be
whispering with an atypical intensity for a reason as unknowable as the
cuneiform hieroglyphs printed upon the clay lions' feet. Catherine sat up
in bed. She would ring Charles. Maybe he would remember. He was
certain to remember a feast of this order!

She became feverish with trying to relive the day, but details kept
escaping her. She was sure the Elgin marbles had been explained. Nothing
else, though. And then, of course, the stated purpose of the visit had come:
the viewing of Uncle James's find.

Good heavens, she thought, it really must have been extraordinary! No wonder her mother had been at such pains to impress upon Charles and herself just what Uncle James amounted to. If she saw it all now, she would be sure to know what it represented in terms of period and importance to Greek civilization, but then all she had sensed had been the demand to be awed. It had been a very small exhibit of gold and Uncle James had dug it up. She remembered being lifted to admire it.

She searched her mind's eye for an impression of what she had seen or been told at the time. It had been a bandeau or a crown, worn once by a priestess in the depths of antiquity. Surrounding it had been some filigree earrings pinned to a white board like two butterflies, and a few rings – all discovered in a tomb, the grave of this dead woman.

Catherine could not remember noticing the tiny myrtle flowers on the crown nor the little winged nikes on their wire clouds of gold, which she now knew to be characteristic of archaic Greek jewellery, yet she did remember with sharp clarity that she had become suddenly, but not vocally, indignant that the grave of the priestess had been robbed and by Uncle James.

As a child, her notions had been very direct and simple; in a sense they still were. There had been a huge palaver about resting in peace when her grandmother had died. Masses had been said. There had been, too, a whole system of indulgences attached to the dead from about the time of Noah onwards, and she still remembered that the *Salve Regina* got 300 days clipped off Purgatory. There were always God's awful punishments, His awful sentences to be considered, and for some reason she had got everything mixed up in her head about the dead priestess (and had wondered on top of this why she had never seen a 'priestess' and had decided that such a personage most certainly would not wear gold).

It was no wonder, Catherine thought now, that she had blotted out this memory, for it had been her first real presentiment of death, its mystery laid bare and exposed. Uncle James had violated the sanctuary of this dead person, for surely a priestess would have been a very holy woman who would have worked hard for a peaceful death by prayer and penance. When, added to this, Charles had made his polite racket about seeing the mummy with its revolting sprouts of hair, its pitiful, weathered, curled-up thinness, she had been even more certain that cracking open a tomb was an insult. Why it was that she and her brother had been taken to admire the spoils of such desecration had been difficult for the young Catherine to fathom. Or had it been something else that had disturbed her that day? What remained foremost in her mind was a quality, a tone. She

37

remembered the occasion only with fear and distaste, and the memory of her uncle was still inextricably bound up with it. It was not the bandeau, his triumph, nor the gold earrings and other trinkets with which she associated him. She classified him, rather, with the steely Pharaohs in the hall whose cold breath, not breathing, seemed to exude, nonetheless, from their granite nostrils in the form of damp. This erect man with his fastidious dislike of mess or noise or children had, she now realized, been paying some debt to her mother or bringing some quarrel to a muted crisis. Even with Charles's ghoulish appetite for horror slaked, the three of them had gone home in the train oddly unified by a silence expressing disaffection: their mother, her back never slacking, had looked grimly out of the window all the way.

Catherine stood now on the pavement in front of Thessaloniki's first-ranking hotel; the faintly scented air from the Electra Palace lobby, of wrapped soaps and shower gel, seemed to cling to her as she tried to summon the doorman, who was spooning rich Americans into a taxi. With a twinge of conscience, she realized that she had not stayed in anything less grand for a period of maybe thirty years. She was sure Uncle James would approve of her lodgings, but she wondered if Father Edward saw her role in the Susannah affair as something of a hopeless camel butting stupidly at a needle's eye. Susannah had, in no uncertain terms, embraced poverty, he had told her.

This annoyed Catherine still more. And when she found herself remembering how liberal she tried to be, in her own quiet way, to various charities, she was ashamed of spiritual pride. She gave an exasperated sigh. She was confused by what to do in this strange city; she was disappointed in herself; she was worried about her decision to divorce Theo, and on top of it she had to go looking for the golden legend of this paragon of a relative she had never really liked in the first place.

She would have liked the Pharaonic dispensation of her uncle's car. Despairing now of the doorman, she summoned her own taxi and, having the advantage of the language, asked her way to her uncle's address near the city walls.

Once seated in the taxi, she started to think she would have liked to stretch her legs and get a sense of the place. She lost patience with herself, however, and settled down. As they nosed their way towards the Via Egnatia, she was struck by how much the scene put her in mind of Roman Byzantium. The roads were straight, the shops smart, the women almost haughty in their bearing, the speech slow and clipped. She smiled. She could see her Uncle James as a consul somehow, ornamented with *dignitas* and *gravitas* and perhaps a little decadent within. He had been educated at Sandhurst, then during the war had taken command of something. Had he been to Burma or India? India, she thought. Afterwards he had taken up archaeology almost as a hobby – or that was the impression he had given. During their long marriage, her husband Theo had constructively burst a few cultural balloons for Catherine. He thought the English most unbearable when they disguised raw ability as a cooked delicacy. He would have loathed the ethereal, mandarin James Vaughan.

The taxi pushed north. She realized with a start that she was thinking of her uncle not as a man but as a walking entry in *Who's Who*. Surely time had mellowed him; perhaps the tragedy had even dignified him with wisdom. He could not be all that bad. She gazed out of the window of the car, thankful, at least, that he probably would not pry into her domestic affairs, or lack of them, as her mother had. They were stuck in traffic now, she and the driver, who was, happily, taciturn, and she looked up at a crumbling Byzantine edifice to her left. Had it been a church? Had it been a mosque? Almost certainly it had been both, and a bazaar as well, for she could see in the ancient structure recesses that had been stalls. Whatever its former function, the spectacularly decrepit walls sank gracefully into large, buttressing beams of wood. Weeds and fluffy grass sprouted from old battlements, but beneath them a large, purposeful population, devoid of tourists, went to and fro, buying, selling, as if no hiatus had occurred in their steady stream for centuries.

Catherine sighed. She would have to let Yiorgia and Spiro go if she sold the house in Chios, and it made her wince to think of this. To be fair to Theo, he would certainly set them up well in old age, but Catherine loved Yiorgia. Could she really countenance not seeing her again? She would promise to visit, but she knew that she would not.

Catherine thought for a moment of praying to Susannah, lighting a candle to her. A family saint, particularly a Vaughan, might plead especially on genetic grounds. What would her statue look like? An involuntary cough of laughter rose in her, causing the driver to start. She extracted a handkerchief from her handbag and pretended to blow her nose. Suddenly, another memory of the strange girl came back to her, quite an early one, she was sure; she could date her life by nannies, so she could not have been more than four years old, for she had been with Nanny Hall. Susannah, in that case, must have been about thirteen, a silent, awkward teenager, but in the bizarre distortion of memory Catherine saw her as being a great deal younger, a fellow child. It was as hazy as it was sad to think of the narrow, half-forgotten face set in plaster, probably with a beatific smirk. Susannah

39

had stood by the Aga to keep warm: that she did remember. Catherine did not think she had been especially given to prayer as Beatrice had always been. She had seemed lost, rather, like a disoriented kitten discovered outside and put in a cardboard box with old bits of blanket. To think that this shivering, waif-like creature had died so horribly disturbed Catherine in quite a new way, and she tried to dismiss it from her mind.

The taxi jerked forward and wove its way deeper into the older part of the city where a formal building of the Ottoman period seemed to teeter on the lip of a vast excavation as if it were about to fall in. The road upwards was lined with shabby housing punctuated at intervals by Byzantine churches, one of which, she noticed, was quite fine.

For some reason it was this and not Susannah's putative sanctity that made her think of Father Edward again. He had told her he would pay a visit today to the famous tomb of St Demetrius and somehow it made her smile to think of him on this modest pilgrimage. It came to her now unbidden that she actually liked him. His purblind, mole gestures, his companionable silence and a kind of goodness about him had somehow rallied her the day before, and it now occurred to her that he had been more than generous to her in exposing his frank views concerning Susannah. Actually, she had the suspicion that he had been a little in love with her. For all the horror of his story and the emotion with which he had told it, Catherine now suppressed a giggle at the thought, then blushed when it struck her what a schoolgirl reaction this was.

She thought again and sobered herself with a twinge of pity. It was not until the train had chugged past the distant Mount Parnassos that she realized the extent of his blindness. With a touching meekness, he asked her to describe what he could not himself see, the substance of the shadows, the distant seat of Dionysos, of Apollo. Catherine was no poet, but her wit had been forced upon the peaks by his necessity; both sombre and pale with snow, they had struck her as being truly singular, and she felt a twinge of guilt now about abandoning him to fumble about in this wholly foreign city where he knew nothing of the language. Yet, he had insisted.

Lost as she was in this reflection, it startled her when the driver jerked the brakes and stopped the car. They had climbed to quite an altitude and she looked about her, astonished at the shabbiness of the neighbourhood in which she found herself, clearly an old Turkish quarter, which after the exchange of populations in 1921 must have silted up with Greeks from a depressed or oppressed class. The taxi had not quite achieved the brow of the hill, and the street wound upwards, packed densely with houses almost medieval in their appearance. Their overhanging balconies shed a gloom over the few passers-by – women in dark clothes and headscarves, scruffy children and grizzled old men with flat caps, hard faces and worry beads. The peeled walls were pitted; great lumps of plaster seemed almost to have been eaten out of them, and empty window frames looked perilously insecure, as if they might crash to the ground in response to the rumble of a cart going by.

Before Catherine could even catch her breath in sympathy for those who had to live with this dereliction, however, the driver jerked a thumb in the direction of the address she had given him. In a walled garden, set back from the road, stood her uncle's residence, for she could apply no other word to the grand, severely shuttered wooden structure before her. It was clear enough from the style of the building that a pasha, or some other Ottoman dignitary, had indeed lived there in the past, and, as Catherine knew, the outward simplicity of the large house would almost certainly belie the opulence of its interior.

Perhaps it was the story of the murder that gave her sharp misgivings about being left to tackle the house alone, but in a sense it was also the result of her long years in Chios that made Catherine feel at once uncomfortable at such a strong reminder of Turkish rule, and this, too, might have been the reason for the taxi driver's curt manner as she paid him. What had happened once could happen again, especially with the crisis to the north. As he roared off, abandoning her alone in front of the heavily barred iron gate, she had the strongest instinct to follow the cab on foot down the steep hill, leaving her uncle for evermore enclosed behind his own barricade. Maybe her letter had not arrived, for she had clearly said she would call upon him that morning. The whole place looked completely closed up, as if everyone in it had gone away for the summer.

She mustered her courage, however, and pressed a buzzer set in the forbidding wall. Although it was hot, her graceful linen skirt felt clammy and heavy against her legs, and the damp curls, which had now escaped the chignon-for-meeting-Uncle-James she had done that morning, clung to her forehead and tickled the nape of her neck.

There seemed to be no response, but as she turned to go she suddenly heard the low, wolfish sound of baying dogs, and at a bound they were there, a brace of svelte hounds, a breed she did not recognize. They had short, reddish hair, protuberant red eyes, and sleek ears: they leapt, male dogs, at the gate, barking and jumping in a chaos of aggression, baring their teeth, their hackles raised.

Catherine shrank back. She disliked dogs, and these seemed particu-larly ferocious, her mother's brother's hounds. At once, a small man with dark, slicked-down hair rounded the corner from the back of the house. He was wearing a tracksuit and a milometer and seemed to have been jogging, for sweat still gleamed on his forehead. As he neared her, she realized with surprise that he must be about sixty years old, for by his dress and his gait she had judged him a much younger man. Perhaps he dyed his hair; he seemed to have a heavy jaw and a weak chin at the same time, and he fixed her with an ironic stare, just short of rudeness. He sized her up as he came down the path. Catherine had a seizure of instant dislike.

'Hi,' he said. 'You must be Catherine Phocas.' He commanded the dogs to sit, and they did, cringing slightly. He was, she realized, an American, and he spoke with an unreconstructed nasal accent. 'I'm Phil Deals,' he added for the benefit of her puzzlement.

He took a chain off and then some bolts. 'Neighbourhood,' he said with a shrug of contempt, perhaps at the ragamuffins in the road who were staring at the scene, their faces dirty, their eyes wide. His seamed face made him look like a wizened apple, a bronzed Rumpelstiltskin, a spirit or a eunuch. 'Hi,' he said again. 'Come in, come in. We're expecting you. Big excitement, big day.'

Catherine entered and regarded the dogs at his feet with her own brand of disdain. The tracksuit of Phil Deals was a chemical blue. He leaned down and scratched their ears, then snapped his fingers and they slunk back. 'The niece,' he said, appraising her. It was as if he thought of everything in inverted commas.

Catherine had expected some pleasantry about her journey, a query as to its rigours, but this was not evidently to be awarded her.

'It's been a while,' he said enigmatically as they walked into the enclosure. She was surprised to see how English the garden was. There were even delphinium plants. But the old house was as Levantine, as Balkan, as it could be. It stood as if astride the plot of land, arms akimbo like a paynim with access to scimitars. The roof, a dull red colour, loomed over her. The cantilevered façade with its half-timbered gables did not express the Tudor ethos at all.

'How is my uncle?' she finally managed to say.

'OK, OK. He's doing all right today. But, of course, since the stroke he's not the same.'

'Stroke? I had no idea.'

'Oh, he had a big haemorrhage a few years back, but he's a fighter – tough as they come. When *was* it you last saw him?' Deals asked in a faintly accusatory tone.

'I was trying to remember that myself,' she said shortly, decisively. She drew the line now at being patronized. 'About forty-three years ago.'

'And so you're here to see him now,' Deals said flatly.

'Yes.' Who was this man?

The silky-eared, red-eyed dogs gambolled at a slight distance and he whistled to them, softly clucking. 'We'll go round the back. Uncle is in his wheelchair in the *sofa*.'

Catherine knew that *sofa* in this context meant a Turkish sitting room, but it annoyed her intensely that he had used this word as if to her ignorance. He looked like a sports coach or a 'resting' film producer. His teeth were discoloured and uneven and he needed a shave.

As deft with keys as a prison warder, he flicked his wrist at the lock of a side door. Catherine glanced into the larger garden which stood at the back and she slightly caught her breath. A labyrinth of enchanting walkways meandered under mature trees and there was the quiet plashing of a fountain. At the end of one perspective, she could see a marble entablature, still, like a blind altar, and potted with geraniums. 'Security-minded we *really* are,' said Phil Deals interrupting her thoughts. 'You cannot *know* what it's like!'

IV

CATHERINE FOLLOWED Deals over the threshold and into the gloom of a downstairs hall. A chilly smell of mothballs hung about the place as if all but the bare essentials for living were wrapped away in dustsheets. Her guide made no acknowledgement of her. He neither smiled nor ushered her in. Instead, he preceded her with a weary trudge as if he were an estate agent with a white elephant on his hands and she a client without means or serious intent to buy. Before them stood a flight of scuffed stairs, monumental with dark, carved balusters, and Deals motioned her upwards.

If the scene of Susannah's murder, execution or martyrdom made its own grim suggestion to Catherine as she ascended, the quick spasm of fear at meeting her Uncle James was worse. Perhaps it was the association with the awful butchery that Father Edward had described to her; perhaps it was the loutish Deals. More likely still, however, was the gathered weight of Lady Simon's unuttered disapproval of her brother. Her poor opinion of him seemed to coagulate in the gloom and materialize into a peculiar dread. Catherine tried to shake this off. A window on the first landing gave on to the lavish garden behind, but it shed little light. High on the wall Catherine thought she spied an oil portrait of Lord Byron, very much in need of cleaning. Whoever it was had posed as a corsair for the picture, and though the dashing costume lent an air of dusty romanticism to the stairwell it also bore the suggestion of old scandal and moral turpitude.

When they reached the top, Deals let out a sigh as if escorting her thus far had been rather an ordeal. It seemed odd that someone dressed like a games master should baulk at such a simple task: his studied indifference to her seemed eloquent with resentment. Catherine felt a sudden jab of irritation. She had not wanted to come. She did not wish to be there. It seemed that in Deals's opinion her visit to her uncle had come both too late and inconveniently, and she wondered if she ought to return to Father Edward with the news that the whole Susannah enterprise was bound to be a waste of time. She could hire a car and show him round the region. Maybe she would drive him to the Meteora, for instance, or, although she was not sure a Catholic priest would be welcome on Mount Athos, perhaps she could park him there; she would not, blessedly, be able to accompany him.

44

She looked up at an imposing set of double doors capped by a neo-classical pediment; pretty, spindly furniture graced the landing – an antique mirror, a hall table, an inlaid chair, all perched as if in anticipation of a footman to complete the picture.

Deals knocked abruptly and, without waiting for an answer, flung the doors open, giving the gesture full dramatic emphasis. 'Your uncle!' he said.

Catherine drew in a nervous breath. Before her, at the far end of a handsome drawing room, sat James Vaughan, propped in a wheelchair against a shuttered window which was partly opened to let in a little light and air. 'Uncle James?' she said uncertainly, but he did not move.

For a moment, it was hard to believe he was alive. He was exactly frail, almost inhumanly so. Like a vacated cocoon, his body seemed to hang tremulously, prey to the slightest gust of wind. His eyes were large, pale blue, and wintry, his lips thin, his cheekbones angular, and he remained very still. At length, with a large effort, he turned his head a fraction and wheezed out some kind of reply to her greeting.

Catherine moved closer, in danger, she realized, of gawking at this spectacle. Her uncle's chest was concave, his shoulders fallen, but his hands and arms appeared to have escaped the general devastation of age. He had curiously powerful forearms, perhaps from pushing the wheelchair. And as she stood in front of him, presenting herself for the promised reunion, her eye lit upon his hands. He had subtle, nimble fingers, long and spiritual, except for the unsettling detail of long, curved nails which had been filed rather like a woman's. This filled her with an odd repugnance. The large darkened room seemed stuffy. A rancid smell lingered over it, half-human and half-animal. She wondered if her uncle and Deals kept goats somewhere beneath the window. The delicate furniture, which stood as if etched from the shadows, and an elaborate crystal chandelier seemed, in this atmosphere, the etiolated affectations of a provincial life not far removed from the farmyard.

James Vaughan looked vacantly at Catherine, and for quite a while. Suddenly, she wondered if he had Alzheimer's disease. Was this the reason for Deals's brusque irony? The family she represented must indeed seem uncaring to him if he alone had been bearing the burden of her uncle's senility. However, just as she was about to turn in perplexity to Deals, her uncle's eyes narrowed, and he seemed to take her in. He peered, scrutinizing her. 'Are you Isabelle's daughter?' he said – and clearly.

'Catherine,' said Catherine. She crept a little closer as if she might break him with the vibrations of too definite a step.

45

'Kind of you to come,' he said. 'Isabelle's dead.'

Catherine did not know if he sought to inform her of her mother's death or if he were merely stressing its reality. 'Yes, I'm afraid so. She died in February.'

He nodded. 'You do not in the least resemble my sister,' he said.

Oddly rebuffed by this, Catherine felt tears prick at the back of her eyes.

'Come closer. More like Maman, I think. Here, let me look at you in the light.'

Phil Deals went to the window and threw the shutters fully open almost as if he were uncovering sins known to him but forgotten by Catherine herself. She felt uncomfortable, exposed. She stood before her uncle in the graceful room as though she were seven once again and at the British Museum, surrounded by tall and shadowed pagan deities.

'Yes, she looks like Maman. Do you not agree, Philip?'

Deals squinted at Catherine and shrugged. 'James, I never knew your mother.' ('I continually remind him of this,' he said to Catherine as an aside.) 'But I'm prepared to say she does resemble the photographs.'

There seemed to be satisfaction all round at this. She had been identified, ringed like a bird.

'Then, of course, there is George Simon,' her uncle added. 'Your father,' he said, reminding her as if this were needed. 'A baronet,' he said to Deals, 'a cut above me, you see.'

'How intolerable!' said Deals sarcastically.

Catherine began to feel as if the Mad Tea Party were underway, and she the butt of countless buried cross-references between the Mad Hatter and the March Hare.

'Your father was a kind man!' Her uncle spoke with a disoriented suddenness, as if the memory had waylaid him, giving him a vivid jolt. 'Poor Isabelle.'

There was an edge to this remark that made Catherine feel that her uncle was getting at her mother in some way. A weary, mocking sigh escaped him as if to stress the ambiguity of his remark.

Catherine was suddenly seized with the idea that both men were being deliberately rude to her. 'May I sit down?' she asked stiffly.

'Ah, of course, of course . . . Please. You must forgive me, Catherine. I have become unused to visitors and am quite a recluse.'

Catherine flushed with shame at her own bad manners. Truth to tell, she had always had a spiky disposition and had often been told that she was

46

brusque with people. Her uncle began to mobilize himself, twisting the wheelchair this way and that in a flurry, it seemed, to locate a suitable chair.

'Philip!' he cried, 'let us kill the fatted calf. Can there not be cakes and coffee for my niece who has come so far? We must open these gloomy shutters. *Kiria* Phocas must see the *sofa*, the salon.'

'*Amesos*!' Phil Deals cried. It meant 'at once', and was the characteristic reply of Greek waiters in response to an order.

'Thank you,' Catherine murmured, mortified to realize that this charade they enacted was probably meant to humiliate her, 'but I have had coffee and do not wish to disturb in any way the rhythm of your household, Uncle James.' With a twinge of pity for his frailty, she added more gently, 'I'm sorry. I was not thinking about how unwell you have been.'

'Nonsense!' cried her uncle, galvanized, it seemed, by the surly look of Deals. 'Philip, *do* be an angel and bring some semblance of civilization to these proceedings. The fair Catherine is welcome, and *will* be welcomed by me.'

Although she was still embarrassed, she was surprised at the way Deals did his bidding. Efficiently, he opened the shutters of the other two French windows which dominated the room, and a flood of light streamed in.

'You see, we're not exactly Miss Havisham,' her uncle said. 'If we live in darkness, it's really more to do with the damage the sun does to the fabric.'

Catherine was up on this sort of thing, having restored the house on Chios. She nodded. 'One can't be too careful,' she said with feeling. 'What a beautiful room!'

Everywhere the tone of gold silk was picked up by the polished wood of slender chairs with backs and arms so dainty that it seemed impossible they should be sat upon. Tables and lamps and vases abounded. In a niche, there was a marvellously painted *trompe-l'oeil* showing a formal garden, which led the eye to a distant palace, worthy of a sultan, or perhaps someone more exalted still. It was as if the combined longings of Louis Quinze and Suleiman the Magnificent had created this gem of a room, where intricacies and intimacies might be woven undisturbed. It was as Occidental as it was Oriental. It was where East and West met.

'So glad you like it,' said her uncle. He did seem genuinely pleased.

Phil snorted.

'Get thee gone!' James Vaughan cried, clapping his hands. 'Off with you and *do* bring the coffee, Phil!'

Deals, in his now completely incongruous tracksuit, stomped off, humphing and hawing as he went.

'Sit!' her uncle commanded. He indicated a wing chair, a lesser one that did not look as if it belonged quite yet in the Victoria and Albert Museum.

Catherine was by no means one to bend in any wind that blew, but she did as she was told almost despite herself. She perched lightly on the edge of the chair and folded her hands on her knees.

After a moment's deliberation, her uncle grasped the steel rims of the wheelchair and thrust it forward with a grunt. He parked in front of an antique ceramic stove, an ornament in itself; the tiles were covered with fine tracery as if to lend warmth and decorum to the suite of a begum. He leaned back in the chair and regarded Catherine with his cold blue eyes. She wondered how it was she had imagined he was gaga.

'You musn't mind Phil,' he said at last with the *dégagé* air of a perfect host. 'In his way, he is my personal guarantee of privacy, as you have clearly discovered for yourself. One hardly needs the dogs to keep visitors at bay! Very tediously he continually reminds one of how much he does for one – and he does do a lot. I often have to ask myself, though, who else would have him?'

Now that the light streamed into the room, Catherine took in her uncle more fully. He was wearing a blue silk cravat tidily knotted under a faintly soiled shirt that looked as if it had come long ago from the Burlington Arcade. An Afghan rug lay on his knees and a cardigan was draped around his shoulders, giving his thin torso the look of an emaciated mannequin in a smart men's shop. Wisps of white hair hung about his temples where liver spots stood in large clusters. The only thing that remained from her early memory of him, however, was his disdainful air. It had softened and become more feminine, more exquisite, but the quality of haughtiness was the same.

'Who *is* he?' she found herself asking. Her nervousness, the strain of the last few days in Greece, had wrung her out to the point of protest.

Her uncle waved his slender hand. 'Oh, the tiresome little man is my nephew – officially, that is. I suppose that makes him your first cousin by marriage. He is the son of my dead wife's elder sister. She married a ghastly man from Idaho or somewhere like that . . . No, let me see, Detroit. He gives himself airs about that. *Can* you imagine! He came on an impromptu visit some twenty years ago – and stayed. I think it may be the longest visit in history.'

Like an old harmonium operated by bellows, her uncle's windpipe seemed to have cleared with the exercise of talking. Small gestures from his curiously taloned hands suggested a former expressiveness. 'Do you remember my wife?' he asked, rather as an afterthought.

'I'm afraid I do not,' Catherine said. She wondered if it were too soon to broach the subject of Susannah. The idea made her feel very uneasy and she shifted around in her chair.

'Do you not? I felt sure you had met her. Mind you, she died very young – of a weak heart. She had rheumatic fever as a child. I am quite certain, however, that we came to stay with your parents before her death, and I distinctly remember you as a very pretty little girl.'

Catherine was not as taken with the compliment as she might have been. It seemed not so much a generous remark as one made, obscurely, at someone else's expense, perhaps even at Susannah's. Again a memory of her cousin's sickliness came to her, defining her with a white, pinched face, lacklustre hair, and a quiet withdrawal from life. Of course! It had been Susannah, not her mother, who had had rheumatic fever as a child, and this was why she had been 'delicate'.

'Ah, let me see,' he said, elevating the fine head to a position of studied recollection: 'it was just before the war.'

'Well, I wasn't born until 1943. You must be muddling me with Beatrice,' Catherine said. 'She was about the same age as ... uh ... Susannah.' Her eyes flicked over him as she spoke, but the mention of his dead daughter's name seemed to have no effect. 'Of course, it might have been Theresa, who is directly above me. I'm the one above Charles. I was remembering only yesterday that you took my brother and me to Simpson's and around the British Museum.'

'Oh, yes, Beatrice . . . an attractive child and Isabelle's eldest. It would have been Beatrice. What is she doing now? It appals me to realize that she must be nearly sixty.'

'She is the Prioress of a Carmelite Monastery,' Catherine said, watching how this went down.

'Oh dear! What a waste!' her uncle said. 'Or are you frightfully religious? My poor sister certainly was, and a good influence too, I'm *quite* sure.'

'I'm not unreligious,' was all Catherine would say. 'But we're all quite chuffed with Beatrice and think she's done rather well.'

He gave a dry smile. 'Well, I'm a hopeless pagan, I'm afraid. Comes from digging up too many heathen idols, I expect. Then, of course, there was my darling *mother*, whose slavery to the Church gave me a permanent will to be entirely free from it.'

49

Catherine was taken aback at the venom with which he spoke of her grandmother, whom she was supposed especially to resemble in his eyes. 'Well, I'm sure Beatrice would remember Aunt . . .' She was so flustered that she had forgotten the name of her uncle's wife.

' . . . Nancy,' he said, having let her sweat for a moment. 'Not a proper name really, is it? Nancy Schuyler, she was . . . Flapper deb from New York and heiress to a manufacturing fortune.' He seemed almost triumphantly to proclaim that his wife had been a notable fool. 'Phil was fond of her,' he added.

'I do remember Susannah,' Catherine found herself saying. It thrilled her just as skiing did: she had jumped into wanting to hound this vain-glorious popinjay and rattle him somehow.

Before she could assess the effect of her words, however, Deals arrived bumptiously with a large tray set beautifully according to the ordinances of Greek hospitality. He had changed, too, and was wearing a polo-neck shirt and neat duck trousers. 'Here we are!' he said. He laid everything out just so on a brass table, of considerable antique value, Catherine noted. He passed round the little cups and pastries with the ceremony of a wife. It dawned on her that they were possibly a couple, and suddenly a whole range of clarifications presented themselves to her. If this were true, then it was no wonder they mistrusted an emissary from Isabelle Simon, who would have wholly anathematized such a union. No wonder, too, she herself had been relegated to an hotel from which vantage she would not be able to pry into their domestic arrangements. What was more, the whole mystery of her arch-conservative mother's subdued horror at her brother was explained.

Now she saw it! Uncle James had made a stab at heterosexuality in his ill-starred marriage to Nancy Schuyler and the fruit of this union, Susannah, had lived as a reproach, in some hazy way, to his true sense of himself. It struck Catherine at once that having his daughter turned into a Catholic saint might be for Uncle James the last straw. She would stand eternally beaming on a plinth, an everlasting condemnation of his life. Her uncle was an ironist, she could see, but possibly not enough of one to see the joke in this refined twist.

'Did I hear you mentioning Susie-Q as I was coming up the stairs?' Deals asked in that arch, brittle tone which he could apparently not resist. He had, quite obviously, been listening at the door.

'Delicious,' she said, swallowing a mouthful of truly light, sweet pastry. Her gorge rose, however, at the manner in which he had mentioned

Susannah's name. A fetid memory of reported details returned to her, of limbs hacked at. Where had she died? Maybe she had died in this room.

'Glad you like it.' Deals drew out an untipped cigarette, hand-rolled, by the look of it. He lit it and blew an aromatic stream of smoke into the room. It hovered as a haze, like a genie from a Turkish lamp. 'She is a cousin we share . . . or shared. We have Susannah in common.'

Catherine looked from one man to the other. It seemed extraordinary that neither reacted to the name of the dead woman with a recognition of what she must have suffered. Of course, they must be used to it by now, but all the same . . . 'James was telling me that you are Aunt Nancy's nephew,' she replied, her tone of voice noncommittal.

'I knew Susannah very well,' Deals continued. 'She stayed with us every summer. We had a house in Northern New Jersey. Darling Uncle had his digs and books and conferences, so Susie stayed with us instead. Isn't that so, James?'

If Catherine was astonished by this almost naked accusation of neglect, her uncle seemed unfazed by it. Whatever crucial position Deals occupied in the household, he also seemed to serve as court jester, one who had limitless powers of frankness. 'It's come to light that she was very fond of my mother,' Catherine said, not knowing why she intervened.

At this, an icy ripple of laughter came from her uncle. There was something so shocking, so inappropriate about this that Catherine started, making her demi-tasse clatter against its saucer. As difficult as she herself had found Lady Simon, there seemed something altogether unseemly about this cynicism from the recently dead woman's only brother. Catherine had put up with every kind of interference from her mother, and this had played a part in her separation from Theo. All the same, her pity for the dead little bones of Lady Simon rose within her at the expression of contempt on James Vaughan's face.

She found herself looking at Deals, perhaps as if he might provide an interpretation to the recondite language of her uncle's apparent callousness.

To her great surprise, a flash of empathy, of indignation, leapt from his eyes, as if at last he had found an ally worthy of the name.

'Another cake?'

'No, thank you.'

Deals shot a mephitic glance at his charge in the wheelchair, shrugged and blew another smoke ring. 'There's a lot you need to know,' he said *sotto voce*. Catherine noticed that the whites of his eyes were yellowed and venous and it was this that made him look somehow like a wise reptile.

He looked at her again, no more sympathetic than the lizard he resembled, but, curiously, she realized that he meant to have her for a confederate, though in the service of what conspiracy she could not imagine. He seemed to assume a bond between them, and she had no idea how this had come about.

They both looked at her uncle . . . their uncle, after all. He had fallen asleep.

'There he is, snoozing away. Unsettling, isn't it?'

'Did you make these cakes yourself?' she whispered, not really knowing where to look for social common ground.

'I *can* cook,' he said evasively.

'Well, I will have another one after all,' she said. 'And then, I wonder if we could find a place where we can talk. There are one or two things I would like to discuss with you, if you don't mind.'

'Whatever it is,' he said dryly, 'I can guarantee I have a right to know.'

V

JAMES VAUGHAN awoke with a start. The shutters were open, the sun was at its zenith, and he was alone. Where was Phil? Where was his niece? The coffee cups still stood on the table and the air was utterly silent. He put his hand to his forehead, which pricked and tingled. The sun had burnt a livid red patch into the delicate, fair skin along his left side, and his face throbbed slightly, emitting little beads of sweat. He must have been sitting there for over an hour, abandoned to the elements. 'Phil!' he cried, but there was no reply. A familiar stench rose from his trousers where urine had soaked them in his sleep. He gave a sob of frustration. 'Phil!'

Why was the silence so profound?

Depending on his mood, Phil could be fastidious to the point of mania; on the other hand, sometimes he would leave James untended for what seemed like long stretches of time, and then scold him for the accident. All of a sudden it struck him that it was unlike Phil to have let it happen on a drawing-room day. Drawing-room days were few and far between now. There had been no way, however, of fending off the heartless Catherine, and so Phil and the boy had had to heave him up the stairs from his bedroom. Phil had been as rigorous as Nanny this morning, and in fact often reminded James of that bleak individual; she, too, had often forced James to the lavatory when he hadn't the slightest inclination to go, but then, of course, she had been worse to Isabelle for she had hated girls.

He surveyed the tray. Cold dregs of coffee congealed in the cups and pastry crumbs seemed to have been strewn about the burnished surface as if the children of the nearby slums had entered the house. Upstairs, downstairs. In their upstairs life, Phil hated to see dirty crockery left about. Downstairs was a different existence, like a foxhole, and took James back to the war, the nomadic existence of freedom, of his 'misspent youth', as Phil was wont to say.

James struggled to get his bearings. What happened nowadays resembled being in a rowing-boat where he had mislaid the oars: the drift often found him bumping against dark shores, banks upon which there stood features of the wrong journey, as if the current could flow backwards. He was talking to Isabelle, but she had blonde hair, and she was getting married, a frightened girl in white. There were no sentimental tears on

Maman's face under the imperial cloche she wore, only relief at the suitable match. He was thinking that she could now spend more time with her dogs. His mother had kept a fleet of them, a curious breed of Belgian barge dogs called Schipperkes, which were small, black and nasty. Isabelle had had a veil, a hood of flowers like Ophelia about to drown, and it had finally fallen to him to tell her 'what to expect' on her wedding night as Maman had omitted this. Poor little Isabelle! She had been so shaken; yet, mysteriously, she and George Simon had become a devoted couple, excluding perhaps even their children and certainly James himself from the depth of a bond which had been meant only to be superficial. Good God! What year had that been? Some time before the war at any rate . . . was it '34?

The boat collided with the bank (as it were) and he fell, jumbled, into the present.

Isabelle was dead.

Why hadn't he been told?

She had died in February and the arrogant daughter had waited until April to write to him, mentioning the event *en passant*, just because she happened to be visiting Thessaloniki. Not, of course, that he minded. As Phil had pointed out, his sister had left him high and dry for the last twenty years. These things hurt and then they stopped hurting. In his experience, women enjoyed the exercise of high moral disdain more than they did any other faculty.

Now he grasped it, why he had seen backwards into Isabelle's marriage. Isabelle had had dark hair, but Catherine, her daughter, was fair. He had been to Catherine's wedding too; she had married a Greek with the pure olive beauty of the Levant. The ceremonies had got muddled. Like her mother, his niece had resembled the crouching Rossetti maiden Mary fending off the advances of the Angel Gabriel. Isabelle had not wanted to see him, though. She had not even written to him after Susannah's death.

Was it really Catherine who had come? Or had she been one of what Phil called his 'spooks'? Sometimes he saw things that were not there, remembered things that had not happened. Phil sniffed through James's unknown territory like a guide dog. Perhaps he had invented Catherine. Was she with Phil? Even distracted by a visitor, Phil would not have gone off with the house unlocked; especially with a visitor, he would not have left James and the drawing room in such a state.

'Phil!' This time he bellowed. There was no reply. James listened, and gradually came to hear nothing but the sound of his own terror singing in his ears. Had there been talk about Susannah? What had been said? He had no idea that Isabelle had been fond of Susannah. If she had been so fond of Susannah, she might at least have had the decency to send flowers to her funeral. Susannah had never told him she was fond of Isabelle. She had stayed at Isabelle's house a certain amount in her childhood, but that did not mean she was fond. Then, Susannah was the sort of person who never told one things like that. Isabelle, of course, had become blighted by religion in middle age after George Simon died. She had always been a bit 'pi', but she had never fooled James, not even when she had finally come to delude herself. So it had been Isabelle who had poisoned Susannah with so much 'morality'. He strained again for any sound at all.

Where were the dogs? They had been out earlier, for he had heard their deep-throated, panicked barking at the stranger at the gate. They cruised the area, patrolled it. Phil was an excellent dog-handler. He knew dogs. They responded absolutely, even to his unspoken commands. Usually when they were out, James could hear the click of their claws on the terrace, the chink of their choke chains . . . their panting as they completed the circuit of the grounds and came near the house. Phil would softly whistle, cluck. Now, there was no sound of them, nothing. It was possible to poison dogs. Phil feared it. One of them had gashed a neighbourhood child who had got over the wall into the garden, and Phil had said he was frightened the child's father would throw over a piece of 'arsenic meat'. With a thrill of horror, it came to James that any one of his enemies could do this; and especially those among them who thought he still possessed the Head.

He pushed the wheelchair forward with his powerful arms and swiftly gained the escritoire where he kept his old service revolver. In fact, there were guns hidden all over the house. After what had happened, Phil had thought it wise. James remembered the location of each and every one – a little nervously, for he knew how to use them and what they could do. Phil, who had only a fascination, cleaned them, often lovingly. He would oil the arsenal out in the garden, carefully removing the parts and putting them back together again. On this occasion, James was glad of Phil's foresight.

Resting the weapon on his lap, he pushed the wheelchair forward to the door and sat alert, especially for sounds in the study down the hall. There was nothing in the noonday hour, not the cry of a bird nor of a distant child nor a breath of wind. After so many years, he was able to sense Phil's whereabouts in the house kinetically. Either for some extraordinary reason he had gone out . . . or he was dead.

Oh, Phil! he thought.

Slowly, the little ooze of a new fear began to grow and take hold.

Suppose the woman he had just met was not Catherine Phocas at all. She could have seen Isabelle's death notice in the paper and realized that her story would not be easy to check. Phil had shown him her letter and helped him to write the reply, for his hands were so shaky now. But this did not necessarily mean it was Catherine to whom he had replied. Anyone could pinch a bit of headed stationery, or even have some made up if the stakes were high enough. A 'Catherine', not *the* Catherine, could have been produced out of thin air with only a few sketchy lines to go on, an entry in Debrett, the right sort of hair and accent. What better tool for his enemies than a well-bred, middle-aged Englishwoman? She had not even remembered Nancy, and had made the sly reference to Susannah, engaging Phil's confidence in this subtle manner!

Of all the torments Phil had devised for James, his most refined was Susannah, one that he saved up for special occasions. He revelled in his horrid nickname for her – 'Susie-Q' – and would utter it with a particular relish, as if it tasted good. And Phil had felt like a spot of torture today . . . oh yes, from early that morning. He had punished with the flannel and with the hairbrush. And so, when this imposter had come, he had risen to the bait. Phil loved to have an audience. With an audience, his sadism knew no bounds. He had played straight into this woman's hands, and even now he might be lying slumped and bleeding on the floor while the woman efficiently rummaged, looking for evidence of the Head's whereabouts. Her anxiety goading her, her frustration mounting, she might come looking for him. A half-landing and the hall were all that stood between him and torture. Well, he was ready for her.

'Phil!' he tried to call, but the name stuck to his tongue like dry ice and nothing but a terrified wheeze emerged. Suppose Phil were not dead after all but was planning to leave with this woman. He threatened it often enough – to go and leave James all alone.

James listened carefully, perhaps for the low murmur of female entice-ment. Phil could be bought. James never knew how much money he still had from the Schuylers and old Deals. He was impetuous, a gamester, but maybe not with money. Susannah used to say that he would gamble his life away if he could. Why had he not thought about it before? There were buyers enough. He knew. Oh yes, there were buyers, all right, and the stuff of blackmail lurked about the house. He had almost forgotten how the blueprints of the Church of the Holy Sepulchre, which lay in the safe, might be used to incriminate him unfairly, to say nothing of his research on the Dionysos site. And there were other papers as well. Even before Susannah's murder, there had been rumours. Some Orthodox fanatics had blackened him as a heathen, which of course he was. The destruction of Christendom itself, however, had never been his foremost aim. All he had wanted to do was excavate in the grounds of one mediocre fourteenth-century church! Even though that was in the past, these people had long memories. They hadn't forgotten the Battle of Thermopylae, much less St Paul's mission to the Thessalonians. To say nothing of 1204 . . .

As for the Dionysos Sanctuary which he had discovered, the Church mendaciously claimed to this day that St Paul had preached at the site (they owned that land too, merely a field) where an early Christian community was said to have had its base; they maintained, furthermore, that James's findings were to be interpreted as proof of the existence of a rudimentary basilica, and not a pagan temple at all. Suppose they knew that James had surreptitiously discovered more since the theft of the Head. Phil himself had gone out, photographed and sketched, and from this evidence James had slowly, painstakingly, pieced together the Dionysos Sanctuary.

Sometimes, in order to flee the 'spooks', in order to make them let him alone, James would take sanctuary himself in the imagined temple.

He tried to think about it now, but to conjure it might be to endanger it. Slowly, the fragments of lopped-off Doric entablature, the vestiges of post-holes, had built themselves into a woodland shrine in the hills. In archaic times, it would have been a clearing in the forest, where the women of the region would have flocked, leaving behind them their distaffs, the stiff entailment to a rational social order. With dark unreason in the moon-light, they would have cast aside restraint, bloodying their jaws with torn meat, gnawing at bones, displaying their very unsanctimonious true nature, their sex, to Dionysos, himself dismembered and twice born. How the god had revealed them, finding his way through the veneer of self-righteous-ness to the pulse of frenzied, orgiastic abandonment! The site was still a place of great power, of that James was certain: Phil was often reluctant to go there even now, and when he came back he would be in a mood for days. From the sifted evidence, it was clear that devotion to the telluric Dionysos had grown in prestige and grandeur. He had proof from the missing Head. Over a century before the founding of Thessaloniki, the Sanctuary had been established.

At first, he had rather despised Dionysos. Everything in his back-ground and education had been built on discipline and reason. His early chance meeting with the god's artefacts had drawn him into a fascination almost with his own contempt for the slovenly wine-stained barbarian, an infant god, not unlike Jesus in some ways, who had tried to rescue his mortal mother from Hades, thus mirroring the Assumption of the Virgin. But, bit by bit, the scandalous androgyny of Dionysos had drawn him closer, not to the mindless hedonism which Phil enjoyed but to a greater depth. Dionysos was a god who stood apart, who touched the angles of madness and chaos in nature.

On some days, when somehow it seemed permitted, the Sanctuary seemed to lift itself darkly around his mind. There, the god crowned his bride Ariadne with flowers and placed her in the heavens; there the Maenads sang paeans of praise. Sometimes he could make it all happen: the torches, the rushes, the sacrifice, the wine; and, when he could, it did not matter so much about the Head. At these times, James could leap like the flame among the sacred participants, then transmogrified, purified from the afflicting oppositions of male and female, he could feel himself ascending.

At times, Phil seemed to know when 'a retreat' was needed. James never told him what went on in the private cave, but Phil 'smoked dope', a soldierly habit he had picked up while pushing a pen in Vietnam. When things really oppressed James, Phil would offer to share, and this facilitated the journey.

They were capable of anything! James had a horrid vision of black-robed, black-bearded monks swarming on Phil like flies, directed by one gesture of the woman who called herself Catherine. He shook it off. It was unlikely that they would act so directly.

The edge of his panic reached a pitch in a cry of frustration. If only he could get down the stairs! No, that had to do with another time. He was in the drawing room now. If he manoeuvred the wheelchair just a little closer to the door, maybe he could hear movement in the study. James fingered the gun in his lap. If he gave way to temptation and moved, then they would be able to hear him, not he them. And who was to say what would happen? There had been blood before and it could flow again. Daily, nightly, he dreaded it.

It was not as if his enemies were confined to the Orthodox Church. In fact, the whole discipline of archaeology itself had become little more than a political football in Greece, especially since this 'Macedonian' crisis had arisen. Phil kept him informed. Little Skopje to the north had put a picture of Thessaloniki's landmark, the White Tower, on their worthless currency, and this had not only resulted in the port being closed to them, it had also brought out a lunatic obsession with Philip of Macedon. James often thought bitterly on his misfortune. His Dionysos Sanctuary lay a mere two miles from his house and was barely beneath the soil. It also happened to pre-date Philip by a century. These days in Greece, the passion for emphasizing the Greekness of the Greek ruler was so intense that he could imagine the city fathers digging up even Agia Sophia or the shrine of St Demetrius if the mere shred of Philip's tunic lay buried beneath. Well, of course that was absurd. He knew it was. Still, the point remained. Again, if he had been Greek himself, if he had been a native archaeologist like Andronicos, then none of the confusion about the site or the Head would have arisen.

It was this that rankled more than anything – the discovery by Andronicos of the Royal Macedonian Tombs of ancient Aigai, now called Vergina, a tourist trap! As Phil often pointed out to him, no one knew more than he about gold hordes, so why was it that Andronicos had not asked James to attend the excavation of the burial chamber? Andronicos had been a hero after the find. As a dead hero, he was almost as unassailable as Philip of Macedon himself.

Even before the recent Balkan nonsense, there had seemed to be no ancient stone that could be left unturned and none without some Byronic cause lurking underneath it. Once the Melina Mercouri types had got wind of the rumours about the Head of Dionysos, James had been frozen out of the archaeological fraternity. Although he had not been fully discredited, there were those who suspected that he still had the Head, those who would do anything to get it, and all in the name of 'patriotism'.

Only Phil knew about the sketches and where they were. If James's enemies were as powerful as he believed them to be, they could make it well worth Phil's while to hand over the papers and his few slides. In fact, even if the woman did happen to be Catherine Phocas – perhaps *especially* if she were Catherine Phocas – her personal fortune must be vast. Wasn't her husband the shipping magnate? A Greek? He could have been persuaded to join forces with the scheming 'patriots'. With his enormous wealth, he could find just the right temptation for Phil. Not many people knew Phil's little weaknesses, but a rich man could find out. Phil would go, gloating in the role of Judas, enjoying it.

James, now febrile with anger, started to catalogue this new and convincing evidence of Phil's deviousness. It would not be the first time his trust had been betrayed. In fact, his whole life had been a saga of cruel disappointments. He might as well die at the hands of these cutthroats, he thought. They had butchered Susannah in the hall, they might as well slaughter him in the drawing room, just like a game of Cluedo: Miss Scarlet and Colonel Mustard. Actually, he was a retired major. He would show them how a British soldier could die.

All at once, he was brought up sharply against Susannah. He had meant specifically not to think about her, but there he was with flashbulbs popping and questions being asked. He struggled hard. Once in her thrall, there was nothing but her. He wrestled. One slip into the memory of his daughter presaged a voyage to Hades, his little boat pulled down the rushing gorge, as if he were being pulled into it after her or by her . . . drowned, all rational thought broken up like the spars of a useless raft. He battled harder. He fought and struggled free.

Almost more frightful than her treachery had been the irony of her final clinging, her clinging like a child. Indeed, there had always been something in her that had pulled him down: her neediness. A scent of her, which was the scent of hunger, lingered in the room like the smell of burnt almonds which sometimes predicated an attack of her, but he was free this time, he thought . . . yes, he knew it. He tried to breathe more deeply and the heavy revolver fell from his lap to the floor with a crash.

Before James knew it, Phil was in the room as if he had materialized out of nowhere.

Standing before the wheelchair, his arms folded across his chest, he took in the scene. 'You old moron! What the hell do you think you're doing with that gun!'

Although James shuddered with relief to see him, he refused to speak. He glared at Phil.

Phil sniffed the air, wrinkling his nose at the scent of urine. 'Oh, my *God*! I can't leave you alone for two minutes, can I?' He shook his head, scooped up the revolver from the floor and inspected it. 'Well, at least you left the safety catch on,' he said, 'but I imagine that was a close call.' He shoved it back in the drawer. 'So, you were going to drill the fair Catherine full of holes, were you? It's unbelievable!'

James said nothing.

Phil muttered to himself and bustled about the table, piling the crockery, sighing, fussing with crumbs. If the atmosphere was rocky, it was familiar. Like ill-matched castaways, they had come to endure the inconvenience of each other in choppy seas.

'Where were you?' James burst out at last. He heard the fear and strain breaking his voice; he had intended to be peremptory, even minatory.

Phil stood, weary arms akimbo on his hips. 'I *talked* with your niece. I *rang* for a taxi. I *put* her in the taxi. OK with you?'

'I . . . she . . . *is* Catherine, isn't she?'

'Well, who the hell do you think she is? She even looks like you. Do you think Susie's Nemesis has finally rolled up? You know and I know that

60

Susie's a lot more subtle than that! It's the silence which really gets to you . . . and not knowing.'

'I do wish you would not call my daughter "Susie"!' James cried, regaining control of the haughty tone that Phil detested. 'And, I can assure you, I have nothing to fear from Nemesis.'

'Well, we're on our high horse today.' Phil sighed. 'I suppose you don't want to know what the fair niece is up to. You will never ever guess in a million years, and as you're in such a foul mood, waving guns around and the like, I'm not going to tell you.'

James was not, however, yet prepared to eat humble pie. He glowered petulantly into the middle distance.

Phil lifted the heavy tray with ease and balanced it on his hip. With his free hand, he dangled the key to the drawer in front of James's nose. 'From now on, this gun is out of commission; it stays in there. This stays with me.'

'What is she here for, then?'

'Wouldn't you like to know! All I can tell you is that we had a long talk, James. *Long*!'

'What a lot of power your little secrets give you, Phil.'

'Sometimes you fill me with such contempt, such loathing! Your uppity niece will have you squirming, all right!'

'I really can't imagine how, Phil.'

'It's exciting, it's dramatic. It isn't anything you expect.' Phil jeered all of this in the sing-song voice of a bad boy. 'You'll hate it!'

James pulled all of his forces into him. 'I hate you!' And he saw he had struck with unbelievable strength.

There was the hung silence of shock and Phil blinked hard.

'I said "I hate you".'

There was another slow moment, then Phil peered at him closely. 'Your head! Your skin! What have you been up to?'

'You left me in the sun.' James was triumphant. 'Am I badly burned?'

Phil put down the tray and left the room without a word. He soon returned with a bowl of cool water and a flannel. Tenderly he bathed the sore skin and James flinched, basking nonetheless in his nephew's acute remorse. Phil never said that he was sorry but James knew when he was sorry. Things would build up until they culminated in something like the sunburn, then Phil would suffer almost egregiously and the balance of power would be brought back to a level of near-equality.

'Better?' Phil asked at length. 'Come on. Let's get you changed.'

VI

CATHERINE HAD found her way back to the Electra Palace Hotel, not by taxi but on foot, as if by walking she could spin one ordered thread of meaning out of the heaps of contradictory evidence she had heard that morning.

She had been as delighted to get away from her uncle's house as if she had been locked in his cellar. As she walked, however, her release offered her little illumination; for, as she sifted through the snippets she had gleaned from her visit, they seemed to elude her like so much thistledown blown from her mind. By the time she arrived back at the hotel, she felt no nearer to the truth than when she had started out that morning.

Without a map to guide her, she had aimed to follow the ancient, crenellated city walls down towards the harbour but had managed to get herself lost, though not seriously, in a disorderly maze of streets upon which layers of architectural history displayed themselves with slovenly abandon. Along the way, it would have been quite possible to come across a temple of Pan, an early Christian basilica, or a bit of minaret poking between the serried bunkers of post-war flats. Catherine, however, paid little attention to the scene. The more she tried to make sense of what had happened to Susannah, the more she found herself unable to follow any process of thought. Against her will, she was swamped in a reaction so instinctual that she could not ignore it; everything about her uncle's household filled her with unreasoning fear.

Catherine had spent many years in silent thought, partly because she had never believed anyone would be interested in her opinions. Everyone had always seemed cleverer than she was; she had married soon after leaving school. Because of this, she had little confidence in her natural wit. Bold thoughts and sound intuitions came to her, but she shrank from the risk of venturing too much on them, and thus she often retreated on to the safer ground of being practical.

Perhaps because she mistrusted herself, she had forced herself to become scrupulously fair-minded. In recent years she had discovered a capacity for strong feeling but, because this usually manifested itself in rage, she was not sure that she should give it a free hand. The result was that she often talked herself out of her true responses to a given situation only to find herself in a false position later on. This, in turn, would make her angry and she would end up behaving in a far more irrational way than she would have done if she had listened to herself in the first place.

Although her first response had been indignation at Phil Deals, she tried to argue it away. As she threaded her way down the steep, narrow streets of Ano Poli, she compared the two men. Phil, in fact, seemed to be the lesser of two evils. This made things worse. Surely it was rash to impute evil either to Deals or to her uncle – rash and harsh. It had been the very worst aspect of her mother to condemn all those who did not fit into her tight Procrustean thinking, and, although Catherine was aware that her own manner was sometimes wooden and off-putting, she was determined not to become a Cross on which all should die who did not agree with her.

Having said this to herself, she took yet another wrong turning and found herself immured in a close crowd of buildings at the end of which stood a venerable Orthodox church, voluptuous with domes and cross-hatched arches, dedicated, it said on a small board, to St Catherine. This show of cosmic irony might have made her smile but, wringing her hands in vexation at getting lost, she retraced her steps and was once more in the thick of her unreasoning enmity. What was her uncle on about? Just who did he think he was?

Annoyed with herself and him, she searched for a way out of the cul-de-sac and, finding a downward path, took it. After a few moments, she discovered herself in a larger thoroughfare where passers-by making their way home to lunch stared covertly at the attractive woman with her stiff bearing and graceful clothes. Without realizing it, Catherine always looked as if she had stepped out of some wider canvas. Her handsomeness made her look famous or historical.

Oh, how he made her flesh creep! She could hardly bear to think of the horrid old man. It was almost as if he had sloughed off a skin or, more accurately, had hatched out of his old military shell into a full-blown serpent coiled to strike. She had been mesmerized by his venomous languor, no less terrified of him, she realized, than when she had been seven and he the most conventional of men. Even the thought of her uncle's beautiful things made her shudder slightly as if his spindly furniture and sumptuous stuffs had been arranged to conceal damning evidence of something unclean.

That was it, she thought as she strode down a flight of steps that seemed to lead towards the city centre. It was as if he and Deals had studied grandeur, manufactured elegance in order to maintain their lives over the squalor of Susannah's murder. It was not as if they had come to terms with the tragedy; they seemed, more, to ignore it, as if her spilt blood had no more significance than any other irksome stain. It was the same with her mother's death. Her uncle had not only ignored the event at the time, he had made his recently dead sister the butt of his mockery. She shuddered, thankful that she had not been asked to stay. She wondered what it would be like to spend the night in a house where a woman's brutal murder seemed still to cry out for vengeance; if what she had later gleaned from Deals was true, her uncle's callousness was almost inconceivable.

Catherine once more struggled to overcome her fear. A lamb in an abattoir, no matter if the hygienic arrangements were perfect and the butchers played Muzak, was no less led to slaughter. She slowed to a wandering pace and stopped. Perhaps James Vaughan actually had murdered his only child. Perhaps he still lived on at the scene of the crime in order to conceal evidence of this. Catherine checked herself severely. How could she think such a thing!

She immediately dismissed the notion and came to her uncle's defence. He might present the mask of a contemptuous old cynic, but this could easily be a defence against his own pain and her prying eyes. Her husband Theo had too often in the past accused her of being unfeeling, especially at times when she had felt too deeply for words. What was more, the old man was ill, perhaps near death. Maybe the stroke had frozen the expression on his face. Maybe he was in pain. Phil Deals might have been lying, manipulating her so she would see her mother's only surviving brother in a bad light.

Catherine was still faced with her intractable dislike as she picked her way through the unfamiliar streets. Where was she? In her dudgeon, she had drifted west and was now navigating major roadworks over which it was necessary to balance on planks. Every now and then half-excavated pockets of earth yawned at the sides of the pavement as if the city were in a continual state of being exhumed or as if the ground beneath her were in perpetual motion. This was not far from the truth. She remembered with a thrill of alarm that an earthquake had devastated Thessaloniki in 1978. Most of the population had been evacuated in time, but Theo had been very distressed by it. So had they all. Chios was also in an earthquake zone. When she peered, however, into one of the small chasms underneath her feet, she thought she spied the remnants of a Byzantine tombstone propped against the raw earth. Although no one was about, it appeared that a dig was in progress.

As she picked her way around the hole, a small but desolate memory of her mother's grave unnerved her. She had never thought to be grateful for the undertaker's art, but somehow the Astroturf surrounding that dismal shaft in the ground had been a welcome euphemism. She twitched the thought aside, and wondered instead where Susannah's body lay. Had she been buried in Greece or shipped home to England? It struck Catherine that, now this investigation was afoot, they'd have to dig her cousin up. They did that with putative saints, didn't they, to see if the flesh had corrupted.

A story that had haunted her at school came back to her. She had even had nightmares about it. Who was that barmy old nun who had told them, their little mouths agape, about Thomas à Kempis? It had preoccupied Catherine for . . . oh, ages . . . that on uncovering his coffin to check the degree of decay they had found long scratches on the inside of the lid, which proved that he had been buried alive. How did the story go? He had not been canonized because his last desperate stuggle for air demonstrated insufficient resignation to the will of God. Catherine gave a long shudder and drew a deep breath. Had Susannah really offered her neck to the sword? Meekly? She felt a stab of guilt that she resisted this as noble.

When Catherine had lain down to rest for the afternoon as was the Greek custom (and yet no longer her habit), her eyes refused to close and she stared blankly at the ceiling. If her cousin had died 'a good death' (as the nuns used to call it) in the old house, surely she would have a different sense of the place. She sighed. Her religious upbringing had been a package deal with saints and martyrs safely confined to heaven; with virtues as knowable as told beads, each one as efficacious and tangible; with vices vicious and merit meritorious. If there had been little elbow room, there had been little doubt, too, of where one stood exactly. It had all been mapped out precisely like the Roman thoroughfares of the ancient Byzantine city she had just crossed, with Latin as its sacred tongue and imperial structure as its rectifying edifice. If someone died a spectacularly holy death, then a spectacularly holy rainbow ensued upon the storm of that last anguish. One *felt* it, the numen, the glow, smelt the odour of sanctity, absorbed a peace exuding from the spot. One did not emerge from any truly sacred spot with a sense of foreboding, and even disgust. One did not feel compromised.

Catherine poured herself a glass of mineral water and readjusted the sheet she had become entangled in. She wished she had brought a blind-fold to exclude the light that pierced the rich, thick curtains. She was too lazy to get up and pull them to. Just how had she compromised herself? If anything, she had been extremely straight, especially with the poor crooked little Phil Deals. The conversation she had sought with him had backfired, and now she wondered if she had ruined things for Father Edward.

Phil Deals. Oh, why couldn't she just drop off and doze! He had led her into the airy garden with its lush succulents and deep vines. As in Ottoman estates of the grand past, the arrangement of the paths and plants and fountains was informal, complex and luxurious, and they had wandered, the dogs panting and clicking at their heels, to a low stone bench that stood near an old Islamic ablution basin which had been converted into an ornamental piece of garden statuary. She had expected, from the somewhat conspiratorial manner in which he had coaxed her to take the air, that he had taken a liking to her and had something juicy to impart. Indeed, she had been mildly pleased with her progress, feeling that she had gently fomented the right atmosphere into which she might eventually introduce the reason for her visit. It was thus with considerable surprise that she found herself the subject of his own brazen inquisition.

'So, you've come about Susie,' he had said when they had seated themselves. 'I thought somebody might eventually.'

Catherine had been too startled to confirm or deny this.

'Well, you can't tell me you've come about Uncle. Anyone with any sense leaves Uncle strictly alone, which is where it leaves me looking after him. I mean with no sense. Alone, too, as a matter of fact.' Phil huffed, but his animosity no longer seemed directed at Catherine. 'God, he was rude to you! When I think you've just buried your mom! What an old scum-bag he is. You have no idea.'

Catherine's friend Marina was an American, as was her sister-in-law Rosamund, but Deals's broad, slangy diction brought to mind neither. It revived thoughts of Missy, Theo's former mistress and her grounds for divorce. Of course, this was why she had disliked him so at first sight. Missy and Deals both relished the pose of outright barbarian.

'My mother and Uncle James were estranged,' she said a little coldly.

Deals gave her a probing, impertinent look, too bold for her to be mistaken about his disdain for her, but he breezed on as if they were the best of friends. 'Yeah, but that doesn't give him the right to off-load it on you. Don't feel singled out, though. He has a way with him, Uncle does. And estranging happens to be his special talent. He does it, as he would say, "*awfully* well".'

Somehow there was a possessive unction about the way he spoke that goaded Catherine into taking a ridiculous kind of umbrage. His criticisms of her uncle seemed too familiar, almost as if he were asserting his ultimate rights over the old man as his special pet monster. He crossed his weedy legs and, with a boyish air, embraced his knee with his hands and swung his foot back and forth, whistling lightly as if for the dogs which lay cocking their ears lazily on the gravel path. She began to wonder if money was involved and Deals was her uncle's heir.

All at once, his insouciant manner so exercised her that she found herself plunging before she had thought out the consequences. 'As it happens, I *have* come about Susannah,' she said with a buttoned English chill that would have done her uncle proud.

Deals released his knee and unpuckered his pouting lips. 'See? I knew it. Sue was very special. I'll lay you ten to one, though, that Uncle thinks you're a secret agent. I'll give you a multiple choice: CIA, Hezbollah, the International Archaeological Conspiracy, or the Greater Orthodox Church Swindling Society.'

Catherine said, unable to resist a thrust of repartee, 'I happen to be a Vatican spy.'

'Oh, Holy Molloy!' he crowed. For a moment, she thought he was going to get up and cut a caper. '*Really*? I'm thrilled.'

Catherine at once regretted her self-indulgence, but there seemed to be no going back. In any case, beating about the bush was not her forte and she was relieved to be rid of the secret. 'The truth is,' she said, 'that since her death Susannah has picked up a distinguished reputation of her own . . .'

'You're not telling me they want to make her into a saint.' He paused, amused to the marrow, it seemed. 'You aren't, are you?'

She shrugged in assent.

'Jesus wept! Susannah Vaughan, this is your life!'

'Is it so unbelievable?' She found herself actively interested in the answer to this without regard to Deals's absurd manner.

'Ah!' he said, making a steeple with his hands under his chin. He looked for all the world like a goblin. 'Well, that's a matter of opinion. Come on, tell me, be straight with me. You aren't really coming from Head Office on this one, are you?'

All of a sudden, Catherine found it a relief to have the might of the Church, if not fully behind her, at least on the side of her mission. With some gravity, she said, 'I am here in Thessaloniki with a priest who knew Susannah and he is making the initial investigation for a Cause to be instigated. That means—'

'Oh, I know what it means,' he said, swatting at the air as if at a noisome fly. 'His name isn't Knight, is it?'

Catherine nodded, surprised.

67

'Susie's Svengali. Guru? She used to talk about him anyway.'

'Well, he's here,' Catherine said, at a loss with this description of the gentle priest.

'And you're the foot in the door.'

Catherine discovered that she had had about enough. 'There really is no need to be so disagreeable, Mr Deals. I came to see if it was feasible to discuss Susannah with my uncle and, as it is not, I shall report to Father Edward that we had better start looking somewhere else for the information he needs.' She stood. 'I'm doing this for my sister who is a nun. I have other ways to spend my time, and I will trouble you no further.'

All at once, Deals's shoulders slumped and he gazed up at her like a reproved child, moping. '*I'm* sorry. *All* my fault. I get carried away sometimes in my own, well, idiom, if you like. You must admit, though, it does seem a little incredible. Plus, James will have a fit, you know.'

Catherine stayed on the ball of her foot, turning, wholly bemused by his shift of manner. His voice was plaintive, his hands joined in beseeching her. A low growl came from the dogs as she shifted her bag on to her shoulder and he absently snapped his fingers at them.

'God, I could use a drink; not that I normally indulge. Could you use a drink?'

'No,' said Catherine.

'Look, sit down, won't you? I'll talk to your Father Whatever if you like. I'm not promising Uncle, though, because if you want "estranged" you've got "estranged" in him and Susie. I mean, his track record is not good. His mother, his wife, his sister, his daughter, his colleagues. You see he actually holds Sue's death against her.'

Catherine sat. The man deflated had become a child. She felt as if she were sitting with a strange little boy lost at a bus station. She would not have been surprised to see him swinging his legs from the bench or to hear him demanding an ice cream.

'He holds her death against her?' she asked incredulously, then wondered once again if Susannah's death had been willed, a form of suicide.

He shrugged, again in a childlike way, a little man trying to ward off blubbering or rage. 'Did you like Susie?' he asked her suddenly. 'I mean, if we're going to go into this I want to know she was liked. I want to know how you saw her. She was like a sister to me.' He paused, reconnecting with his adult surface. 'You have no idea.' He shook his head and she was astonished to see real tears mist up his eyes behind his glasses.

'I didn't like her particularly, no,' Catherine said. 'But then I didn't know her, you see. She was older than I was, and whenever she came to stay I was usually away at school. She seemed rather dreary, to tell you the truth. She was always ill.'

'You're telling me! Ill? She was a mess! Poor Sue, so they want to sanctify you!'

Resistant as she was to him, Catherine nonetheless caught a note in his voice that corresponded to her own deepest misgivings about the project. There was something horribly intrusive about the whole process, almost diminishing. 'Father Edward liked her,' she murmured, suddenly feeling ashamed that she had taken such a hard line.

Deals sighed. 'I don't know why she ever joined the Catholic Church. She was one of these crazy people, you know, who couldn't get out of bed in the morning without falling into some sort of crisis – self-inflicted, I may say. I always knew it gave her masochism a structure, but now they intend to reward that. What a bummer!'

'Well, they say she effects miracles.'

She could see that he was subtly pleased. 'You hear that, boys?' he said to the dogs.

Catherine woke, having finally dozed off, to see the sun slanted now, late afternoon. She sat, feeling blowsy, and drew her knees up to her chest, encircling them with her arms while she shook off the unpleasant effects of sleep. Her room, though well appointed, was like all hotel rooms; it seemed sterile, a place for solitary transients. She at once felt lonely and a little afraid. She rose, padded to the shower, struggled for self-mastery under the cleansing flow of water, and determined to ring home. Xenia might be worried about her. She had understood that this trip might bring about the final split with Theo, but Catherine was worried that she concealed a child's distress under her brand-new maturity. In any case, Theo might have been in touch with her and, though Catherine had never discouraged him, he was seldom indirect and he could upset Xenia without the slightest intention of doing so. Charged with motherly zeal, Catherine put in a call to the Bayswater flat, only to hear her own crisp message on the answering machine. She had not allowed for the time difference and Xenia, of course, was still at college. Catherine gave her number and sent her love.

She put in another call to London, this time to the office of her brother Charles. His secretary told her that he was in a meeting and Catherine felt stupid to have no concrete message.

As a last resort, she tried the number Father Edward had given her the night before of his borrowed rooms in Frangon Street. There was no reply, and the telephone sounded flatly as if echoing the emptiness of the space around it.

She gave up on the prospect of any human contact, dressed and set out again, armed with a map of the city and a cheap guidebook she picked up at the kiosk in the hotel lobby. She had no real idea of which way to go, so she set off in the general easterly direction in which the White Tower lay. The city was beginning to come to life again after the somnolent lull of afternoon. Shutters went up in the more ambitious shops which lined Tsimikis Street and the tables on pavements began to stir with an assorted clientele of desultory trippers, shoppers early for the evening scrum, and the inevitable elderly men whose only role in life seemed to be as essential extras in the slow drama that unfolded around any *cafenion* in Greece.

The scene, although not Thessaloniki itself, was all too familiar to Catherine; restively, she changed direction and, as she strolled north towards the Via Egnatia, she felt the heaviness of her own situation descend upon her. The simple action of retrieving the Greek language from her memory seemed to unearth aspects of Theo that pinched. They had spoken to each other in a polyglot way, finishing sentences in English which had begun in Greek or vice versa.

She had waited for years, hoping vainly that her mind would be made up for her by Theo, but this had been an evasion of a duty to herself.

Again, the sound of her own voice on her answering machine resounded flatly in her ears; again came the clutch to her stomach at Xenia's absence. It was five years ago that Missy had lured Xenia away, five years ago when she had exacted her brutal vengeance on Theo, five years since she had wrecked their family. But it was no longer Missy who was at issue, it was the fear itself, the lack of trust which was embedded like nuclear waste in the ground of Catherine's being. Oddly, she could forgive Theo the adultery, but not the lies, not the deliberate misleading. Suppose he did want to save the marriage. It had taken her all this time to find the courage not to immolate herself upon his wishes.

Her cousin Susannah might have found the towering heights of spiritual fulfilment in sacrifice, but Catherine had learned too well that she herself grew lower. In fact, what contented and connected her now was the very smallness of her life: her business, her family, her friends.

VII

UNDER THE blur of angels in the dome, Father Edward had been still for long, protracted moments, a time extended and curtailed by a flicker then a flash of their long white wings, their dancing feet. That he could not fully see them made the rhythm of their bright mosaic forms more credibly alive.

It was the Ascension (that much he knew). In keeping with Orthodox formality, the Mother of God and Apostles gazed up at a Christ seated in majesty on a rainbow; perhaps because of this very constraint, they seemed to whirl in circular ecstatic motion, fixed along the fathomless trajectory of the universe to a time defying time, wheeling to the measure of the stars. For some reason, the mosaic in the dome moved him almost intolerably, as if he were painfully in love and had been granted some kind of token that was too vague to interpret as a personal sign of favour.

He had taken refuge that evening in Agia Sophia, the Church of the Holy Wisdom, after a strenuous morning in the Church of St Demetrius and, even though he had been anxious about Catherine's meeting with James Vaughan, he had avoided ringing her as a delaying tactic. It was almost as if he had spent the day with Susannah herself, and somehow he wanted to hold on to the encounter before he made the inevitable move of letting go. He had followed, in a way, her own favourite itinerary. Susannah had been oblivious to schisms and internecine wars. She had been, perhaps, a little too inclusive in her love for all religions. If the Orthodox resented the Roman Church, she had blithely ignored it. He had come to Agia Sophia where he was now sitting because she had liked it, and had found his way to St Demetrius earlier because she had admired it.

When his sight had begun to fail, Edward soon realized that he was always better off entrusting himself to the mercy of the shadows rather than making a vain attempt to see, to act as if everything was normal. Whenever he strove for clarity, he became panicked by its absence and fear made him clumsy. In accepting his limitations, however, he moved better, more swiftly. Over the years he had developed a system of mapping land-marks in his memory and in this way was able to infer what he could not see from the shapes he could identify.

The worst of his morning's quest had thus not been his blundering attempts to get to the martyr's shrine, the pride and joy of Thessaloniki. It had been, rather, the shrine itself, and the curious sensation that Susannah had accompanied him. It was almost as if she had discovered that he was visiting and was determined to latch on.

He did not, of course, for a minute think that she was haunting him, but he had nonetheless been struck with a surreal idea of her presence, rather as if she had slipped from the pages of a novel by Bulgakov or Henry James. He would not have been the least bit surprised to come across a black cat walking upright and discoursing upon philosophy, nor to discover himself in the grip of some pathological delusion. Without meaning to, he had found himself addressing her mentally, making comments on the passing scene rather as if they had been on holiday together, old friends who needed few words between them. Maybe the special character of the city evoked her to him. It seemed a place of contradictions, with layer upon layer of agonized history. Mellow buildings with a *fin-de-siècle* air contended with aggressive modern ones. The traffic was grotesque, and yet small pockets of great antiquity lay in odd corners. Despite his disability, he had found his way all right, far more quickly and efficiently than had seemed possible. What was more, he had travelled by the most interesting route, past the Arch of Galerius, the Rotunda and the ancient forum. It was almost as if Susannah were giving him a guided tour. She pressed at him somehow, as if she were surging forward in joy at their reunion.

Edward wondered if he could honestly say that Susannah had had an early fascination with martyrs. It was something of a two-edged sword, that one, for preoccupation with violent death could be a problem, especially in her case. Perhaps the Bishop would see it differently, however. If he were to bring evidence for the initiation of a Cause, it might say something that she had shown devotion to the early Christian martyr Demetrius, patron of the city where her father had chosen to live. He remembered it because she had often mentioned worshipping at his shrine, and for this reason he had prepared himself to visit the basilica by reading before he had left England what little he could find about the martyr and his cultus. It seemed a place to start.

Even though he knew the church was modern, his mind's eye had projected a building more venerable and intimate than the vast, barn-like structure erected shortly after the war on the site of an earlier church, which had burnt to the ground. It seemed unexceptionally Byzantine in design, but somehow the marble plaza in front of it glared, the bare elevation frowned in eloquent severity. On entering, he felt self-conscious. He had been determined to wear his Roman collar throughout his stay in the Orthodox city, partly because he had heard of a breakdown in ecumenical communication from his friends and he did not want to imply shame of his faith by dressing in civvies. However, once in this bastion, sacred, after all, to a saint martyred by Galerius and thus pre-schismatic, he began to feel uncomfortable and out of place. He was not sure what honour to devote to the icons that stood ranged about the porch. The church was virtually empty save for a few old women who punctiliously lit candles and kissed the images, crossing themselves in the opposite direction from the way he did himself. He slid in and, buying a candle from a shadowy aged woman, made a clumsy veneration to an image too blurred for him to see.

The cavernous interior of the church was bathed in a greenish light, giving it a slightly forlorn air. Modern frescos of the Virgin and various saints leapt, rigid and garish, from the pillars of the colonnade leading to the altar. He found himself grateful for the bright colours of the postured images, easy to read for their emblematic clarity. For the first time since he had arrived in this alien city, he felt lost and a little afraid. In the distance, a solitary woman stood praying. Susannah clutched at his heart.

He shook her off. He remembered that there were some fine, ancient mosaics embedded in the wall somewhere in the vast edifice, but he was sure he would not be able to see them. For a moment, he wished he had brought Catherine as a guide, but at once he knew himself a coward. A sense of darkness, not blindness, invaded him, and once again, as many years ago, he was heavy with the whole freight he carried with him of Susannah's death. He sat for a moment on one of the spindly chairs that lined the nave and tried to put the burden back in the place where he had stored it for so long; but, realizing the futility of this, he allowed it into his heart. Although he had said a Mass for her at the time of her death and remembered her anniversaries, she was one of his dead whom he had not quite buried.

He had baptized her. Her pale face had been streaming with tears. She had been weak, fragile from having had rheumatic fever as a child, and it had left her with a pellucid skin. Of course, her murder upset him! However could it not? The sacrament had been no formula to her; she had actively sought to be born again. She had looked at him like a lamb brought to slaughter, dying as she was in Christ.

He supposed he had better see if he could find some evidence of St Demetrius. Like Susannah, he had read, the martyr had come from the upper class but had been a Roman prefect, not a rich neurotic. He had been, so the pious legend went, exceptionally good-looking. This was not true of Susannah, although she had been magnetic, charismatic – quite literally, he supposed. As he was sitting, he had the irritating sensation of her fluent self, moving just out of the corner of his occluded field of vision, and so he got up and walked around. She had had light hair and dark brown eyes. He was not sure she had ever been as crazy as she thought, but the spiritual path she had so doggedly followed had forced her into dropping the knotted cargo of her past, and this had given her manner an extraordinary lightness. It had charmed him to learn from Catherine that Susannah had been mad on horses as a child. So had his sisters. He could see her wan face lighting up as she galloped in the fresh, clean air. She had been physically graceful and, perhaps because of her early ill health, courageous. She would have had a good seat on a horse. So, he imagined, would have Demetrius, whose life-sized image he eventually found; it was painted boldly with gold leaf. The saint, wearing a bandeau, a martyr's crown perhaps, was armed to the teeth with a sword, a shield and a spear. Edward solicited his aid a little half-heartedly.

What was all this saying? Why was he curiously unmoved to be on the spot where perhaps she had even had divine intuitions of her end? Surely, it was only human to react with horror at the death she had suffered. The Roman martyr had been stabbed to death as she had been, but his friends and family might have felt differently about his dreadful end. Perhaps they had even rejoiced in it in that age of heroic faith.

Reading was a labour for Edward; he had to fit little telescopes to the lenses of his spectacles. The gain, however, was that he remembered each detail he mustered. He had gleaned, for instance, that the bloodstains from Demetrius's death were miraculously preserved on the floor somewhere in the church. Holy oil was said to have bubbled spontaneously from a well, healing unction to all who needed it. Edward rather enjoyed the theatrical props of medieval thought, which seemed poetic statements in his view of a truth beyond the reach of science.

Cures! Edward had gone to Lourdes for his eyes. He smiled at the recollection of a sudden peace descending on him by a stall selling tacky neon Sacred Hearts. Resignation had come to him thereafter. He glanced again at the stern bright icon of the martyr and it brought him back to the task at hand. He wandered through the silent, empty church, a little fortified.

All of a sudden, she was there kneeling, seen and unseen, on the floor in front of a glaring marble structure, the tomb of the martyr, perhaps, and she was weeping. It unnerved him. Had she come here to pray just before her death? Presumably the saint's relics were housed in the shrine. Had this been her Gethsemane? Perhaps the prayers of the beautiful young man had enabled her to follow his example and die by the sword.

The bright marble shrine was obviously meant to be visited, and so Edward gingerly went in, making a surreptitious Roman sign of the Cross. He almost had to fend off the blaze from the gold and silver of the sumptuous reliquaries – a silver coffin and a gold Patriarch's crown. On impulse he kissed the glass case in Susannah's memory. Perhaps she really had prayed here; perhaps this really was a key to unlocking her mystery. He sighed. He somehow could not see this shrine inspiring a real martyrdom, even though the saint himself might have done. Not for the first time, he wondered what Susannah would think of his thankless task as an investigator and was rewarded with a memory of her laughter. As she had grown older, she had developed a sense of humour, a sort of gaiety. He could hardly bear to think about it.

He was just about to go, when his ears were assailed by a strident English voice. A small flock of British tourists was assembled outside the little sanctuary earnestly drinking in the words of a guide, who without respect for local sensibility seemed to be deriving great pleasure from mocking the lavish reliquary.

It seemed the saint's supposed relics had been conveniently found quite two centuries after his death. In any case, if there had indeed been a saint, he had certainly not died in Thessaloniki but elsewhere. The famous holy oil had been piped and olive, not miraculous and redolent with the odour of sanctity. The mandarin personage who uttered all of this was dressed in an impeccable linen jacket. He shot a look at Edward's Roman collar and for a moment Edward had the bizarre impulse to stick his thumbs in his ears and waggle his hands like a child. As he left the church, the significance of the episode struck him. Was he saying the same thing in his heart about Susannah? Patronizing her colossal need for God?

At lunch time, he paid the necessary courtesy call to the presbytery of the Catholic Church, which was in the same street as the flat made available to him for the duration of his stay. He wondered how the priest, a Father Pavlos, fared. He was Greek and his second language was Italian. They communicated with a lot of affable gesticulation, both of them reprieved from having to spend long hours together. Edward supposed that Susannah would have to be gone into with the local clergy. After all, they had buried her, had they not? Some medieval proof might have emerged at the funeral. Edward was glad that he could not address this and many other inquiries to Father Pavlos. Perhaps Catherine would interpret for him at some later stage. The idea of asking questions like this embarrassed him.

Edward found a sudden relief in the restrained baroque enclosure of the church and its immaculate courtyard. It had the ambience, somehow, of a Spanish mission, wonderfully un-Byzantine: a statue, ironically enough, of Our Lady of Lourdes stood dressed in blue familiar robes, with praying familiar hands clutching a rosary on a pedestal in a grotto made of tiered paving stones. The church itself was as neat and plain and as rationally constructed as a Latin prose – no domes, no icons, no smoky depths. A verger was washing the marble floor: the tabernacle drew from Edward a suddenly heartfelt genuflection.

But, after agreeing to say an early morning Mass in English on Sunday, he was out again on the unfamiliar streets, and once more he sensed Susannah. It was almost as if in some mute way she were pleading with him . . . or for him.

'What is it you want from me, my dear?' he found himself saying softly to the empty air, then felt a fool. With a little ripple of happy inspiration, it struck him that, of all people, the last who would ever want the honour of proven sanctity was Susannah. She had had a nice sense of irony and had hated ostentation. To be left alone to get on with God might, in some odd sense, have been said to be her dearest wish. If she were to be canonized she most certainly would not want marble canopies or golden shrines.

Maybe that was it. Maybe she was perched invisibly on some wisp of wind longing to tell him to abandon the search and give up the struggle before it began. It came over him again that he missed her. He could see her (this time with his imagination) scurrying into the church he had just left, a faded skirt slightly askew, her hair pulled back any old way, and any old cardigan buttoned in any old way, bent on her devotions and possibly a little late, so out of breath. One could never discredit her eagerness for religion, but – he checked himself as if he were even now delivering his own mortal wound to her – her success at it. He shrank from the memory of her acknowledged faults with a wince of pity for them. Watching her progress had been like watching a child in a kitchen attempting to make an elaborate cake out of an enthusiasm for cooking. The thought of people going into all of that, probing at her weaknesses, made him want to swing blows, get on a horse, ride with armour for her. Oh, they would bring it all out, surely, the . . . well, what? What had she actually done that was so awful? Nothing, really. He blushed for her and shut his mind off as if he were hearing again whispered sins, whispered, embarrassed disclosures.

Edward pitied the poor weak flesh. More often, he saw malice writ large over the tiny lapses of those with a conceit of their own virtue, but never with Susannah. She had dealt with both frailty and malice openly. Her spiritual struggles had been confrontational, Armageddon all the way. But that, of course, had been very long ago. It shocked him to realize that she had been in her forties when she died.

But, as she had then in her youth, now she seemed to worry at him. He had the distinct impression of her gnawing away at something. Was she not at peace, then? This thought really did disturb him. And yet (taking the fantastical notion of her ghostly presence at face value) they seemed to travel serenely enough down Frangon Street, under the shady trees that grew there. Since her murder, he had considered only the horror of it. At last in the strange city where she had met her bloody death, her end seemed oddly the least of her.

Ever since he had known Susannah, she had talked about Thessaloniki; and, now he was here, it was bound to be interpreted through her eyes. As the years had gone by, he had seen her slowly detach herself from it, as surely as she had detached herself from other things. Good Lord, it had been so long ago – not her death, but when they had, well, worked together. She had shed attachments as other women shed pounds, her able mind paring away what did not apply to her purpose, the junk and clutter of feelings which got in the way. Often he had wondered, after she had moved on to found her community, if she wasn't one of those troubled people who find it easier to give love to strangers than accept the demands of intimacy, but then she had been such an odd fish that it had been difficult to categorize her.

Edward had to admit that he was very curious to meet her father. In the beginning, when Susannah had been so much the ugly duckling, they had talked a lot about James Vaughan, but by the time she had turned into a swan he had seen her infrequently. After her murder, he had ruefully dwelt upon the last time he had seen her, feeling that he had not quite said goodbye to her. She had dropped in on him at a time when he had been genuinely busy; and, now he thought about it, she had told him about the earthquake in Thessaloniki and how she had been distressed about it. This had been very much in passing, all said with that lightness of tone she had come to adopt in her later years. He remembered thinking how fine she was, her features had eroded to show the strength which had been born out of so much weakness. She had blown through his day like a breeze, not holding him to their old acquaintance. Apparently she and the old boy had had something of a row. In fact, in regard to the earthquake, she had mentioned the ground shifting under her own feet – all with a little laugh. Edward had not listened very carefully. He had been in a hurry. He had never seen her again.

Oh, there had always been so much coming from Susannah, so many questions, so many observations: her life had been immense, full. There had been a lot of money about, that he had known, and although she burned a different fuel, and had ended up giving it away, wealth had formed her expectations. For all her modesty, she had held the imperious belief that her needs would be met, her wishes obeyed. She assumed people would do things for her. This was almost certainly the way in which she had founded the Bethany Community upon which her chief claim to fame now rested. Although he had seen her only infrequently after she had begun this project for the mentally ill, he had no doubt that she had bulldozed its way into being, confident in the unconscious faith that she was worthy of other people's sacrifice. Edward was suddenly ashamed at the uncharity of this thought. Susannah had had the ruthlessness of the single-minded, but she had never been arrogant.

It came back to him, after this wide ellipsis of thought, that her journeys to Thessaloniki, through which he now dimly made his way, had been her humbling. During the time he had known her well, she had gone annually, faithfully, regularly to visit her father and she would return shattered, her ego in rags, torn by him more effectively than a discipline made of thorns. But that had been in the distant past.

He had never known quite why her father had made her suffer so much. Nowadays, the press wrote about abuse in families with lip-smacking shock and in prurient detail. As far as Edward knew, James Vaughan had never laid a finger on Susannah; but, thinking back on it, Thessaloniki had been a place of dread for her. And he suddenly recalled how urgently she had wanted to be at peace with the old man.

By evening Edward had had enough. He felt saturated, as full of Susannah as a sponge which has absorbed the large spillage of a subtly intoxicating brew. He made his way to The Holy Wisdom, Agia Sophia, which had been founded in the eighth century. This seemed far enough back to go for his own detachment; its severe façade made it look ideal for sober reflection.

On entering, however, he had been caught by the loveliness, the holiness, of the interior. And, as he sat with his intention to sum things up to himself, a curious balm of peace and self-forgetting drifted in upon his meditations.

He was, in fact, so fully held in this calm and elongated flight from time that he failed to notice the entrance of Catherine Phocas. When he finally did spot the hazy female form standing a little apart and towards the iconstasis, he gave a start. It was Susannah to the life, as if he conjured her up before him.

Catherine turned, for she had waited for him to see her. She had stepped into the church to pass the time rather than from any particular interest in it, and she had been somewhat taken aback at the jolt of pleasure she felt at seeing the gentle priest sitting there. The truth was that, although they had planned to meet for dinner, he was far from her thoughts. Standing now in the ancient basilica, which had to her the immense familiarity of long Orthodox use, the more personal familiarity of his Roman collar and his peculiarly Western stoop kindled in her a feeling of relief. It was almost like seeing old Christmas trappings from childhood – bits of tinsel, crèche figures – in a disused box in the attic. Indeed, his head was held in the mild and unassuming slope of St Joseph bent in devotion to the infant Jesus. For a moment, unexpected tears caught at her throat. She *was* close to the surface, she thought. He had put her in mind of her own father whom she had loved and who had died shortly after her marriage to Theo. It was as if in Edward she had caught a glimpse of him.

At once, she realized how tired she was, emotionally exhausted, and when Father Edward looked up at her with his sudden, dazzled smile a great weight seemed to shift from her. She was not, after all, alone in the strange city.

'How are you?' she asked, slipping in next to him where he sat. He frowned slightly, shook his head and blinked as if trying to dislodge some thought. 'I'm sorry, did I disturb you?'

'Not at all,' said Edward, both saddened and relieved that it was not Susannah after all. 'I was just about to go . . . to ring you. Happy coincidence.' Above the altar in a golden apse was a dark mosaic of the Mother of God, solemn, complete. He could make out only the shape, but a sense of purity reverberated on the air, and he knew why Susannah had liked this church, visited it.

'Did you . . .?'

'How . . .?'

Their polite questions clashed and they both apologized for interrupting.

'How did I get on at my uncle's house?' Catherine said at last. 'Let's go and get a drink or something . . . take a walk. I met with limited success.'

The church was sunken, so that it was about three metres below the busy concourse of the trading city which swept by its austere and ancient bulk. They had created a paved garden in front of it where palms and pines offset somewhat the harsh architecture. Children played there in the early evening light, calling to one another as they chased about intent upon some obscure game. With a twinge, Catherine remembered Xenia as she had breathlessly scrambled around with the neighbours' children near the house in the Kampos of Chios where she and Theo had lived, where once she had thought she had a family. Mute with nostalgia for this time, she glanced at Father Edward and noted that he seemed no less preoccupied than she was herself. As they made their way up the steps and back to the street, a limousine drew up to the pavement, and Catherine glimpsed a baby swathed in white baptismal robes. Its entire family seemed to crush into its ritually fluffed, tulled, flounced little body. The infant looked as if its life depended on getting out of the car and to the font inside the church below. Ahead of her down the busy thoroughfare, a life-assurance company advertised itself in lights, promising guarantees different from those envisioned by the Church fathers. Catherine had been to countless Orthodox baptisms of other people's children, and she remembered Xenia's own with pain. She had tried too long to deny her Greek experience and had met with too much success, perhaps, in blotting it out. Slow, obedient days of long liturgies in hot churches came back to her, weddings, funerals, baptisms of neighbours, where she, the Roman, had stuck out as vaguely apostate and barbarian, the thin end of a Popish wedge, a dim memorial of Frankish conquests.

She steered Father Edward across the road and made towards the harbour.

'Did Susannah ever tell you about a cousin of hers called Phil Deals?' she asked.

'It's been so many years . . .'

'He knew all about you,' said Catherine. 'He called her "Susie-Q" and you her "guru".'

Edward flushed.

'He is on the American side of her family and so brash that the glare quite blinds one . . . oh, dear!'

Edward touched her arm lightly. 'It's all right.' She was very embarrassed. 'No, really. I'm quite used to it.'

She laughed nervously. 'I'm not the family diplomat,' she said.

'Actually, I do remember,' Edward said. 'Susannah's aunt was married to some automobile magnate, I believe. Susannah was attached to a cousin;

she called him Phil. You see, she spent her summer holidays in the States. Especially after her mother's death. In fact, it all comes back to me now. He wanted to marry Susannah.'

'Good Lord! I could have sworn . . .!' She shifted a look at him. 'I thought he was gay.'

'I don't think so,' he said abruptly.

'Oh, no, I've done it again!'

He realized she thought she had shocked him. 'No, truly, Catherine, you haven't. You see, I can't really discuss . . .' Edward remembered that Susannah had thought she would 'save' Phil, but not from homosexuality. Edward had warned her against the attempt. 'But I can see why he calls me a "guru" in the ironic tone you suggest, because I tried to give her a way to say no without rejecting him. She was not in love with him. Why should she have made a loveless marriage? It would have been wrong, intolerable.'

'She was self-sacrificial from the outset?'

He smiled. 'In a way of always expecting a ram to appear from a thicket, perhaps.' He noted her puzzlement. 'Abraham and Isaac. You remember. She wanted a graceful way out of it, and that graceful way was me!'

'My marriage wasn't loveless to begin with. It died on me.'

Edward decided that, although she wanted him to hear this, she did not want him to take her up on the muttered remark. In any case, they had arrived at the long sweeping shore where soulless modern shops and bars lined the embankment. The sea looked desolate now and glared too openly in the fading light. Rush-hour traffic went by the front, gassing them with fumes.

Catherine decided they should sit at a little table in the endless rows of little tables outside a line of indistinguishable cafés.

'Am I to understand that this Deals chap lives with Susannah's father?' Edward asked when they had ordered some wine. 'Did you manage to see both of them?'

'I saw my uncle, yes.'

He tried not to peer at Catherine, but he thought he saw the muscles of her face flex oddly and she seemed glad of the wine when it came. A sea breeze blew her fine hair up and out behind her and it glinted in the sun.

'Deals seemed to think it funny that Susannah is now to be regarded as "an exceptionally holy dead individual". This is hard enough to take, I know, but he says my uncle would be *angry*.'

'Ah,' said Edward. 'That stands to reason.'

'How could anyone possibly be angry at hearing his child was a saint?'

Edward burst out laughing. 'Have you ever known one?'

'Only people who think they are.'

'Disqualified in Round One. The genuine article generally suffers too much for any such vanity.'

'Having met my uncle, I can imagine that Susannah must have had some intensely unhappy moments.' She shivered a little in the brisk gusts from the gulf.

'She had breakdowns,' he said, 'which she saw in metaphysical terms.'

'Did you see them in that way?' Catherine asked, suddenly interested.

He shrugged. The evening light on the water made curtains in his eyes like an aurora borealis. The cool wine from Samos tasted good and the fresh wind lifted his spirits. 'I was never sure. Undoubtedly she did suffer, but with Susannah it was often hard to tell the difference between the neurotic and the sublime. There was a visionary aspect, which was a strong feature of her inner life, and centuries ago nobody would have thought twice about it. Susannah was a well-educated woman, however, and most of her torture derived from being only too aware that she might be mad. Whatever one can say about her, though, she accepted the hand she had been dealt and made something of it. If she was crippled she was bound to feel pain and she was a lot more than merely stoical. Sometimes I think she let God take over precisely because she was such a mess, and in this way her problems came to be more perfectly resolved than if she had relied on anything less to help her. This was the principle upon which she built Bethany. She was quite open about this, and, in fact, wrote an article saying something to that effect.'

'That's what Phil Deals called her,' Catherine said: ' "a mess".'

They finished their wine and rose by mutual consent to stroll along the front in the direction of the White Tower. The shore curved round handsomely, somehow dwarfing the heavy flow of traffic which snaked along in the dusk. A large posse of well-dressed middle-aged Greek women was making its way in the opposite direction towards the Plataea Aristote-lous, a vast tract of tarmac around which were ranged an equally vast number of *zacheroplastaeas* and cafés. The evening *volta* had begun; there was seeing and being seen to be done, and passers-by glanced at the odd pair, Catherine so striking in her smart long skirt, the stylish cardigan she had designed and made herself out of the finest cotton yarn which she had caused to be dyed to her specifications. She huddled into it against the April night air and the ladies made a mental note of it. Next to her, the stooped priest in his thick glasses loped, hands braced out oddly, an habitual strategy he had adopted to avoid a fall. Together, they looked like the relics of an endangered species, anxiously bucking the waves of a more zoologically successful herd.

'Did this Phil Deals say he would see me?' Edward asked her as they went along.

'Didn't I say? I would call him avid. But don't expect any respect for your calling, or any sympathy with the nature of your inquiry. In fact,' she said with energy, 'he is quite the rudest man I ever met! Sly, manipulative . . . Oh, I detested him! I'm sorry. I keep trying to be on my best behaviour for you and then I let myself down.'

She stabbed forward on her elegant sandals. Edward was amused by a sudden mental picture he got of Catherine as an enraged mythical being – not a goddess, perhaps, but a spirit with potential nonetheless for being whimsically vexed.

'I detested both of them, in fact,' she continued. 'There, I've said it! And the house. It's a lovely house, done to opulent standards of high taste and correctness of period and so on . . .'

'Is he prepared to discuss Susannah's death? Did he have anything to say about it?'

She was fully exercised in her little burst of passion. 'The house, as I was about to tell you, speaks of it in volumes! Their lives express something unspeakably malign, and I say "unspeakably" because I have no way of explaining it to you. But there is no shrine to her there, and you'll have a job to make one. I'm sorry, I found it very disturbing – almost as if . . .'

'What?' He remembered the letter, the one the Mother Prioress said she had read dated a few days before Susannah's death, the one which was supposed to contain 'a shocking revelation'. Could it be there was something suspicious after all? If this were so, it seemed extraordinary that she had insisted on clinging to the letters and not letting him read them.

They had reached the White Tower. As they crossed the busy road, Catherine grasped Edward's arm and whisked him past a hell-bent lorry. 'Oh, please watch out, Father Edward!' she cried. Suddenly, floodlights snapped on and the ghostly edifice, with its beetling crenellations, was sharply defined against the evening sky.

'Do you want to go in? I think it's open. It's a museum with icons and so on. Might as well.'

She was worried, he saw it, by the force of her own outburst, and he wondered what else was troubling her that had made her so angry that day. He nodded, humouring her, and they went through a small door at the base of the high tower.

Catherine bought tickets and a rough guide from a bored official and together she and Edward began the long climb. 'This tower,' she said, interpreting from the sheet of paper, 'is 105 feet high and was built by Venetians or Turks in the fifteenth century . . .' She continued to peruse the guide as they trudged upwards and, after a moment, she gave a sharp bark of laughter. 'You will never guess what it used to be called and why! What an irony. I dragged you in here to escape your question.'

They went aimlessly up the turret and at random walked into a little room to the left where icons were displayed.

Catherine was insensible to their appeal. 'In this place,' she continued, 'Mahmout II had his janissaries massacred in 1826, and because it was called the Bloody Tower after this event he had it whitewashed. There really seems no escape, does there?'

Edward saw a filmy spectacle of glowing colour, St George piercing the dragon, Elijah in his cave. The forms were familiar as Gospel words, easy to read without literacy, by the eternal shapes they made.

'What I was trying not to tell you,' she said, 'is that I feel sure Deals and my uncle are trying to hide something about Susannah's death.'

He wished he could see her better. Her whole stance, however, evoked real distress as if she were the proverbial maiden in Western paintings of St George. He thought carefully about this. 'You mean to say—'

'I mean, and it has only just struck me, that it may be more than simply psychologically inconvenient to have us here poking into Susannah's murder.'

He made to descend. He was tired and out of breath. She followed him. He lightly touched her shoulder as they went down the spiral stairs. 'Do you read a lot of thrillers? I used to.'

It occurred to Catherine that anyone else might have offended her by this statement, but there was no patronage in it, just the priest's mild observation that she might be letting her imagination get out of hand.

'Well, it's an unsolved murder after all,' she said. 'And surely you are trying to solve it in one way. Unless we know who did it, how can you tell if it was a martyrdom or not?'

'Oh, I've never been sure that we could prove it a martyrdom *per se*,' Edward said. They stopped at a lower plateau and wandered into a room full of detached Byzantine capitals and chunks of frescos rescued from the huge puzzle of ruins that lay below the surface of the city. 'Martyrdom is quite a technical term in its way. It has to be established that the victim died for the faith, because he or she was a Christian; and in this case, no other proof of sanctity is needed – no miracles, signs, wonders. Susannah would have had to have been given a choice – you know, like St Thomas

More, or even St Demetrius, whose tomb I saw today. Worship the Emperor or worship God. Now, if it could be established that a band of Muslim fanatics had insisted she renounce Christianity and embrace Islam or that Marxist zealots had killed her because she was defending some sacred object or territory, then there would be no difficulty in getting her canonized. As it is, however, the best we can hope for is that she was heroic. It would add to the balance of evidence and be persuasive along with her healings and cures.'

Catherine shivered into her cardigan although it was warm in the turret room. 'I would have thought after what I saw today that it is possible she did die because she was a Christian,' she said, 'or because other people were not.'

Edward shrugged. 'Not quite the same thing.' All the same, a little tremor of excitement passed through him at her words. He wandered blankly, trying to divert himself with the exhibits. Catherine drifted past him, making the same attempt.

'Susannah!' All of a sudden, Catherine cried out as if in recognition of an old friend. She had gone ahead of him through an arch towards an arrow slit window.

Edward trembled in earnest. 'What?' he asked faintly.

'Look! Come here, Father Edward. This is surely more than coincidence.'

Blindly, he followed her voice.

'Susannah!' she cried, triumphant, and his heart pitifully sank as he drew next to her. Before them stood the stylishly lit relic of a painted mausoleum, a little house for the dead, an empty tomb.

He squinted heavily and was only just able to make out the peeling fresco that Catherine had discovered. Painted in an arch stood a female figure in robes, hands raised in victory or praise. She was flanked by two resentful-looking men in togas, who cringed beneath her outstretched arms.

'Listen to this! "The painting depicts the well-known Old Testament episode of Susannah with the two Elders who unjustly accuse her of adultery. Susannah invokes the assistance of God and proves her innocence by means of divine intervention. The subject is used as proof that Man is saved through faith in God. This representation is unique within Greece . . ." '

A terrible sadness afflicted Edward, but he tried to be polite and inspected the dead girl's memorial rather in the way he had seen art buffs scrutinize a painting in an exhibition. It was a lively enough spectacle, what he could see of it, but empty in comparison with his crack-brained hope that some vision had been vouchsafed to Catherine, or, more idiotic still, that Susannah had escaped in some way, gone into hiding, and had now returned in the flesh. He wanted to sob in vexation. Had he really allowed himself to think that he had ever been detached? Surely, he had been; indeed, she had often praised his detachment.

Catherine stood in the shadow, at a respectful distance from the pain she sensed in him. The poor old fellow seemed so helpless, floundering there with the picture he could hardly see; his head bobbed, intense and quivering. Against her habitual restraint, she had the urge to touch his shoulder, even to put her arm around him and console him, but that would never have done, she knew. Nor would an apology for unwittingly exposing in him some raw nerve.

After a moment, he straightened himself.

'Maybe it's a sign,' she said lamely.

He gave a slight, ironic shrug. 'In a way,' he said. After a pause, he added, 'It comes back to me. This tomb painting meant a lot to her. I had forgotten, you see. She mentioned it to me several times . . . that she had seen it here and that it was unique. Her name, you know. She was often too introspective.' He said this with almost bitter vehemence, but checked himself and continued in a more even tone. 'And, of course, the persecution by the Elders seemed an analogy to Susannah, in terms of her own life . . . Though I really don't know why,' he hastily added.

'Let's find something to eat, get some dinner,' Catherine said quietly. 'Come along . . . Please?'

'She thought of the figure as rising from the grave,' he added. 'On to the resurrected life, if you see.'

'Food!' said Catherine.

'Food,' he replied.

VIII

MARINA CROUCHED on the ottoman in the sitting room, her fingers curled around a mug of tea, and regarded the dank sky over Oxfordshire with a stupefied eye. A high April wind shattered the petals of the cherry trees, scattering them in drifts around her garden; the tops of the evergreens bounced and tossed, and a draught sifted in, rattling the window panes of the old and comforting house. She sipped the tea – it seemed a pity to waste it once it was made – and wished that Paul would come home early from the hospital. She was excited, agitated. Her mind was in four or five places at once, and her memory was unearthing large fragments of a time she had mislaid. To have heard about poor Susie and Phil Deals, of all people . . . And from Catherine! On this day of all days, when she had been striving to achieve more positive feelings about her mother's latest visit! It was almost like a sign calling her to incorporate a lost part of an American past into her present life, a history she had for the last six years rejected, a childhood she had negated.

Although Maureen had departed for home the day before, a shadow of her seemed to curl itself around the furniture, fingering the nice old sofa, straightening the dicky table, plumping the faded armchairs and the handsome needlepoint cushions that Catherine had made and given them for Christmas. Maureen, for this was what she called her mother, thought the house shabby. She competed with Marina over little points of order, if not style, and over Paul, for whom she had an almost obsequious respect because he was a doctor. Marina guiltily dreaded the phone call Maureen would almost certainly soon make, telling her that she had arrived safely back on American soil, a phone call filled with household hints, and 'tactful' innuendoes about how to keep a man.

This was the fifth time Marina had seen her mother, if one disqualified birth. She had been reunited with Maureen only six years ago. Looking back on that first visit to New Jersey, Marina still felt freshly the terror and relief she had experienced when her mother had opened the door of the split-level ranch house of which she was so proud. It was almost unbearable to contemplate even now that Maureen's whole family had assembled with a banner and balloons: Maureen had locked Marina in her arms and, for the first few hours, would not let go of her hand, which

87

she had patted and squeezed and smoothed as if it were a baby. Paul had not been directly involved at that time; he and Marina had not made up their minds to marry even though it had been on the cards. Now they were married, Maureen came to them, and maybe this was what had made the troubling difference.

Well, he had warned Marina even then that the drug of love for her salvaged parent might wear off, and indeed their reunion had, it now seemed in retrospect, been like a major operation after which the pain of truth began to have its way. Although they both still strove to 'catch up', as Maureen put it, the fine-line distinctions between them which had at first seemed so trivial now widened and deepened, making the most ordinary conversations awkward.

In some way, Marina ruefully knew that she expected too much from Maureen, and would have done with any woman who had stepped into the vast mysterious shoes she had provided for her long-lost parent. She longed for Maureen to understand everything about her by a magical intuition: her first marriage to Arthur Holt, and a life spent in England in consequence. More dangerously, she had wanted Maureen to enter into the childhood which separated them.

But mere physics, the laws of time and distance, militated against them both, and there were things they both failed to grasp about each other. The publication of Edgar Jolly's biography of Arthur, making him into a major poet, had been a case in point. Maureen had been stunned and puzzled by it, not because she had been shocked that her new-found daughter had achieved infamy in print, nor even that she, a Catholic, had been married to a divorced man. It was more that she could not understand the literary tone, the level of discourse upon which her daughter's life with Arthur Holt had been dissected. It was Maureen's unenlightened belief that the widowed Marina had bettered herself in marrying a psychiatrist second time around; she thought it a step-up from Arthur, which, of course, was true enough in its way.

Marina glanced up at the coloured photographic portrait of her mother that she kept loyally in a prominent place since they had met. Especially for the visit, it stood on the mantelpiece, and Marina wondered if she could forgive herself if she now moved it to the tallboy in the corner. Maureen posed in a gaudy, flounced blouse; the picture was both touched-up and touching for the theatrically made-up eyes that hunted like those of a bad icon, drawing the beholder into some involvement with the sitter's pain. Maureen had genuinely suffered from having given birth to Marina at the age of fifteen. Marina had been adopted by a wealthy New York family. Six years from the reunion, they did not know whether to treat each other as mother and daughter or as sisters, but they were finding out that they could never really be friends. At sixty-one and forty-six, they very well might have been.

Each successive visit seemed to drop a notch nearer to the truth about what both women really meant to each other, and each time Maureen's resentment of Marina's adoptive mother asserted itself more strongly, like a stone statue gradually unveiled. Of course she had every kind of reason. And of course it was true, too, that because she had been denied the rights of motherhood over Marina, she was bound to be a little controlling now. Marina knew that. She accepted it. But this had little effect on resentments of her own which appeared to have an awful autonomy. No matter how unreasonable this was, she still felt Maureen had abandoned her.

Perhaps Maureen, sensitive for all her lack of education, had picked this up, and she took it out on the family of East Coast swells who had assumed Marina into their midst. Both the justice of Maureen's cause and her guileless, pitiful envy were almost too painful for Marina to bear, and in consequence she had slowly excised her adoptive family from her memory. It was as if, by merely thinking about the people who had formed and educated her, Marina hurt Maureen. Childhood trips to the Metropolitan, Opera or Museum, private schools, charity balls, the Upper East Side, country houses, Bach, skiing, Shakespeare, Europe, the very thought of stocks and shares, had to be obliterated, not only from Marina's tongue and mind, but from her very history. And this was why hearing about Phil Deals by chance that afternoon had filled Marina with a guilty, childish pleasure.

After all these years of longing for her, Marina could hardly bear to believe that her natural mother had any faults at all. Surely, Maureen did not envy Marina her present happiness with Paul. It was Maddy, Marina's adoptive mother, whom she envied, of course. The most wounding implication was that Maddy, with all the money in the world, had failed to instruct Marina in the simple tasks which any real woman was required to know. It was obscurely Maddy's fault, for instance, that Marina had run off with Arthur. As for the miserable marriage itself, Maureen would have trained Marina up to be a better wife. Now, of course, that she was the wife of an important doctor, an even higher duty called. Marriage was Maureen's only horizon, perhaps because her first child had been born so traumatically out of wedlock. Kevin, the husband she had finally 'hooked', was a contractor. Maureen would fuss over Paul as if he lacked something. Marina neglected Paul; Marina did not want her second marriage to fail as her first had done, now did she? And why in the name of sense had Marina gone into business with her friend Catherine, especially as she had no need of the money? Wasn't it risking a lot not to be on call for Paul when he came home so tired, so full of the world's cares? Maureen was jealous of Catherine. She disliked Catherine's subtle designs, the baggy sweaters Marina had so triumphantly marketed to Harrods at so exorbitant a price. Marina became bitterly aware that Maureen could never have afforded such things; it put a shameful light on the whole enterprise.

Although neither Paul nor Catherine had actually said that Maureen's limitations were those of the lower-middle class, it was what they meant when they averted their eyes and told Marina what utter nonsense it was to mind *what* Maureen thought. Perhaps it was not a class judgement on their part. Paul had no truck with that kind of attitude, and Catherine had lived in a weird, self-imposed exile all her life. Marina was quite sure that she herself was above any considerations of class. In fact, for some time after one of Maureen's transatlantic visits, Marina would become painfully feverish about the bathroom towels which did not match and aware that her elegant chintz 'looked old'. That she herself never wore lipstick and slopped around in jeans seemed to be asking for it, for desertion, contempt or another woman. Arthur Holt might have used her as a model for a Greek goddess in his poetry, but at forty-six Marina was pushing her luck not to take more trouble with her appearance.

Marina whipped a lock of wiry, flaxen hair from her face, put the mug down and stood, stretching. She pressed her nose against the diamond-clean window and watched the empty gravel drive as if willing Paul to drive home into the countryside where the deafening wings of wind hurled the trees and clouds about, drowning the babble of madness he heard daily. The house was vaguely Georgian. They had two happy dogs, setters, which liked to go walking with Paul. Marina not only loved Paul, she was *in* love with him; it terrified her to think of losing him. When her mother was there, she felt like a frantic moth beating at him as if he were a lamp beyond the darkness of her unworthy self. Maybe she did not do enough to gain his love, maybe he was humouring her when he told her she had nothing more to gain. The whole idea made her feel as shaky as someone on a tightrope looking down. In their five years together, they had weathered first the publication of Arthur's biography, and then her childlessness. It was already too late for Marina, who tried to conceal her hot flushes and frayed nerves not only from Paul but from herself, trying to convince herself that this missed month or that one signified a pregnancy. The fecund Maureen, with her brood of Marina's half-brothers and -sisters, had not failed to commiserate with her on this score. What a shame such a gentleman as Paul could not have an heir!

For all of her wider insecurities, however, Marina's impatience to see Paul that evening had nothing directly to do with them. They jangled under the surface of a more immediate concern with Catherine's trip to Salonika, with Phil Deals.

With his Jungian leanings, Paul would be entranced, she thought (she hoped), with an extraordinary coincidence, and one which had astonished Catherine as well. On the somewhat thin pretext of finding out how the plans were going for the shop they meant to open in the Fulham Road that autumn, Catherine had rung to chat. In reality, she was worried about Xenia, worried about Theo, and was having a predictably stiff time of it in Salonika with her uncle. Catherine had mentioned in passing a name which had rung a faint bell with Marina, Phil Deals. And when this small tremor had finally agitated her memory, the whole of it had opened up into one vast chasm of recall. Not only had Marina gone to dances in New York with Deals's younger brother Geoff, she had actually known Susannah Vaughan. How shocking, how horrible to think that poor Susie had died in such a terrible way!

Marina was impatient. When something like this happened, she longed to tell it all. Bottling things up was not her problem, which was perhaps why she was good for both Cat and Paul whose Englishness made them bottle a good deal. Good Lord, Geoff Deals! What had happened to him? she wondered. Maybe Catherine would find out. When he had been a freshman at Yale and Marina had been a senior at school, they had danced away a whole night to Lester Lanin in the St Regis Hotel. Her girlfriends had been awed that she was going out with Geoff Deals, but they had known each other as children, and had simply used each other from time to time as a shelter from the opposing sex. Maddy and Leila Deals had been chums, brought up in the same area. Whenever Maddy took Marina out to the country to stay with her 'grandmother', they would go over to have lunch with Leila in Far Hills. Mr Deals had been very rich and maintained a house there, along with his other houses (there was some mid-Western connection), for his New York wife in which she could entertain her friends and so on.

The minute these Scott Fitzgerald memories cropped up, Marina tried to squash them. The Deals house was hardly a palace, was it? It had been pretty big, though. Country houses like this had been erected in New Jersey during Carnegie times as summer retreats from New York; they glowed like a string of false jewels in the salubrious air of the Watchung

Hills. Marina's adoptive 'grandmother' had lived in a stately shack on Mine Mountain, aptly named, for it was a bastion of old money, a Republican stronghold. People like her true grandmother and Maureen had lived in the townships below.

Mrs Deals, who had been Leila Schuyler, came from an old Dutch family from New Amsterdam, while Deals had been a car magnate . . . that was it. It was her breeding and their combined money that kept the family floating so high. He, a bit of a Gatsby, had spent much time in Detroit, where his wife felt ill at ease.

Marina's unregenerate Daisy self now waltzed again in these heights as it once had done literally, for there had been brilliant parties underneath silken marquees, and she had been asked to them all. As for Susannah, Marina did remember her – not framed by billowing white curtains, but just as if she had been. Of course, Catherine had talked about her cousin; she had even asked Paul to look into the spectacular cures attributed to her intercession. The reason the penny had not dropped before was that no one in New Jersey had ever called her 'Susannah Vaughan'; she was 'Susie'.

She had not thought about these people for about thirty years! The Dealses had been part of the wallpaper of her life, not an emotional connection. They had simply weaved in and out of her parents' ambit. If she remembered correctly, Geoff had been an afterthought, probably a 'mistake', a late baby, a brother to Phil and two sisters, Geraldine and Jenny. Gerry and Jenny. Imagine!

Well, now, how did it go? Gerry had run off with someone – a cowboy, was it? – and had moved to Montana or somewhere like that. Marina remembered that well enough because Maddy had used her as an example of folly personified. (Poor Maddy had been incapable of even imagining Arthur.) Gerry must have been about twenty-two when she had committed this heinous social crime. Jenny, on the other hand, had been the object of Marina's devotion, a childhood crush. With immense condescension, Jenny had permitted the little girl Marina to witness her dressing table, a vision of white organza covered with potions and unguents. When she had actually brushed Marina's long hair with one of her silver hairbrushes, Marina had thought she would die of happiness. It had been a moment of transfiguration to see her own face in Jenny's glass as if it were older than twelve. Jenny and Marina had both been pretty, and this had been the unspoken bond and why Jenny had conferred such a blessing. In 1961, Jenny had been in the cattle market where Marina herself was soon to go – deb parties that lasted until 5 a.m., decisive battles in which being pretty

92

and rich cast the die for life. What *had* become of Jenny? Marina had no idea. One thing was certain, though: she had very much disliked Phil. Gerry had as well, and it had all seemed a little cruel to Marina but not unfair.

It was Phil who had been the odd one out, and Marina supposed all at once, as she sat in her Oxfordshire house, that if she had been an unhappy child, which she had not been, for all of that came later, she might have found him disturbing.

Maddy and Mrs Deals must have been insane to let Marina and Geoff racket about with Phil, a man in his early twenties who had acted like a slightly disturbed child. Marina shuddered. People had not thought the same way then, though, you had to remember, and certainly Phil had never done them any harm. Well, he wouldn't to his own brother, would he? Or was that naïve?

He had been a little homunculus, stunted but not abnormally so. He had worn heavy black-rimmed spectacles and had a squint or a limp or something like that. He constantly wore black, and this was because, she now remembered, he was supposed to be artistic in some way. He must have been in on the end of the Beat Generation. She could imagine Phil reading a thumbed copy of *On the Road*. Yes, he had given poetry readings in coffee houses in Greenwich Village, she was sure of it, for Geoff had talked about it disdainfully when he and she had been teenagers. At that time in her life, Marina had been sure that being a poet was of a higher significance than anything. (Well, she'd had to repent in leisure of *that*!) It was certainly better than being a beastly banker, which was probably what Geoff was at the moment. No, *of course*! He would be running his father's firm, or whatever was left of it. It was probably the American end of a Japanese takeover now. In fact, now Marina thought about it, she remembered that Geoff had confided in her about his brother's situation at a dance one evening in New York. This had been when the poetry came into it.

It seemed that Deals Senior had washed his hands of his elder son and had pensioned him off, leaving the colossus of Detroit for Geoff, the baby, to manage on his retirement. It had been a real Jacob and Esau conflict, and Geoff had had the decency to feel remorse. All of this had been before anything had happened to ruffle Detroit other than Tamla Motown. There had been no Japanese mergers, the riots in 1968 had not yet taken place, nor had the entirety of modern American history, Vietnam. Had there been such a time?

Back to Phil. Someone had tried 'to make a man out of him': his father, a boor. And now he was in Salonika, of all places, dancing attendance on Susie's father, who was almost certainly not a boor.

All right, the Deals house had been shamefully palatial and ugly with it, an erection of mock Tudor, not unlike places in Surrey. It had lawns and tennis courts, a pool and disused paddocks, and this had been where Marina and Geoff would play when Maddy visited Leila. There had been old, smelly hay in the paddocks, more dust than substance, and they would bound about in it. Geoff, for all his sins, had a strong imagination, that was what she had liked about him, and they had played roles from the latest epic movies. Somehow, it seemed that Phil would always appear during these games, a shadow at the stable door, hardly moving in his black turtleneck and jeans. He acted as if he happened to be passing, but his face and neck would be tense because it was a fib, Marina knew. But it didn't matter. He would generally offer a child-treat such as the view of a bird's nest full of eggs which they mustn't disturb or a glass of real lemonade which he was going to make in the kitchen. Phil, the pied piper, had taken them round his mother's acres in a complicated game of follow-my-leader, which was much more ingenious than anything they might have invented for themselves. He had been to Marina then quite simply an odd fish, someone who didn't match – a Peter Pan, but not by Disney. In the company of adults, his mother and his sisters, he would become sombre, dead almost, as if his true self had been snuffed out by puberty. 'I think my brother *likes* you,' Geoff once said to her when she was about nine. It had made her feel all funny.

Now she thought about it, Marina's heart ached for the poor oddity. There had been something hazardous about him, but she did not think it had been actively malign. He was the sort of man who might have had bizarre impulses, but she doubted that he had ever put them into practice. Indeed, he had always seemed to hold his face in front of his soul like a mask, as if to guard others from seeing the monstrosity that he was, as if he might do even the most casual observer some damage. Marina sighed. She rather hoped Phil had found some Macedonian forest where he could caper undisturbed on his dainty goat's feet, a sanctuary where, protected, he could also do no harm.

Marina took her mug of unfinished tea and popped down the hall into the kitchen, where she considered what to defrost for dinner. It was a mercy Paul had no interest in food, for she had no interest in cooking. Lately, she had exhausted herself night after night feeding Maureen with dainties she had spoiled or burned in her ham-fisted way. Spaghetti. She bunged some frozen mince in the microwave to thaw. Bolognese. He liked that. She rummaged for tomato purée in the cupboard. Banjo and Turnip thumped their tails against the stone floor. Soon they would be rioting. She had a conversation with the dogs and scratched their ears.

It was Susie (not Susannah) whom she now saw before her inner eye, rather in the manner of a remembered dream.

Leila Deals had had a Somerset Maugham 'verandah', which had surrounded the half-timbered house with anachronistic abandon. It was as if Marina were floating over the past, looking down. Susie the martyr was reading in a rattan chair, settled in cushions with a green floral print. The verandah overlooked the tennis court, where the sisters Jenny and Gerry, dressed in cut-offs, were lobbing balls. Susie was older than the girls, a pale young woman, quite an adult, of course, to Marina as she had been then, but Marina saw her now through adult eyes. Susie's pallor, amongst women who never studied anything more taxing than how to get a tan and maintain it all the year round, had made her stand out, as had her fine mousy-blonde hair and her beautiful and slightly protuberant eyes. Above all things, she was remarkable, of course, for her accent, and Marina would creep up close to Susie just to hear her talk. Of course, now that Marina looked back on it, Susie had been terribly young, but even then she had seemed old with her correct manner and English ways. She had read incessantly and used to smoke, turning pages as if she were consuming the contents and blowing out the ethereal residue of what she had not needed to know. Maybe she had been reading the Bible or the *Confessions* of St Augustine, but Marina doubted it. Susie had seemed to use a book as a portable visor, a defence against an invasion of Dealses.

In a way, now Marina thought of it, Susie had been necessary to Mrs Deals's establishment. There had always been the vague suggestion that Leila was very well connected in England and so the reserved girl smoking on the verandah had the curious mystique Marina attached to movie stars or foreign royalty. It was also understood that she was not well, and this had added to Susie the otherworldly glamour of a Victorian heroine.

Or had it been more? In recent years, Marina had returned to her childhood Catholic faith after a long and painful absence. Paul, a convert of long standing, still had fits of zeal interlaced with rationalist panic, but Marina, bathed in an unspoken *rapprochement* with God, felt more a kind of eternal gratitude. Still, she reckoned that a higher charm than glamour must have attended Susie if in later life she had become a saint; a deeper distinction than breeding should have graced her if she had had the guts for martyrdom. Marina searched for it in memory, uneasy with the temptation to supply a nimbus. When Susie looked at you with those prominent eyes, dreamy, and slightly smudged underneath as if she did not sleep at all well, the look stayed with you. Was Marina imagining this now?

Susie rarely smiled, Marina remembered that, but for some reason this had not communicated severity. There had been, more, a gravity to her. An oddly gentle observer, she seemed to weigh what she saw, and if she did not participate no one appeared to mind: she seemed to have a general licence to withdraw.

In order to forestall the dogs, Marina got out a couple of tins and an opener and doled out their food. The kitchen was simple, plain as an old shoe, with nothing to distinguish it but the view from the window of the vegetable patch Marina had started last year. In fact, she had wanted to put her back into it today, but the weather was foul and increasing in foulness; it had started to rain heavily. 'You're not getting much of a walk tonight, I can tell you,' she admonished the dogs as they wolfed their supper.

It had been unfair to impute snobbish motives to Mrs Deals. She winced as it came back to her now with a measure of shock that Susannah's mother, and this had been Leila's sister, was supposed to have taken her own life.

Now, how had she heard such a story? Surely, Maddy would have sheltered her from anything so unpleasant. Marina fell to chopping onions. These things got about. The tragic English girl was bound to have been explained by someone, and the hushed tiptoeing around her might easily have been accounted for if the rumour Marina remembered had been true. Geoff might have told her, or maybe even the wondrous Jenny, who had adored anything sensational. In those days, an unhappy childhood had been the distinguishing mark of a rarefied soul, one purified by suffering. Even mental illness had had a kind of cachet . . . Ann Sexton and Sylvia Plath had exchanged symptoms by mail, vying with each other in feats of madness, of derring-do.

The dogs pricked up their ears at the unaccustomed sound of Marina's grim hilarity. The demons Paul had to exorcise daily were nothing if not sordid. She looked at her watch. Where was he now if not rummaging around in somebody's hell, trying to wrestle a way to the surface? Obsession, depression and schizophrenia repelled him. He regarded them as fiends which fed upon his patients; he stunned them with lithium and Largactil and tried to salvage what was left.

Which somehow brought her back to Phil. Absently, she scraped onions and garlic into some oil and started to fry them. The aroma rose and she added some basil. She had not needed nor wanted to cook that evening. Even the marriage did not require this. She had spent twenty

96

years being a doormat to Arthur for whom she had slaved. Although they would eat it, the spaghetti was neither for Paul nor for herself; she did it for the absent Maureen, a penance, not only for the sin of her memories, but for the false premises on which she had built them.

The last time she had seen Phil, and Susie for that matter, had been at a garden party given by her adoptive grandmother in her honour. The occasion for it had been her departure to England, where she was to study at Oxford. The irony had not escaped Marina that she had come full circle, for she now lived near the city where she had first met Arthur. But that was beside the point. Marina's real grandmother had once been her adoptive grandmother's servant, and this was the reason Marina had been given to Maddy. The secret, of course, had been kept from Marina, and when she had finally found out, her perspective on the genteel doings of her false grandmother's household had been necessarily and radically changed. It was therefore not without pain that she remembered the silver trays passing under the noses of the guests assembled to wish her a good journey. Champagne had circulated one way, smoked salmon and asparagus rolls another, as if it had been an upper-class English wedding. She was almost twenty and had worn a pink linen dress bought by Maddy for the occasion at Bergdorf's. Her 'grandmother' had had a 'couple' then, Portuguese, and it filled Marina with deep sadness to think whose place they had taken. No wonder Maureen was angry!

Whatever her feelings now, Marina had been quite a featherbrain then – well, perhaps more brains than feathers. She had only acted a part which had been expected of her. As a fluffy blonde, she had enjoyed the highest status. A girl had not had to be a brain surgeon in those days; Oxford had been camouflaged as a dilettantish adventure for Marina, and it had only been a summer school course after all. At college, where they tried to take her seriously, there had been talk of its leading somewhere else, but Maddy and her grandmother had seen it as a way of meeting a nice Englishman, preferably titled, or at least finding her way to Henley or Cowes for a few good parties.

It was all very well making these excuses for herself, blaming history and the gilded cage for her callous indifference to any serious issue, for she had taken the *mise-en-scène* for granted, and she remembered enjoying the party, the attention she was getting. Susie, on one of her annual visits, had been especially invited because she was English and Marina was going to England. Marina had been meant to ask Susie what to expect.

What to expect! She wished she could talk to Susie now about just the sort of voyage she had made. Marina dumped the meat into the frying pan and stirred furiously; she opened a tin of tomatoes and tipped them in.

Susie must have been about thirty at the time. She had come with Phil as if with a date, and they made an unusual couple, to say the least. The guest list was composed of forty or so family friends, diverse in age but uniform in appearing indisputably well-bred. A few of the *jeunesse dorée*, who were supposed to be missing Marina when she left, were sprinkled round like sparklers on an elaborate pudding. It was many years after Marina had left America for good before she realized how incongruous was the little enclave with everything the country itself stood for. Later, she had taken such a terrible battering from Arthur, a Socialist, about this rank capitalism that she had become ashamed of it, and this even before Maureen. Her careful education had left its mark on her, however, like a gently pressed thumb – just as it was meant to do.

Marina wondered what she would now make of Phil and Susie if she could meet them as they had been that day. Even then, Phil, who was surly, clearly angry at having been dragged there, looked like a Communist. His unfriendliness to Marina took her aback. He kept in Susie's orbit all the time, as if she were the mother ship and he her satellite. As for Susie herself, she seemed to cringe from the opulent surroundings as if they might infect her, as if they weakened her in some way. For the most part, she huddled in a feathered garden sofa, hunching away from the group, thin, with little child bones, like a bird blown into the wrong place by a storm. Marina supposed that she would place them now as intelligentsia . . . Susie, an ex-public-school radical . . . and of course she would be wrong.

That day, Phil had danced attendance, fussing around Susie. On the edges of the party, which flowed counter to their seriousness, they seemed to be discussing something too important or high-minded to be shared. Perhaps this was why a rumour had got about that, first cousins though they were, they had fallen in love and intended to break the news of an engagement to a horrified Leila Deals.

It had been a hot day and the party had been held in the portico with its view of the formal garden and the hills beyond. Marina had turned from a pretty child into an attractive woman. Men levitated when she entered a room. She remembered standing by a slender column, suddenly conscious of the power sexuality gave her, proud of it. She had felt that day anything she wanted could be hers. She had not known then that she would come to want Arthur.

She and Susie must have crossed tracks that day like trains at a junction, each with a different destination.

Somewhat irritably, Marina put the lid on the sauce, and wandered back into the sitting room. Had Susie's gruesome death been blindly chosen? She put the question another way. Had Susie chosen it, but blindly?

She remembered getting up her nerve to cross the terrace and join them so that she could get the required chat about England out of the way, and had been embarrassed to find them arguing. Susie had blinked slowly up at Marina, her concentration broken. It had been one of those awkward situations in which retreating was ruder than toughing it out. Susie had asked her what she wanted to know, and Marina had twittered something stupid; all while Phil tried to distract them, interrupting the conversation with jokes, demanding attention like one of the dogs wanting a game with a ball . . . although Marina wondered if a sarcastic dog were not a contradiction in terms.

Marina was impatient with the idea of destiny seen as an impersonal force. In her own case, she had been blithely unconscious of her true capacities and would have thought it absurd if anyone had told her that a year from then she would have broken up a marriage and run off with a man twenty years her senior. It would not have occurred to her that the beauty with which she had then been so innocently pleased could have been used and abused by Arthur, nor that it would become infamous as a force for destruction. Marina's doughty theology admitted only of free will. It was self-knowledge she had lacked so terribly; her life of ease had flattered her into believing she was a nice person, not the egoist she secretly was, the spoiler she would turn out to be.

So, taking that angle on Susie, it was possible to believe that the seeds of some inordinate, godly impulse had already germinated in her; that the aloof and somewhat wary English cousin of the Dealses had already made a choice with the hidden logical outcome of a violent death. And if Susie's mother truly had committed suicide, it was tempting to think of a pattern, not of fate but of subterranean election.

At that time on the terrace, embraced by the slim columns of the portico, Marina had been aware of Susie more as a rough guide to the British Isles than as one who might eventually plead for her across the more radical bourne of death. She had privately noted that Susie's outfit left something to be desired and she had wondered if she would be expected to be dowdy in England. Susie had worn a skirt and blouse to the sumptuous party on the terrace, her long hair caught up off her neck in a simple clasp. She told Marina about Oxford; she herself had studied at Cambridge, but ill health had prevented her from taking a degree, and Marina had thought her a little dismissive about the whole exercise. Now she knew why. Spiritual giants rarely grew in such soil where snarky dons and Augustan poets flourished.

Susie had been much keener on some group she was forming in the 'East End', as if Marina could identify it when all Marina knew about London had centred on Buckingham Palace and the National Gallery. Looking back on it, Marina realized that Susie must have lived in Hackney, or somewhere like that. Although Susie had given her an address, she did not have a phone, which had amazed Marina, and she had described her flat as 'public housing'. Yes, she remembered now it had been Hackney. There had been no inverse snobbery about this or even pride. Susie had laughed and said words to the effect that she had become interested in dangerous criminals because they had no place to go. In fact, there had been something slightly dangerous about Susie. One remembered her calm eyes as if she had been a seafarer who had known voyages into places of which it was preferable not to speak.

Thinking about it, Marina flushed. She remembered herself as she had been then, a fizzy, spoiled, rich girl, a little tiddly with champagne. Despite the weird, caustic interpolations from Phil, who had clearly wanted to get rid of Marina, Susie had been kind, but the gentle thrust of a sidelong glance had intimated to her that there was more to England than Trafalgar Square and that the English might not be wholly vanquished by Marina's airs and graces to date. There had been no cruelty in the suggestion, no accusation of barbarism, but Marina felt she had horsed up to Susie in rather a silly way.

Was she giving Susie a prophet's eye in retrospect? At the time, she had been a bit floored by the seniority and foreignness of Susie who, albeit graciously, had warned her that she must not be misled into thinking the common language signified a common mind. In itself, this was a banality, but a deeper gaze from Susie had swept her up at the time. For one curious moment, she had wanted to be with Susie, to be like Susie, and she had impulsively volunteered to offer some help at Susie's refuge. Of course, Susie had accepted, with that little half-smile of hers, and of course Marina had forgotten completely about it, remembering it only now because she was glad she had at least proffered something.

The point was, and Marina now saw it with the relief of working out a puzzle, that she remembered almost exactly the tone and quality of the encounter, even though it had occurred nearly thirty years ago. She had not thought about Susie, nor dwelt on her; she had lost touch with her adoptive family's connections during the long exile of her marriage to Arthur and had not even heard of Susie's death; but, like a harmony reverberating on the air or the light from a dead star, Marina's recollection seemed to have an existence almost beyond itself: it was perfectly clear, not the conversation nor its content, but the being, the presence and indeed the interior beauty of Susie herself. There had been no particular epiphany that day, but Marina wondered if perhaps there was one now.

Glancing out of the window, she spotted Paul's car coming through the gate at the end of the drive, and so she hurried to the door to greet him. With a pang, Marina wished that Susannah had known she had, at long last, ended up with Paul, for if she had prayed for Marina that afternoon so very long ago, she could not have been more pleased with the result. Marina smiled a little to herself. Maybe she had.

IX

'YOU'LL NEVER guess!'

Catherine looked up from her breakfast to find Phil Deals standing in front of her table in the dining room of the Electra Palace. He was wearing an open-necked shirt and a neat, lamb's-wool jumper was thrown over his shoulders, making him look vaguely Italian.

'May I?' He sat and summoned the waiter, from whom he demanded coffee in bad but idiomatic Greek. 'Uncle has decided he wants to meet your Grand Inquisitor.' The waiter brought the coffee and Phil shoved some drachmas at him across the table like a poker player.

At the best of times, Catherine regarded each new dawn with mistrust and she needed some time in which to adjust a coherent working philosophy for the day ahead. She stared at Phil, her process having been outraged. 'Good morning,' she said frostily.

He was enjoying it. He sipped at the coffee and winked over the cup. 'Breakfast conferences are all the rage these days, I understand,' he said. 'As it happens, I'm triple-parked outside. The traffic in the city is a nightmare. I thought you and your holy man wouldn't mind a lift up the hill. Is he here with you?'

Catherine shook her head. 'The Church found a flat for him.'

'Then we can swing by and pick him up. Finish your egg, give him a buzz, why not? I'm sure he'll be fascinated by Uncle.'

Deals repelled her like an insect. He actually resembled one with his stick limbs and irritating whine; he had a pointed jaw as if he had concealed mandibles and ate nasty things with them on the sly. Triple-parked, was he? She took her time, spreading Euro-jam slowly on her cold toast for revenge. 'The oddest coincidence,' she said. 'A friend of mine knew you years ago in the States. Marina . . .' but suddenly she couldn't remember Marina's maiden name. 'She married Arthur Holt.'

'Not Horner! Well, blow me down! Small world. She was a fetching kid, a bit of a Lolita, if you know what I mean.'

Imploding with rage, Catherine said through her teeth, 'She is my best friend.'

He shrugged. 'Why are the English so uptight about sex? If she was talented at art you wouldn't mind me saying so.'

'She was a child when you knew her.'

' "Thank heaven for little girls",' Phil said. 'What's she up to now? I was a fan of Holt's and couldn't have been more thrilled that I had known his lady, a woman of such distinction.'

Catherine counted to ten under her breath. He was merely an elderly *enfant terrible*, the sort who did not realize he had grown too old to be deliberately outrageous. 'She is married to a psychiatrist. They are very happy.'

'A shrink . . . My God. Poor little Marina: from the sublime to the ridiculous.'

'Do you really have to be quite so offensive?' Catherine's outburst drew the embarrassed attention of some Germans at the next table.

He paused, thought. 'Yes. Yes, I do. I have to. Now, do you want to come or not? That honking out there is at me.'

'I will ring Father Edward. Perhaps, during that time, you could move your car. And, as you have been frank with me, I shall be frank with you. I am doing this for his sake. He actually is, as it happens, "a holy man", and a very nice one too. What is more, he is virtually blind and he deserves both your tolerance and your respect. I refuse to expose him to taunting and bad manners, and so I will have an undertaking from you that you will at least attempt to be polite.'

'Attagirl!' he said. 'I like spunk in a woman.'

The haughtier she became, the more she felt like Groucho Marx's pouter-pigeon adversary, the pompous socialite who provoked his anarchy. But she lifted her lip. 'Well, you have it in me,' she snarled. She had learned, oh, at long last, that she did not have to be 'nice'.

He was, indeed, slightly taken aback, but he rose to look after his car. '*Ciao*!' he said and slouched off. Out of the window, Catherine could see that the offending vehicle had caused complete chaos. Phil raised his hand in blessing at the furious Thessalonians . . . a cool dude.

Catherine assembled her belongings in her pleasant room and rang the priest. She wished he were staying at the hotel. They had had supper together the night before at a taverna which sprawled outside an ancient bazaar, propped with beams so that it would not collapse. The proprietor took an interest in them because he had lived in England for some years and had returned to Thessaloniki to look after his aged parents. Possibly because of Father Edward's Roman collar, but more probably because of his evanescent quality of benevolence, the restaurateur began to talk about religion. He was Jewish. In the evening air, musky with the faintly Oriental scent of Near Eastern cooking, Catherine remembered stories of

Byzantium, where theological disputes had been discussed on every street corner like football scores. Father Edward drank it all in along with retsina from a keg. Thessaloniki had once been called the Second Jerusalem for its vast Jewish population, some of its survivors still speaking a medieval Spanish dialect. They had lived in harmony with the Greeks until the coming of the Nazis, who had massacred eighty thousand of them. Only a few families remained now and a synagogue or two out of hundreds. As he spoke, his voice took on the unspeakably sad air of a well-thumbed psalm; Catherine and the priest had listened, breathless.

At last, in a grand, ecumenical gesture, the restaurateur had claimed St Paul as a somewhat eccentric coreligionist, who would have visited the early Jewish communities as a Jew. Catherine had watched, touched and moved by the spread of wonderment over the priest's face, his friendliness to the proprietor, the way he had made the man expand, tell his story, recount the tragedy.

During the long, slow meal, she too had found herself talking. Perhaps it had been the good Eastern food on her plate, perhaps the exercise of the Greek tongue that day, but she was put painfully in mind of Theo, and ended up telling Father Edward about her husband, and how he had betrayed her. He had been gently appalled at the story of how Missy had kidnapped her daughter . . . Missy's daughter, as it happened, too, for Theo's ex-mistress had been discovered to be the biological mother of the adopted girl. Catherine was too reserved to let her hair down completely, but she had woken that morning relieved. She had given him the essentials of the story, almost for safekeeping. Someone else had it now, not her brother Charles, nor Marina; it was more as if she had taken a threatening letter to the police or had called in the army to look at an unexpected, unexploded bomb.

In fact, as she now stood waiting for him to answer the telephone, she found herself anxiously wondering if he were all right; and, when he finally replied, more anxiously anticipating some subtle form of snub or rejection. And so, it gratified her not a little that he seemed all the friendlier for their conversation, and that he was particularly pleased to be meeting Uncle James. She found herself admitting to him that she had been rude to Phil – and more, that she was often short-tempered. Although she could not see Father Edward's face, Catherine felt a constructive mildness emanating from him, like a welcome breeze on a hot day. If she had to spend another morning with her uncle and Phil, she was relieved that he would be there with her.

For all her earlier fantasies about James Vaughan's high status and his chauffeur-driven Rolls, Phil's car turned out to be a jaunty, messy Fiat full of old clobber which he heaved into the boot to give her room to sit. He tackled the swift, snarled traffic, crashing the gears and nosing his way through gaps with careless bravado. Catherine sank into the seat and folded her arms across her chest, saying nothing as he made his way towards Frangon Street . . . the old French quarter, she thought. Greeks, Romans, Jews, Crusaders, Turks, Germans . . . who had *not* had a historical presence in the city? Bulgarian Slavs? Albanians? They, too, surely were woven somehow into the loose cloth. She stuck out her chin and glanced at Deals out of the corner of her eye. His face was set in an expression of self-satisfaction. He had enjoyed ruffling her composure. It amused him to torment people, she imagined, to egg them on. She could not imagine what earthly connection there could have been between this man and Susannah, or how he could seriously have thought of marrying her.

An idle memory came back of Susannah now, like something in a dream. She had been musical, hadn't she, like darling Xenia: like Xenia, vulnerable. Was she thinking of her daughter or was she thinking of Susannah strumming the piano, humming lightly to herself as she played Lady Simon's untuned Bechstein in Sussex? The thought was gone, but there remained an impression of someone shy who was perhaps very unhappy. And Catherine remembered a subtle mobility about her plain features that made them alive and interesting.

'Is this it?' Phil asked, coming to an abrupt halt before a block of flats. It was a solid building, constructed at the turn of the century, vaguely and decorously Viennese in style. The street was lined with trees and this lent a bosky air to the surroundings, making it an enclave apart from the roar of the city.

She nodded. 'I'll fetch him,' she said. For no apparent reason, Phil fumed at the wheel as she got out. The street was quiet, and although they had exchanged sharp words this had not appeared to bother him. It was more as if he habitually responded to some inner audience, a drama in which he acted whatever role took his fancy at the time. It pleased him now, she thought, to act as if he were sweating in a traffic jam.

Father Edward appeared almost at once at the ornate door and Catherine resisted an impulse to embrace him as she would an old friend. He smiled diffidently at her, straining to catch her expression through his heavy lenses, and she forbore to lead him down the steps to the waiting car. He looked more frail than she had remembered.

'Good-morning,' he said to Phil through the window. 'I'm Edward Knight. You must be—'

'Phil,' said Phil. 'Hop on in.'

Catherine ground her teeth and got into the back while Father Edward fumbled with the mechanics of simply getting into the small car. 'It is very kind of you and Mr Vaughan to see me,' he said.

Phil shrugged and revved up. 'All in a day's work,' he said. The car bounded forward as he let out the clutch. 'As a matter of fact, you and I go way back even though we haven't actually met.' He eyed the priest maliciously as he cut into the traffic on the main road.

Edward said nothing, but inclined his head.

'Sue was my best friend. You were the big *influence*. We often disagreed, you and I.'

'I am sorry to hear it.'

'You always won.'

'I was not aware,' Edward said after a moment's thought, 'that there was a conflict on that kind of order, nor one strictly between you and me. I was Susannah's religious adviser.'

'You can say that again!'

Catherine opened her mouth to speak, then decided to remain silent. To her surprise, the priest seemed more capable than she had imagined, more able to take Deals in his stride. Next to him, Phil was somehow diminished. His harsh voice made him seem like a barking gargoyle, a minor imp consigned to the upper guttering of a large cathedral.

'I loved her!' Deals continued indignantly.

'Who could not have loved her? Susannah was greatly loved by a good number of people.'

For some reason, it took Catherine aback to hear this. It had been assumed in the family that her cousin was a sort of poor relation in the respect of being unloved. Everyone knew she had inherited money from her mother, but it had been rendered worthless in a subtle way by her having been abandoned; no one had said this, it had simply been understood. Indeed, Catherine remembered that 'poor' had been her cousin's epithet. 'Poor Susannah is coming to stay this Easter.' Or, 'My beastly brother forgot poor Susannah's birthday again. At least I managed to send her a cake from Floris.'

'Well, you'll soon find out the answer to that conundrum,' Deals replied. 'Uncle didn't love Susannah. And if you ask me, which you will, whether I think Susie was a martyr, I'll tell you just exactly on whose altar she was sacrificed. I have pretty strong ideas about who carved her up and I don't mean the butchers who killed her.' Suddenly, he lurched the car, cutting across two lanes of the Via Egnatia in order to make a right-hand turn. He was punishing them, harrowing his passengers like a schoolboy. He glanced at the priest to see what effect this display had made.

'I am sure we will get to that very large question in time,' Edward said, a little pompously. 'It is quite complex . . . as you suggest.'

'On the contrary, it is elementary, my dear Watson,' Phil muttered.

Mercifully, he fell silent as he drove them up the steep hill which appeared to rise almost vertically in front of them on the way to the upper city walls. The medieval street, more prosperous than the one in which her uncle lived, was lined with gabled overhanging houses, most of them tactlessly modernized, Catherine noted, so that they looked like mock Swiss chalets. The car laboured in first gear; there was an unpleasant tension in the air as if Phil were willing it. Perhaps he was simply sulking, she thought, because the estimable Father Edward had refused to get entangled in his game of lures and tricks and theatrical flourishes; but, glancing at his profile from the back seat, Catherine noticed a grim set to his jaw, a thin, sharp smile. At the summit of the rise, he turned left and glided slowly down a somewhat gentler incline. He pulled on the hand-brake so hard that they jolted forward. 'Right. We're here,' he said.

'Uncle awaits you in the garden,' said Phil when he had unlocked the gate. 'A little fresh air never goes amiss if you have any dealings with him. And I have been slaving away over a hot stove since the crack of dawn so that he can offer you the sort of hospitality he believes should come from a little sultan like himself.' He flounced ahead of them, flourishing his keys from a belt chain, and the dogs bounded out to greet him. 'Hi, boys, what's cooking?' he said. The dogs fawned and prowled, but ignored Catherine and the priest as if at some invisible command.

Not being able to contain the enormity of Phil any longer, Catherine threw a look at Father Edward, then, realizing he could not catch nuances of expression, she found herself digging him in the arm with her finger-nails. He looked startled and she flushed, embarrassed that she had behaved so familiarly.

'Sorry,' she muttered.

She was shocked to see genuine suffering in his magnified, distended eyes.

'Ah yes,' she said, 'it struck me too . . . yesterday . . . this is where she died. Of course, of course.'

'It wasn't here, not in this garden,' he said. 'Was it?'

'I don't think so. I think it was in the house,' she said, not really knowing. She wanted to add that the day before she, too, had been haunted by the ugly question of where Susannah was supposed to have died; that her gorge had risen rather than her tears; and that she wanted him to exorcise the horror of it in some way. All this, she knew, would cause him pain, and so she suppressed it.

'Of course, it was,' he said in confusion. 'I am glad not to have to go in there.' They wended their way deeper into the garden after Phil. 'Do you think he really does know who did it?'

Catherine was not a sentimental woman; even as a child she had been a bit acerbic. In fact, she often thought these days that she had married Theo precisely because he had never mooned over her or pawed at her, but had liked the arm's length at which she habitually kept herself. They had been silent partners, direct in their manner with each other when the need arose for conversation. A fugue of things unsaid, however, had worked disaster in the end.

For this reason, it puzzled her that Father Edward appealed so strongly to the affective side of her nature. Perhaps it was his precarious grasp on the physical world, his floundering, that brought out a wish to protect him, but this alone did not account for a sympathy for him that had blossomed almost overnight like an ungainly flower. She now found it almost unbearable to hear the broken tone in his voice when he asked this question, and so she merely shook her head in order that he could not hear the pity in her voice.

Catherine dealt with the weakening feeling of compassion by being cross with herself. Why had it not occurred to her that visiting the spot where Susannah had died might be difficult for him, might cost him much? During Xenia's long illness and slow recovery, she had come to see for herself how terrible it was to witness the suffering of someone she loved. And, because she was not Xenia's natural mother, Catherine had felt the burden of her own pain more keenly for its not being in some way official.

For Father Edward, surely it was worse. Was it even recognized that he could have anyone emotionally important to him except close relatives? Who would have comforted him about Susannah, a woman, after all? Especially if she had secured a place in heaven, how could he grieve at such a fixed bliss? How could he shudder against the mauling which might have elevated her to Paradise? Instead of talking about her own problems, she should have drawn him out in some way, shown him that she intuitively grasped his pain without drawing the wrong sort of attention to it. As a child, she had lived in her mother's awe of priests, thinking them angelic beings filled with a terrible potential to destroy, a potential they would not unleash if one was particularly kind and respectful to them. From her youth up, she had kept to her Catholic faith, but she had been forced to come to terms with it independently because she had lived in an Orthodox country. Now, however, and perhaps for this reason, she apprehended the humanity of Father Edward as his most powerful attribute. It had been crushed and refined, she thought, a coal pressed into a diamond. A generous love for him filled her. She knew she was somewhat awkward, but she would try to make this horrible visit easy for him.

So busy was she with these thoughts that she did not notice that they had arrived at the centre of the maze of paths to a splendid terrace where her uncle, literally, lay in wait for them on a small divan which had been moved out under the shade of an arbor twined with jasmine. Pots of Easter lilies stood about, giving the arrangement the faint air of an altar. This impression was curiously deepened by the sumptuous Oriental rug which was thrown across her uncle like a quilt. He rested on piles of over-stuffed cushions covered with old bits of other, perhaps even finer, carpets, so that he sat nearly upright. He was cleaner, tidier, than she had seen him the day before, and he wore a fine lawn nightshirt and a shawl around his shoulders. Catherine wondered if Deals and her uncle had anything else to do but dress up and show off to each other. But for the continual move-ment of his eyes, her uncle looked like an illustration from a story by Conan Doyle, not a real human being at all.

As she and Father Edward entered the glade, a young Turkish or gypsy boy leapt up and scuttled backwards towards the bushes, dropping a large fan with which he had evidently been cooling the swaddled old man, whose face seemed to have become very red overnight as if his anger had been switched on and had been given time to heat up like an ancient boiler.

'Oh, hi, Ali,' Phil said wearily to the boy, who quickly retrieved the fan. He stood before Phil in a pose of tremulous servility. 'I do wish he wouldn't grovel so,' he said to Catherine and the priest. 'God knows I pay him enough.' He clapped his hands and the child ran off in the direction of the house. 'Don't worry,' he added, 'his family blesses me daily, and he knows I couldn't cope without him.'

The old man, meanwhile, blinked at the sunlight and his visitors with an even-handed malevolence, as if the entire scene might be willed away, dissolved in his withering stare.

As no introduction was forthcoming from Phil, Catherine took command. 'Uncle James,' she said, 'I hope you are well today. I have brought Father Knight to see you.'

'Right! Well, as I can see that you'll manage just fine without me, I'll get on with Ali and some refreshments,' Phil said huffily. 'You'll do better without me, James,' he muttered to the old man. 'Believe it.'

Catherine did not deign to apologize and Deals wandered off in the direction the boy had gone, smiling again his cryptic wooden smile.

'How do you do?' Father Edward said to her uncle. 'It is very good of you to see me, Dr Vaughan.'

The old man scrutinized the pair for some time before answering. 'I am better today, thank you. I hope you had a good journey. Please be seated.' He graciously indicated some wrought-iron chairs which stood near his divan. 'But I do not have a doctorate, I am merely a gifted amateur.'

Father Edward and Catherine sat. Catherine was surprised at the change in her uncle's manner and relieved by it. A pressure somewhere had been taken off.

'Your niece has been enormously helpful,' said Edward. 'I could not have made the journey here without her.' He smiled at Catherine and she felt childishly pleased, like a schoolgirl given special mention in Assembly. 'But your gifts as an amateur, sir, have surely given you a special position in archaeology. I read a monograph you wrote on Macedonian gold many years ago and it has stayed with me.'

Catherine was surprised by the priest's unexpected urbanity and naughtily amused by it. She wondered if the old crow would drop the cheese for the fox who flattered so patiently.

'I thought you came here to talk about my daughter,' her uncle said sharply.

'Indeed, I have,' said Edward. 'I knew her well.'

'But you have found the time from saving souls to read learned monographs.'

'Well, one needs some form of recreation. And, of course, I read Classics . . . at King's . . .'

Catherine was thrilled at this neatly placed lob and quickly looked at her uncle to see how he would return the shot.

'Susannah told you about the monograph on gold, and about Dionysos too, I dare say,' the old man said with contemptuous finality, as if this disproved any or all of Father Edward's credentials.

'That is true. She did. But—'

'She thought I was a Satanist!' he snapped. 'Or something of that order.' He pulled the shawl around his shoulders and tightly folded his arms.

'She was proud of you, but, whatever she thought or felt, I read your work and formed my own opinion.'

In the fullness of the garden air, Catherine noticed that her uncle appeared more in his true proportions. The old rooted vine which sheltered him cut him down to size, as perhaps Father Edward did too. Even the brisk social scuffle had not taken away the gravity of the priest's sorrow. It seemed to linger still, pulling his shoulders down, weighting the furrows in his cheeks; his moon-like eyes blinked slowly, rhythmically, unseeing. Next to him, her uncle seemed an insubstantial figure, almost comic in his outlandish clothes, his *fin-de-siècle* mannerisms. They were both thinking of Susannah, but Catherine wondered how it was each of them saw her in the privacy of his own mind's eye.

'Philip tells me you think my daughter was a saint,' the old man said peevishly. 'But I suppose you think it's all right that she hurt me very deeply. After all, what am I but a heretic? *I* don't count!'

As if he had heard an odd strain of music, the priest leaned forward. 'I am not sure what I believe about her yet. That is why I am here. And I certainly believe that you "count", no matter how unorthodox you may have become. Either everyone matters or no one does, if you see what I mean.' Although he did not stroke her uncle's hand, Catherine felt as if he might have done. Indeed, the old man withdrew slightly as if he had been touched. 'Tell me,' Father Edward continued. 'Do you think she was? A saint, I mean, a Christian one?'

'If you mean to ask if she was immensely pious, yes, she was.'

Catherine noticed that her uncle barely addressed the priest. He spoke, rather, to himself, as if there were a continual stirring within him of a cauldron upon which he was fixated. He was like one of those fairy-tale characters who is doomed to row a boat for ever from shore to fixed shore, or like Sisyphus with his endless rock. She wondered suddenly if he were obsessed with Susannah, the child he had seemed to reject.

'In other words, you think she was guilty of spiritual pride,' his inquisitor answered. 'It would be, wouldn't it, pride, to be immensely pious . . . like the Pharisees who prayed on the street corners with their large phylacteries. Or, worse still, hypocrisy.'

The priest was so pleasantly crisp and precise in his definition that the old man seemed taken aback enough to give the matter some actual thought. 'I am not sure about that. She made no display of her devotions. She scuttled around furtively at them like a scullery maid after a forbidden "gentleman caller". It made one's flesh creep. She padded about clicking rosary beads; she slunk out to Mass at infernal hours of the morning, every morning. No, her piety was genuine enough in that sense . . .'

'But it nauseated you. Was it religious hysteria, then? A sort of badly sublimated libido?'

Vaughan sat up, discreditably excited, Catherine thought. 'Yes, in a way! I think you may have it there.' She noticed too that Father Edward's eyes were dull, as if he had had to numb himself in order to proceed to this awful place.

'A misdirected Dionysiac urge, you might say?'

The old man looked sharply at him. 'Oh dear,' he said, 'for a moment I thought that, *malgré* your calling, you might be amusing. Susannah hadn't the abandon of a Maenad. She would never have been capable of sinking her consciousness into anything so collective as an orgy, nor yet anything as immense as God, presupposing, of course, that there is such an entity; in fact, if you are going to present me with that tiresome old chestnut of Nietzsche, all of that "Apollo versus Dionysos" nonsense, I shall send you packing.' He said this in a pleasant enough way, as if it were a manner of speaking. 'And, as for misdirection, surely you yourself might have done that. I understand from Philip that you advised her.'

'For about five years . . . yes.'

'And might one ask what kind of advice you gave so fragile an individual?'

Father Edward flushed but said nothing.

'Did you advise her to come here on her last journey, as it were?'

Catherine noticed her uncle pausing almost daintily over this question, a spider with a fly.

'Susannah had two other spiritual directors besides myself – a Dominican, I believe, and a Jesuit who was her confessor at that time. Both have subsequently died. Although she and I remained friends, her life became overstretched. Her work took over and I rarely saw her.'

'She was a social worker,' the old man replied, falling back on his cushions as if the very thought exhausted him. 'In my day, saints slaughtered dragons or oozed with myrrh; they levitated or received stigmata. One liked that about them.'

Catherine was about to intervene. All at once, her uncle's affected dress and manner made perfect sense to her. The day before, she had thought him pitifully ill; today, he performed in another costume. Like an Indonesian puppeteer, he cast shadows on the wall, illusory shapes, sharp, exotic figures to distract the eye from his real purpose, which was to demolish Edward. He had probably been operating Phil Deals from the beginning, and he was almost certainly getting the better of this encounter now. Catherine could not understand quite why she saw the contest as unfair: it was surely not unequal.

'Susannah was not a social worker,' Edward said bluntly. 'And, as for oozing myrrh and slaying dragons, there are plenty of signs and wonders in Susannah's case.'

'How extraordinary!'

'Well, quite. But, tedious though it is, I am inclined to believe that virtue is its own reward.'

'Heavens to Betsy!' Phil cried. He returned down the garden path preceded by the small boy. They both bore trays laden with fruit, ices, little cakes. There was both plenty and excess and it might have tempted a Caravaggio to paint the picture. 'Did I hear "signs and wonders"? Did Susie fly? Talk to the animals? What fun to think that sanctity might be a bit of a circus!'

For the simple reason that Phil's entrance had broken a certain air of concentration, Catherine had somehow expected her uncle to silence his egregious Caliban. What she observed instead surprised her. The old man suddenly became pale and withdrawn.

Perhaps Phil was Ariel instead, for he regarded the dilapidated Prospero with the scorn only a really ethereal being can confer upon someone who shows too strongly the limitations of mortality. Catherine wondered if he was angry at her uncle for getting old.

'Uncle doesn't really want ocular proof of Susie's miracles,' Deals said. 'It might mean she was still hanging out here after all, *in reality*, and that would be very inconvenient. If he couldn't control her alive, how much more difficult it is to rule a spirit.' He was very jaunty in all this and turned to the old man. 'James, the genie is out of the bottle whether you like it or not. This is major. You have to cope with it. It isn't going to go away.'

'Do you mean to say that Susannah haunts the house?' Catherine asked because Father Edward hardly could. Indeed, he gave a start.

'Well, there are knockings, bangings, you know, probably the neighbourhood kids. James likes to say he thinks the art theft industry takes a close interest in the house, don't you, James? We're *not* well-liked in Thessaloniki, and this is because they think James got rid of the Head on the sly . . .'

' . . . which is completely untrue!' the old man cried.

'Of course, of course. We hardly need the money, now do we? Both of us being beneficiaries of Aunt Nancy; or, rather, my Grandfather Schuyler. It's just that you didn't get round to cataloguing the Head before the thieves got to it, did you, dear? Which is why it was such a cinch to off-load it.'

'Isn't he ghastly?' her uncle appealed to Catherine. 'If I take any notice it gives him just what he wants. He knows perfectly well that I intended to catalogue the Head as soon as it was possible to do so.'

For some reason, despite his languid style, the strain in her uncle's voice made it grate. Deals's expression became hooded, and Catherine was at once alert to a collusion between the two men which now seemed even deeper than she had supposed.

'There were only two people who knew it was here,' Vaughan continued. 'The first is, of course, the wholly ineffectual Phil, the second, and my Judas, was St Susannah. If she has survived death, which I do not believe for a moment, the only reason she would visit this house would be to ask my forgiveness. As a complete heathen, I see no need to give it. For a petty scruple, she destroyed my life – and, in letting in the thieves, she destroyed her own.'

Catherine glanced at Edward, expecting his outrage at her uncle's summary dismissal of his only child. Instead, he was opaque, still but for the slow blinking of his refracted, spherical eyes. 'Go on,' he said, 'go on.'

X

EDWARD WAS surprised when he saw Catherine coming up for Holy Communion, and oddly touched when she received it from his hand. He had not expected her to be there. He was a little embarrassed too. He had had to read the lectionary through his snap-on lenses, which always made him feel like a spaceman. The Gospel had been the Raising of Lazarus, for the Greeks were still observing Lent. Although it had been announced that the Mass was to be in English, he felt disoriented in the church and uprooted even from the liturgy. His homily had been inadequate to the greatness of a theme which seemed all too apposite. 'Jesus wept.' He had concentrated on that.

Susannah's funeral had taken place in this church. Her coffin must have stood where the communicants now filed up towards him. The sound of her voice came back to him; it had been full of expressive inflection, and her throat had been stopped with knives.

Catherine received the Host on her tongue, eyes shut. Of course, he was glad she had made the effort to come to Communion, especially so early, but he had thought to have some time to himself, literally *sub specie aeternatis*, this Sunday morning, in order to assimilate the events of the day before. Edward relied more and more on the little space of peace after Mass to recollect himself into a necessary silence. It was a way of absorbing God and being absorbed, of letting go all preoccupations.

This day of all days, it had seemed important to make a radical detachment from the knot of complex thoughts and feelings which were bound up in his visit to James Vaughan's house. The immediate temptation was to analyse what was going on between the two strange men. The more he tried, however, the more he suspected that the role of analyst had been assigned to him as if by some invisible casting director. Imperceptibly, he had become an actor whose part it was to be flattered into believing he understood the scene. Without knowing why, Edward had the unpleasant sensation that he was meant to serve the hidden demands of some larger plot the two men wove around the death of Susannah and he was determined not to be manipulated into the script.

Now he had seen Catherine in the church, however, he supposed he would have to meet her after Mass. When the last communicant, a Filipino, had gone, he peered into the small and scattered congregation to find her. She knelt, a hazy praying form, and he was at once filled with gratitude for her presence.

When he had cleaned both paten and chalice and when he had sat for a moment of thanksgiving, he found himself thinking instead of how much he liked Catherine. She had an unconscious dignity which informed her smallest movements. The day before, when she had sat by his side in Vaughan's garden, her rigour had brooded over the dark, absurd proceedings as if an examination were taking place and she, the invigilator, suspected cheating. Knowing that she was in the church, Edward was drawn inexorably back to the odd performance of Vaughan and Deals and, despite his intention to meditate, he was unable to resist its glittering distractions.

At least now there was *a* story if not *the* story to go on. If anything, it presented a tantalizing conundrum. Edward had spent the previous evening actually writing down permutations, his head bent close to the paper under a searchlight of a desk lamp. Indeed, this morning his eyes still smarted with the effort and his head ached. In the watches of the night, he had finally broken down. He had always given unconscious credence to the modern old wives' tale that tears brought relief. In this case, they had not.

Who killed Cock Robin? I, said the Sparrow, With my bow and arrow ... When finally he had slept, the nursery rhyme, in the arch voice of Phil Deals, had whirred round in a dream, and he had woken with the fantastical notion that Deals had crawled into his mind to keep warm during the night, a shivering minor demon who spouted everlasting nonsense against the bold, ugly reality of Susannah's murder. Now, even with the sacrifice of the Mass firmly between him and all evil, the shape of Vaughan's testament came back into his mind. It was hard to fathom the truth of his insinuations.

If Susannah had wittingly courted murder, then there was little point in pursuing his inquiries: however, he was intuitively convinced that she had not.

Even if she had been an unwitting victim, gulled by confidence tricksters, her death merited nothing but pity: however, he believed it merited more.

Her father's suggestion, however, that she had connived in a theft, for whatever motives, no matter how lofty they might have seemed to her at the time, reduced her Cause to ashes: and yet, ironically because of Vaughan's damaging testimony, Edward started to believe for the first time that Susannah might have died for a deeper and better reason than he had originally supposed. Unless she had radically changed, her father's story was false. Susannah had held any kind of trickery in abhorrence.

Vaughan, Catherine, Deals and Edward had shared (if that was the proper word for it) a light lunch under the trees. An atavistic distaste for breaking bread with them had dried his mouth and killed his appetite. Compared to Susannah, the two men seemed like small boys, who had simply not understood the seriousness of what had happened to her, children who were pretending she had only popped out to the shops. And maybe that was it; maybe they only missed her, their proper queen. Susannah had grown into a formidable woman, and for this reason it seemed almost bathetic that she should have been brought down in this house of games.

At the same time, he had been uncomfortably aware that the Mother Prioress, after all a member of the same clan, had had a point in getting him to visit Thessaloniki. As he sat in the garden nibbling at the ogre's fare before him, a very large piece of the whole puzzle of Susannah seemed to fall into his hand, and yet, maddeningly, he could not place it. Her father had been a Cross, that she had said often enough, but had it been the one on which she had died? That seemed to reduce her terribly. Whatever the answer to that question, Edward had the sense that she had been rendered helpless in this place, as if her achievements had counted for nothing.

All along, he had had the sense of Susannah walking there, threading her way through the labyrinth of trees, an honest woman trapped in the palace of Minos. Her family difficulties had always seemed somewhat abstract to Edward, but now, faced with her father, a whole experience of priesthood bore her out in her distress. For all the elegant show, it was like visiting sour-smelling homes where poverty-reduced families existed in a casual viciousness too abject to condemn. Like them, Susannah's father and Deals lived on the margins, unmeasurable by any standard but their own.

It was tempting to think that some single Minotaur lurked at the centre of the carefully constructed maze demanding him to be Theseus, but Edward doubted it. The unwholesome tone, however, was almost audible. Corruption had been accepted in the household as a necessary evil. Every gesture, each blurred movement of the two men, seemed to suggest an exhausted decadence. In such an atmosphere, Susannah's bright vigour must have seemed officious, her very integrity moralistic. Worst of all, the love in her, which had once seemed so inexhaustible, must have looked like mere sentiment. With more than a thrill of horror, Edward had envisaged it spilt there, not her blood, but something altogether more precious.

After the meal, Vaughan had propped himself up against his theatrical riot of cushions and, as if this had been a signal, Phil produced a frisbee, which he deftly flung at the boy Ali and the dogs rather as if they had been the same species. If Edward had demanded an apologia from Vaughan (as Catherine had said later), there might have been some toe-hold in the cliff. This, of course, had been the genius of his tactic, as Edward had begun to see for himself.

And, as Catherine later pointed out, the long, rehearsed monologue had been like a statement prepared for the press. Perhaps, for its dry precision, it originally had been. When, the previous night, Edward had come to write it down, the words had assembled themselves on the page like a biography . . . the story of Vaughan himself, the narcissistic father who could barely spare a word for his murdered child. And all the while, Phil tossed the frisbee the small distance of the artificial glade into the snapping, accurate jaws of the dogs.

In 1945, it seemed, Vaughan, then an army officer, had been detailed to Northern Greece during the civil strife which had followed on the heels of the Second World War, and during a time in which he had been stationed in Epirus he had been alerted to some strange markings near a cave in the mountains where he and his men had flushed out a band of Communist guerrillas. He had long taken an interest in archaeology – in fact, he had belonged to a few learned societies even then. As he and his men had been investigating, Vaughan had noticed worn grooves – for door posts, he thought – near the mouth of the cave, and, on entering it, what seemed to be remnants of a mosaic floor. It was his instinct that this was an unusual configuration but, unable to act upon this intuition at the time, he had marked the cave on his ordnance map and returned in 1950, ostensibly on holiday, to make a tentative search. To his amazement, he had discovered a cache of gold which seemed to have been hidden during some archaic raid or war. Having notified the Greek authorities, he then continued to help the professional archaeologists when they arrived and, together, they had uncovered the now famous tomb of the 'priestess' of Dionysos; the prize had been the golden diadem they found perched askew upon her mouldering skull. It had been an important find, for it had established a link between Scythian and Greek techniques of working gold. In addition to this it seemed to suggest that the cult of Dionysos had flourished in Epirus in a more sophisticated way than had earlier been thought. The diadem of the god's priestess – or so she was thought to be –

had given insights into the possible nature of the cult, and was in itself a thing of considerable beauty. Vaughan had co-operated completely with the Greek government and the gold was now on permanent display in the Archaeological Museum in Athens.

Having made such a success of this discovery, Vaughan had extricated himself from the army so that he could devote his entire energy to archaeology; and, although he had been to Sandhurst and had no academic qualifications in archaeology, his papers, monographs and a book had come to be respected universally. A knighthood had been within his grasp.

Vaughan had wanted, however, to explore the cult of Dionysos in Macedonia, and so he decided to move to Greece and buy the house in Salonika. Whatever privations he had endured for the sake of his research, semi-permanent exile, the reign of the Greek Colonels, he had kept up a house in Chelsea for the sake of his daughter. He was at pains to point out that both his life and hers had been, at that time, full and constructive . . . if not entirely happy.

When he turned to draw Susannah into his chronicle, Vaughan had paused, giving a little cough as if to mark a parenthetical change of subject. Although Edward had wrestled the night before with the striking discrepancies between Susannah's own story and her father's, it finally occurred to him that it was better to let the two narratives run concomitantly rather than tease out each point of contradiction and try to resolve every one.

Susannah had been born, Vaughan told them, in 1935. That at least was true. He had met her mother, Nancy Schuyler, the year before at a house party – something to do with the Cunards – and they had eloped rather than face a family wedding. Nancy had been a devoted mother but, because of ill health, had unwillingly relied on nannies. They had lived happily in a flat in Kensington until the war broke out and Nancy had taken Susannah to the States for safety. At the war's end they had returned but, shortly afterwards, Nancy died, when Susannah had been eleven. When later Susannah had gone to Roedean, she appeared to be happy. She had done well and had even seemed to take some pride in the school. If during some of her holidays she spent time with her relations in America, it was of her choosing, not his, for she had never fully recovered from the loss of her mother and had suffered her whole life in consequence. Her Cambridge career had been truncated by poor health. If it was true that he and Susannah had not always been on entirely friendly terms, this had been for a variety of reasons, the chief of which, he believed, was her necessary sole dependence on himself – that, and a neurotic inability to come to terms with the reality of her motherless existence. When she became a

Catholic, he had not opposed this as she might have suggested; in fact, he welcomed it that she had, at last, embraced something of him, something of his family, in doing so, for her mother had come from Protestant stock and had not shown an interest in any religion. In any case, whatever the difficulties between them, he and Susannah had never become wholly estranged and she visited him annually when he finally decided to sell the house in Chelsea and live permanently in Greece. Susannah had wanted to live in Hackney anyway.

Edward remembered why the Chelsea house had been sold. Susannah had packed it with her foundlings, much to the anger of the neighbours. He let it pass, however, and the old man went on.

The very fact, he told them, that she had based her life in England had proven to him that she valued him and what he stood for. Of course, he had been very much aware of her crusading activities on behalf of the mentally ill and applauded them. He wished to correct the impression he might have given that he had contempt for her good works. Just because he did not believe she was a saint did not detract from her achievements as a welfare worker, and he had privately nourished hopes that she might gain an OBE or some such recognition for what she had done in founding the Bethany Community.

All of this, Catherine said later, had been delivered loftily from his divan in a manner designed to resemble portraits of Socrates toasting his enemies in hemlock. Indeed, when he had finished his exposition, he extended his glass to Phil for wine, and Phil, oddly silent during the entire discourse except for his rhythmic game with the dogs, obliged him. When Vaughan had slaked his thirst, he continued, in such a way that Edward nearly imagined the rustling of lecture notes, even though the speech had been made to appear impromptu.

Whatever was decided about the ultimate value of Susannah's life, he wanted it put on record that his anger at her was no generalized, petty spite, but in regard to a specific set of events, it was both powerful and just. Things she had done, which he did not wish to specify, had led to the theft of a staggeringly important artefact.

In 1979, a year after the earthquake, Vaughan had been collaborating with a team of Greek archaeologists on a site in the north of the city. The project had been variously funded; in fact, at the time of the theft and the murder, Vaughan and his Greek colleagues had been expecting a professor from the University of Pennsylvania Museum to arrive with expertise and more money.

The excavation was in a field belonging to a small monastery and adjacent to its church, the Church of the Transfiguration. Although the Orthodox claimed it was an ancient Christian foundation visited by St Paul, Vaughan was now certain that it had been, in fact, a temple to Dionysos which had been destroyed and built upon in the manner of many Greek churches on pagan sites. A good example in Thessaloniki was the Church of Panagia Halkeon – Our Lady of Coppersmiths – which had been founded on an ancient temple to Hephaestos and Kaviros.

Although many such churches did have early Christian associations, the monastery in question, he believed, had been built late in the High Byzantine period as a satellite house to Vlatades; this was a much older monastery of true historical interest because of the patronage of the Byzantine Empress Anna Palaeologina and the mystic sect which she had fostered there. By the time the Transfiguration Monastery had come into being, the Dionysos temple had long been a ruin. Some of its ancient marbles, he believed, had been incorporated into fifteenth-century walls. What was more, he was quite sure there was no evidence that a Christian or Jewish community had existed there in the first century AD.

At the time of the excavation, Vaughan was convinced that the archaic site had once been consecrated to Dionysos, and he had based his theory on a then recent and analogous discovery of the Temple of Ammon Zeus in Aphistos in the Halkidiki Pensinsula nearby. There, an older shrine to Dionysos, yet to be uncovered, had yielded a lovely fourth-century head of the god.

Vaughan's colleagues argued that there was no evidence to suggest this. In the first place, as Thessaloniki had not been a city until the fourth century BC, their interest in the site was primarily in its age: it was fifth century BC, it seemed, and the ruins suggested that there might have been a Classical settlement. Now, of course, they utterly denied it. More to the point, however, it had then been their bigoted view that the cult of Dionysos had come late into Greece from Phrygia, Thrace or Lydia. Even though there was evidence of the god's worship in Homer, scholars such as Nilsson and Harrison had confused the time when Dionysos had ousted Hestia from the Olympic pantheon and taken her place. It seemed unlikely to Vaughan's narrow-minded colleagues that the site they were excavating could have comprised a Dionysos temple because they simply did not want to believe it.

Vaughan, of course, was no stranger to this kind of controversy. His theories on the origins and nature of Dionysos agreed with those of the unpopular Walter Otto, whose masterful attack on scientific orthodoxy made many enemies. With spectacular cynicism, the anti-Dionysos camp on the dig claimed that a small oracle of Zeus might have been in the field, in imitation perhaps of Dodona, though far less ambitious, of course. In this sly way, they refuted Vaughan's evidence of Dionysos. A disruptive god like Dionysos, only lately admitted into the pantheon at the time the site had been constructed, would hardly be simultaneously honoured at a small oracle of Zeus. In fact, they were only encouraging the flow of money for the project by turning a blind eye. The Americans were Nilssonites to a man.

Whatever the argument, it was an evening in the Greek Holy Week those many years ago when Vaughan, then mobile, had, rather on impulse, driven his car up to the site in order to have a leisurely look round. His Greek colleagues had all been dashing about in an effort to get to their homes for the Easter holidays and none of them lived locally. In fact, he himself had been expecting Susannah to arrive the following day and he felt he would be too preoccupied with her visit to make any progress on the excavation. Of course, he would not have continued digging without the help of his colleagues, but her visit would mean that he could not even get on with some necessary paperwork. It did happen to be a beautiful evening, however, and he had felt the need to stroll and think about the site away from the Holy Week racket in the city below. In fact, as far as the 'monastery' itself was concerned, there were no tolling bells, processions or services. No monks lived there any more, only an ancient female porter who would unlock the place for the infrequent visitors wishing to light candles or to see the dim and second-rate, late Byzantine frescos along the dank walls.

Just before dusk he ascended and, having walked in the garden below the monastery church for a little while, he had an urge to look over the site. They had fenced it off but he had a key, and so he let himself in, to take a look in the gloaming at the barely perceptible walls the team had already unearthed. A morbid thought had struck him at the time, and he often wondered with a shudder if there had been an element of omen in it. As he gazed at the ruined marble foundations, the ordered rubble had suddenly appeared to him like broken teeth still white in a fragmented human jawbone.

If the vision had been ominous in one way, it was happily portentous in another, for as he looked down and away from the crooked rows of marble gleaming so oddly in the fading light he spotted a curved object of a whiter, finer marble protruding from the ground in a declivity which had been caused by the recent earthquake. Various bits of antique rubbish lay exposed along with it, and amid this detritus it had lain concealed. He scrambled down the decline and, in the growing dusk, dug away with his penknife until at last the most perfect Classical Head of Dionysos had emerged from the roots and earth and potsherds into his trembling hands.

If ever Edward longed for his vision to be fully restored to him, it was during the moments of silence which followed Vaughan's story of his finding the marble Head. He needed to see the old man's face, peer through the masked expression to the eyes. He had heard, almost, the stuff of myth . . . or had it been fiction?

All too clearly, Edward had seen it in his mind's eye – the resurrection in Holy Week of a beautiful god. In the twilight, in the dusk, in the dark time of borders between day and night, consciousness and sleeping, the old man held the pure, the ambivalent, the young Dionysos in his hands. What extraordinary excitement, what a marvel! It was as if Maenads had tumbled from the monastery complex above in hot expectation of their deity, who, beardless, bore his thyrsus, who unclearly sexed was wrapped in leopard skin, accompanied by leopards, by gambolling animals and satyrs. It was as if the elevation of the Head had made Dionysos manifest in one breath-taking theophany.

Whatever Edward was later to believe, Vaughan's account of his finding the Head of Dionysos remained with him. In fact, every other element of the story was reduced next to the intensity of the old man's vision of it. His voice had been charged with the memory of ecstasy. The pagan god had existed for him more powerfully than his own child.

What, then, had touched Vaughan? Into what element had he been transported? It was not that Edward was so naïve, so narrow, to suppose that religious experience could only be Christian, it was simply easier to measure such experience. Whatever form it took, the content gave way to close analysis . . . and not only the content, but the effect. If someone were to have a vision of Jesus, and Jesus were to order up a murder, which was then committed as a result, then *ipso facto* Jesus could not have spoken. Conversely, if the effect of hearing a crucifix speak made a man into St Francis of Assisi, it was safe to assume that it had.

What, then, of Dionysos? Given that Edward could not credit his existence, did the god exist for Vaughan? And if so, how so? As a force of nature? As the master of divine intoxication? As the deity of theatre? or of madness? If Dionysos had 'spoken', had Vaughan acted? Something in the old man's eyes might have told him, something of a gesture, unconscious yet profound, might have given away the nature of his vision, the quality of his response. And yet, Edward could not see, nor did he dare move for fear of startling his subject into the knowledge that he had seen as much as he had.

But Vaughan had already hastened on with his story. He had taken the Head, wrapping it in a piece of sacking and carefully marking where he had found it, for given its obvious, extraordinary value he had no other course of action open to him. He had taken it home, where he had put it in his safe – no ordinary lock-up, but one of museum standard.

The following day, Vaughan had sent Phil to meet Susannah at the airport, a task he normally performed himself.

At this, the frisbee whizzed by Edward's ear, making him jump. With his mannikin's grin, Phil had leaned forward in order to display an ironic eye. Either Vaughan had decided to ignore this gesture or he had not seen it, because he seemed intent upon establishing in minute detail what had been contingent on her arrival.

Curiously, he lunged forward, his frail hands gripping the rug which covered him so that Edward braced himself for a substantial revelation. In a low, rasping, oracular voice he spoke: Susannah had resented his decision not to meet her, and had been even more offended by his distracted state when she reached the house. He could think of no other way to explain her subsequent behaviour. It was only when that day he could no longer contain his excitement that he had confided in Phil and Susannah the reason for his agitation. He had taken the god, so beautiful it might almost have been Aphrodite, from the safe and shown them: how it bore the marks of Dionysos in every particular; how it had been carved and polished; how the leopard claws of his robe nestled in the god's neck like five thorns in the ripe stone flesh; how, indeed, it had been made in the early part of the fifth century; how it just emerged from the archaic period with the faintest ghost of a smile . . . unique in the entire world, a keystone in the iconic canon, an unsurpassed work of art.

And if Edward, so clearly disbelieving of Susannah's connivance in the theft, wanted a motive for such seemingly extraordinary behaviour on the part of one so given to holy practice, Vaughan could supply it. Of this exquisite, nearly breathing marble, she had been . . . jealous.

Suddenly, Edward became aware that the scattered congregation in the church was shifting and coughing, and so, a little embarrassed by the time he had taken over these unholy recollections, he blinked and stood, shuffled over the blessing and dismissed the pious early-morning crew of French tourists, Filipino servants to Greek families, and the small spattering of Greek Catholics themselves, into the sunshine. They trickled away, and when he returned from the vestry the church had emptied. For a moment he thought that Catherine herself had gone, and this filled him with a kind of dreariness that he had not experienced in a long time. He hoped he was not becoming reliant on her in the wrong way. He allowed himself to smile at this for a moment. It was hard not to like such a doughty woman. Among other things, she had mentioned in passing that one of her ancestors, a Crusader, had passed through the city in the eleventh century with Raymond Count of St Gilles on the road to Constantinople and Antioch, bound for Jerusalem. Edward could see her swinging a broad-sword with the best of them – and it was heartening to feel that she might do so on his behalf.

But she had waited after all. She was sitting in a rather squashed manner in a side aisle before the Blessed Sacrament and, when she spotted him, she hailed him a little miserably. 'I don't think I should have taken Communion,' she said. 'Is it terrible? It was sort of an impulse. I haven't been in a very long time . . . even though I go to Mass every Sunday.'

Edward was amazed. It had not occurred to him that she might be unworthy of the Sacrament. He softened hugely towards her.

'I haven't done anything worse than I have already told you. I don't have a boyfriend or anything like that. But I am so angry at Theo . . . I've been up all night just thinking about him.'

'It's all right,' he said, 'I can absolve you if you like, but I'm sure—'

'Please do so . . . at once . . . will you? I shall suffer if you don't.'

He sat next to her and, as bit by bit she unburdened herself, the faintest note of Susannah struck his ear. The integrity of Catherine was not so terrifying, nor was the humility as profound, but the woman was genuine, of that he was now sure. When the ritual was accomplished, she blew her nose and he realized she had been crying. 'I feel much better,' she said, 'much.'

He smiled, happier himself. 'There!' he said. 'It really does help, doesn't it?'

She nodded. 'Father Edward, the original reason I came was to tell you that I've hired a car. It's parked outside. What is more, I have not been idle since yesterday. There is someone I think you ought to meet.'

She strode with him from the church, setting the pace, ebullient, perhaps, with sanctifying grace, or maybe hot on the scent of mystery. Edward found it extraordinary to believe that she had been the gilded wife of a merchant prince, the child of a family which included James Vaughan. Susannah had once told him how snobby her English relatives were, even Lady Simon, her aunt. She had been Catherine's mother, and a large theme in her Confession.

125

'I have,' she said, swinging through the doors and out on to the marble plaza outside the church, 'thoroughly discredited Uncle James . . . as though you wanted proof.'

A side of him had wanted it, but he had not realized how much until the relief came with her remark.

'You see, it occurred to me that there was no way at all that my uncle could have legitimately clung on to that Head, even over the Easter weekend that year.'

'And . . .?'

'And so I rang round a bit yesterday evening when you had gone to rest.'

He had used this excuse to be alone, to stifle the horror and suspicion left with him by Vaughan's story.

'You see, if you know Greece and anything at all about archaeology, one name of all names springs to mind: that of Andronicos. It was he who discovered the Tombs at Vergina in 1977 – you know, Philip of Macedon and all that *gold*. In fact, it all happened not so very long before Susannah's murder, and it made huge headlines all over Greece. I remember it. And, of course, Andronicos lived in Thessaloniki. There is no earthly way that anyone reputable who had found anything of any value could have failed to ring him instantly and ask for his advice. What is more, there is a renowned archaeological community in the city, attached to the university. There are no circumstances in which the Head would have been safer with Uncle James than in the museum, and no reason why he could not have got at least ten eminent experts to unlock its vaults – Christmas, Easter, any day at all . . . in any weather! The Greek intelligentsia is no more pious than any other anywhere else. What is more, I think even a monk from Athos would have stirred himself for such an important discovery.'

Of course, Edward had heard of Andronicos.

'Andronicos is dead,' she continued, 'but he wasn't then. My married name and my Greek are a help and so I grasped the nettle and telephoned around. When you are ready, I am taking us off to the ancient site of Pella. I have made rather an important discovery myself, and I think you will hear an entirely different story when we arrive.'

XI

PAUL MASON'S mind was jammed with the immediate: small tasks left undone, letters unwritten, overstretched budgets about to be axed, sterile meetings, appointments missed or interrupted. No single patient dominated his thoughts; no single issue was uppermost. Each frustration locked instead into the next, like so many railway carriages stranded on a bridge in the heat and ground to a halt. He liked his car, a Citroën; Marina told him he needed it and he supposed he did. Every night he shut himself into it and the hospital out. He was getting better at resolutely ending a stale day; more adept at realism. The CDs had been his wife's idea: tonight, he selected Brahms, which blasted forth harmonic solutions, over and against the dissonant jabber of his consulting room.

Paul tried not to be fed up. The second training in psychiatry had been his idea, and above all it would let Marina down to tell her he had brought his former sense of failure to his new career. It was, after all, this lack of self-belief that had led him into crisis as a GP before he met her, not the job itself. He thought he had faced this out in analysis but he had never been successful at eradicating the shadow of Herakles under which he laboured. A *Boy's Own* rule book, full of heroic ideals and tasks, had always operated his unconscious thoughts, but knowing this did not stop a childish disappointment at himself whenever he failed to save the day. That morning, they had sent another schizophrenic out on to the streets – or, rather, into 'Community Care' – one of many, probably harmless: the television set had told him he was Jesus Christ.

Paul eased the car on to the main road and pointed it towards the whisky awaiting him at home. He drank more now, not much more than he should . . . but still. He glanced at the seat next to him, glad that he had remembered to get the book that Marina wanted on the Bethany Community. There was a rather austere photograph of Susannah Vaughan on the front – oddly, he could see the resemblance to Catherine – and, during a moment with a Clingfilm sandwich in his office, he had leafed through it.

He had come upon many Susannahs throughout his professional life, and it was a type he rather liked. They were generally misfits themselves, women in full flight from an upper-class background, which nonetheless served them well in twisting the arm of authority on behalf of the outcasts they befriended – battered women, young offenders, the homeless. Susannah had started by taking ex-mental patients into her house in Chelsea and, as time went by, she had expanded, making Bethany of a little string of hostels, one of which, he noted, was nearby in Chipping Campden, not twenty miles away from Oxford.

Paul vaguely remembered that Bethany had provoked some controversy at its inception. It had been radically unscientific, an attempt to produce a healing environment. Now, the programme sounded unexceptionable, worthy in every way. The founder had concentrated on hard cases, her aims rather like Mother Teresa's. She had stood by incurables without expectation of reward, in order that they might spin out their barmy days with dignity. She had taken on violent cases, and with them the risk. The insane, she believed, should be treated with full human dignity rather than like insects under a microscope. Paul shook his head at this inoperable religious fantasy. From the snippets of her writing included in the book, however, it was clear that Susannah had loved her charges and had rather enjoyed their freakish behaviour. Paul could see that; from time to time he had shared that sense of his patients. Not often, though; perhaps not often enough.

According to the bland and badly written book, Bethany had evolved over the years. Now, there was an excellent training scheme for volunteers – he'd heard of it. A stint at Bethany often paved the way for professional qualifications. This all seemed very noble to Paul, and useful too, but not earth-shattering in its originality. He rather liked the sound of Susannah, however. The few excerpts from her writings on the Community were free from pious rhetoric, and seemed to proceed from a sound and practical basis. She had started as a romantic idealist with a mission, but in the end she had seemed happy to draw upon the skill of professional advisers.

In fact, partly because his curiosity had got the better of him, he had rung the nearby Chipping Campden community on behalf of poor schizophrenic Tom, that morning's casualty, only to find the house was full. A rather nunnish voice had answered the phone, once a girlish soprano, he imagined, now dried to a middle-aged husk, emotionless, without timbre. Such women in such outreach jobs never failed to amaze him, little tight, grey knots of virtue. How was this army of women recruited? It operated in every charitable sphere. Where did they come from? They were the sort who made grown-ups 'rediscover' their childhood with clay modelling on religious retreats; they sold Christmas cards made out of pressed flowers and they studiously reused envelopes; they held jumble sales. Their collective voice on the telephone, their presence at the threshold of any refuge, tended to wilt the most earnest inquirer. However, he wondered, did they get mixed up in the Armageddon of the mad or apply themselves to the baroque confusions of the homeless poor when the deepest disorder they knew was a muddle over the gas bill? They followed in the wake of such as Susannah; they glued themselves to sadness wherever it was, almost wistfully, he often thought, as if the bold life of disturbed passions, the flamboyant inability to cope, represented some orgy in the moonlight to which they had not been asked.

He glanced at Susannah's picture again. She seemed to glance back. The book had been written by one of her disciples after her death. If she had the homely aura of the morally serious, there was something even humorous in her prominent eyes. Paul noted that, although she wore a crucifix, the picture she made was not of one professionally good; perhaps he really had become cynical, but his own trek into saintly endeavour some years ago had left him with an allergy to a certain kind of holy self-regard. The apparently nice distinction, however, between primness and simplicity was, in fact, vast, and indeed, from St Susannah's oddly inviting half-smile, he could imagine talking to her, unburdening himself. What would she have done today with poor Tom, who, having been shot through with medication, would at once forget to return for more? He would surely be 'a-cold' this wet April night on some by-road near Oxford – for he always slipped the clutches of Social Services; or, if he found shelter now, it was only a matter of time before he was off into his weird and wonderful landscape peopled with angels and demons. Paul was stung by the real-ization that Susannah would have taken Tom home, or trudged the roads with him; for that, of course, was the way Bethany had started. In the afflicted she saw Christ, and so it seemed only natural to ask Him to stay with her.

Paul rued the little goad of envy he felt, but he was glad that he saw it for what it was. He had made a different choice and had a Georgian house and a Citroën car. Like Susannah, he had kept himself single for large combat for long years, but either he had lost the battle or had won some-thing else, for he had married Marina. The assault of feelings on his suppressed heart had not made this an easy solution. Over the years, he had become high-minded, set apart from anything messy and personal. He had forgotten that he could be ugly, selfish, petty, and in consequence he had secretly formed a high opinion of his moral character. Marina's first marriage to Arthur Holt, on the other hand, had given her insight into the sometimes Dantesque nature of marriage: together they had had to work things through, mostly on each other's mistrust. Privately, he was glad they hadn't had a child to get caught in the struggle, and he wished Marina would let the subject drop. For the most part, he was grateful for her, however, and now that he was drawing near their house his anticipation at seeing her made him smile involuntarily. He was thankful his disruptive mother-in-law had gone back to the States. It was a good sign that last night Marina had been full of this Susannah business rather than her mother's visit. As a therapist, he knew she should talk it through; common sense, however, told him that the best way to deal with the prying old besom was to act as if she didn't exist unless she actively had to be acknowledged. He wondered how the Blessed Susannah would have reacted to that! As he parked the car in the drive and scooped the book up, it struck him at once that she might have agreed. There was a certain toughness and shrewdness in her face. She might have seen through manipulative behaviour, he thought, and would probably not have tolerated it.

Marina and the dogs bounded out to greet him in the rain, like one fierce, tumbling, bright ball of living creature. He was guilty of liking her because she was a blonde; her beauty still absolutely had him under its thumb, and he surrendered gladly to her embrace and the wet gambolling animals which slithered like seals around his trousers, covering them prob- ably with mud.

'You'll never guess what I did today!' she said when he had heaved down briefcase, book and mackintosh on to the bench in the wide tiled hall. There was always a range of clobber strewn on it and about it: Wellington boots, dog and garden paraphernalia, unopened circulars, forgotten bits of dry-cleaning. More often than not, Marina had a story waiting for him – a conversation in the village, a book she had been reading, the latest on the new shop. The patter of normality was like a massage to sore temples. He always loved to hear about her day. He had initially been worried that she would languish during his long hours, but she was wonderfully self- occupied, and had a strange resistance to boredom.

'What did you do? I can't guess. Too shattered.' He walked into the sitting room, had a drink. She curled bare toes underneath her on the sofa, his chest and shoulders sank with gratitude into the armchair.

'I met Susannah's miracle! At least, one of them.'

'No! Coincidence abounds.'

'Not at all. I was so fired up by remembering her that I drove to Chipping Campden, "on spec", really, to visit the Bethany Community. I thought of you. While I was there, a psychiatrist rang and asked if they could find a place for one of his patients.'

130

'It *was* me.'

'How wonderful!'

'You simply walked in? Simple as that?'

'Simple as that.'

'I have never met a miracle before,' he said somewhat acidly into his whisky. 'What was he like?'

'She! . . . It was the woman you talked to on the telephone.'

He stifled a laugh at the thoughts he had had in the car.

'What's so funny?'

'Nothing. I'll tell you later.'

Marina giggled deliciously and leaned against the cushion, her bright hair kinked by the damp weather making an aureole round her head, her long throat nearly irresistible. Whatever she did or said, she included him, making him a companion in her travels no matter how short or inconsequential they were. She was talented at love in its smallest expression. It was her especial genius.

'Well, it's all pretty medieval, but she's quite amazing really. A miracle is by definition, surely. Heather – that's her name. She's tiny and she wears huge spectacles. She reminds me of a baby owl, someone not fully fledged but on the way.'

'A lot of my patients are pretty medieval: their visions could be painted by Hieronymus Bosch.'

'Oh, you are in a mood!'

'Actually, I am,' said Paul. 'I'm sorry.'

Marina studied Paul, though gently. His hands were knotted and his glance flickered round the room like shutters slowly opening. He made heavy weather of his work, narrowing himself, she thought, to too fine a point of objectivity. It was his way of dealing with anything absurd or upsetting, and he did it well. Marina knew that, under it all, he had an intuitive power which saved him and on which he operated more than he would allow, but he was of a certain age and education that forced him on bad days into a clinical directness. Sometimes she felt he supplied reason in so large a measure because his patients had lost theirs. It was a fruitless compensation which exhausted him. 'Awful day, eh?' she said.

'It was a Bedlam day.'

'Bedlam was medieval,' she said, 'so you ought to be ready for this!'

His hands relaxed on the chair and he smiled.

'In any case, I thought you had a weakness for miracles – bits of the True Cross, weeping statues, that kind of thing.'

'Well, as phenomena . . . the primitive psyche . . .'

'Precisely so! That's just the point of Bethany in a way. It's a bit like homeopathy; it uses madness against itself, "an holistic approach", they call it. I found it refreshing.' A glimpse of Susannah flashed across Marina's mind, the remembered girl turned into a woman dredging away at Chipping Campden. She had redeemed a condemned Jacobean manor with the gross wealth of Nancy Schuyler. Heather had shown the rooms and then the grounds to Marina and had wept a little, shivered a little, when Marina shared highly edited memories of Susannah. The house was lovely, peaceful in a hollow near the Rollrights, an ancient stone circle Marina had known about but never visited. Large primeval trees sheltered the sanctuary, Bethany. A photographic portrait of Susannah hung in the communal sitting room, giving it all a faintly cultish aspect. It seemed to glance at Marina accusingly, as if she had not responded to some subtle call, as if she had abused her own wealth and privilege simply by looking after her own. Susannah, her patrician brow, her fine nose, her lean cheeks, might have come from the Great West door of some French cathedral. An absolute simplicity characterized the smallest aspect of her appearance. As if refined by fire, she had transmogrified from the brooding, reading, smoking young woman on her aunt's porch into something like an icon, planed, intense and abstract.

'All right, all right, I have a weakness for bits of the True Cross if you like! If it makes you feel any better. I can bear the suspense no longer. What about Heather?'

'If what Heather says is true, she used to be stark raving bonkers. She most certainly isn't now. She's the receptionist.'

'In what way did this lunacy manifest itself?'

Oddly, Marina thought, Heather had left her with an impression of beauty, even though she had been devoid of conventional attractions. 'Well, she claims to have had everything, "an infestation" she called it, "like the seven devils of Mary Magdalene", she said . . . autism, compulsions, mainly, I think.'

'Difficult to treat. What was her history?'

Marina and Heather, who was now the very picture of pure reason, had had a cup of tea in the kitchen, where from time to time various weathered-looking inmates drifted amiably in and out. An understated sense of kindness and acceptance had seemed to permeate the place. 'It's a little hard to believe now, but she told me she had spent most of her life in and out of hospitals, having graduated to them from Barnardo's. When she wasn't sectioned, she'd sleep under Waterloo Bridge. She was violent, as many of their residents seem to be – or to have been. She had been diagnosed subnormal, but she seems to have had the wit to elude her captors, because she kept escaping; she said they beat her and drugged her and put her in side wards. Old story: she would get out, then forget her medication. She was a prostitute for a while in King's Cross, and finally she wound up in a hostel in London, not a Bethany. The interesting thing is that by the time Bethany took her on, Susannah had died and so Heather never knew her. And that is where the *miracle* comes in.'

'Oh, do tell!'

'Well, it seems that poor old Heather was placed in Chipping Campden rather as a last resort in lieu of a custodial sentence. She had stabbed a care worker in a place in Soho . . . I mean there was no lasting damage, but it was enough and quite the last straw. She doesn't remember a lot about her first few weeks at Bethany, but she says that bit by bit the place got to her. There's a nice rhythm to the day, it's all very soothing. No patronizing, she said, and that seemed very important. She felt for the first time in her life that she was just allowed to be crazy and that that was creative enough in its way.'

Paul laughed. 'I know what she means, but it is rather R. D. Laing after all, isn't it?'

'Not really. There's a lot of structure . . . In any case, Heather said she began to feel a bit less angry, less threatened. They didn't make any attempt to eradicate her compulsions. She had a thing about washing . . . but they sort of made a big deal of it, as if this was her particular pro-gramme – something special which she must fit in with her other obligations to the community. The whoring they didn't like, however, and eventually there was a scene about her seductive behaviour. Well, things went from bad to worse, and, although once Bethany takes someone on they say they never kick them out, I suppose there are limits. Heather went completely berserk. And this is where your miracle comes in! There she was, raving away, and just as she was picking up a heavy ashtray, about to belabour the Bethany worker over the head, she heard a voice so clearly that she dropped the bludgeon and fell to her knees . . . the voice, naturally enough, of Susannah.'

Paul sighed and rolled his eyes.

'I know, I know, but the whole point is that it worked! Heather thinks she heard the voice and the voice instructed her to desist. What is more, it told her to pray for nine days asking for a healing, and a sign which would confirm the truth of Heather's vision.'

'Heather was raised a Catholic, I assume. A novena of prayer is a nice, old-fashioned devotion.'

'Paul, Paul, do let me have my fun! That's what is so lovely. Whatever religious education Heather had, it was strictly middle and broad Anglican – no frills.'

'My darling Marina, if she could pray for nine days, then she wasn't as ill as she claimed to be. It takes a lot of concentration for someone in that state.'

'So it did, so it did!' Marina cried. 'She told me she completed the "course" only with the greatest effort.'

'I'm sorry, I don't mean to upset you,' he said, reaching out his hand in a gesture.

It hadn't struck Marina that she was upset, but he was right: she was. The drive to the sequestered house in its misty hollow, the odd little person with her large glasses, her neat little folded hands, her bizarre story, the remembered face of Susie made iconic in the simple communal room, had churned her up, disturbed her. The day's experience seemed to make obscure demands on her. If Heather had been cured, then at what price? Marina stiffened at the notion that Susannah's blood had been the remedy . . . an old and primal form of sacrifice.

Still, she felt she had to defend Heather's story. 'Well, whatever the ramifications, the long and short of it is she obeyed the voice, she is entirely in her right mind and has been for years, and, what is more, the sign appeared.'

'Tell me!'

'I'm telling you . . .'

'*Pax*!'

'*Pax* . . .' Marina looked at Paul sheepishly. 'I suppose I simply want it to be true. At another level, however, I find it threatening, worrying. Not because I am afraid of being credulous . . .'

'Which you think I am . . . afraid of.'

He had said this pleasantly enough. 'A bit . . . No, I'm more afraid that it compromises God somehow. I don't really know what I mean by that. All I know is that it makes me uncomfortable. It's like those evangelical meetings at Earl's Court or those people who "speak in tongues". I shy away from it even though it makes me feel guilty. Susie made me feel guilty. I began to think that maybe I should have become a nun or something.'

He laughed out loud. 'Tell me the sign.'

Marina tittered nervously and raked her fingers through her bright hair. 'Well, at the end of Heather's "novena" of prayer, the selfsame thing happened in the Bethany in London, this time to a young schizophrenic man who had set upon a visiting woman doctor. He had his hands at her throat, when Susannah communicated with him. This time no concentrated effort was required. He was healed on the spot. This was five years ago, if Heather can be believed, and he has never relapsed once.'

'And so we have a brace of miracles already! Enough to be getting on with, I should say. I can't think why Catherine has to be roaring round Greece looking for more evidence.'

Marina rose from the sofa and idled towards the door and their supper. 'You don't think she was a saint, do you?'

Paul stretched, then followed her, giving her a swift hug, which she returned. 'I would not presume to make such a judgement. I'm not entirely sure I know what a saint is.'

'Cat knows . . . I spoke to her earlier before you got home.'

'She's decided that Susannah must be canonized?' Paul asked. 'You know and I know that Catherine is in no fit state to judge anything much, what with her ghastly mother's death and a divorce looming.'

Marina smiled. 'Ah, that is my real surprise. Cat has not made up her mind about Susannah. It's this Father Edward she is travelling with. Now, *he's* the saint, she says.'

'Truly?'

They ambled down the hall towards the kitchen in married complicity. 'Truly!' Marina laughed.

XII

'I CAN'T help being curious,' Catherine said when they had finally cleared the dismal outskirts of Thessaloniki. 'What were these amazing signs and wonders that Susannah is supposed to have brought about?'

She had felt a burst of relief at unburdening her conscience, but now she cravenly wondered if she had gone too far; had she needed to say quite so much? Of course, his opinion of her was not the point; indeed, a really good person would be pleased that he knew her for what she was. Still, she did not see how he could think well of her again: Catherine Phocas, rich, pampered and spoiled, aloof from the human condition, brusque, critical and cold. Now she had admitted to these bad qualities, it seemed no wonder that her marriage had failed. Since she had left Theo, she had stoutly defended her position. Given the gravity of his fault, she had refused to take any responsibility for hers, and because anyone who knew her story had always put Theo squarely in the wrong she had even come to think of herself as rather noble. In order to survive, she had had to brush self-doubt aside and had treated bouts of it as morbid.

There came a point, however, when it was dishonest and discreditable not to see the other side. Catherine glanced at her eyes in the rear-view mirror and saw herself for what she was, a woman at the borders of old age, on her way to a lonely death . . . well deserved for her habitual intolerance of others. The most damning evidence of this was that she did not want to forgive Theo even though he had initially wanted forgiveness. And, if she were to be really truthful to herself, she had to acknowledge that she had spent years of their married life maintaining a safe, impenetrable distance between them.

The worst of it was that Father Edward had been so kind to her, had even tried to find excuses for her. Had she isolated herself out of a fear of rejection? he had asked her. Wounds as deep as hers needed time to heal. How feeble she must appear to him!

And so it seemed to Catherine an apt self-imposed penance to heap coals of fire on her own head. Apart from everything else, she grudged her holy cousin's spectacular success with God; as an antidote, therefore, she raised the subject of her miraculous life, determined to admire it. Although Susannah might have had bad impulses like anyone else, she had taken the better part, struggled against them and won. An inner picture came to her of dragons at Susannah's feet, each one neatly skewered. Like the Greek icons which had surrounded Catherine throughout her married life, there was something fixed about this vision, proclaiming, as it did, Susannah's eternal goodness with a rigid lack of compromise.

The road in front of her was straight, the land flat. Even though it was not the Via Egnatia of old, it was still possible to imagine that the armies of Rome, of the Byzantine Empire, of the Crusades, of the Ottoman Empire, had all marched upon it, perhaps jingling and gleaming in the hot sun, perhaps simply wilting in it. Through Rome and Dyrrachaeum, they had come to Thessaloniki, bound for Constantinople, Antioch and for Jerusalem, but the city had stood its ground, its walls thick palisades against intruders. Imperial tenants had come and gone, leaving the city rich in battered experience.

They had reached the open country; Catherine put her foot down and the Audi she had hired, a nice car at the top of the range, sped forward with slick ease. '*Did* she levitate?'

Edward was wondering yet again who had killed Susannah. What sort of anger could have called out such savagery? She had always taken risks, the Lady with the Lamp, seeking out the lost. She had started from humble beginnings, giving soup to the homeless, soup which she made herself and doled out from thermos flasks. From this dangerous, solitary pursuit, she had graduated to living with self-confessed, violent maniacs. Surely, none of her grateful mental patients had followed her to Greece in order to dispatch her!

Susannah had always read the Bible as if it had been written with her specifically in mind, particularly the most strenuous bits. She had been especially drawn to the Book of Daniel with its esoteric prophecies. The ends of things had always appealed to her, the Day of Judgement. Edward imagined that she had first been attracted to the prophet's dealings with Susannah and the Elders, but she had broadened her interest. The Children in the Burning Fiery Furnace had become a favourite source of meditation for her, and of course Daniel in the Lion's Den. Oh, she had made endless uses of this text; with it, she had shut the jaws of her own appetite for savagery. In the end, it had come to be an analogy for her descent into the feral chaos of the mad, a dizzying journey made possible only by faith.

Was it conceivable that some paranoid schizophrenic could have assembled the cash and mental organization to pursue her? It seemed unlikely. Perhaps not satisfied with her efforts in Britain, she had tried to spread her nets in Macedonia. Maybe some unfortunate Greek had stopped her good efforts for ever.

The sound of Catherine's voice gave him a start. 'Levitate?' he asked her.

What a question! Catherine thought. Did Susannah levitate? No wonder he seemed pained. It only went to demonstrate how shallow she was. She was quite as frivolous as Uncle James, who had made the same, derisive remark the day before. 'I'm sorry,' she said, even though it hurt her feelings that he had become so distant.

'Sorry?'

'I think it was flippant of me to ask that.'

'Ask what? Oh dear,' said Edward, 'I was miles away. I did not hear what you said.'

'I shan't repeat it, then,' Catherine said briskly, but she was goaded to do so. 'I simply wanted to know what these amazing signs were that my cousin seems to have produced. You mentioned them yesterday, but you didn't say what they were. She didn't walk on water, did she?' Ahead of her a harrowing machine trundled into the road and she slowed the car. There! She'd done it again. Well, *she* was no saint. That was for sure. A pure spurt of irritation shot up to stain her new state of grace.

'Oh,' he said sheepishly, 'I wish you hadn't mentioned that. I really shouldn't have said it, but to tell you the truth your uncle and Mr Deals—'

'Drove you to it?' she crowed with unseemly triumph.

Edward made an effort to shake off the creeping suspicion that Susannah might have driven someone, even someone quite sane, to uncontrollable fury. 'I'm afraid I really did exaggerate. They seemed so dismissive of her. There *is*, however, an uncorroborated story about scent. They say that the house where she lived with her patients is filled with the perfume of jasmine every year on the anniversary of her death. Unseasonably, of course. But it would be very easy to produce this effect.'

'Someone has an aromatherapy burner, I'll guarantee it,' Catherine growled. 'My friend Marina goes in for those things – you know, scent which has healing properties.'

'Is jasmine healing?' he asked faintly. There had been a sweetness about Susannah. He had forgotten. He remembered it now with the story of the scent. Surely he was being too hard on her. For all her spiritual virtuosity, she had been like a ghostly bride in her shining innocence. He could hardly bear to think of her tenderness.

Catherine overtook the harrowing machine. She sped by the flat fields, the immemorial land. Long ago, it had been a marsh where Philip of Macedon had hunted, spreading fowlers' nets. 'I have no idea.'

'Are you familiar with *The Bacchae*?' he asked suddenly. 'I knew that Pella had some association for me and it only now struck me that Euripides escaped there from Athens. Do you know the play?'

'It has to do with some chap being torn apart by his own mother, hasn't it? Theo and I went to a gala performance once. He fancied himself as a patron of the arts at one time.' She blushed at the bitterness still in her voice. 'All I can remember is that we went to Epidauros and it rained! I was frozen.'

'It's a subtle work,' Edward said. 'I read it at university. It hinges on the failure of the victim to acknowledge the divinity of Dionysos. I never thought it would come in handy.'

'Oh, Father Edward, you don't think . . .'

He blinked, suddenly frozen by the horrid similarity between Susannah's case and that of Pentheus.

'Whatever I might say about Uncle James, I really can't see him engaging in some sacred orgy. You don't think Phil . . . I wouldn't put anything past Phil.'

But he was thinking of it in a less literal way. 'If I remember it correctly, Pentheus is a very righteous fellow, strait-laced, observant of religion. But when Dionysos, an actual god, arrives at his court, he appears to be dishevelled, foolish, of no consequence to Pentheus. It is a religious idea we ourselves believe, that the divine immanence presents itself in humble disguise . . .'

'And so you are saying that, if one is too proud to recognize it, the power of it all tears one apart?'

She was too close to the mark. 'Or perhaps that the forces of nature need to be addressed, respected. There is some truth in what Susannah's father suggested. She was not very good with her basic instincts.'

Catherine slowed the car, for a sign indicating the ancient site appeared. 'He did not say that! He said she was incapable of abandoning herself.' She signalled for the car park which lay ahead. On the opposite side of the road there were a few columns marking the site. A rich kingdom by the sea had once stood on the now dry fields, the birthplace of Alexander the Great. 'I must say, I can hardly see the Maenads prancing about here,' she said, sharp in an obscure rage.

'I don't know where I got the idea, then.' Edward felt his jaw tense.

She drew in and stopped the car with an emphatic tug of the handbrake. A small museum stood in front of them, but they seemed to be the only visitors. It was here that she had arranged to meet the archaeologist, Dr Passides. 'I'm sorry,' she said again.

Edward too was sorry. 'Susannah troubles you, doesn't she?' he asked her softly. 'Why is that?'

Catherine felt more than usually exposed by this little fit of temper. In fact, a kind of emotional nakedness made her fold her arms across her chest. She said nothing, but she had a sudden impulse to bang the steering wheel with her two fists and scream with incoherent vexation.

She felt the ghost of a touch on her shoulder. 'I ask you because she troubles me too. And, to tell you the truth, she always has. But, as I really don't know why, I thought maybe you, who are a woman, after all, might have fresh insight.' He paused, smiling to himself suddenly. He had forgotten her confession, but it struck him that she was still embarrassed by what she had revealed and needed reassurance. 'And, Catherine, don't worry about what you told me earlier . . . in the church, you know. I have quite enough faults of my own to be getting on with. They really do keep me fully occupied.'

'I had no idea I was quite so transparent,' she said truculently, but her shoulders dropped. She felt mollified, like a child who had been given a sweet. She frowned. 'I expect I am a little jealous of Susannah. I feel there is something else, but I can't define it.'

'It was her power.'

Catherine was startled by the note in his voice and looked round. His face was contorted by some odd emotion. His purblind eyes blinked as if they were sore. If anything, he was more exposed than she, indeed more vulnerable.

'Do you think it could be that?' he continued. 'She had enormous power, which she never really acknowledged to herself. I'm not saying she abused it, nor do I think I resented it. But look at me . . . as a man. Please, just as a human being. I'm not an aggressive sort of chap. I never was . . .'

Edward turned his head and stared at Catherine with startled, seeing eyes. He had spoken without thinking, but it was true. One way or another, in weakness or in strength, Susannah had dominated . . . well, every situation, really. There was no getting round it. And it had taken this blunt, honest woman, who had no pretensions to high virtue at all, to elicit from him the admission of a simple, human reaction.

'Oh, I can well imagine,' said Catherine, although she could not formulate with any precision what that imagination was.

For a moment, they were held together in a curious intimacy. It was interrupted, however, by an abrupt knock on the window. A sharp-

140

eyed, puckish individual, presumably Dr Passides, addressed the wind-screen with his knuckles. For some reason, his face was the picture of delighted conspiracy. '*Kiria* Phocas?'

Catherine and Edward both gave a start. She opened the car door quickly, caught guiltily in the act of breaking her reserve.

'Father Knight?' Dr Passides asked. He looked with great curiosity at Edward, as if at a highly unusual specimen of pot.

Catherine, dressed as always for the part, got out of the car. She wore a simple, tailored skirt and blouse and good sandals. 'Dr Passides?' she said somewhat grandly.

The archaeologist nodded. Everything about him from his stocky build to his brisk black eyes seemed to bristle with energy as if he were mildly electrified. He put his head to one side like an inquisitive bird checking out a worm hole of some potential. 'I believe I have met your husband,' he said.

Although Theo was no dilettante, he was rich enough to be an amateur collector of classical antiquities. They (or rather he) owned nothing large or vital to the nation's interests, but he had one or two fine pieces, mostly vases. 'Theo is in New York,' she said curtly, but she felt a little flare of pride in her husband and it took her by surprise. Before Missy had wrecked their marriage, they had enjoyed the gentle pursuit of amphorae together. She smiled in a nervous attempt to cover her bad manners, and was more than a little relieved when she sensed the archae-ologist had got the point.

His eyebrow went up. 'Ah! Well, it was many years ago.' He took in the stooped, slightly untidy priest, his mouse hair fluffed in the breeze, his goggly eyes. 'We shall speak English?'

'Please.'

All at once, they were completely absorbed into the ionosphere of the voluble Passides. If Edward had wanted to muse introspectively on the infancy of the noble Alexander or on Euripides, the great exponent of Greek tragedy, there seemed little chance of his being able to do so.

Dr Passides waved his hand towards the site on the other side of the road. Haughty Pella seemed almost razed to the ground. 'Shall we look at this later on? Perhaps we will. Do you want to see it? But of course, you have really come about poor Susannah, and I am delighted to be able to tell you all that I can about her.'

He did not draw breath. Before they knew it, they were whirled towards the museum, up the steps, past a somnolent guard, until they ground to a sudden halt by a lofty marble wall. It was, the archaeologist told them, the reconstruction of the elevation of a luxurious town house which had once stood in the ancient capital city. A polite question from Catherine about the nature of this once imposing dwelling set Passides in even faster motion, as if he were operated like a gymnasium treadmill with increments of speed. After rattling off an alarming number of facts and figures about the exhibit, however, he turned his attention to the purpose of their visit with the transition only of a waved hand.

'I always thought someone would eventually come to ask some questions,' he continued. 'James Vaughan is your uncle?'

Catherine was about to speak.

'On the telephone I gathered you were not overfond of him?'

She gasped for words. 'I—'

'He is an old man. You must have pity. In fact, we all have pity for him here, although he does not know it. He thinks we are all plotting against him, but we are plotting *for* him. That is what he does not understand; yet maybe he is too proud, and that I apprehend.'

Edward peered desperately at Dr Passides, trying to make some kind of sense of him. He had never in his life heard anyone talk so much. The man's mind seemed so quick and mercurial that it drove his tongue to continual, articulate utterance. To get a word in edgeways seemed a task of the order of reining back the wind. The effect was mildly effervescent.

'The whole tragic business of your cousin Susannah was very odd indeed. *Very* strange. This is a tight little community. Nothing else was talked about for years and so everyone has a theory, but I actually knew her, and I am afraid I may have played an unwitting role in her unfortunate demise.' Here, he flicked a glance at Edward as if in passing deference to a priest. 'You see, there was a delicate issue at stake, and although obviously I told the police after her murder, I doubt that you know anything about it. If you do, then you can stop me.'

There really seemed no hope of that. A British couple, tourists, had arrived and were making their way around the museum, uttering euphoric cries in English over the exhibits. Catherine had the odd idea that she had seen them somewhere before and wondered if the man was a journalist friend of Charles, her brother. This seemed too awful and she cleared her throat in an attempt to warn the archaeologist that he might be overheard.

But Dr Passides plunged on. 'I was very friendly with Susannah, though not, of course, in any improper way, for she was a . . . How do you say it in English? *Agami*?'

'Celibate!' Catherine cried, feeling she had gained a beachhead.

'Quite so. And I am a family man. But she was so, how can I put it,

142

like a plant . . . wilted? shrivelled? I used to water her from time to time, you know, give her a drink, lunch . . . I think she was determined to be hard on herself wherever she was, but she was especially miserable here in Thessaloniki. Everybody knew Susannah. She would come here, year in, year out, with a duty to her aged father, and we all felt sorry for her. Everywhere, she was followed around by—'

'Phil Deals?' Catherine and Edward said in chorus.

'Exactly. Phil Deals. I do not know what you make of him. It is not for me to say. It would be cultural perhaps. I have lived and worked in England and in the States, but never have I met—'

'Neither have we!' Catherine thought he looked a little crushed at her intervention. All at once, she realized that she liked Passides; his ebullience suddenly took hold of her, and she waved him on, rather like an express train.

'I am relieved to hear it. Now James, as everyone knows, is a man of distinction and Greece owes him much for his great work in the past, but . . . how to put this with tact . . . in recent years, in fact from before the awful death of his daughter, he was declining. Here in Greece, we are respectful of old people. They rarely go into homes. Poor Susannah knew that something had to be done about her father and she was very worried about it. She was not a nun, but she was like a nun. Although there was family money, she had given hers away. How could she look after him in her place for mad people? Everyone recognized her dilemma. Everyone but James, of course, who thinks he is at the top of his powers even now. But also everyone recognized that the man who was looking after James – Phil – was a bad influence on him. There are those who knew James in the past who claim that Phil had changed him out of recognition. James, who had once been such a major force, had come to live on the margins. The two men are utter crackpots, and everyone knows it.'

'Good Lord!' Catherine raised her eyebrows at Edward.

Dr Passides paused. They all looked at each other for a moment. Nearby, the British couple were inspecting an architectural model of the stoa from which the elegant marble wall had originally come.

Notwithstanding their presence, Catherine held up her hand like a stop sign and leapt into the breach. 'I myself remember my uncle from my childhood. He was different then, very military and precise. In fact, when I arrived here, I was disturbed by the transformation in him. I'm afraid I concluded that he and Deals had an . . . arrangement, that we had all missed a . . . tendency.'

Passides guffawed. 'Susannah denied that this was true. I used to think her attitude towards them prudish, and so I taxed her with it once. She was quite shocked at my suggestion. No, according to what she told me, Phil is more acolyte than he ever was a catamite. But, whatever the nature of the bond between them, Susannah was deeply concerned about her father's health. Even before the murder, he was obviously unwell. He was in his seventies then, but very frail, and he had some mild form of dementia which would come and go. I understand it still does.

'Susannah claimed it worried her that Phil did not look after her father properly, and maybe this was true, for he was found wandering once or twice. He had high blood pressure, and nothing was done about that. However, I think it was more because Phil had taken over her place in her father's affections, and although she seemed to care about this odd cousin of hers she was critical of the way he behaved. He seemed to make her very nervous. It was almost as if there was something dangerous about the situation. They may have made her miserable, but she wanted them to come to live near her in England where she could keep an eye out. I always thought she felt both of them had to be watched, but I have no idea why.

'Of course, Susannah would still be alive if she had had her way. Each time she visited, she would come up with new schemes. Each time, Phil and her father would reject them. I do sometimes wonder how it is they manage, and how they feel now . . . if they wish they had listened to her.

'Now she is dead, of course, Phil does everything for James, who has lost the few friends he had, including myself, because he is locked away behind those gates. Whether Phil is treated as a son or a servant I can never make out, but he has gained the upper hand bit by bit. It is almost as if there is some kind of blackmail going on . . . The last I heard of it, your uncle believes that we have all turned against him; and as this is not true, Phil must have insinuated this belief. But about the origin of their relationship, Susannah could be very mysterious. And because she was so high-minded, she would never allow herself to talk about it, even to have a little laugh at it all.

'But this is beside the point of what happened on that night. It could have some bearing, but I am not sure it does. I can only tell you my part of the story.

'A few days before she died, Susannah rang me at my home saying there was something very urgent she had to discuss. It was near Easter and we were preparing to fly to my mother's for the holiday. My wife was annoyed when I told her that I must meet Susannah, but she had been in such agitation over the telephone that I felt I had to comply.

'Well, I reluctantly agreed to meet Susannah here at the site because

144

this is where she insisted we talk, and the reason will become evident in a moment.

'She arrived here in a state of great . . . panic? distress? It is hard to describe it. Her face was white, and she was very angry. I was very puzzled indeed, for she usually had . . . how can I put it? . . . distance . . . from all the mundane things that bother everyone else. She was a little remote, a little lacking in humour, but *au fond* she practised what she preached, and it was often remarked that she had the patience of a saint with those two men. I have to stress to you that everyone thought they were mad, you know, real eccentrics. And nobody took them particularly seriously. I only wish now that we had.

'Anyway, Susannah was blazing. She was one of those relentless people who get an idea in their head and thrash it to the ground. Her hands were shaking, her eyes staring out. She insisted that I open up the museum – here, where we are now standing, and so, sensing how upset she was, I unlocked the doors and we came in. Now . . . I will show you where she took me.'

Like awed children on a school trip, Catherine and Edward trooped into the next room after the unstoppable Passides.

A stunning image hung on the wall before them. It was no less than the naked Dionysos clasping his thyrsus and decked with vine leaves. He royally ascended, as if into air, borne on the back of a rampant leopard. Couched on the back of the beast, the god's young body seemed as intimate and sinuous as a girl's. It was a vast fourth-century mosaic which had been taken from the site for preservation, but it was so vivid, so beautifully restored, that for an illusory moment Catherine thought it was alive.

In the blur before his eyes, Edward saw both god and creature moving just as if they had whisked in front of him and pounced away into the thick wall. It startled him. He and Catherine moved closer to the mosaic and scrutinized the image in all its lithe simplicity. As one, they turned to the now silent Passides with the same mute question.

He opened his arms in a wide shrug. 'Susannah began to pour out a long tirade of impenetrable questions. What did I make of Dionysos? How could I explain Dionysos to her? What did he represent to me? I could not understand what she was driving at. You'd say anyone else was hysterical.

'Of course, I had to tell her that Dionysos meant no more to me than, say, Cinderella means to you. His myth and his cult are of great interest, and obviously I said so, but she was trying to discover something more, something to do with religion.

'Because of what happened later, I have tried to remember the conversation in some detail, but it was extremely garbled. It seems she'd had a terrible row with her father, who had accused her of hypocrisy. Worse still, for her, he attacked her religious faith in itself, telling her that it suppressed the truth – the truth, what is more, of Dionysos. For some reason, this made her particularly angry and upset. We all know that Susannah had great devotion to her mental patients, but he challenged that too. He told her that she was doing them actual harm, that the whole exercise was a wallow in her own self-pity . . . and so on.

'At first, I thought this was all there was to it and, although I was sympathetic to her, I could not quite understand how I fitted in. I am not a specialist in mythology, nor in family quarrels. Even if I had been I could not have untangled it all. She was beside herself.'

'Except for the curious line on Dionysos, it was nothing he had not said to her before.' Edward spoke quietly, but Catherine and Passides turned to look at him. 'It was his regular little form of persecution . . . and, from the time I knew her very many years ago, Susannah tried to regard it as grace. She regularly took his outbursts, just like nasty medicine. Often, I thought she courted them.'

Passides looked down at his toes for a moment. 'That must have made her maddening!' he said with some asperity. 'I'm sorry to have to say that, and I hope it does not offend you.'

Edward felt subtly ashamed of Susannah, but he could not deny the truth of what the archaeologist said. 'She would have done better, I think, to see the situation in the round. It was her own father who was attacking her, after all. The quarrel had a dynamic different from what she wanted. It was morbid, psychological, not the stuff of martyrdom.'

Dr Passides put his head to one side and regarded Edward with a different kind of respect. This oddly pleased Catherine. 'But, as I was going to say, the quarrel was not all,' he continued. 'In fact, that was the least of it, as it happened. She was only providing a background to what she really had come to tell me.

'According to her, she arrived in Greece to find Phil and her father refusing to speak to each other. I can imagine that the atmosphere in that household was oppressive at the best of times, but Susannah told me it had become intolerable. She took Phil aside and demanded to know what the matter was.

'Well, this is where the story breaks down for me. There is so much contradictory evidence that I do not know what to believe myself, but I will tell you what I heard from Susannah herself, and you must make up your own minds. Apparently, Phil told her that James had discovered the now infamous "Head of Dionysos" at a site to the north of the city where he had been working with a team funded by the University of Pennsylvania Museum. I say he was working . . . what I mean is that he was only tolerated. He had an honorary place because of his reputation. This, James does not know or, if he does, he will not admit it to himself.

'Whatever James's position with the team, however, Phil Deals told Susannah that her father had taken the artefact from the site, without consulting anyone, and hidden it away in the safe in his study. Day after day, like a miser, he would lock himself away with it, even speak to it. Phil would hear him muttering to it through the door. And, contrary to what James himself has always claimed, this seems to have been going on for nearly a month.

'Now I and others like me have a strong suspicion that the Head did not even exist. Although some photographs of it later emerged, it would be quite astonishing if, as James has always maintained, he discovered anything like that from the fifth century BC in Thessaloniki . . . and from that particular site. In the first place, if he had, he would have been the first to catalogue it, take pictures of the position, calibrate the actual excavation. It would have been a very exciting discovery, as well he must have known. But he did not take any of these steps.

'If it is true that he discovered the Head the very day before Susannah arrived on her fateful trip, it is just about forgivable that he locked it away in his study because he thought he was unable to contact anyone who would put it in the museum safe. After all, I suppose he could not take the risk of letting the thing lie about exposed. Even re-burying it would have been a bit of a risk. However, this version of things falls down when first of all Susannah told me he had had the Head for a month, and secondly when one remembers how long James has been a part of the archaeological fraternity here. He could have got in touch with me or with any number of other people – at Easter or at any other time. When Andronicos opened the Tombs of Vergina, he left a guard over them all night long rather than risk damaging the treasures he was unable to move.

'What is more, James was far too senior an archaeologist to have risked his reputation in the way he seems to have done. If he had uncovered a great work of art, by Phidias or some such, surely he would never have simply moved a thing of such apparent value from a site without getting detailed, confirmed data about its exact provenance . . . unless he had completely lost his mind. Or unless, of course, he found nothing of the kind.

'When we add to this the curious fact that James has spent the last fifteen years trying to convince the authorities that a major sanctuary of the god lies buried beneath the monastery, it seems insane that he destroyed the very evidence which would make one take him seriously. Even if the Head did exist, it could have come from *anywhere*, do you see?

'James must know full well that he would have covered himself in glory if he had gone through the proper channels. As it was, the excavation lost its funding, partly because of the sordid quarrel which followed the news stories after the murder, but much more because, on further exploration, there really wasn't anything there. I understand that he has even attacked the Church for sitting on evidence of an early temple. Half the ancient churches in Christendom have pagan antecedents. And everyone knows that permission to excavate consecrated ground would never in a thousand years be granted to any team, no matter how high-powered. In any case, it was really difficult to believe that such an artefact had come from that particular site. First of all, the monastery church is believed to have been built on the ruins of the synagogue of an early Jewish community, and it is therefore very unlikely that a cult idol would have been kept even as a souvenir. Even if there had been a ruined pagan temple nearby, which is now supposed, it dates from much later. Needless to say, James refutes this. Of course, Dionysos worship might have been observed there, but almost certainly not in the early fifth century . . . and not in that place.

'All of this, you see, adds up to an inevitable conclusion. Either the Head was never in James's possession in the first place, or it came from somewhere else! If he had come by it illegally, then why would he draw attention to its theft after Susannah's murder? It makes no sense.

'Now, for many years I have wondered if James is simply too proud to accept the charitable interpretation we have put on his actions. I myself think, and others agree, chiefly the police, that he imagined the whole thing in a kind of brainstorm. He had long wanted to restore his former greatness; he wanted this very much indeed. He lived in that house in Ano Poli like a great lord, expecting the world to beat a path to his door, and everyone knew he was consumed with envy when Andronicos discovered the Vergina Tombs. So when Susannah arrived the bits of evidence about Dionysos that might have been circulating in his mind came together. By her own evidence, he used to taunt and tease her. Then, as a result of the trauma of her murder, he imagined what he had invented was really true. There seems no explanation of why she was killed, and so the idea of a theft occurred to compensate for it. Is that far-fetched?'

'But Phil and Susannah surely saw the Head for themselves!' Catherine cried.

'I was coming to that. Obviously, the first thing I asked Susannah on that day was if she had seen the Head. It was then she told me that James had refused to show it to *anyone*. Even Phil, she told me, had not actually seen it. Indeed, he later gave evidence to the police that he had not.

'All we actually have now is some slides taken against a dark backdrop. They are not even from James's camera. Then, however, they had not come to light and Susannah had not seen them – unless, of course, she was lying, and that seems . . .'

'Impossible?' said Edward wryly. 'It virtually is.'

Passides laughed. 'So . . . the problem for me on that day became a great deal easier. There seemed very little point in ringing the police when we only had the reported words, spoken in anger, of a cracked old man to go on. And, as Susannah herself pointed out, Phil Deals seems to take great pleasure in making up stories. I began to think that the whole thing was some such nonsense. I advised her to challenge her father, ask to see the Head, get photographs of it if she could, and if it was what he claimed it to be I would speak to him myself after the holidays.

'The problem for Susannah had always been her father, as you probably know. Even she knew it in a rueful kind of way. To this day I do not know if what she had to tell me was more to do with her emotional confusion or with an actual situation. However, even though I tried to persuade her that she was being cruelly deceived about this artefact, she had it in her mind that her father was in danger.'

Edward gave a little cry. 'Ah . . .' It was too much to hope for. 'That someone would murder him for the Head?' Perhaps she had died in defence of the old man after all.

Passides thought for a moment. 'It was moral danger she feared most of all. I do not think she mentioned his dying. If the Head did not exist, then she was frightened for his sanity; if it did, then, to Susannah, more than anything else the question was an ethical one. Forget that he was very old, a little senile; forget that he might have been teasing her in some silly way. In her eyes, he was stealing – and stealing, what is more, in the service of idolatry. Now, not since the days of Iconoclasm do I think there could have been a more passionate argument in Thessaloniki. Susannah spoke like a saint – one of those frightening ones who live in a cave at the top of the Meteora and scare the living daylights out of sinners!'

Catherine and Edward looked at each other and then at Passides.

'Is that why you are here? Because you think she might have been one?' The archaeologist fairly gurgled with delight. 'Well, if it proves anything to you at all, she came here with the express intention to rescue her father from the ultimate sin of worshipping a pagan god. And, although it never occurred to me before, I suppose if she died in an attempt to prevent him, then it would make her a glorious martyr, eh?'

'But she did not, did she! You say the Head did not exist!' Edward snapped. 'I apologize. It is an emotional subject for me.'

Passides scrutinized the priest closely, paying microscopic attention to the smallest inflection of his expression. 'The Head may not have existed, Father,' he said after a moment's careful thought, 'but the issue did. You see, she *believed* it.'

XIII

CATHERINE SAT up in bed. It was dark and the effect of her pill had worn off. She tried to focus on the bedside clock, but she could not make out where the hands were. She had been too vain to get the bifocals she now needed, and she resolved to redeem this on her return to England. It did not matter what the time was in any case. The dull pain she had tried to obliterate with Temazepam returned with interest. In the past she had always refused such anodynes. Although the Greeks took Zantac by the crateload for their knotted stomachs, they disapproved of anything stronger than aspirin for life's other agonies: this had reinforced Catherine's own Spartan sensibility. After her mother's death, however, something of the ramrod had gone out of her spine. There was no Lady Simon to see pain as obscurely *infra dig*, no Theo to find endurance prophylactic. Without the two of them, she had come to feel it. Why not act on it? Why not stop the sleepless nights if one could? She had gone to bed that night wide-eyed with emotional exhaustion. The faint spark she had nourished for Father Edward, a hope of affection, of friendship, had been doused summarily in his now absolute preoccupation with Susannah. Now she was awake, the pain identified itself and with categorical certitude. She was lonely.

Not wanting to turn on the light, she got out of bed and went to the French windows which led to her balcony, opened them and stepped out into the night air, still chilly with spring and damp from the sea mist rising from the Gulf.

Whatever time it was, the Café Olympia across the Plataea was still going strong. A throng chattered, spilling from the pavement on to the road. From her aerial perspective on the sixth floor, it looked like a heaving ant hill or an African watering hole. The rest of the square was dark and silent. She drew her dressing gown around her. Why did the late-night revellers choose this one place? Night after night she had been dimly aware of it. Why choose one tiny bar when the entire population of the city might stand in the huge space below her, when equally pleasant cafés lined the square? Every now and then, Catherine had the feeling that blind instinct ruled the human race more tyrannically than most people supposed. On the news, with which she had tried to divert herself earlier, a Greek report biased in favour of Serbian activity to the north in Bosnia had given support to this theory of species loyalty she now observed in the café-bar below.

Scanning the harbour, which curved below the base of the square, she idly watched for ships. During her early married life, she had been excited to see her new name, Phocas, on the hulls and funnels jostling in Greek ports. She looked out at the Gulf; a lone craft, its lights far away, slid past on the horizon, as ghostly in the faint sea as the *Marie Celeste*.

Catherine leaned on the balcony. It startled her to realize how young she had been – only eighteen – when she had married Theo. She had been four years younger than Xenia was now. Could it have been that her pleasure at the ships had been that of a child, not a bride? She had been given the best, the grandest life-sized toys to play with. Although she had in no sense married for money, what it bought had given her a glittering veil for her shyness. She had been amalgamated into her husband's empire like a foreign princess who was meant to represent something of a conquest for the ruler, and if she had been young, she had been given no chance to grow through responsibility. It had seemed a wonderful game, particularly after post-war privations, that she had merely been meant to reign beautifully. That she had had to exchange sex for the privilege of being Theo's eighteen-year-old empress had filled her with a little girl's mute horror she had never expressed, not even to herself. She gave a slight shudder. She remembered the wedding now, the virgin sacrifice.

Lady Simon had tried to stop it. She had said Catherine was too young, and had told her she was immature. Theo was ten years older and sophisticated with it. Her poor mother had been a kind of Cassandra. Her foretellings had been true, her divinations accurate: but the way she *put* things . . . Catherine would never be able to live among the Greeks, the cultural gap was far too wide. Money was not everything . . . and yet romance did not last. Catherine wondered if the Pythoness at Delphi had uttered cryptograms just to make her clients attend to the message by having to work it out. Her mother had had a way of reducing her deepest prophecies to truisms. Her false premise had been that she had classed all foreigners as 'wogs'.

Catherine had seen Theo in that far-distant time as her true love, dashing and exotic. She had a vague memory of having seen *Gone With the Wind* at the cinema, where Vivien Leigh, whose hair she had admired, had been assumed into Clark Gable's arms up the broad staircase into the filmic dark. Theo had been a handsome stranger with a faint accent. Catherine had been going to do the Season, but she had been smitten with Theo at first sight. She had met him at the party of some neighbours, a barrister friend of her father who specialized in maritime law and whose client Theo had already become, even at twenty-eight. Until that time, she had been biddable. Marrying him after their whirlwind romance had been her only open rebellion.

Having been sent away to school at the age of six, there had been few toys for Catherine, but a lot of herding. She and the other new girls had cried like little beasts in a cold stable her first night in the dormitory, and she had rescued Violet Hogg's teddy-bear from some bullies. Violet had gone on to be bullied still more, but never Catherine. She had learned very young how to put distance between herself and the crowd. In fact, she had invented a way of doing it, imagining a desert of which her small form was the epicentre. The picture she had learned to create had become so practised and vivid that she had been able to call it up at will in order to achieve privacy. She had forgotten this.

Theo had never been in anyone's herd, pack or pride, and maybe this had been the attraction. The sea had surrounded him ... *oi thalassa* ... Catherine remembered this first, onomatopoetic Greek word she had learned and how beautiful she thought it, just her idea of turquoise water sensuously lapping a white, sandy shore quite unlike the Sussex coast of her childhood. In the end, it had felt no different.

Now she thought about it, the sea had always encroached upon her life. Even poor Marina had once remarked that she thought she had been named after this pure and elemental force until Maureen had set her straight. It turned out that she had had sex with Marina's father in a boat yard on a trip to Atlantic City.

Theo had often said how treacherous the sea was for he had sailed it. She and Marina, however, had missed the tide. In that they had allowed men to define them, they had not fully embarked upon the twentieth century and now it was nearly over.

Catherine started to shake herself gruffly out of self-pity, but she decided to splurge instead. Why not? Wasn't her habitual antipathy to this vice something of a vice in itself? Father Edward had pointed out to her that morning that the anger she so regretted might be a function of unexpressed grief. She had not mourned: not for the marriage; not for her mother; not for the horridness of Missy, of having discovered that Missy was Xenia's biological mother; not for the anguish of Xenia which she had had to witness as a result of the lies they had both been told. At least, that is how she had interpreted his words. Well, she couldn't cry. All she could do was to look down from the balcony at the vast concrete space below her made emptier by the gabbling, heaving café in which some sort of life, albeit collective, flourished. She had received Absolution and Communion that very day, though not in that order. It offended Catherine deeply that there was an impulse in her thighs to jump. She firmly moved indoors and switched on the light. She might as well work at her tapestry or read her thriller for a while.

She looked at the bedside table where lay her dim airport paperback. She had brought it to Greece among many. She read thrillers avidly. The more formulaic they were the better she liked them. A good 'tec', lots of bodies, lots of suspects with equal motive and opportunity, and she was happy. She had read so many since her parting of the ways with Theo that she could often guess the outcome, and she deliberately put her mind on hold so that she could be surprised. A rich display of violence, guilt and discovery slaked some Fury in the bottom of her soul. She was *in* a thriller now, though, was she not?

This thought woke Catherine entirely. Susannah's grisly death was so far removed from her usual fix of gently bred policemen and rarefied crime that the comparison was absurd. The archaeologist that day had told them the search into who had done it, why it had been done and when had been exhaustive. No blood on Uncle James, no blood on Phil, their clothes, sink, basins, floors . . . No hairs nor fibres on Susannah that belonged to them, no suspicious lapse between the time of death and the phone call to the police, only a few heavy footprints in the garden made by a pair of shoes mass-produced in Greece, shoes which had not belonged to either of the men, or even to their size of foot. No murder weapon. Only the evidence in the wounds of such brute strength that only a man of considerable size could have inflicted them. No Attic deity, no hard evidence of one, no other valuables stolen . . . no motive.

Except the non-existent Head.

Catherine grappled with her work basket; she was no latter-day Miss Marple. She put the basket back, fidgeting unbearably. Her thought was a thread, not through any labyrinth for Father Edward's Theseus: really there was no Minotaur to slay. It ran, rather, through her own desolation like a ball of yarn unwinding across the blank Plataea outside her hotel. It made Catherine shudder that the hacked body was connected to her own. They had shared the same grandparents. It was in this sense that the Head was immaterial. And it was in this sense too that it mattered very little whether or not Susannah had been outstandingly virtuous. The veins and capillaries knit together in her mother's womb had been ruptured, violated; the bone splintered, crushed to the marrow. If the Church, which made such vehement argument for the sanctity of life, were to celebrate this obscene way of leaving it . . . Catherine frowned. Perhaps this was why the petty legalism of a Cause made some kind of sense – it was not how or why Susannah had died but for what that needed inspecting.

Well, let them get on with it! she thought. Neither Agatha Christie nor the Holy Office seemed to be addressing the questions she herself really had, questions that pressed upon her and oppressed her more and more each day they stayed in this odd and indestructible city. Catherine had never gone to university, not like her brother Charles nor his wife Rosamund, nor like Theo. For years they had all whizzed books over her head, making educated remarks with ironic point. Her years in the unofficial purdah of the marriage had, however, stimulated thought. Indeed, without philosophy, she could not have survived as long as she had. Like Rapunzel in the tower, she had let down her gold hair to secret cogitation on large matters, and so it struck her now to question what set of circumstances had constellated the event of murder. Each actor in the tragedy had started off from a different place bearing his or her own inscrutable potential to the scene of the crime. What catalyst had locked all points on to the engine of mayhem?

If only she had a snapshot of Susannah, something more objective than childhood memory to go on, something from her adult life. Beatrice, who had known her best of all, had been plunged into a convent by the time Susannah had launched on her eccentric career.

Theresa might remember something! Now wholly unsettled by her thoughts, Catherine sprang from the chair, sought her half-moon spectacles and looked at the clock. It was 3 a.m. Greek time. It would be one o'clock in England, and she could hardly ring Theresa, who rose at five to milk the animals, or whatever she did with them. Catherine had a devilish wish to do so all the same and her fingers itched for the telephone. Theresa was deliberately blunted. She only affected a heaviness of manner and speech. She had given them all a miserable time at their mother's funeral just in order to score a point. At the door, she had said to Catherine, 'Poor Mummy, so *raffinée*. How dreadful for her to have had to live with me.' It wouldn't do any harm to wake Theresa up.

Catherine unflexed her fingers from the receiver. Her second sister was an eternal Bolshie adolescent, and would deliberately mislead her about Susannah just for the sake of thumbing her nose at the very idea of sanctity. She had liked to torture their mother by refusing to go to Mass. She hadn't had the tact simply to fade out like Charles; it had been an unspoken confrontation every Sunday.

155

Well, when had she herself last seen Susannah? All of the sudden, Catherine jumped with a little gasp, delighted with the result of her nocturnal sleuthing. Susannah had come to her wedding! That was it! Of course. And she had given them a surprisingly nice present. Catherine could not remember what it had been, but she did recall having been startled by this virtual stranger's gift. What had it been? There had been so much tissue paper at the time, so much work with lists and dresses and bridesmaids and invitations and whatnot. How many asparagus rolls, that sort of thing. Theo had quietly paid for the champagne. Everyone had been very much embarrassed by this necessity and had been skilfully disparaging to him as a consequence of his generosity.

Catherine was uncomfortable about remembering that day. They had borrowed Lord Aubin's house for the wedding because he was a relation, her mother's cousin, who had inherited the jumbled pile that went for a family seat. It was hardly Chatsworth, but one would have thought so from the way her mother talked about it. The reasoning behind this was that Lady Simon, and presumably Uncle James, had been baptized in the chapel, which was old, devolving as it did from Norman times. It was, of course, quite unusual for a recusant Catholic family to have such a venerable ecclesiastical pile at its disposal, but the property had zigzagged across generations, falling into Anglican hands during interesting times.

The house itself was mainly Carolean, for the family had flourished during this period. Catherine supposed that Susannah might have used this ancestral model as a precedent for martyrdom if any of their forebears had actually died for the Faith, but they had managed to keep their heads throughout. There were Tudor bits and Victorian bits of house. Whatever could be said of the family's consistently unwise choice of architects down the centuries, a sense of history prevailed in the portraits hung on the glum panelling: drear old ancestors in ruffs, flabby ancestresses in yards of silk with fichus round their double chins, their vapid eyes proclaiming bland assurance.

The chapel itself resembled a dungeon rather than a place of worship. Heavy, chevronned piers supported the barrel vaults. Past Vaughans and Aubins lay beneath the absolute flagging, and the famed Crusader and his wife were couched on eternal stone. The walls were so thick that a hydrogen bomb could not have shifted them and they oozed with damp, especially from November to February. Catherine had had a winter wedding. In the summer, the house was uncertainly managed by the National Trust, and that more for the gardens than for anything else.

Theo was supposed to have been bowled over by the borrowed *Brides-*

head finery. Secretly, he had been, for it had started a boasting match between him and Catherine's mother that had ended only in his tactful absence from the family fold after Xenia's illness. However, then he had been quite independent – disdainful, really – of all that it implied. This had made Catherine nervous. She had wanted to stand up to her mother and marry in their own parish church instead, but not even her father could be enlisted against the stupid snobbish choice.

Catherine remembered that even the flowers had looked appalled by the wintry conditions of the ceremony, refrigerated blooms though they were. Somehow they had managed to make the chapel look more drab than it normally was with its grey glass mullioned windows which excluded more light than they let in. Her dress had been a moonbeam, though: that she had never regretted. As it was winter, there were little tippets of white fur round the high bodice, which had given her rather the air of a medieval princess, particularly in the setting.

Given the unpleasantness of inter-family feeling that had built up, it was a wonder that the marriage had taken place at all. Theo *had* no family and so he had fought the battle on his own with a few supporters from the Greek community in London who thought he should have been married in the Orthodox Cathedral in Bayswater instead. The groom's side of the chapel had been nominally filled by overdressed, overweight matrons from Athens and Chios, who had in one way or another known Theo's parents before they died; there had been friends of his uncle who had left him the makings of his shipping fortune.

Catherine's side had filled up the empty pews. There had been schoolfriends who, like her, had left the sixth form at St Winifred's that July. She had been the first bride, and they all longed to catch her bouquet; being married in those days had been a high aspiration, though not quite as high as in her mother's day. Catherine remembered seeing the backs of their hats as she sheltered on her father's arm. Her brother Charles, then sixteen, had worn a morning coat too large for him but, even with his Adam's apple swimming in the roomy collar, he had managed to make the Greek contingent look foreign.

Catherine had made her vows with a numb mouth, as if she had been to the dentist. It was only now that she had the courage to allow this unwelcome memory that the image of Susannah began to emerge as if from a brass rubbing. After the long nuptial Mass had been said and sung (Lord Aubin, 'Cousin Henry', they called him although they barely knew him, had arranged for a small choir as part of his gift), she and Theo turned to face the congregation man and wife. It was then she had spotted Susannah sitting behind her mother who had been too angry at the mismatch to weep and who wouldn't have done so anyway. If Uncle James had been with Susannah, Catherine did not remember it. She was surprised now to recall the sharp gratitude she had felt for a small moment. Susannah had worn a rusty hat and a suit dated to the point of absurdity, and this had given her the aspect of a fairy godmother in the Arthur Rackham setting. She had been praying – praying for Catherine (she liked to think) – for when the recessional music had started, Susannah had glanced up and had given Catherine a wonderful smile.

Perhaps it was a distortion to think that, alone among the glossy company with their smart sixties gear, this dowdy fifties woman had *known what was going on*. The glance, the smile, though brief, had been one of affirmation that Catherine had just done something large which had nothing to do with smoked salmon, cake, and lists at Peter Jones. Whirled away after the march from the scaffold, Catherine had seen Susannah only from a distance at the reception where the panelled walls, embalmed from the time of Charles II, had absorbed the din of guests. She had been speaking to Theo, hadn't she? Catherine was sure that could not be really true; the two, Susannah and Theo, had been so much on her mind that it was easy to twist this ancient memory from the varied strands of the present. Perhaps she had been talking with some of the lonely, socially oppressed Greek friends of Theo, people who should never have been snubbed – firstly, because they were human beings, most of them more civilized than her mother, and, secondly, because Catherine had later gone to live among them. Their lasting impression of the upper-class English wedding had made mountains out of the obstacles she would have climbed more easily without it. Or had Susannah been talking to Lady Simon? What Catherine did piece together now was a gentle presence, not at all the ruthless monster of virtue she had come to construct these last few days. She could not imagine that Susannah castigating an enfeebled old man for 'idolatry'.

Suddenly, Catherine wanted to talk to Theo. It came over her, a sharp craving. Was he still in New York? She forgot when he said he would be returning to Athens.

No, it was an illogical thing to do, and it might even compromise her position. Should the threat of loneliness weaken her resolve? She had thought long and hard about breaking her ties with him. It would be misleading him to ring him with trivial questions, but she had an idea now that the family had appealed to him for help with the Greek authorities at the time of Susannah's death, since he knew everyone.

After all, in New York it would only be about seven in the evening and he had left her the number of his hotel, the St Regis.

Well, was she now saying to herself by wanting to hear his voice that divorce was too messy, she too lazy, too cowardly, to wreck the delicate maze of connections they had constructed between them since the wedding day she had so vividly recalled? For all she knew, he was still seeing Missy.

And yet she picked up the telephone and in rapid Greek explained to the operator what number she wanted from the retrieved piece of paper in her shaking hand. She was breathless. Her chest was tight with the pounding of fear. She had hated him enough to kill him. Suppose he had lured Xenia over to New York. Suppose Missy was draped over his bed. Catherine could almost hear her lolling Southern tongue mouthing whispered ridicule at the put-aside wife to whose child she had been bodily mother.

The telephone purred, once, twice. Yes, Mr Phocas was staying at the hotel. Catherine nearly rang off.

'Hallo,' Theo said in English.

'Theo?'

'Catherine.'

'Yes. How did you know it was me?'

He said nothing.

'I am ringing from Thessaloniki . . .'

'You said you would be there.'

'This is an inconvenient time.'

'No, not for me; for you, perhaps. It must be three or four in the morning.'

She could not gauge his tone. It was guarded but not unwelcoming. He was sixty now and had become a little portly. Perhaps the lawyers had been on to him. Surely there must have been legal conversations following her last call.

'I couldn't sleep.'

'I have been thinking about you, Cat, quite a lot. Why did you call me? Is Xenia all right?'

'As far as I know.'

There was a pause. Neither of them knew what to say. It seemed stupid in the face of this overwhelming feeling to mention Susannah, her excuse for ringing him. 'I had a reason, but it really was a pretext. I realize now that I wanted to hear your voice.' She heard an odd sound of swallowing on the other end. She wondered if he were crying, but then dismissed the thought. It seemed dishonourable somehow to ask him if he had a cold.

'Well, what was the excuse?'

There seemed a terrible, rocking power on the line, as if some mammoth storm in space were invisibly battering the satellite which connected them.

'Did I tell you about Cousin Susannah? Surely I told you why I was coming here.'

'Catherine, you also asked me for a divorce. It was difficult to concentrate on anything else at the time.'

'What have you been thinking about me?'

'After all of our years together it is hardly thought, Cat.'

'You're angry with me.'

'No. Go on about Susannah. I remember Susannah.'

'*Do* you?' Catherine asked nervously.

'You said something about visiting that old gargoyle of an uncle . . .'

Catherine laughed despite herself. 'I did not know you had even met him!'

'He came to our wedding . . . with his daughter. They are both indelibly printed on my memory.'

'He was unkind to you?'

'Far from it. A real philhellene. He wished to discuss Homer, the Homer Stone in Chios. He was happy that you were doing the right thing in marrying a Greek with connections to the possible birthplace of Homer.'

'Then why do you say he is a gargoyle? He is, of course.'

'Never mind.'

Her voice failed her. She had never been frightened of Theo. Personally, he had treated her like a china doll. She was frightened of herself, however. 'They are thinking of canonizing Susannah. I seem to remember that you dredged up some Member of Parliament when the case was being investigated in Greece . . . for Charles. They want to know if it was a saint's death. Not a martyrdom exactly. You don't remember anything about it, do you?'

'She was a saint,' said Theo. 'You can tell by the eyes.'

Catherine had a vision of him standing by the telephone in his socks. He was a burly man with heavy hands. Whether he was dressed or not, she associated his tone with nakedness.

'But you are mistaken about her death. I had nothing to do with the investigations. I only read about it in the newspapers. You're upset,

Catherine; I can tell by your voice. Can't you leave thoughts of brutal murder to someone else? There has been enough brutality in our lives.'

Catherine was near to tears. 'Do you love me, Theo?' she asked. 'It's not a fair question, so don't answer it if you don't want to.'

'Yes,' he said.

'I'm very far from a reconciliation, you know.'

'I know that.'

She was openly weeping. 'Can you remember what Susannah gave us for a wedding present?'

'She gave us a gilt angel from Florence. It belonged to her. She told me she had always thought you were unique, a nice thing to say to a bridegroom, perhaps.'

'Oh, it got lost! I know the one you mean.' Suddenly, the loss of the little, delicately wrought figurine, an unusual piece, horrified Catherine.

'To lose a gift from a saint. That is unlucky,' he said.

'I didn't even like Susannah. I had no idea she thought me unique.'

'She said you had a strong character, that you were honest and unspoiled.'

'I haven't been able to remember anything about her.'

'She was more my age.'

'Theo, this is such a mess.'

'Do you want me to come to see you in Thessaloniki? I am flying back to Athens tomorrow morning. Would you like to meet?'

'Not yet.'

'Go to see the Church of Nicholas Orphanos . . . and Ossios David. They are very beautiful.'

'I met someone today who knows you. Dr Passides, an archaeologist.'

'Oh ho! We were shipmates! Back in the fifties.'

Theo had always prided himself on learning his business from the water line up, as it were. Catherine suddenly felt exhausted. As if he sensed this, he added, 'Shall I ring you from Athens some time during the week? I'll be at the flat.'

She said nothing.

'I am glad that you called,' he said.

'I don't know why I did.'

'Yes, you do,' he replied, but all the triumph that might have been in that remark before was gone. His voice was oddly gentle.

XIV

A HERD of sticky schoolchildren was massing in the central hall of the Archaeological Museum and Edward stood aside as their numbers swelled. Batches of them swarmed in geometric proportions as the coaches outside released them. It had rained that morning and was still spitting. The distinct pencil smell of the damp young bodies filled the air. They chattered, girls and boys, cautiously boisterous, under the watchful eyes of their mentors; they seemed exhilarated at the prospect of visiting the treasures of the tombs, the bones of the illustrious dead . . . or perhaps they were simply happy to miss a morning of school. They were armed with little notebooks for a project. Edward looked away, having caught himself out in too painful a wistfulness. Privately, he had always thought he would have made a good father. He really must send his nieces and nephews postcards. He quietly lived for the idea of them, his sisters' children, all grown. They had children of their own now. The very thought of them made him smile; it buoyed him up, giving him a necessary footing in what he somewhat guiltily persisted in regarding as the real world. He had come to the museum to meet Phil Deals, on neutral ground, as it were, but he had not yet arrived.

Edward felt stiff with anticipation. However he tried, he could not conquer the odd, atavistic horror the American produced in him. He had, of course, not shared this ungovernable distaste with Catherine, for it would only serve to make her own worse. In any case, the smallest word might tend to reveal to her things he had heard about the man in a privileged conversation.

Edward tried not to think about those things Susannah had long ago told him about Phil, things uncommon which had nothing to do with homosexuality. Surely, he was condemning the man without judge or jury on hearsay evidence from a woman who had always been given to exaggeration and extremes. To offset the evils of a reactive kind of censure, he had spent the morning praying for Phil Deals: for success in his every legitimate venture, for his health, his happiness and well-being. He firmly meditated now on Phil's virtues. Here was a man who had sacrificed his life to the care of an elderly relative by marriage. What was more, he did this without respect to financial or even emotional reward. Susannah had invariably spoken of him with fondness and respect. Although not in love with him, she had certainly loved him. If what she had said about the man's unfortunate sexual proclivities was true, then it was possible he had brought his impulses under control, perhaps with the pain of Gethsemane. Perhaps he had immured himself with the old man as a form of self-imposed discipline and expiation. His foolish manner might so easily be a brave front put on over much suffering.

No, Edward was sure he did not judge the man on the basis of a suspected aberration. Phil had woken him at seven that morning with the idea that they should meet alone. He had been full of cloak-and-dagger mystery; his voice had almost swaggered down the line, as if the two of them might enjoy playing some game of spies, rules set by Phil, King of the Castle. It was the man's insolent childishness he abhorred. It was a neat form of social aggression that would always go unpunished because it seemed humourless to object.

Edward tried to consider how his sleepless night had been the result of faithless anxiety. A better Christian than himself would have left Susannah's Cause in the hands of God, from which it must necessarily proceed in the first place. Rather than nurture a grudge against Phil for waking him after he had been tossing and turning until 3 a.m., it would be kinder to wonder if the poor man actually might need to confide. Often the moment of decision occurred to people at inconvenient times. Perhaps he had a valid wish to talk . . . simply that. People were often hostile to priests for this very reason. Sometimes they veiled their true anxieties in bravado, angry at themselves for wanting absolution.

He sighed. For all his urgency on the telephone, Deals was now half an hour late. Edward had been glad that Catherine had agreed not to come to this meeting, but now he wished she was with him. There was no reason to be frightened of Deals and yet he was. He felt suddenly frail and weightless, threatened even by the little boys who squeaked their plimsolls as they dashed heedlessly, darting with no real aim around the marble floor.

All at once, without his conjuring it, an image of Susannah came to him as if he held a locket with her picture in his hands. It was the sort of thing one dreamed and yet he was awake. There he was, vivid in his own mind's eye, a younger man, fully sighted, holding in his palm a miniature set in gold. Her slender form, obedient to an inner demand for rigour, stemmed stiffly up to bear her high-carried head. Although younger than he, she had the appearance of an ancestor, as if in some sense she had generated him. Her smile was the enigma of the dead, her eyes inviting his confidences. Oh, how he still missed her! Now that he had met her father, he realized that the whole warmth of her being had sprung almost by necessity from the frozen desolation of her early life. She had been and was still as a flame to him which had burnt out carnal response, transmuting it into an exalted kind of love . . . Platonic, he supposed.

He looked up. Phil Deals was standing in front of him, too close, staring into his dim eyes.

'Well, hi there,' Phil said. 'Have you been waiting long? I got held up.' He was dressed in a loud tie and a checkered jacket, just short of looking literally clownish. His hair was slicked down with something like brilliantine. All he needed was a balloon to make him look as if he were on his way to a birthday party.

Edward blinked and started in surprise. He was near enough to catch the sharpened smile that went with the man's tone. It was almost as if Phil had been watching his thoughts, and he backed away, saying nothing in response to the other man's apparently polite inquiry. For some reason, it seemed that to acknowledge Phil's apology was to collude in a small but significant lie. Edward was instinctively certain that Deals had made him wait in order to achieve the maximum advantage in the conversation.

'It's mobbed,' Phil continued, waving at the children, who were starting now to file into the exhibition of the Vergina treasure. 'The Greeks are keen on justifying the sacred nature of their borders. Did you know that there is a big Serb presence here in Thessaloniki? Fascist thugs! All the kerfuffle about Skopje has to do with getting a pan-Orthodox union at the end of the day. Look at the map. So, Philip of Macedon and Alexander the Great have to be pushed down the throats of kids who will learn to hate, maim and kill anyone who does not worship at this particular ethnic shrine. There is even a Museum of Macedonian Struggle in this town. I kid you not! You should see it. There are dioramas of Balkan bandits in skirts and mustachios, tribesmen passing as the legitimate sons of ancient civilization.'

Phil waited for Edward to speak. When he did not, he grinned out of the side of his mouth. 'Not interested in Greek politics, are we? Well, we all may have to be one day. I hate the place.'

'Then why do you live here?' Edward said sharply.

'My, my! For reasons best known to myself. Except, of course, you must know them, or some of them, given your intimacy with Susie-Q.'

Edward decided not to be drawn on this.

'She didn't tell you? Well, I will, then. Cards on the table all round. I'm an exile, a bit of a Roman Polanski. Trouble follows me wherever I go, but it would never do to have the family embarrassed. In order to get me out of a scrape, I followed Susie here and got me a job with James. He was ecstatic; not so Sue. I bet you thought he and I were lovers, didn't you? Everybody does. Well, we're not. Not that James wouldn't have liked it. Yukky-poohs. It's just not me. You know what he used to call me? Very grand, this . . . his "Private Secretary", as if he had been the Minister for Fisheries or something, but really I'm his dogsbody as you can see. I don't need the money, but the plain fact remains that I need a good home. Old Fido. When he's gone, then what's to do?'

Edward tried not to press his lips angrily together. He imagined a stole round his neck, a crucifix in his hand. He leaned into, not against, the bitter wind of talk.

Phil brandished his hand towards the schoolchildren as they formed themselves into an untidy crocodile. 'Yes, look at them all, look at the kiddie-winks. I didn't plan our little outing this way, but heigh-ho, there you go. A chocolate box for Phil, all the girlies. To me, they're ravishingly lovely. Are you shocked?'

'Yes,' said Edward.

'They have this discreet smile, this unopened look, like the archaic statues, the *kore*. After they start to bud, it's no good for me. I'd like to see them this way for ever, which is why I so loved Susie. She was eternally un-grown, like me. We shared the same . . . syndrome, though sex never had anything to do with it with her. She never got there. Except with you. She was in love with you.'

Edward thought: If I am to be tortured let it be by You not by him, for You, no, *with* You.

'Dazzling Daddy! She did it all to please you.'

But Edward blinked, conscious only of numbness. 'Daddy . . .?' he said.

'Well, do you prefer "Abelard"? You deserted her, abandoned her. Susie and I had no secrets from each other. You pushed her away and she became more feverishly virtuous, more of a virtuoso talent in fervidness. I may be a pervert but I get respect for having smarts.' He glanced at the schoolchildren as they funnelled into the exhibition. 'She began to believe it was really God who had motivated her all along, while I prefer to regard myself as merely whacko. If it doesn't make you sick to think of my little problem, let's follow the kids inside. Believe me, I am just as celibate as you are, so it's no threat to them. We can be two little old eunuchs having a stroll. God, I hate the Catholic Church! I drool over my little girls like an old dog with no teeth, a Lewis Carroll with fantasy Alices. Now, that is. I fell once long ago. Oops! Never again, but this doesn't make me Moses with the burning bush. It makes me an ironist.'

Edward's legs moved as though he were drugged and only partially feeling. It was as if he were being dragged in chains after Phil, his captor, who wittingly and gladly knew the pain he was inflicting.

'You think I'm the devil, don't you? Well, I am. I'm going to harrow you like hell because you deserve it. You guys think I'm a monster; well, I'll show you "monster".'

They were surrounded by the schoolchildren.

'This is agony, rapture, for me. They are all covered in velvet down like pussy willow in the spring time, hidden, reflecting on an inner dream, still unrealized, their nascent womanhood . . . which, incidentally, scares the hell out of me. I find actual women acutely repulsive, y'know, moist, bulbous.'

The children, reaching the end of the corridor, burst into the room ahead of them, like dragonflies escaping the odious eye of a toad.

'They're your hostages, then,' Edward said.

'What *do* you mean?' Phil asked.

'These children. You are talking to me about them in this way because you think I will be too frightened for their sake to cry out against what you want to say to me about Susannah. Just the idea that you are talking about them with what you call candour and I call lust is enough, isn't it? It will silence me, make me afraid, bully me into submission so that I will take anything you say as truth, so that I will be subject to you.'

'Well, well, James did remark that you were a smart cookie, or words to that effect. There is another possibility which you haven't considered. If they weren't here, then maybe I would kill you.'

They moved into the smooth, impressive hall where the furniture of heroes ranged the walls, the glassed-in artefacts of royal tombs. There was gold everywhere, Edward dimly saw, gold glowing in the refulgence of expert lighting design.

'Shall we pretend to look at this?'

'I am looking at it,' Edward said, 'but I am also trying to understand why you want to kill me. Did you murder Susannah?'

'Good heavens, no! You did.'

Edward peered at him. 'What did you say?'

'You killed her. I told you that I knew whodunnit. You done it. That is why you are not safe with me.'

'*I* killed Susannah?' The weight of grief at having heard she had loved him suddenly detached itself and slid like clay, smothering him. He was being buried alive in misery.

'Let me tell you how it works, Hercule Poirot. Now, Susie was an intellectual, kind of a mystic, really, like Simone Weil, tough, extreme, Jewish . . .'

'Jewish . . . ?'

'My mom, her mom. It was the family's dirty little secret. Sue didn't know. Our grandmother was Jewish, and old Schuyler made her convert, conceal it. Can you believe this? It's true. It gave Sue her religious intensity. Me, I'm anti-Semitic. I hate myself. Susie, she liked Jews. Also, she was amazingly monotheistic for a Catholic.'

'We are monotheistic.'

'This is not a theology seminar. This is a trial and you are in the dock, buddy.'

'Go on.'

'Right. So this neurotic, nervy, bright lady comes to you and sicks up all her troubles in your lap. This little girl. This child. This child of God. And your handle on this ought to be to make her grow up, see her straight through.

'But you never did that. Instead, you gave her paranoia, her obsessional mind a vehicle for self-destruction. Where Susie needed love, you gave her sacrifice. Where she needed common sense, you gave her dogma. Where she needed light thrown on old James, you gave her the mud of pathological obscurity. You built the structure of her doom as certainly as if you had been a Pharaoh erecting a pyramid in which to immolate her. Each time she exposed herself to danger, you applauded it, and so she sought more danger still. You gave her the ruinous advice she needed to delude herself into thinking she was a saint when she was just a wee bit bonkers. From a rich, bright looker with everything to play for, she became a pauper, a scrawny frump with about as much realism and prospects as an old bag lady. Susie was not a saint when you finished with her, she was a sex-starved weirdo, and if her gross death had not occurred here it would have occurred somewhere else. She wanted it, she yearned for it. Her masochism found an outlet in you. You gave it permission and so she died. And, if you think I am going to tell you how, then that's a secret between Susie and me and she's not talking!'

Edward struggled not so much for air as for metaphysical balance. If Phil had hauled him into a cell and inflicted violent but imperceptible wounds on his person with neat bludgeons, he could not have felt more violated. Even the tactful lighting of the museum seemed to swing before his eyes as a naked bulb disturbed by the thrust of an arm raised, the laughing chatter of the children assailed his ears like mockery. Without thinking, he reached in his mind for something, anything, to stabilize his reeling head. *Begone, foul spirit, in the name of Jesus. Begone . . .* He snatched at a phrase he had long ago learned to sling at the devil.

For a moment, Deals loomed forward. With his clown's tie, slicked hair and an incongruous look of almost transfigured malevolence on his face, it was as if he had acquired some special bliss.

'Gotcha!' he said. Then, turning on his heel, he flounced away as buoyant and *dégagé* as ever. 'Catch you later,' he trilled. 'Except you probably hope I don't.'

Edward stood immobilized for quite some time or at least it seemed so. It was not so much Phil's words that stunned him, it was the intensity of his hatred. Bit by bit, though, it trickled slowly through, like blood, that Susannah had said these things to Phil, had thought them. Had she? He tried to compose himself. Without knowing what he was doing, he turned and tried to pull himself together. In a trance, ridiculous now, he found himself gazing into the cases of exhibits, moving between them as if he were on wheels. He could not think. An enormous golden urn, decorated to the highest degree of Hellenistic opulence, seemed to strike him as oddly apposite, although he couldn't quite think why; it depicted the sacred marriage of Dionysos and Ariadne. He peered at it, trying to get the drift. The god held his bride, a mortal now immortalized, around her waist, she veiled in a marriage *peplos*, he naked. In a similar configuration above, he yearned after her with his outstretched hand while she slept, waiting to be realized, woken into eternal relation with him. Edward felt absurdly calm, as if he had dreamed Phil. Stiffly he moved to view the great shield of Philip of Macedon, its circumference too gigantic for a mere man to hold it. The meagre bones of the old boy lay in another case and Edward said a reflexive prayer. Elsewhere, there were diadems, shivering with oak leaves of pure gold and perfect, shimmering myrtle flowers, their delicate stamens poised and quivering in response to the slight footsteps of children. He felt his head nodding curiously and said remedial prayers, dumb and thick on his tongue as he whispered them.

It was in front of the neat golden casket containing the bones of the king that he began to founder. The famous sun of Macedonia with its many pointed rays pulled his old, unfocused eyes into its centre and it began to spin like wheels of Ezekiel, like Elijah's chariot . . .

'Sir, are you not well?' a little voice piped up at him. There, by the grace of God or some other means of support, stood a child of about ten, a girl from the school party, who spoke with practised English and smiled with unstudied charity.

He nodded.

'Let me get my teacher,' she said, and before long a chair appeared and a glass of water, and kindness, concern, enveloped him like a warm rug. The child stood at the side, not wanting to crowd him, the children in general respectful of the unknowable pain of a stranger. She had, he observed, an intelligent, sober little face, her skin the tone of olives, her curly brown hair made glossy and biddable by a mother, he presumed, who loved her.

His anguish for Susannah hit him with the child's solemn smile, her transparency. But, having fallen among Samaritans, he could bear it and survive.

XV

CATHERINE CAREENED through the traffic in the hired Audi, remembering Greek driving kinetically. She was a warrior queen on fire, blazing a path through sullen queues of vehicles that dull Monday morning. She used her horn and called down long-forgotten curses. She arrived at the museum and jerked to a halt in front of it. With lipstick, she wrote a note in Greek for the universal company of traffic wardens and stuffed it in her windscreen. 'EMERGENCY' it screeched in red. She thought better than to try to express what its nature was.

She slammed the door of the car and strode across the wide plaza and up the graded steps. A museum official had rung her at the Electra Palace and had put Edward on the phone. He had sounded very weak and muddled, but the upshot of it was that Phil had struck. In Greek, the official had told her that the priest, who had refused an ambulance, looked very unwell; he was resting in her office.

'Ekaterina Phocas! It is not really you, is it?'

Catherine blinked. 'Yianna?'

The dark, attractive woman who stood before her smiled in welcome. They had been friends long ago, during her early married life. At that time, everyone had been casual, everything interesting. Try as she might, Catherine could not remember her surname. Yianna, then, had some form of shipping pedigree and this is why Theo had known her. She had been studying then in Athens, training as an archaeologist. Catherine seemed to remember that they had lost touch during the early seventies, the era of Colonels and torture, when many Greeks avoided the situation by living abroad. She and Theo had spent that time in England, and Yianna had gone to the States to get a doctorate at Harvard.

A sharp and pleasant recollection of Yianna's flat in Athens came to her now. She had lived *la vie de bohème* at the top of her grandmother's stately old house in the Plaka, camping out among the overpowering Biedermeier furniture while she studied and smoked and gave shambolic parties which Catherine, wistful at the other girl's freedom and brilliance, had secretly adored. Nearly thirty years on, in her Hermès scarf and smart shoes, Yianna seemed to be running the museum.

'How is Theo?' Yianna asked before Catherine could prevent it. 'Are you here together?'

Catherine made a helpless gesture. 'Not now. Are you well? You are looking so well. Are you the Curator here?'

Yianna winced slightly at her *faux pas* about Theo. 'No, no, only an assistant. But you must be concerned for your friend. He seems to have recovered somewhat since I rang you. He is lying down.'

'Oh, that is a relief!' Despite his age, his blindness, and his calling, Catherine was struck by the possibility that her connection with Father Edward might be misinterpreted. Theo, she remembered gloomily, cast a long shadow in Greece. For all she knew, Yianna might think the priest the discreet companion of Catherine's lonely autumn years. 'Father Knight and I are visiting my Uncle James. Perhaps you know him as he is an archaeologist, James Vaughan. It is too complicated to explain, but I am helping him with some research.' She was embarrassed that she had said too much, given circumstantial, consequential detail where none was needed. After a pause, 'If I had known you lived here, I would have rung you when I arrived,' she said.

A kind of sympathy emanated from the other woman's intelligent eyes, as if she had not only heard the words but read the confusion. 'I do know your uncle. I had no idea you were related to him.'

'My mother died recently,' Catherine said, and found that she wanted to burst into tears. First there had been Theo's voice the night before, and now there was Yianna bearing with her this happy memory of the old times, of youth in Athens, which had then been exotic to her, of Yianna's kindness to her when she had been struggling with the language, the customs, and had felt like a sore thumb, an idiotic balloon-head in foreign clothes, a reputation for stand-offishness clinging to her as a palpable aura.

'I am so sorry. I met her once. You perhaps do not remember. It was in Chios, when you were restoring the house. She was everything I ever expected of a grand English lady. Such taste, such wonderful manners.'

Standing there on the polished museum floor, which was now empty of children, Catherine felt like a statue. Then, with a huge surge, it came to her to tell the truth. 'She was the bane of my existence.' It felt like dancing to say this.

'That always makes it worse, doesn't it?' her old friend said.

Catherine wanted to go further and say, 'She hated everything I ever did,' but she thought better of it and simply nodded.

'Imagine her being the sister of James Vaughan! I would never have guessed.'

Catherine knew she need not ask Yianna's opinion of her uncle, for that was conveyed readily enough in the eyes. He would have made himself hated. 'Did you know my cousin Susannah?'

Yianna frowned for a moment. 'Oh, the one they call a martyr? No, I never met her, but of course I heard all about her. She used to feed the homeless people who collect near the market. Everyone there knew her. They still talk about her. It was before the Albanians came down to Thessaloniki. Now, we have refugees of all kinds . . . Russians, too, can you believe it? At the time, there were only the usual, gypsies and beggars, a few crazy people. The stall-holders say she was a saint. Your cousin, Ekaterina!' she exclaimed admiringly.

Catherine felt feverish shivers of excitement. 'This is extraordinary! You have no idea, Yianna! This is the reason for Father Knight's visit. They want to canonize Susannah. We are looking into it.'

'Well, if the Agora is anything to go by, she is part of a long city tradition . . . St Paul, St Demetrius!' Yianna laughed, clearly glad of a reprieve from the earlier heaviness and stickiness of their reunion. 'In fact, someone told me that old Yiorgos has something of a shrine!'

'Yiorgos who? Where is this?'

Yianna clapped her hands with delight at Catherine's excitement. 'Oh, he's a very familiar figure. I have no idea what his surname is, but you can't miss him. He runs a coffee stall – in the market, very near your hotel.'

Catherine was breathless.

The two women walked towards the offices. 'How convenient to have a family saint. I am afraid mine will never produce one.'

'They grow, Yianna, in wild outcroppings of rock – high, cold places where only goats feel comfortable.' And Catherine, pleased with this remark, threaded her arm through Yianna's with a remembered gesture of chumminess. She was absurdly happy to hear this affirmation of Susannah's sanctity. It seemed a redemption, suddenly, of something she had never before seen as sad; hitherto her family had had no spiritual imagination, only obedience to the totems of a thin-blooded, eccentric clan.

Father Edward was lying in the shuttered room on an old horsehair sofa, and immediately Catherine saw him she thought with a shock that he was dead. His body lay there stiffly, very still. With his spectacles off, his nose seemed beaky, his eyes sunken, and she gave a start, guilty at her selfishness, her gossip with Yianna. His yellowed hair lay in ropy strands across his forehead, lank, like hanks of yarn. Swiftly, she knelt beside him, but he opened his eyes and smiled with a wan gratitude. 'Thank you for coming so quickly,' he said. 'I did not think I could manage, not even with a taxi, to get back to the flat by myself.'

'Do you need a doctor? Are you all right?'

'I will be, in a moment . . . This lady has been so kind . . .' He indicated Yianna.

'Did Phil hit you? Did he knock you down?' she whispered in English.

'Only metaphorically.' He smiled. Catherine wondered if he could see her, for his eyes were blank.

'Can you walk? I have the car outside.'

'I think so.' He sat up slowly, readjusted the heavy frames on his nose, clenching his eyelids together reflexively, stretching them open. 'Catherine, this is too kind. I am so sorry. I blacked out and now I am afraid I can't see at all well. Hysteria, I think.' He gave a dry chuckle that chilled her.

'He has had a terrible emotional shock,' Catherine explained to Yianna in Greek. 'I was telling her that you had a shock, my dear,' she translated for Edward. Her hand went to smooth his hair. It was wet with sweat. 'Yianna and I knew each other in Athens long ago. Isn't that marvellous?' She found herself babbling at him as one did at frightened children and, as she did so, she was helping him to move, getting him to his feet, then carefully supporting him all the way across the hard floor and down to the car. With many promises to see Yianna before she left, have a meal with her and her husband, promises she knew she probably would not keep, Catherine started up the car and drove as if she were carrying a crate of eggs back to her hotel, where she knew there was a lift and where help, if needed, could be instantly obtained.

Edward lay on Catherine's bed and woke slowly, a beached fish gasping from time to time, his eyelids fluttering. She had drawn the curtains for him and was sitting decorously on the balcony. Through the crack of light in the open French windows, he could see her blurred form; she was bent to her sewing – the rhythmic movement of her hands suggested it. Despite the modern conveniences of the Electra Palace hotel, there was archaic reassurance in this thought, that a feminine hand drew wools through canvas, slowly building a picture, painstaking, a mosaic of colours, and that her consciousness enveloped him loosely, in patience, not questioning him, not giving him the third degree about Phil. Any husband who betrayed a woman like this would be a fool, he thought. She was a throwback to the Proverbs, a good woman beyond the price of rubies, who puts her hand to the distaff and the spindle and who opens the same hand to the poor . . . It was he, Edward, who fell into that category now, and whose needs she had met with unquestioning generosity. She had called for a doctor, who had come and given him a sedative and who had promised to return if his eyes did not improve after a rest. He blinked them now, not really wanting to put on his spectacles to find out. In the museum offices, he had had the sensation of eclipse, not signifying the wisdom of blind Tiresias. He had reeled in and out of an hysterical obscurity as he had lain upon the couch, an Oedipus, he thought, sightless from years of willed unseeing.

Edward gave a long, cold shudder and forced himself to fumble for the heavy glasses that lay upon the bedside table. If he could see Catherine's sewing hands even in a blur, then the occlusion must have been temporary – unless, of course, he had had a mild stroke as everyone seemed to fear. He grasped them and put them on. The room began slowly to come into focus. No, it had been an emotional reaction, he was sure of it. The doctor had wanted him to go to hospital, but he had bargained his way out of that. Yes, he could see, and even though the blind panic came muffled up through the receding effects of the medication, he did feel rested now, and better.

Perhaps she had heard him move, perhaps she came responding to some intuition. 'How do you feel?' she asked as she slipped in from the balcony.

He nodded, not really wanting to speak, but she seemed to require it of him and so he replied that he felt almost recovered. Catherine moved to the telephone, picked it up and spoke. 'I'm ordering you something to eat,' she said, 'something light.' He nodded again, too weak still to object. He had not eaten all day and had no idea what time it was now. She again withdrew, presumably so that he could gather his wits, use the bathroom. He found his way there and splashed cold water over his face.

'Come and sit outside with me in the fresh air,' she said when the food arrived. In fact, she had got the hotel to rustle up some grilled fish and a glass of wine. Sitting on the balcony, he found them very restorative.

'Now,' she said, clipping off a thread and resting her hands in her lap, 'tell me what happened. Do you think you can?'

His own hands felt useless. He flapped them somewhat on his knees. 'I'm afraid there's not much I can tell you,' he said. The thought of Phil and the little girls nauseated him. Perhaps because of that he found his memory clenched shut. There had been a dreadful accusation . . . no, more. It came slowly back, a heavy train of thought. He painfully wanted to talk, and yet it was as if one of his natural functions had ceased and, when he opened his mouth, nothing came.

'It's all right, I can wait,' she said. 'And you mustn't feel any pressure. It might make you feel better, that's all.'

He gazed over the balcony wall towards the sea. To his surprise, the sun was setting in the west. A faint, murmurous clamour came from the square below. It was evening and the Thessalonians were taking their preprandial stroll. 'Phil Deals threatened to kill me.' Edward knew this was a distortion, but it had come out that way.

'What! I'm ringing the police!'

Edward shook his head. 'There is no need for that. I hardly think he will act on it.'

'He nearly achieved his end if you ask me!'

Despite the painful intensity of his feelings, Edward more or less managed to smile to himself at Catherine's hot defence of him. His earlier sentimental picture of the ideal needlewoman popped like a cartoon bubble in the face of her battle-axe ferocity.

'He accused me of causing Susannah's death.' His words extended directly from the wound; they were out of his mouth before he had thought about them.

'I don't believe it! How were you supposed to have done that?'

'Oh, indirectly, of course. I'm supposed to have egged her on, encouraged her in a way that led to an empty martyrdom when she, well, was out on a limb emotionally speaking.' Edward found this difficult to say. Suddenly, he felt annoyed. It had been his business to preach Christ Crucified, not to treat Susannah's inner wounds.

What, then, should he fear from Phil Deals's attack? He half expected Catherine to splutter in outrage. She looked at him for a long time in the dusky light.

'Did you?' she inquired. Then she reached out her hand in an ameliorating gesture. 'I mean to say that Phil is so bizarre and the accusation so absurd that you must feel accountable in some way . . . to have reacted so strongly to what he said.'

There was an electric buzz. The hotel sign had switched on and the word 'Electra' lit up just below the balcony parapet, shining back to front, a tasteful blue.

An impulse to jump into confidences took Edward by surprise, but he reeled back from the precipice feeling the impropriety of the situation. It might scandalize Catherine were he to speak as frankly as he needed to if talk was to do him any good. He was alone with a woman in an hotel room, and in her debt as well. He moved restively. 'I tried to preach the Gospel to Susannah,' he said, uncomfortable with this evasion. 'She understood it better than I and was prepared to give more than I. She was, quite simply, a better person.' He could not see Catherine in the growing dark; the suddenness of the Aegean night took him by surprise. He felt her, however, a palpable consciousness, not hostile nor even dogged. Although she had dropped back into her chair, he could feel that her mind still hunted and questioned.

'Forgive me,' she said after a moment; 'you are still very tired, shocked. I don't mean to pry.'

He waved the apology away. 'I . . .'

'While you were asleep, I took the liberty,' she continued, almost as if she preferred nothing to his avoidance of the truth, 'of booking you into the next-door room here. I am certain that it would not be safe for you to spend the night alone in a flat in your condition, even if you were at home. Now you have eaten a little, you probably want to rest some more. There is a telephone by the bed and the staff all speak English. It's probably better than a Greek hospital, where I should be expected to nurse you anyway, and if you do not feel better tomorrow, why then we will fly home together.' As she spoke, she got up and bustled around.

Edward felt he had let her down. 'That is very kind of you, but surely—'

'Father Edward, you really mustn't worry about anything. That seems crucial. Frankly, the price of a room here is merely a drop in the ocean to me, if that is what is bothering you. Whatever else I can say for my husband Theo, he still supports me, and very well. Besides,' she said, stopping her sorting and tidying, 'I . . . feel for you.' She touched her breastbone. It seemed a difficult thing for her to say and he was moved by it. 'I could never forgive myself if anything happened to you.'

He looked up at the kindly, dauntless woman who seemed so determined to stand between him and the terrors of the night to come – and they were terrors, he was frightened. He was frightened beyond all things of confronting again the regret, a regret, now compounded by Phil into an emotion without a name. Suddenly, it occurred to him that he had hurt Catherine's feelings. She had given him a doctor, a room, a meal, but, more than that, offered an ear, herself, her friendship. 'Something already has happened, Catherine,' he said. 'Could you sit for a minute? What I have to say . . . I ask you not to tell anyone.'

She eased herself gracefully, attentively, into the chair. She sat straight and still, like a caryatid ready to bear the heavy roof of some large building. He knew he had done the right thing.

'It is difficult to tell a story,' he began, 'that began so very long ago . . . more difficult because it isn't really a story in any true sense of the word . . .'

'It's a history, then.'

'A history. Yes, I like that. And it is a history so bound up in confidential matters that, if I were to go by the book, it would probably be better not to speak of it at all. Nevertheless, Susannah is dead, and she made no secret of herself, if you know what I mean.'

'How did you meet her?'

Edward took off his spectacles and rubbed his eyes. 'I suppose I was coming up to forty at the time, a dangerous age for a man, they say, and in retrospect it might have been, although I was not aware of it then. I had been teaching at the seminary and was attached to a parish where I helped out. As a secular priest with a salary, I could have had a flat of my own, but loneliness is a problem; and I did recognize that it was easier to avoid awkward situations if I lived in some sort of community. At any rate, it was one of my duties to visit the local hospital, take Communion to the sick and so forth. And I don't think it does Susannah any disservice, rather the reverse, if I tell you that she had been admitted after she attempted suicide.'

'Ah!' said Catherine.

Edward left his spectacles on the table. Her voice was enough to make him see that she followed the drift. 'Well, among others on that ward, I was visiting an elderly woman who was in the bed next to Susannah. After a while I could not help noticing her, how unusual she seemed . . . and how no one came to see her. She would stare at me, quite fixedly sometimes, and her eyes would follow me wherever I went. In fact, I thought she was a lapsed Catholic with an axe to grind. She was very striking, Susannah, a mystery woman. She had features rather like her father's although, I may say, without the same . . .'

'Arrogance!' Catherine supplied.

'If you like. There was something both noble and remote about her. The old lady whispered to me that she had cut her wrists with a razor blade and they were bound up in an awful way. For some reason I remember that the bandages were covered with plastic. She was about to be sectioned, sent to a mental hospital, and apparently she wept every night, inconsolable tears.'

'It sounds rather romantic the way you put it.'

He laughed dryly. 'Oh, Susannah had quite a sense of drama. She wasn't ordinary, you see, and I think she did know that, and to an extent she played on it. However, at that time, she was far too miserable. She had genuinely touched bottom.

'At any rate, we sort of circled around each other without speaking, and then one day she invited me to talk to her. She beckoned. I remember the gesture; it was almost a command.

'I remember sitting down at her bedside with the resigned feeling that I was going to be inadequate. I wondered what had driven her to attempt suicide, and I had it in my head that it was a theological matter, which indeed it turned out to be, although not the kind I had expected. Somehow, I had the impression that I would have to answer for the Spanish Inquisition, the Borgia popes, and I had armed myself with the then new rhetoric of the Second Vatican Council. I needn't have had any fear.

'I shall never forget . . . a sort of awe I felt when we began to talk, not exactly at her, although she was even then quite formidable. There was a sense of something important, that I had met my . . . match? Rubicon? Waterloo? I can't describe it and it seems so foolish in any case to think of things as destined.'

'You didn't think that way. You felt that way,' Catherine said with some acerbity.

'I take your point. At any rate, Susannah talked about what she had tried to do, the worthlessness she had felt and the immense guilt she suffered from having cut her wrists. She told me all about the Catholic side of her family – that must have been yours, now I think about it! How rich they seemed in comparison with her more affluent relatives in America. The security that faith brought had always fascinated her, and yet that safety seemed a temptation to her.'

He paused, but Catherine simply shook her head, saying nothing.

'I had the most awful pity for her,' he continued. 'I can't explain it. Maybe it was because she had no pity on herself. She was hard on herself. Her suicide attempt had had to do with an ontological despair. She had felt her being to be meaningless. In fact, she was extraordinarily stoical in her way. I had the sense that she had fallen on her sword, like an ancient Roman, for some misguided reason, and finally it emerged, as you may yourself know, that her mother had committed suicide when she had been a child.'

'I had no idea! That was completely kept from us.'

'Well, it used to be a disgrace; not that I ever thought it so.'

'I wonder if that is why my mother took so dim a view of Uncle James. Perhaps she held him responsible.'

Edward felt uncomfortable, for now he remembered meeting Lady

Simon briefly at Susannah's baptism, and disliking her. She had stood as a godmother and had drawn much credit to herself for Susannah's conversion by means of an egregious false modesty about the part she had had to play in it. 'It's very likely. I knew that your mother was very attached to Susannah.'

'And . . . Susannah blamed Uncle James for her mother's death!'

He nodded.

'Your mother was admirable in the way she took Susannah in after this sad episode.' He saw no harm in saying that. 'She really came to the rescue. Susannah was allowed to go down to the country to recuperate rather than to do a spell of basket-weaving in some awful asylum. You must have been married at the time and living in Greece.'

'I was. Mummy always took Susannah's part against Uncle James, long before this breakdown. Of course, none of us had any idea why. That was so like her!'

'Well, perhaps as the result of her visit to your mother, Susannah sought me out when she returned to London after her convalescence. I was surprised to see her, but she had remembered our conversations. She had sacked the psychiatrist she had agreed to see; her mind was made up. Nothing would do but that she must become a Roman Catholic. And I was the one to instruct her.

'It is very hard to communicate Susannah's unique combination of vision and sheer barminess. She was convinced that God had brought us together. She insisted that she had lived her life as a sinner and now repented utterly, flamboyantly. Her mother had "sinned" by taking her own life. Her father had rejected the one salvation. She could be very harsh. Only the Church held that life was sacred, and so on.'

'I assume you took this with a grain of salt.' Catherine's voice came warily out of the darkness.

'Oh, Catherine, what a mixture people are! It is part of Phil Deals's case against me that I took the whole thing at face value, but that really is a bit of an irony as I held quite liberal views in those days, and I did recognize that she was probably clinically disturbed at the time. I remember that I tried to keep her in some form of contact with her doctor, even though he did sound a bit of an idiot, to tell you the truth, but she adamantly refused to do it. She was an extraordinarily categorical woman. If she had not been so intelligent and so well-educated, I would have said she was almost primitive. Religion was the solution, therefore psychiatry was not. At that time, she would not countenance the idea that the two things might overlap, or that God could act creatively anywhere He chose. Later she mellowed.'

'So, Phil is blaming you for her narrowness.'

'There is more to it than that, as you will hear. At the risk of justifying myself, what sort of situation do you think I was in? Susannah grew more and more dependent on me. Our meetings seemed to describe a circle of safety for her, almost as if the rest of the world was bedevilled, which it was for her. She was a mystic. She thought it perfectly reasonable that St Teresa had thrown holy water at demons, and when she heard God talk to her He *did* talk to her, as far as she was concerned.

'The worst of it was that I found myself becoming more and more wrapped up in her. Maybe I became dependent on her dependence. In addition to this, knowing that she had had suicidal tendencies put a gun to my own head. I began to feel that I was responsible for her life. I limited her visits, but she left me drained whenever I did see her. In retrospect, I think I felt I was carrying her tragic childhood, her genuine aspirations to God, her actual guilt as well as her spurious feelings of it . . . all at once, and trying to find some balance for her.'

'She sounds extraordinary all right! Extraordinarily manipulative.'

'You are right. But at the same time . . .'

'You loved her!' Catherine spoke softly, identifying it.

'It was what she demanded,' he said after a long pause. 'No, *needed* . . . There was nothing, Catherine . . .'

'I'm sure,' she said, reaching a hand out of the dark. 'And yet, there was everything too, wasn't there?'

'She did get better,' he said, searching the shadows.

'Maybe it was Christ who bore it then,' said Catherine. 'When you said you were carrying it all, then maybe it was not you – well, you and not you at the same time.'

'What a very nice woman you are,' Edward said, suddenly feeling that this was a lot to say.

'I think you showed heroic strength.'

'It wasn't as easy as that.'

'If it had been easy, would it have been heroic?'

'I am talking as if I had been completely dispassionate, Catherine.'

'I see,' she said slowly. 'So you are not allowed to have any feelings?'

'Oh, I'm allowed to have them!' he almost snapped. 'I'm not allowed to act on them, but that is beside the point in this case. It was, until this morning, my belief that *Susannah* had no feelings. I often thought, later, that this was why she was so good with psychopathic personalities, people whom no one else would treat. Oh, with her there was plenty of display – tears, rage, that sort of thing – and oddly enough she was never cold. In fact, before I met Phil Deals this morning, I was remembering her warmth, her vivacity. But I knew and she knew, or at least this is how I persuaded myself, that she was a misfit: a "loner" as they are fond of saying about people who commit awful mass murders. Susannah could embrace, but she could never be held. She shared her entire fortune with the poor, but she could not share a biscuit crumb of human love with anyone, not man, nor woman. It is a distinction we are supposed to applaud,' he said with a bitterness that shocked him. 'She had no friends.'

'She had Phil Deals,' said Catherine, adding, after a moment's reflection: 'There are some little bottles in the mini-bar. Would you like something strong?'

He nodded and she rose, returning promptly with some brandy and tooth glasses.

Edward swigged the thimbleful of Dutch courage. 'It was not until this morning that I heard the truth. The worst of it is that I knew it all along, though obliquely. The reasons I defended myself against it do not bear thinking about, for the consequences, I fear, were dreadful. Phil told me that Susannah had been in love with me.'

'Oh dear,' she said. It came gently out of the dark.

He sat with his hands splayed upon his knees, the pain again cruising through him.

'Would you have left the priesthood and married her?' Catherine asked after a delicate pause.

'I don't know, Catherine. I don't think so. I don't think she would have assented to that in any case, no matter what she felt.'

'But you feel you could have saved her life if you had? Perhaps I am being obtuse.'

'You are not obtuse!' he said warmly. 'But the problem is – and was – more complex than that. I congratulated myself on the way I had sublimated my feelings for her, and maybe I was right to do so. What I had not taken into account was the way in which she might have sublimated her feelings for me. This is what Phil told me. She was in the act of committing suicide all her life, and she finally achieved her ambition. She launched upon her dangerous vocation with my blessing and died with my connivance. All the time she was walking on water, she was longing to drown.'

'Father Edward!'

'Could you please call me Edward?'

'Edward. Do you think,' she cried passionately, 'that marriage or even a love affair would have made this any different?'

An annihilating loneliness almost too frightful to encounter opened itself, its empty arms, like the *shakti*, negatively aspected, of an Indian god . . . the embrace of Durga with her flat dugs and blood-slaked fangs. 'Yes,' he said. Isolation had been what they had shared, after all, he and Susannah, and perhaps they shared it even now. 'I know it.'

'And so you are saying,' she continued, the edge of desperation in her voice, 'that you redeemed her by your own love, then called it God?'

'Something like that. I never knew she would go so far.'

'Are you sure it *wasn't* God?'

'I don't know,' he said. 'I truly do not. And I do not know either if Phil's main allegation against me was even true. He told me I had rejected her. I really do not think there is anything worse to bear than that.'

'Did you? I hardly think so.'

'Well, it was she who decided to move on. Susannah. She went to live in Hackney, and though we continued to meet from time to time I believed the energy of the love had somehow changed, had been transformed, albeit in a kind of crucible, but now I'm not so sure. She did seem to have a genuine vocation. For a while, she thought about joining the Little Sisters of the Poor, but then she was not a "sister"; she was a solitary. In any event, she subsequently took advice from others and they must have had their own view . . . Still, as you said, I wouldn't have been so distressed by Phil Deals if I had not always felt there was a great deal of truth in his allegations.'

Catherine made a noise of exasperation. 'The way I see it, no one rejected anyone else. You both rejected something which you would have ultimately seen as degrading. Surely you see that. Surely you must give her credit for having that instinct. Maybe you can even see that there really was some kind of nobility in Susannah for not having pressed the matter. I don't think she could have lived with a man and, deep down, she probably knew it.'

'She was . . . inhuman,' Edward said. He looked, with wide trust, through fogged eyes at Catherine.

'It strikes me, too,' she continued, without breaking stride for the awful sorrow in his voice, 'that when you say Susannah was a psychopath *manquée* maybe you have more reason to believe it than you think. It was perhaps for that reason, her remoteness, her singularity, that I could never feel much connection with her.'

Edward sighed. 'I communicated much more to Susannah than I think I am admitting . . . and she to me. She did know.'

'I talked to Theo, my husband, last night,' Catherine said.

Despite his woeful dereliction, his ears sharpened at the change in her tone. Over years of listening, he had uncovered the voice of the live wire in people, a voice they often concealed in other, seemingly more urgent trains of thought.

'I was married for twenty-five years,' she said, 'to a man who desired another woman for nearly twenty of them. As I told you. He wants me back. I don't think I can go. The point is, however, that even I do see that he was not entirely free to choose. We're not entirely free to choose in matters of the heart. Sometimes the best we can do is to choose our behaviour. Theo chose to behave well towards me, if I am honest with myself. He renounced the woman after all and I think he tried to be physically faithful to me.'

'Then you have forgiven him,' said Edward, happy for one thing at least.

'Do you think so? I? Even though I can't quite countenance living with him?'

'Yes.' He could not see her face but felt her smile.

'Well then, to celebrate, you must forgive yourself. You chose not to damage Susannah, you could not choose how you felt.'

'Catherine . . .' he said. There was something wonderfully comforting about this ease with her over the great, dividing darkness.

'Yes?'

'Do you remember seeing the tomb painting, the one in the White Tower of Susannah and the Elders?'

'Yes.'

The upthrust hands of the triumphant girl came to his mind, a symbol of Christ's victory over death. 'It was important to Susannah. I told you. She was obscure about it even then.'

'Well?'

'I used to think of the Elders as, well, her awful father, if you will forgive me. But then it doesn't fit, does it? He never abused her, not that I know of. The "Elder" in question was me.'

'Oh, don't be daft!'

'Well, Phil Deals thinks so.'

'Wait a minute! Are you sure he isn't saying that Christianity itself is an abuse? Plenty of people think it is.'

But Edward's inner eye saw the Greek schoolgirl who had rescued him that morning, and the shaft of Phil's import again struck home. 'Susannah was much more damaged than ever I gave credit,' he said, his voice muffled by the weight of her remembered innocence.

'Well, if you are determined to flagellate yourself, then you are!' Catherine said irritably. 'I'm sorry, there I go again.'

XVI

THEO TOOK pleasure where he could these days, mostly in small things. Even though he was anxious about seeing Xenia, he looked up with wry nostalgia at the venerable Bayswater mansion block as if it and he were old friends in reduced circumstances but holding up nonetheless. His daughter was at home and expecting him.

Theo was a man who never let hot iron go unstruck; therefore, after he and Catherine had spoken on the telephone, he rang Xenia and asked her if they might talk. He wanted to see her, to consult her about ways to a reconciliation with Catherine. He had listened with awful trepidation while she turned his proposal over in her mind. He was changing his ticket for Athens to London. Would she object to seeing him?

Theo had an exact measure of his wife's strengths and weaknesses. If she was proud, she was never mean, and he knew he owed Xenia's mistrust of him to himself alone. Just after the separation, Xenia had refused to have anything to do with him, but over the past few years there had been a slow thawing in his child. They had met for the occasional painful luncheon when he was in London, and he had attended a song recital of hers at the Royal College of Music, where he had applauded loudly, a magnanimous Daddy. It had once been his ambition that she should study maritime law at Oxford, where he himself had been educated, but now, in the retrospect of years, he really did see that Xenia had been right. Her voice, once thin and pure, was maturing. And thank Heaven she kept her weight up to give it body.

Theo did not know if it was fair to get to Catherine through Xenia, but he had been open about his doubt on the telephone, and his daughter had accepted, though coolly, that she was prepared to listen to what he had to say.

Although now in his sixties, Theo was strongly built and generally exuded a decisive masculine presence. Nevertheless, he nervously prodded the bell aside his name, Phocas, and the door latch was buzzed off without the accompaniment of Xenia's voice to welcome him or even to inquire who it was. Presumably, she knew. He had not been to the flat itself for the last four years. On his visits to London, it had been easier to stay at his club or at an hotel.

He was a little aggrieved that the proprietors of the building had changed the hall. Perhaps they had written to him and he had ignored it. It was done now in a creamy, sickly beige with chandelier lights on even in broad daylight; mirrors with a marbled effect now reflected him as a good deal older than he had been on his last visit; he was stouter than he had been, though not fat, he convinced himself. His eyes, however, were faded now, dulled in aged creases. He turned away. He had always been a little vain; it was a fault, which, if he thought about it, had brought about this awful exile from his family. There was a small modern lift in the hall, but Theo decided to walk. In his childhood, when he had lived with his uncle in the flat, there had been a caged lift. The whole hall had been tiled and had had an ormolu look which he preferred to the new chi-chi swank. He was sure Catherine had been appalled by it.

Theo and his mother had come to London having fled to England after his father had been killed in the Greek Civil War. He associated the grand old mansion block with a curious mixture of feelings, a sense of unaccustomed physical safety combined with unexpected emotional terror. It had always smelt of brass polish; it did no longer. His Uncle Petros had been a minor magnate of the Howard Hughes school, if not fortune, a miser and recluse, his mother's brother, and he had changed his own name as a condition of the old man's will. Ah, he had almost forgotten what it was. Omeros. Never mind. Life worked out the way it did.

He was, in fact, frightened of Xenia and had dressed with care. When he reached the third floor, he made to ring, but she opened the door to him before he had the chance. There she stood in all her terrible beauty, dressed in jeans and a sweatshirt, suddenly a grown woman, only shorter than he remembered because she was in stocking feet.

'Xenia?' He tried to keep emotion out of his voice. She hovered there for a moment, radiant with some ineffable and unquantifiable feeling, and then embraced him with an exactly applied pressure. She had cut her long dark hair; with her oval face and dramatic, low brow, he tried not to think how much she looked like Missy.

'Papa . . .' She held out her hand as if he were an old man and led him in.

To his odd relief, Catherine had done nothing radical to the flat itself. A sailor, he steered by landmarks. The handsome old hall table was still there; above it a mirror from palmy Greek days. The furnishings had always been a bit more Austro-Hungarian than Hellenic. He smiled meekly.

'You are looking very well,' he said to his daughter, not knowing quite how to address her. 'Are you liking your course?'

'I seem to be doing all right.' They spoke in English. 'You would like some coffee, I imagine. You must be very tired from your flight. Was your trip to New York a success?'

'Oh yes.' It had been. 'I would love some coffee, thank you, Xenia.'

She padded out on her little cat feet to the kitchen and he followed her, feeling like a big sheep. 'Proper coffee . . .' She smiled and put on a stew of grains in a lipped pan, boiling it up with expertise. The kitchen had a high ceiling and was exactly what a kitchen should be. It did not pretend to be a breakfast room and was a little muddled, evidence of Catherine's absence perhaps, for she had always been very tidy.

They did not really know what to say to each other. 'I was sorry to hear of Lady Simon's death,' he said awkwardly.

'Papa! The ancient foe?' Despite her student's mufti, Xenia sailed like a lady into the sitting room with the tray. 'The funeral was ghastly. Poor Mummy.'

'That's more or less what I meant,' said Theo.

'Poor Grandmama, too,' Xenia said, looking down at the coffee she was pouring. Her words, her gestures, were Anglicized now. Theo could see her hands trembling and his were too when they took the cup which clattered against the saucer. Catherine had not got rid of the chesterfield. She had made, however, a nice tapestry screen for the fire and covered the old footstool upon which Xenia propped her socked feet.

Theo simply did not know what to say. He had not until now been fully aware of the picture he had formed in the back of his mind of this moment when he would sit alone with his daughter in the flat, talking as if nothing had happened. Now he was here and she was operating on the thinnest plane possible above the wreckage, he felt a kind of desperation which struck him dumb.

'How is Missy?' She asked this after a second's deliberation. 'It is best to get it out of the way, Papa.'

His heavy chest sank.

'I always have to know where she *is*.' Xenia leaned forward with a look that penetrated all nonsense. It was a method she had acquired from Catherine, her adoptive mother. Missy, her natural parent, would have resorted to wiles or butchery.

'I keep track of her too, Xenia, but not in the way you think!'

'How do you think I think?' she said. It would have been impertinent but for their painful history.

'I don't know. You might think I had wanted her back.'

Xenia had fine black brows which wrote a wry message in quick calligraphy; this was certainly a Greek characteristic, something from him. 'I don't know if that is a dead give-away or not. I was wondering if you had murdered her.'

'And swing for Missy?' he said out of the side of his mouth like a gangster. The joke made them both laugh a little, their eyes rooted on each other like gamblers. 'Missy has married again despite my attempts to have her put in jail.'

Xenia's face was expressive of a peculiar horror. She had had a terrible breakdown after Missy had abducted her. Theo was terrified lest his confrontation with Xenia sent her back to hospital. He could hardly contemplate his own guilt towards his child if this were to happen. Sensing this, she said, 'Don't worry, Pa. Just tell me.'

'Well, I don't think we need worry too much. She has apparently met her match at last. She is living in Alaska with her new tycoon, a Japanese who is building a museum in Nome to house his Oriental collection. Missy has always been a bit of a geisha, but I understand her present husband is quite exacting. He is a karate black belt and richer than I am – even richer than her last husband.'

A little noise of pain escaped Xenia's throat and it reverberated on the air as if someone had hit a tuning fork, pronged but with one vibration of feeling.

'I am sorry to be flippant. It is the only way I can bear it myself, the hatred. You must feel differently about her.'

She folded her slim hands on her denim lap. 'Papa, it *is* painful. There is no way around that. I can't pretend that she didn't give birth to me. I have to balance myself because of her as if I had diabetes.' She cleared her throat. 'The good thing is that I have come to love Mummy very much. Silly none of us ever saw her before, what she was made of. I really do adore her, you see, and I don't want anything disrupting her peace of mind, not even your return, which in some ways I would very much like.' She gave a nervous smile. 'Especially now that I am grown up and want to move away before too long. Next year, I want to share a flat with my friends. She makes no demands, says nothing about being lonely, but I feel it.'

'This is good coffee,' he said lamely. 'Have you spoken to her since she was in Greece? Did you tell her I was coming to see you?'

'I rang her last night after you and I had talked. I have,' she said with something approaching real venom, 'a deep hatred of concealment. As you may understand. I do not keep anything from anyone any more. It is useless telling me a secret. Please never try.'

'Xenia . . .' If he had not kept the facts of her birth from her, Missy would never have had power over their lives. 'I know I was wrong, in every way. If you make me crawl, it will only put things back.'

Xenia pressed her lips together for a moment, then suddenly the surface broke. 'I can't go forward,' she flared, 'unless I know you have actually changed. I can't sue for peace unless I have that assurance . . .'

'Xenia . . . I would hardly have come . . .'

But she was sharp with her interrogation. It had been brewing, she had thought about it, he supposed. 'You came here to see if I would intercede. My mother cannot take the humiliation of your adulteries again. Why should she be degraded? She has friends now, a life. She has even made great chums with this old Catholic priest she is travelling with. Obviously, he has listened to her and has helped her. She told me she has forgiven you, if you really want to know, but that she is not sure she could live with you again. She loves you, you see? Although I'm not sure she knows it herself. Faithful Penelope stuck with her loom while you go bounding about the world in ships. Well, don't expect me to be Tele-machus. I think I'd kill you if you are going to torture her with more of the same . . . even though I'm a girl, not the boy you always wanted.'

She was not frenzied but childish, bursting into tears now as if she were four with her little fists flying.

Theo did not know what to do. Here he was with the person whom he thought he loved the most, and she had suddenly turned into a hostile Fury. He had not wanted her to be a boy, but it seemed beneath him to say so. 'Actually, I thought you might be upset when she went to Athens about the divorce, but obviously you are not,' he finally said, then knew that it was wrong. He was shocked at his own childish reaction to her defence of Catherine, now the preferred parent when once he and Xenia had been so close.

'Papa, I have a life of my own! I am twenty-two years old. A lot of my friends' parents are divorced. It's quite the thing these days.'

For a moment, he suspected Missy in her, the cold shrug a remembered gesture, but her eyes were plaintive, two little screwed-up knots of pain. 'Xenia, my own father was killed. This may happen to many children, but knowing that never consoled me for his loss. Just as I walked down the street on my way here I thought of how long I had known this building. I first came here when I was ten years old; my mother died soon afterwards. She surrendered to her grief.' He gestured at the spacious rooms. 'My uncle did his best.' It unnerved Theo terribly to talk in such a personal way, but he pressed on. 'I am *your* father, and your mother and I both love

189

you. It might be easier to pretend that none of it matters as I did in my case, but I can promise you it catches up with you later on.'

She glanced at him. 'Am I to understand that your parents' deaths were responsible in some way for what happened between you and Mummy, you and Missy? You see, *I* happened between you and Missy.' She was shaking all over now. 'Sometimes I think I am a sort of Minotaur.'

Awful and out of hand as this was getting, Theo was a good businessman and he gauged the strength of any opponent's argument with instinct. Xenia had contradicted herself more than once, therefore he judged that she was unclear as to what she felt. He ignored the bathetic classical reference and charged down the confessional path he had taken. 'I am saying that this arid world I lived in as a child affected me; it made me egocentric and lonely. Catherine had a similar background. Our reasons for choosing each other were not shallow, but they kept us apart when they should have united us.'

'Often, when I was ill I thought it was all my fault,' said Xenia. 'It was I who wrecked your marriage to Mummy, just by existing. Sometimes I felt as if I had summoned Missy up by black magic; sometimes I still feel as if I am a carrier for Missy, like Typhoid Mary . . .'

The old, polished coffee table now stood between them like the Dispatch Box in the House of Commons. Each had a solo agenda. 'Is this getting anywhere?' Theo asked abruptly.

She looked at him with full, wide eyes. 'Yes.' She paused. 'We never spoke before on real terms. The last time I saw you . . . really saw you as my father, you gave me a gold pen to write my Oxford Entrance Exam paper. We were in the garden at Chios. I loved you so much.' She started to cry. 'It was the last day but one of my childhood and I was eighteen then. Two days later Missy turned up.'

He often saw it in his own mind, that last time he had embraced her, the apple of his eye. He nearly bellowed with frustration and reproach. He must not shout at her; he would not. She had become a fretting, vengeful girl playing his admitted sins to her full advantage. How would she grow older? he wondered. Would she be one of those women who could not draw breath without laying blame, whose husband and children would have the full blessing of living with a martyr? Whatever he could say of Catherine, she never 'moaned'. And yet, the pain that lay between him and Xenia all at once seemed too large to minimize by diminishing her in this way. Rather than speak the words that would do further damage, he inhaled them, literally holding his breath. In a long moment's silence, he looked across the room for distraction. His eyes strayed on to a cat, apparently a new acquisition, which lay stretched in soft abandon over an old wing chair his uncle had liked to occupy in the evenings. Theo had not been allowed to speak to his uncle unless spoken to. They would read, the hard, cold, selfish old man and himself, a vigorous boy. He had an urge to rise and clasp the little, luxuriant animal to himself and make it purr in his ear. He looked again at his daughter. 'Your love – the love you speak of for me – was a child's love, Xenia. You saw me as perfect and I saw you as perfect. This would have to change under any circumstances if ever we were simply to . . . like each other, appreciate each other. Maybe you are not perfect either. Is that possible?'

'I told you I am a Minotaur!' she cried with full Greek drama. She was preparing herself for operatic roles; she was a singer after all, he thought.

'You are nothing of the kind, Xenia!' He felt so weary. 'There is nothing I can do about what happened in the past. If you cannot forgive it, then you can't. Your mother and I are a separate issue in any case. We are all in a different place from when we left off, and I came to see you because we have to start from here, all three of us, if there is to be any hope. Now I know how you feel . . .'

'But you don't know how I feel!' she cried. 'You don't.'

'Understandably, you want to protect your mother from further pain.'

'You're no feminist, Papa.'

'Are you?' he asked, suddenly struck with the idea. He could not imagine they had been talking about politics, but perhaps they had been after all, all along.

She shrugged. 'Now Mummy is exempt from your patriarchal good-ness and its attendant hypocrisy, she is capable of independent thought. As a child, I simply remember her as your avatar, a bit colourless really, while all along you and I were in cahoots. That is the change you would have to imagine dealing with. Otherwise, it would be a retrograde step for everyone, even you.'

Theo wished to tell Xenia that his patriarchal goodness and its attendant hypocrisy had fed, clothed and educated her in style; that the exercise of it had rescued her at birth from Missy who had tried to kill her. He suddenly realized, however, with a kind of pleasure that he was too grown-up to try. There were some things she should never know in any case. Why wasn't he angry with her? he wondered. In the past, he would have been. Why was he so patient with it all? Beneath the steel of her educated and articulate tongue, beneath the patina of high finishing, he noticed with a kind of poetic tenderness the still-faint immaturity of her bones as they knit together, slightly knobbly at the joints. Around her eyes was the frowning seriousness when she spoke that he associated with moments of his own youth when he had thought he possessed amazing wisdom.

Feminism! It was today's lens and she saw through its spectacles, just as his mother had seen committing a kind of suttee to be the dignified end of a wife. Even for Catherine, marriage had been a privileged state, the uprooting of which had made her cry the previous night on the telephone. To him, too, it had seemed a privileged state: he had fastened special honours to Catherine, honours which she had richly deserved for her fidelity, her reserve, her high suffering as his adornment. If he had been a lesser mortal, so had men always been in comparison with honourable women. Although he disliked the popular debasement of the word icon, Catherine had been something of an icon to whom he had devoted incense and candles, special attention on feast days. There had seemed no higher thing to do with her, and indeed he had imputed a kind of wisdom to her silence, her remoteness, and had glanced at her from time to time to focus his own resources of insight.

It suddenly occurred to him to say, 'You do know I think of you as her child, as Catherine's. Do you know that? If Missy "turned up", as you say, couldn't you think of it as a kind of liberation for us all?' He had her attention. 'These struggles do not occur without casualties and wounds. The truth now is that you are the daughter of Catherine because you choose to be. And, if I am an unregenerate Balkan male, then I love you all the same.'

Her eyes were liquid for a moment, but she veiled her gaze, an old Greek trick of women.

'And as for Catherine, your mother, it is clear from what you say that she has grown since she has been away from my heavy . . . self. You too, I am sure.

'To tell you the truth, we were very unhappy and I don't think we would have been if I had given her a chance, well, to develop. And of course, if it hadn't been for the awful secret about Missy, we would never have come to live so formally. Secrets, intrigue . . . it is a Byzantine way, don't you think, to hide boxes within boxes and fashion jewelled birds that sing like nightingales . . . in preference to the real thing, or at best to protect just that – which in our case I did think I was doing, Xenia. You see, I wanted to shield you and Catherine from any unpleasantness.' He made to rise. 'Whatever the consequences of this conversation, I am glad we have had it now, although I was not too sure earlier, and for its own sake. Thank you for seeing me.'

She looked up as he stood, her lips again pressed together. 'You have had nothing to eat,' she said to him in Greek. 'You must be very hungry.'

'I am,' he replied.

'I have nothing in the house. Shall we go out?'

'Why not? Kalamares, perhaps.' It had always been a favourite restaurant nearby. Theo thought of its peach-coloured tablecloths, its friendly proprietor, with an unusual relief. He was cautious not to indulge the triumph he suddenly felt. She was looking at him honestly now, as if their conversation had removed barriers for her which were obscure to him.

'In that case, I must change!' She uncoiled her limbs which had become entwined in a tense clutch during the conversation. She glanced aside, and to his relief changed the subject. 'What do you know about this family saint?' She stood, shaking herself loose.

Theo leaned heavily back in his chair, glad himself for a diversion. 'Susannah Vaughan? I met her at our wedding. She was the only person there who seemed genuinely to wish us well. She died when you were a child. It affected me, in an abstract but serious way, like the death of JFK.'

His and Xenia's eyes were averted from each other, but their glances touched from time to time. 'I've something to show you' she said. She sprang across the room to the old sideboard which looked rather like a coffin. Theo remembered that his uncle had kept ledgers there. Xenia scooped up a handful of leaflets and gave them to him. 'I found these in St Mary and the Angels,' she said. 'You know, where Mummy goes.'

A photograph of Susannah was printed on the front, with her name embossed in Gothic letters underneath. On the back, there was a prayer: 'O God who, among your many Graces, did cause the healing of Susannah Vaughan to bear fruit in the care of the mentally ill, grant, we beseech you, that this example of a pious life and holy death may be counted among her Saints by Holy Mother Church, and that our hearts may be kindled with a desire to imitate her love of the poor and her faith. Into your hands we commend our spirit. Through Christ our Lord, Amen.' There was an address in fine print of a society formed in her honour, and it invited those with evidence of her successful intercession to write to them.

'Good Heavens!' said Theo.

'I asked the priest. He said someone must have just put them there. He said she must first be counted Venerable, then Blessed. But I notice he has not taken them away. He said he had known her and she had done much good. What a wonderful face she had!'

Together, they gazed at the rough, photocopied portrait, blurred both by time and amateurish reproduction. Theo restrained his deep desire to put his hand on Xenia's shoulder and studied the picture of Susannah unseeing. He wondered if Xenia, who had been brought up Orthodox, was making a point about Catherine's persistent Catholicism, or even declaring her own change of heart, but he decided not to mind even if this was the case.

'I think she looks a bit like Grandmama,' Xenia said.

He made a second effort to scrutinize the picture. At once, a kind of pity stole over him. The face of the dead woman, touching, somehow, through the fuzzy printing, seemed to reach out with its shy smile, straight in its appeal to him, perhaps for herself, perhaps for Xenia, or perhaps even for him. 'A little like her, I think,' he said out of good manners to the memory of Lady Simon, 'but maybe more like Mummy in a way.' He sketched this compliment to Xenia's sensibilities somewhat falsely over the high brow of the dead woman and down her cheekbone.

'She can pray for us if she likes,' Xenia said, and then, with an almost imperceptible pressure on his arm, she skipped away to change her clothes.

Theo dropped the prayer leaflets on the coffee table and went to the window. The scene through the glass of growing April evening was somehow unfamiliar though he had long known it. A dusky, violet light lay heavy on the air above the endless traffic, and in Hyde Park beyond he could see the tips of trees, their budding leaves illumined.

XVII

IT WAS early in the morning when Catherine set out to explore the market-place, for she wanted to find the old man called Yiorgos among the traders in the lull after they had set up their stalls and before the main crush of shoppers arrived. As a wife, she had often bought the household supplies herself even though she could easily have employed a servant to shop. Although she had enjoyed its benefits, Theo's great quantities of money had embarrassed her and, besides, she had felt an English obligation to 'the village', meaning Chios town. Incongruously a Miss Mapp, she had set out twice a week to the market with a wicker trug, prodding vegetables and haggling like everyone else; it had earned her a reputation for sincerity. She was not like the foreign wives of some shipowners with diamonds and divorces and prenuptial agreements. Catherine knew that eggs were eggs. This had put a nice spin on her position in the community. Despite the barbarousness of her looks and her religion, she had been seen as a decent woman who had her priorities right, and thus had become more an ornament to her husband than the jewels he occasionally had given her for birthdays and, ironically to her, for anniversaries.

Because she was no stranger to the Agora, she knew that she would get on faster without a purblind Catholic priest in tow. So, having pushed a note under his door, she left the hotel and walked northwards along the formal arcade which stretched like something out of the dream of a surreal painter from the harbour to the centre of the city. The eggshell tint of the easterly light basted the flat planes of the arches, casting sharp, angled shadows. Catherine could hear her heels click on the lonely pavement. She was nervous, expectant of some large supranormal event. An early bus, expectorating fumes, ground by, and towards the heart of the city she heard the growing hum of the day's traffic.

She soon found the market, which sprawled untidily behind the severely geometric colonnade. Its activity was coming to a slow simmer; peering into the space before her, she was buoyed up to see the stalls being assembled, the crates and boxes heaved and trundled. Father Edward's story of the night before weighed heavily on her. She hoped he still slept and would not awake until her return, lest he think that she had obscurely rejected him. More deeply still, she hoped too that he would not hold his confession of the night before against her.

The story of the blameless old priest had touched a subdued chord of unexpressed yearning in herself. She supposed that, in this city of ruined mosques and medieval walls, it had the romance of Crusaders' tales or stories from the harem of tragic concubines love-struck by a single glance from the seraglio window. How could he blame himself for Susannah's death? In fact, now she thought about it in broad daylight, it was an unwittingly self-centred thing to do. In a sense, it diminished her cousin's autonomy and failed to address her genuine religious conviction. Still, one always blamed oneself for lost love: of that she was obscurely certain. As if grief were not punishment enough! Catherine shook her head.

Now that she stood, however, at the mouth of the market, she suddenly realized that, for all her bravado in coming out so early, the secret timidity which often undermined her best intentions suddenly dragged her back. Where to find this Yiorgos? It was easy enough to ask, but somehow she did not like to. As she harnessed her bag to her shoulder and stepped into this new territory, the market seemed to unroll before her like a complicated Oriental carpet. Jars of every conceivable pickle glowed yellow and red and green from crowded shelves alongside vats containing olives of every size and description. Heaps of fish glistened on packed ice: squid and octopus, red mullet, tuna. She strolled and the traders observed her unfamiliar form obliquely. The butchers had already arranged their gruesome stacks of sheep's heads, eyeless, grinning, meaty skulls as if in the wake of Tamerlane. The poulterers hacked chickens, strung their entrails out and prodded for the heart and liver like so many augurs. Further on, there were vegetable stalls with aubergines of imperial purple, scarlet tomatoes, sheaves of flat parsley, spinach, greens, all heaped royally. She scanned the halls and walkways, but there was no sign of a coffee stall.

Wandering away from the food, she came upon a square festooned with shoddy clothes: piles of trousers, drifts of cheap blouses, knitted jumpers swinging from racks. She paused to inspect these and shook her head at the poor workmanship. Where should she start to look for this devotee of Susannah? Crones knew everybody . . . always. She searched among the black-clad women of the market; indeed, there was a whole covered shop which seemed to sell nothing but widow's weeds. Something in her rebelled from asking there.

Catherine hung indecisively, shifting from place to place; the market was starting to fill up with customers, seasoned shoppers with string bags determined to get the early worm. By noon, it would be swarming. Just as she was about to despair of her quest, she spotted it, a narrow café sand-wiched between two spice stalls. There was nobody about, but she made for one of the little tables that spilt out on to the concourse and sat, hoping that this was the right place. She had forgone her breakfast in order to get a march on Edward and so she supposed she ought to eat. Her stomach, however, was agitated. After a moment, a frail little man of indeterminate age emerged slowly from a dark hole behind some bright plastic strips, and trundled up to her. Catherine could see that he was cruelly bent with arthritis. She was convinced this must be the market character Yianna had told her about. He had every emblem of this type, looking as he did as if he had been fossilized with the place itself, embedded in it like an ancient snail.

Perhaps this perpetuity or his pain explained the curtness of his manner; making no concessions to her evident foreignness, he asked for her order in a Macedonian dialect. When she answered him in Greek, however, he smiled. She ordered coffee and toast. He shuffled off to fill this modest request; the scent of cinammon and cloves emanated from the spice stalls in the growing heat of day. Catherine decided she must act.

After rather a long time, he shuffled back with Nescafé and rolls but, before she could speak, he appraised her.

'Englis'?' he asked when he had put the tray on the table. It might be, she thought, a kind of apology for his surliness.

'And Greek,' she said in Greek, although she wasn't. 'My husband . . .' She glanced downwards. It was important to draw him out.

'Ah,' he said, admiring the man's taste like a jeweller with a good stone. 'You live in London?'

'And in Athens,' she lied. The opportunity seemed golden. 'I had a cousin who lived here in Thessaloniki, an English cousin. She died here.'

'Here in Thessaloniki?' he exclaimed with appropriate shock at some possible failure of hospitality.

'Yes indeed.' Catherine shook her head. 'It was a very sad business, a murder.'

'A murder!' He made an abbreviated gesture, a sketchy sign of the cross.

She threw up her hands, remembering how to indicate that one could do little against fate. They both shook their heads and tutted. Catherine sipped her coffee and praised the brew. 'Oh yes,' she continued. 'And I would like to visit her grave. She is buried here. No one knew who killed her.'

He shook his head again.

Catherine sighed. He did not seem to be the right man. Looking more closely at his lined face and grey hair, she decided he must be about seventy, but of course he could be younger. Maybe there was a still older café owner. Perhaps he had not worked in the market at the time of Susannah's death. Perhaps he had been a seaman and had only recently settled down because of ill health. 'She died in a very dramatic way, up on the hill . . .'

'Oh, you mean our *martyr*!'

Catherine shared her moment of victory with the shade of Agatha Christie, forgiving her at once for Miss Marple's tweedy smugness.

'You are her cousin?' He was awed.

She raised a hand, palm first, in modest acknowledgement. 'Did you know her?' She thought it best to elicit this without reference to his allegedly famous devotion.

He looked at her for a long moment, quite warily, she thought. 'She came to Thessaloniki twice every year,' he said. 'I knew her. Everyone knew her.' He scrutinized her a little longer. 'You do resemble her,' he finally said.

'I am pleased that you say so. She was a very holy woman.' Catherine tried to calculate the source of his mistrust. Was it her appearance? She had dressed with particular simplicity. Maybe he thought she was a news-paper reporter or even the police. There must have been far-reaching inquiries. 'I last saw her at my wedding,' she added. 'My mother and her father were brother and sister.'

The old man paused for a moment. 'Wait,' he said. Slowly, he hobbled back to the inner room where presumably he rested between customers. Catherine prayed that there would be no more. She could hardly breathe for excitement. After a minute, he returned, carrying a photograph in a black frame. '*Kiria* Susannah,' he said.

Catherine made Greek noises of entrancement, even though she was entranced enough in an ordinary English sort of way. If ever there were a sign of that popular religious feeling that somehow goes with sanctifiable beings, this was it. Susannah, formal as an icon, stood in the market, her arms full of bread stacked like symbols; her lips were parted in a nimbus of a smile. She was wearing ordinary everyday clothes, the sort that simple Greeks could themselves afford, the sort that surrounded Catherine now in the stalls where a growing clientele fingered the goods. Susannah had clearly been asked to pose for the picture, and it had been blown up and framed expensively.

'We looked forward to her visits,' the old man said sadly. 'Each evening when she was here, she came at the end of the market to collect the food that was not sold during the day. At first, we thought that she was one of those British ladies who worry about Greek cats . . .'

Catherine laughed. The tourist cat lobby was certainly a strong one.

'But then we saw that she was feeding the poor. No one knew where she came from. She could not speak Greek well like you, but she was not a tourist.'

'I am amazed that she did not offend people,' Catherine said, for it suddenly struck her how arrogant this behaviour could have appeared. And at once, remembering her own obligations of conscience, she noticed how twisted the poor man's body was; not to be outdone by Susannah, she offered him a chair.

He sat gratefully. 'She had a good heart,' he said, thumping his own chest for emphasis. 'She was meek and gentle. No one minded her. She was not trying to be critical of us. In fact, she tried to conceal what she was doing. I do not think even her family knew. If she had not hidden her good actions, then maybe she would not have died. It was one of those she tried to help who killed her.'

'Do you know that for certain?' Catherine exclaimed.

He shrugged. 'It is what is said. Your cousin,' and here he used a polite form indicating the highest respect, 'had a particular care for the insane, those who could feed themselves but would not. Sometimes she would mix up bread and egg and milk and feed them with a spoon as if they were babies. They say the one who killed her was a man called Alexos, a very dangerous type.'

Could it be as simple as this? Catherine could hardly believe her luck. Perhaps the old man was addled. On the other hand, he gave no evidence of rambling; his rheumy eyes focused on her with an almost clinical stare, as if he were feeling his way towards a definitive diagnosis of her character. She had forgotten the subtle, intuitive flair of Greeks, a shrewdness born out of centuries of unwilling accommodation to conquerors, Frankish or Ottoman. 'Did the police know about this Alexos?'

The old man shrugged again. 'Maybe they knew, but what could they do to prove it?' he said obscurely. 'After the death, he disappeared. There are travelling people to the north, Romanians, gypsies, Albanians, Bulgarians . . . who knows? He could simply have joined one of their caravans. Others have it that he was sent to Leros.'

This was the island near Patmos in the Dodecanese where there was a huge state asylum. The newspapers had exposed it some years before and Catherine remembered with a twinge of horror the photographs of naked bodies being hosed down as in concentration camps. Perhaps it had improved.

'His mother lived here in Thessaloniki,' he said, with a sudden, curious bitterness. 'She could have got him away and destroyed the evidence.'

'Do you think he followed Susannah home from the marketplace?'

The old man gazed at the photograph, saying nothing. Catherine had the unsettling impression that he was communicating with the dead woman through the means of the picture. He searched its eyes.

'She was a woman,' he said at length, as if this demonstrated the obvious. 'Alexos could not tell the difference between women and women.' He gave a shudder. 'And I told you, your cousin was a martyr.'

All of a sudden, everything connected in Catherine's mind. 'A virgin . . .' she said softly, first in English, then in Greek. So Susannah had taken the time-honoured course Catherine thought she would have eschewed herself: death rather than dishonour, an archaic concept.

He made a gesture appropriate to the delicacy of this. 'It was said.' He looked at Catherine carefully. 'She was very innocent, like a child. He was insane.'

'And that is why she was hacked to pieces . . . Of course!'

The wizened man nodded, suddenly a sage with his swollen knuckles clasped painfully together on the table. 'She defended her honour. The honour of her family.' His look gave Catherine the benefit of this heritage.

Catherine thought wryly that the Holy Office could want no more. And yet, given Susannah's nature, it was a reasonable explanation, which in all probability had been given out in the first place by the Greek police. It had been rendered suspect only by the story of the theft. From Thessaloniki, it would have been relatively easy for a certain kind of drifter to disappear beyond the borders to the then Communist north or even across the sea. It remained to be seen whether Susannah had died defending her virginity, but the brutality of the murder and the legend surrounding it of a 'martyrdom' gave credence to an explanation of a failed sexual assault. All of this fitted if the Head of Dionysos had never existed, but what if it had? 'Could this Alexos have stolen anything?' she asked.

'They say so; they say the murderer stole an ancient treasure, but I do not think so. This Alexos was too confused to do anything like that. It is a long time ago, and maybe he is dead.'

Catherine looked up sharply at the suddenly oracular face of the twisted man. 'You know, don't you!'

There was a terrible unease between them, then very slowly he spoke.

'I know that he never hurt anyone else and that he is dead. He was my brother.'

Catherine stared at him for a long time. 'Why are you telling me this?'

'I see her picture every day. I have a light burning. Everyone knows through me that she was a saint. This is what I have done for her. Now, there is no one left to hurt by the truth. You need to know. You are her family. I do not think that you will betray me.'

She slowly shook her head.

'My brother was very strong . . . big . . . He had the strength of a madman . . . But the family took care of it. He was punished.' He winced, and Catherine had an odious mental picture of a felled ox, squealing in terror as it was sacrificed. 'Was your cousin Orthodox?' he asked.

'No, Catholic.'

'It is no different. Maybe to the priests, but not to me.'

'She is going to be made a saint,' Catherine said, suddenly confident of this, 'and she would not want revenge.'

The old man gave a wonderful smile to the portrait. 'Just as I thought,' he said, nodding his head gravely. 'Ask anyone, anyone here old enough to remember her. Sometimes she would be all night down at the harbour with the old drunks and prostitutes. Everyone trusted her. She was very *dignified*. She liked their company, like the Lord. She drew people to her.'

Catherine hesitated. 'If it could be proven that your brother killed her because she resisted him, then it would be easier . . .'

He smiled and shook his head. '*They* must know, up in Ano Poli, up at the house where she died. I am sure they know more than I do. As for me, I am not certain that this is why she died exactly. I swear it. But in my soul I know.'

Catherine sighed. 'Well, I suppose we could say that it is known among the people . . .'

'Lady,' he said, 'what proof is there but *Kiria* Susannah herself? But, if you want, I will write what I have told you, and when I die my statement may be opened. I have no children, and my sister's children all live in America in big houses. They do not remember me.'

The face of the old man was contorted. '*She* brought you here,' he said. 'I have been waiting for someone like you to come for many years. She will have her justice.'

Catherine went to the nearest kiosk and picked up the telephone which stood, a reminder of her Aegean past, on a shelf amid the racks of newspapers, and dialled the hotel. After a few rings, Father Edward picked up the receiver, and she was amazed how relieved she felt to hear his voice.

'Edward?' she said, having to swallow down the 'Father'. 'Are you all right?'

'Thank you, I slept very well. I am much better. Thank you for your note.'

'I've had spectacular success,' she said. Briefly, she told him what the old stall–holder had said, including his promise of documentary evidence.

'Why, that is extraordinary! It would seem our business is ended, then,' he said, but his voice sounded flat.

Catherine's head was buzzing as if she had unleashed a hive of bees. An acute feeling of falling short of the whole story stung her. 'Look,' she said, 'I have some things to do, and I shall be gone for another hour or so. I suggest that you rest. I wouldn't go out. I . . .' It struck her that Phil might have been in earnest with his threats. He was mad enough, she suddenly thought, and he really hadn't anything to lose. 'Well, you never know.'

'You're not going—?'

'I'll see you later. Goodbye!' she said briskly and put the telephone down. She had never been so resolute, but now that she had taken the reins she felt slightly self-conscious about it. Nevertheless, she fished the keys to the rented car from her pocket, and walked the necessary mile to find where she had put it for the night. She had a ticket. She ripped it off the windscreen and shoved it down on the seat beside her. Some things never changed. Spiky with nerves and irritation that she had left her reading glasses behind in the hotel, she voyaged out into the growing stream of cars, without the benefit of being able to consult the map which lay in the glove compartment. She pointed the nose of the car vaguely to the north-east, only to find herself forced into a westerly direction by the one-way system. Here and there, memorials of an opulent past loomed, old Turkish baths with graceful domes, a vast neoclassical mansion with pierced windows and balconies sugared with wrought-iron. It was extravagantly Levantine and Catherine could not help but admire it.

She lurched through the traffic, like some confused homing pigeon, hoping to get her bearings and right her course. Suddenly, the famous Rotunda came into view, just above the Arch of Galerius, which was swathed in scaffolding and green netting. This time, she had gone too far east. At last she found a gap and nudged the car into the right stream; she swung past the ancient forum, and found herself once more in the Upper City, where suddenly all was quiet. Catherine realized that she had forgotten to bring her uncle's address and she could not remember it. The streets rose almost vertically up towards the old acropolis, where the thick, crenellated Byzantine walls shone fiercely in the morning sun.

She drew the car to a halt in a relatively horizontal spot where it did not seem in danger of actually toppling down the hill. Wearily she got out, and now, thinking her plan misconceived, looked around her. To her right, she spied a tiny church tucked behind the crumbling houses. A finger-post announced that it was Ossios David, the Church of Holy David, and at once she remembered that Theo had recommended it when they had spoken on the telephone. She smothered a sudden flame of anxiety. Xenia had told her that Theo was flying to London. What did he want? What was he going to say? Catherine silenced herself: she had schooled herself harshly never to interfere between the two of them.

Out of curiosity more than anything else, she scaled the steps that led to the little church, thinking that she could at least catch her breath and on holy ground too. She had flapped up the hill like a demented moth in her pursuit of Phil and her uncle, and if she was not yet able to find the house maybe it was a blessing in disguise. An elderly woman, the ubiquitous and eternal keeper of Greek sacred places, nodded at her approach and shoved a leaflet into Catherine's hand. The church was very old, fifth century AD, and the mosaics had been covered with cowhide to save them during the fevered time of the Iconoclasts. The aged guardian wearily brandished the key, and Catherine followed her inside the dark building. The old woman snapped on some lights, then left, clearly satisfied that Catherine would do no harm to the fabric of the church.

She was struck, not exactly off balance, for she had been in an unbalanced mood, by the loveliness of the mosaic in the apse above the altar. It was a very unusual depiction of Christ as a beardless boy, seated on a rainbow, His right arm stretched upwards, a youthful, inclusive gesture; in His left, He held a scroll. Around Him, the beasts signifying the Evangelists emerged from the bright cloud of His glory as if they had somehow been happily stunned by it. Catherine squinted at the leaflet: it was the Vision of Ezekiel. She shook her head sadly. It had been made when Christendom had been united, long before the Great Schism, but despite its age the colours were fresh as morning, wonderful, glittering blues and greens and tints of rose . . . nothing sombrely Byzantine. The mosaic was startling, alive, as if, after secret, shameful doubts about it, its maker had come to the obvious and evident conclusion that the Resurrection really after all had taken place, and would take place, and maybe even did – in small and unregarded ways – take place in the drift of ordinary life, proceeding as it did from the timeless source of energy which fizzed out of the mandorla.

Just for an instant, she was reminded of the couchant Dionysos riding on his leopard, the one Passides had shown her and Father Edward, but although there was a similar sense of youthful repose in the limbs of both figures, a similar androgyny, there the resemblance stopped. The mosaic seemed to draw her into its cloudy nucleus, just as if she had been told a secret impossible to give away for its lack of cognates in a human tongue. At once, she felt revived and at peace, no mystic, simply a tired human being, restored to a state of balance and normality.

Catherine sat for a moment on one of the carved wooden seats ranged along the wall and blinked at the wonderful Christ bathed in His glory. Her mind suddenly whirled free from the confusion of the last few days. In fact, she admitted to herself, she had been in a dreadful turmoil for some months. Her mother had died and she had not allowed herself really to think about how uprooting it had been. It seemed hypocritical to cry, but now with a deep pang she saw how irrevocable it was that they had denied each other love. A shadow of the old, elegant lady seemed to pass through her and she shuddered; the matrix of her own being was now displaced. She had gone into hospital for a trivial operation and her heart had stopped. Catherine had been to see her a few nights before she had died because she had been visiting Charles and Rosamund in London. Not even the smallest inkling of the abyss that would separate them had charged their goodbye, only the familiar, ceremonial kiss, the inquiry about Xenia, the veiled query about Theo.

Catherine looked again at the ambiguous Christ with its almost feminine grace. She had spent her entire life making sacrificial offerings to her mother, secret ones designed to meet the old lady's approval; her only rebellion had been to marry Theo. Suddenly, she had the urge to start a formal, keening wail. Susannah had received this royal bounty, her mother's love, for free. Was this because she had made the right sacrifice? Susannah had offered everything to God, of Whom the gleaming mosaic figure on the wall was just a shadow. She had risked everything on this one gamble, and gone beyond the need for human affirmation. It seemed cruel that she had gained it almost inconsequentially . . . Lady Simon, Edward, even the old man in the market loved her.

The implications of this struck Catherine, but not unkindly. *She had been waiting all her life for life to happen.* It was always just about to occur, or had occurred. Susannah, on the other hand, had occurred in the moment. She had been faithful to time, not history, for where the Alpha began and the Omega ended was one and the same for the true student of the inscrutable alphabet, the seemingly garbled language of God.

In a flash of intuition, Catherine saw herself in the outstretched moment of not wanting anything to be that wasn't. It seemed enough to be integral to what was now, and with a long-drawn shuddering breath of relief she saw her cousin for the first time feelingly, more surely than if she had entered the church and sat down beside her. An immense understanding came to her of genuine being, not a spirit who did magic tricks, nor the victim of some masochistic urge. She had been, after all, generous and, like a particle of the shining mosaic, she now lived indestructibly, both static and phosphorescent, a part of the whole body and necessary to it, a woman who had reduced the proportions of her ego to the thinnest substance through which the uncreated light could shine. Somehow, even the brutal murder seemed to make sense; it was as if some primal demi-urge, some primitive instinct in life she had abandoned, had needed the blood of Susannah. Indeed, it had been bound to happen. The ancients would have perfectly understood it: Andromeda had been chained to her rock, St Catherine, indeed, to her wheel.

Catherine shivered and shook herself. In all the reports, nothing had been said about a rape. Susannah must have struggled horribly, and no one had come to her aid.

A feeling of lightness and freedom suffused her despite the growing and unpleasant certainty of what had actually happened in the house that night. With one last look at the mosaic, she realized that it had been necessary to Susannah to resist her attacker, not out of prudery nor even purity.

All of a sudden, Catherine knew that her cousin had indeed been in love with Edward, perhaps quite deeply, but she had severed it as sharply as she had surrendered her own life because she had loved something else more . . . no, someone. Was it really possible in this age? God had been both her destiny and her delight.

Catherine stood, calmer now and ready to face her uncle and Phil Deals.

The truth was beginning to take form, and in an ugly pattern.

XVIII

THE BOY Ali had no English or he chose not to speak it. Even if Edward had spoken Greek, he could not have made himself heard above the dogs, which hurled themselves, snarling, against the chain-link fence. He had come up by taxi, on a hero's errand, to protect Catherine, for he had been sure she meant to visit her uncle alone. Now, however, he felt he made a poor Herakles against this Cerberus: the two dogs looked as one in their whirring visceral rage.

'Is Phil Deals at home?' he cried over the cacophony.

The child looked quite at home with the animals. He was too far away for Edward to read his expression, but his body was slack and still.

In a moment, he thought, Phil would arrive at the gate, warned of a stranger by the noise. It struck Edward now that all Deals needed to do was to slide back some bolts and the wretched animals would tear out his throat. Phil could always explain that there had been a mistake; Ali had forgotten to lock the gate; Edward had looked like an intruder to the dogs.

Where, then, was Catherine? Was she inside already? With the savage animals unleashed she would be stranded in the house; the two men could do what they liked with her. The horror of Susannah's death was frozen to a density within him, almost as if it were a memory, and it repeated itself. He gazed unseeing into the terrible compound.

He wondered if the murderer had really been this Alexos whom Catherine had mentioned on the telephone. And, if this were true, had it really been Susannah who had let him in? Maybe Deals had 'slipped' again with another child. Maybe Susannah had confronted him and it had been all too simple to hire a down-and-out to silence her.

'Let me in!' he cried, shaking the fence despite the gnashing teeth of the dogs.

The boy said something, shrugged, then ran away back to the house.

'Edward!' A voice behind him made him whirl round. For a fraction of a second, he sensed the presence of Susannah herself, released, transmogrified. When he saw Catherine standing behind him, he was at once relieved but, oddly enough, no longer disappointed.

'Catherine! Thank God!' he said.

'What are you doing here? You must be mad!'

206

The animals redoubled their fury, and then for no apparent reason it seemed to abate.

'I could ask you the same question. I came because I suspected you might come here. I did not think you would be safe.'

Catherine looked Father Edward up and down and suppressed a smile. With his bottle glasses, his studious face, his rusty black sleeves waving in the air, he looked no match for a tabby cat, much less the snarling curs behind him. Somehow this made him all the more endearing, a Don Quixote in a craven world. 'I came alone because I didn't want you to be exposed to any more. I thought *you* wouldn't be safe,' she said.

'Well, neither of us is.'

'Oh, dearie me, callers!' They turned, startled by the insinuating voice of Deals. 'And me without a bite to eat in the house.' Either he had come very quietly to the gate by a circuitous route, or he had simply materialized. The dogs had retreated at the nearly imperceptible motion of his hand. He scratched their hackles, then slowly drew the bolts. 'We got dog meat, though, so don't worry. You're not on the menu.' He snapped his fingers, in total control, and the animals slunk away, growling, as the heavy gate opened. 'I guess you'd better come in. What's the difference? No big deal,' he said. He was wearing jeans and a sweatshirt, and for the first time Catherine saw how old he really was, a fragile vessel for all the malice he contained.

She was frightened, but she sailed in and down the path as if she were not. 'Father Edward and I will be leaving soon. We have come to say goodbye to my uncle,' she said, inventing it on the spur of the moment.

'Oh, we *will* be disappointed!' Phil cried. And at some level, she subtly thought, he might be. 'I'm awfully sorry,' he continued, 'but Uncle isn't up yet. He is not able to receive.'

Now faced with his tormentor, a slow enlightenment crept upon Edward, and he let it rise upon him until he saw the way. The Head . . . of course. 'However that may be, I need to see him,' he said.

'Need?' said Phil. 'You need?' His face was distorted with hatred. The dogs crouched at his feet, heraldic, as if their aggression had found its true expression in their master.

A strange dissociation split Catherine. She both feared and did not fear, almost as if she were floating above the scene. In this serenity, she remembered what Passides had said about her uncle and how none of his colleagues had been able to get past Phil to see him. And, although she did not forget her promise to old Yiorgos, she said, 'We have new information about Susannah's death.' She gripped her hands tightly together, bluffing. 'The police are on to it now.'

'He does not want to see you. Can I make myself plainer?'

'Then I would like to hear it from him,' Edward said. 'If he is too ill to tell me that, then he should be in hospital.'

'I thought we had a little chat yesterday. I thought we established some ground rules.'

'Well, of course, you did threaten to kill me, but I suppose what was sauce for Susannah is sauce for me.'

'I did not kill Susie!' Phil screeched.

'I wish to see her father and I wish to see him alone.'

'You don't know what you're doing!'

Even at the time, it struck Catherine that the spirit that fired her to tackle Deals was not alien to her basic nature. What had attracted her to Theo so many years ago seemed to rekindle; she had chosen to marry, in her mother's eyes, a Levantine buccaneer perhaps because she was a little bit of one herself. Boarding this ship, she blazed with a fine rage. 'As a matter of fact, I think we do know what we are doing,' she said. 'I think we need to be assured of Uncle James's welfare and, if we are not, then all sorts of trouble could follow. Greece is a member of the EU, you know. And then . . . my husband . . . might well take an interest.' She caught her breath at this last. Had she made a decision counter to the decision she thought she had made? Perhaps she had seen a glimpse of it the first day she had met Father Edward in Athens.

'You're lying!' he said. 'You don't give a damn about Uncle.'

'Actually, I can see myself becoming very worried about him indeed.'

'Great!' said Phil. 'That *will* make a nice change. The way you guys have treated Uncle in the past must be a world record. What are you going to do? Put him in a nice Sunset Home? He'll love it.'

'It's not about that, Phil,' she said quietly. 'You're his gaoler. And I want to know why.'

For Edward, the sensation was not unlike sailing. He leaned back and let her billow forth. Certitude . . . She knew. Of course.

Phil rocked slightly, caught off balance.

'Let us hear it from him that you are not,' she continued, 'and without the benefit of your interpretations.'

'I never heard anything so ridiculous! You think I'm going to let you put an idea like that into the head of a sick old man? You must be joking.'

'There are two ways of looking at the keys, Phil.' Alive to the drama of it all, she stabbed a finger at the jingling bunch in his hand. 'Anyone would naturally assume that you and my uncle had every reason to lock the world out. But I think you have a better reason to lock Uncle James in, and that has something to do with the night Susannah died.'

She had half expected, indeed she had hoped, that he would deflate at this, just as he had done when she had challenged him the first time they had met. Instead, he grinned with a purposeful leer as if some wonderfully obscene riposte had occurred to him and he was savouring it before spitting it out.

Then, capricious as always, he seemed to change his mind. 'I suppose I don't see any harm in letting you inside,' he said. 'Maybe it is about time we did have a little chat about Uncle. You might be getting more than you bargained for, but it's really up to you.'

'I insist on it,' said Catherine.

'Very well . . . You'll be sorry.' He intoned this like a child in a hide-out where no grown-ups were allowed.

'If you are threatening Catherine, I cannot countenance her entering this house!'

'Oh, *relax*,' said Phil.

'I assure you, I could be even more pompous in a court of law,' Edward said. It struck him more forcefully than ever that the seemingly arbitrary leaps of the games master were wonderfully designed to put every opponent at a disadvantage.

Phil rolled his eyes. 'OK, OK. You and the fair Catherine are to remain unmolested. Think of it. Why would I molest you anyway? I have nothing to hide and, although that may not go for Uncle, you will have to make up your own mind on that score. If you would have done anything other than I have done, then I'd love to hear it.'

With a theatrical flourish, he unlocked the house; Edward and Catherine followed him in.

The downstairs hall was quiet, almost unnaturally, so it seemed to Catherine. She peered around its gloom, wondering where her uncle slept. She had bluffed her way in only on a hunch that Phil had been mistreating her uncle, but, now she was there, the suspicion grew. Why hadn't she taken it seriously that Susannah had been genuinely worried about her father? Her cousin had operated on such a high moral plane that the anxieties of real life seemed beneath her. Catherine peered dimly at a shut door at the end of the passageway and remembered the general arrangement of this sort of house. The kitchens, she supposed, were ahead of her, with perhaps a courtyard beyond. Around it would be arranged the ground-floor complex. Perhaps his bedroom was in there.

She glanced at Edward. Even in the shadows, she could see he was pale. 'Could you tell me exactly where Susannah died?' he asked Deals, his voice thin and peremptory.

'You're standing on holy ground right now.' Phil spoke as if they had been ghoulish sightseers.

'Thank you,' said Edward. He was ashen. 'And so her body was dragged here? Or did she crawl here from somewhere else?'

Deals jerked his thumb at the shut door beyond them. 'She was in the kitchen. Listen, do you really want to know about this?'

'Why was she in the kitchen?' Edward pressed on.

Phil's face was impassive. 'She was cooking Uncle his supper. I was out for the evening, and this is well and truly established. My brother Geoff and his wife came to Thessaloniki and took me out to dinner. You can check if you like – that is, if you can get through to him. He's the head of our very, very big family firm, and could probably eat Mr Phocas for breakfast, if you're thinking of making too much out of this, Cousin Catherine.'

'Could she have been cooking food for anybody else?' Catherine suddenly asked.

'Oh, you mean Susie's everlasting soup kitchens?' Deals seemed relieved. 'Uncle didn't like it. He said she encouraged the riff-raff that way. In fact, the police thought it was one of her clientele, attracted by rich pickings.'

'The thief, you mean,' said Catherine.

Their eyes focused on the rug as they spoke. In contrast to the other furnishings of the hall, it was relatively new, a replacement, perhaps.

'He got in through the kitchen window, did he?' Edward asked.

'I thought Uncle *told* you. She let him in . . . whoever it was.'

'And he stole the Head of Dionysos,' she said with a faint interrogative note in her voice.

Together, Catherine and Edward lifted their gaze to Phil, who looked at them with unadulterated disdain.

'He didn't, did he?' she said. 'He didn't steal the Head.'

'What's it to you? It was fifteen years ago.'

'He didn't steal the Head because you did,' she said with an awful finality. 'Didn't you?'

' "Curses! Foiled again!" ' said Phil, snapping his fingers in parody. 'You want to know the story? I'll tell you the story.'

'The truth would be better,' said Edward. The chill of the hall seeped into him. Here he was; she had died here, dragged from the kitchen. Had she screamed? Maybe she had begged for mercy. A primal loyalty to her, wider than he had ever suspected, opened in him, a love beyond mere predilection. She had not been raped, that he knew for sure. He knew Susannah for sure and, for this brief elected moment, utterly.

'At the risk of sounding like Pontius Pilate, I'm never sure what truth is,' Phil said. 'Come into the murder room if you like. If you can digest it, I'll make you some coffee, give you a "bickie", as James so endearingly calls it.' He strode down the hall and flung open the door. Before them was an old-fashioned kitchen with grease hanging from the ceiling, smelly dog beds, a sink full of washing-up. The light from the courtyard beyond was dimmed by the dirty windows. 'Cheerful, isn't it? We didn't have the heart to redecorate.'

Phil scraped back three chairs from around the cracked formica table in the centre of the room and put the kettle on to boil. Catherine and Edward sat rigidly, their backs resisting any comfort. 'Look at you two,' he said, 'like a couple of social workers. I can see you don't admire the hygiene of my kitchen.' He stood, his arms folded over his chest. 'But then it is more hygienic than it was. It took ages to mop up the blood.'

It had been a long time since Edward had sized up an antagonist, for he had never been given to battle, even crusade. What was more, he had literally to pray for the grace not to take revenge. *'A pure heart, create . . .'* He could not help but notice, though, that Phil's weakness was betrayed in the cocky stance he took, centre stage.

Deals smirked and leaned against the sink. 'Are you ready for what happened? Then here it is. The night Sue died was Easter Saturday, just before the Orthodox Vigil was at an end. I met my brother Geoff and his ass of a wife in town and, because of the Lenten fast, it was hard to get a meal, so it took us a while to find a restaurant. The Jewish Passover *was* over that year, however, and we managed to get a bite down by the harbour. We stayed a long, long time over our meal, because there are always a lot of things Geoff wants to know about me, and part of my condition of freedom has always been to give him an update every year.'

Catherine was puzzled. 'Condition . . .?'

'Well, an A-plus to the Venerable Edward. He may be a witch doctor but he isn't a grass. Never mind. I digress. Apart from being my brother, Geoff is also my meal ticket. Every cent I have is trussed up in trust. We negotiate. James never gets involved. That's *my* condition. Anyway, we were eating this meal for a long time, and it was only when I started to hear Easter noises that I decided I'd never get back if I didn't make a move. The *Epitaphos* was doing its rounds – you know, they parade the icon of the dead Christ around on a bier. Its being almost midnight, I split. Geoff and his wife wanted to see the picturesque scene . . . not for me!

'I got back home just before the fireworks began, about 12.15, just after the start of the "Christ is Risen" bit. So I can *time* it. They were setting off sky rockets just as I walked in the door. A great illumination for Susie. I would have fallen over her body in the hall if it hadn't been for the pyrotechnic blaze.' He sighed. 'So, what's to do? Shock, horror. Touch nothing, I decide, and I call the goddamn police. Try getting a Greek policeman on Easter. Susie was dead, that was obvious, but where was James?'

The kettle screamed on the cooker. Phil yanked it off the heat. 'Tea? Coffee?' He seemed almost drunk with the power of the moment.

'Go on!' Edward thundered.

Phil shrugged. 'So what do I do? I'm a bit of a hero here. I follow the trail of blood; I find it starts in the kitchen. I take the claw hammer. I go upstairs, and what do I find? There is James, crouching under the desk in his study. He hasn't got any blood on his clothes, so I think "Whew! He's alive," and then, "Thank God he didn't do it," but then I see the Head. He's got it wrapped up in sacking, Dionysos. He's got it out of the safe and he's hiding it, whimpering like an animal. He thinks I'm the burglar.

'But then again he's not deaf. Susie must have screamed and screamed. He had a gun. He could have saved her. He was mobile then. He's a good shot and he had the advantage of being upstairs. Instead, he runs to Dionysos. He saves Dionysos. He thinks the guy is going to make him open the safe, and so he opens it, makes it look like it's been broken into already and he hides with the Head.

'Now, surely you realize that James had to be punished for this grotesque act of cowardice, and I was on the verge of doing it myself with the revolver he didn't use, when the thought occurred to me that the punishment must fit the crime. So I take the Head from him and I quickly stash it with some neighbours who've made a nice little income for their silence for many years. Worth it to me at the price and I get the devotion of genuine gratitude. In the time it takes for the cops to come, James and I make up a story about the burglar. We say that James fainted dead away and that Susie was forced at knife-point to open the safe. When the police have finally gone back to their lamb soup and coloured eggs, very cross indeed about being called out on Easter, when Susie's body has finally been removed, and when we've all been questioned to death, I slip out, just before dawn. I take the Head with me to the harbour and, in the deepest part, I throw it in. Now, James finds it hard to remember the batting order

212

here. He still gets confused. Sometimes he remembers I took it, sometimes he thinks art thieves came back for it. Sometimes he thinks that it is still hidden in the house and that they will come and get it. Sometimes he even thinks Susie took it. So now you know.' Like an exhausted virtuoso, he bowed his head.

'Dear me, Phil.'

A reedy voice came from behind the door that led to the courtyard beyond the kitchen. The door had been standing ajar, presumably to let some air into the rancid place.

Deals whirled round.

Sitting askew in his wheelchair, half-dressed in a pair of stained pyjamas and swaddled in a dirty rug, James Vaughan entered the kitchen accompanied by Ali. His bedroom, Catherine realized, must have been across the atrium with its well and pots of herbs and flowers. The child must have told him they had come. 'Dear me, Phil, that *was* an interesting story.'

Phil laughed. 'Who let you out?'

'The dogs were barking, were they not? Young Ali here took pity on me and helped me into my chair. Good-morning, Catherine. Good-morning, Father Knight. Please forgive my appearance.' He turned to Phil. 'So, it was my cowardice, was it?' The old man's intensity made his frailty glow as if he were a paper lantern. 'You're prepared to say that to Isabelle's daughter? How could you tell such lies?'

Deals's eyes were fixed on the old man. A curious energy ran between them, an almost palpable current. 'If I tell lies, which I am not admitting for a minute, I've learned from the Master,' he said. They were utterly absorbed in each other, as if no one else were in the room.

The old man was the first to break the circuit. 'It is and always has been beneath my dignity to explain myself in this matter,' he said, and for the first time Catherine could see in him the flicker of an ancestral strength she recognized, one which perhaps they both drew upon.

Everyone had forgotten Edward, so when he spoke it was unexpected. Catherine thought she would never forget the quiet impact of his words. 'Under what circumstances would you think it morally permissible to lie, Mr Vaughan?' he asked. 'St Augustine has said it is never permissible; I am sure Susannah never told a lie, and that was disquieting, wasn't it? One never dared, almost, to ask her what she thought because she would tell one straight away. But, in practice, most good people would tell a lie to protect someone else. Isn't that so?'

213

The old man, as crazed as King Lear in his tattered, striped pyjamas, looked sharply at Edward. He scrutinized Phil, who gazed at his nails.

'It is not a good idea to lie even for this reason,' Edward continued softly, 'as I believe the present situation demonstrates. You did not find the Head of Dionysos in the field as you told me, did you? It came to you in another way, and it had nothing whatever to do with Susannah's murder, did it?'

There was a complete silence.

'You see, I myself might have been tempted to do exactly what you did. In fact, that is the reason I can see so closely into the situation. At the time I lost my sight, I was researching a book very important to me, and it horrified me to realize just how far I would have gone to finish it if I had had the means.'

Vaughan narrowed his eyes mistrustfully, but he motioned Edward to continue with a wave of his hand.

'Perhaps you thought I was flattering you when I told you I had admired your monograph on Greek gold, but I did admire it. So much so that, now Catherine and I have investigated the matter, I can only conclude that you were supplied with this wonderful Dionysos by someone who might act as if he had only the vaguest idea of the rules and disciplines of archaeology. Mr Deals gave it to you, didn't he? Quite some time before Susannah's arrival. And he claimed it had come from the site you were exploring with the University of Pennsylvania Museum. The story you told me was, in fact, the one he told you. He said he had gone there and had found it by accident. Whether you believed it was true, I am not sure, though I think you may have convinced yourself in the end. Maybe one day you think one thing, the next day, another. I am sure of this, though: you must have taken him to task for having removed it in such an unscientific way, for, of course, with no proof you never *will* know for sure where it came from.

'Once it had been dug up, moreover – and I'm sure Mr Deals provided enough bogus evidence to persuade you – it must have been difficult to know what to do with the Head. Your reputation would have been at stake if it had been thought you had taken a valuable artefact from its context, and you knew that Deals would get into trouble if it was admitted that he had done it. He had defiled the evidence that would have added real value to the Head, no matter who had found it, evidence which would have proven the site to be of greater antiquity than was supposed. In fact, under Greek law, it is probable that he would have been prosecuted, because it would have been hard to persuade anyone that he hadn't intended to sell it on the black market. What is more, the scandal might have implicated you. So you were in a quandary. You couldn't catalogue it, but you couldn't take credit for the find unless you did. Worst of all, bringing Mr Deals to the attention of the police would not have been in anyone's interest – and for a variety of reasons. Perhaps you even tried to get him to put it back where he said he had found it.'

Somehow, even Catherine had not expected Father Edward to be such a formidable adversary, but Deals and the old man were taken completely off guard. It was as if a large bird of prey had parted the fetid air in the kitchen. The owlish priest with talons swooping at mice.

Perhaps aware of his advantage of surprise, he softened his tone. 'Cruel as it seems to expose this now,' he said to Vaughan, 'I am quite sure that the end of this delusion can only be to your benefit. Your reputation rests on sound scholarship, sounder perhaps for the fact that you are a self-confessed amateur. The Head never was found at the site. I think Mr Deals here has access to a great deal of money and he bought it, didn't he, perhaps as a little "joke", and probably from some crooked dealer, whose speciality is antiquities of doubtful provenance. I imagine Mr Deals gave it to you nicely caked with earth, "distressed" to make you believe that you were on the way to a major discovery.'

No one said anything. The two men were completely motionless.

'The reason Mr Deals got rid of the Head the night Susannah died,' Edward continued, 'was primarily that her murder gave him the oppor-tunity to do so. Once the police started to investigate, the truth about the Head would have come to light, and he had meant it to be a very private joke indeed between the two of you. Possibly you felt that in many ways you would have been better off without him. Susannah evidently thought so. At least, I know she wanted you to move to England because she told me she did. Once you had the mysterious artefact within your grasp, however, Mr Deals was in no danger that your domestic arrangements would be disrupted. In your heart of hearts, you knew its provenance was false, but you were tempted beyond endurance by the hope that you had made yet another major discovery through Phil Deals.'

'Good grief! Shades of Father Brown!' said Deals. 'This is unreal.'

Later, Catherine identified this as the moment when she really became afraid. Between the three men there was the force and power of the hunt. Edward's eyes rested on Vaughan as if he were calling him out of some terrible black cave.

'When Susannah came to stay,' he continued, 'it took her a while, but, saint or not, she was most certainly not stupid. She finally arrived at the truth, and she tried to tell you. You did not want to hear it; you would not hear it. Doubtless, she told you to get Deals to confess. I imagine this conversation was consequent on your showing her the Head the night she died.'

Vaughan looked from Phil to Edward, leaned forward as if to say something, but evidently thought better of it.

'In fact,' Edward went on, 'I believe it was for this reason that you had taken the Head out of the safe that night. You were trying to make her see its beauty, but Susannah could not see that, could she? She could only see it in absolute terms for the harm it was doing. Is this what you can't forgive her? I imagine it is, and I can understand just what you felt, believe me. However, Susannah happened to be right, as so often. What had started as an apparently innocuous game between you and Deals was turning into a very dangerous situation and she advised you of this in her inimitable, uncompromising way.

'In the middle of the discussion, however, you and she were inter- rupted by a noise; she went to find out what it was; she saw that it was one of the poor whom she fed in the city; he seemed to have wandered up the hill after her; and so, not wanting to turn away anyone who was hungry, she went to get him some food. It is perhaps because she was distracted by your quarrel that she failed to grasp the man's highly unstable state of mind. From what Catherine and I have just learned, he tried to rape her. She resisted him, possibly dragging herself into the hall to get to the telephone, or even to warn you. Whatever happened, I believe that she did not have the opportunity to scream, for when she tried he cut her throat to silence her. In his frenzy, he butchered her; then, aghast at what he had done, he ran away.

'Now, it is my conjecture that you probably had no idea what had happened. I imagine you thought there were actual burglars, and it never crossed your mind that she had been killed until you saw her body at the bottom of the stairs.'

'Go on,' said the old man. His voice was barely audible.

'What you made of what you saw, however, interests me greatly. It is my intuition that, in that one moment of horror, you saw . . . not so much Susannah's death, but a sacrifice. For your entire professional life you have looked for evidence of this god's cult. In some ineffable way, you thought the violent dismemberment of Susannah had been actuated by Dionysos. Like Pentheus in *The Bacchae* she was an "unbeliever" who had meddled too far in the secrets of the god. And so appalled were you by this inescap- able metaphoric circumstance that you agreed to the sacrifice of the Head –

in reparation and because Deals had subtly convinced you that it was your fault, *its* fault, that she died. He may even have convinced you that he had chased the thief and murderer away. Whatever he said, I am sure you had lots of permutations to choose from, stories that contradicted each other on small points, just to keep you guessing.

'God alone knows what you went through that night, but I believe that you lied to cover Deals's tracks, thinking in your understandable confusion that the murder investigation might reveal all sorts of unwelcome truths.

'One awful irony was this, however, and I am not sure how Mr Deals managed to live with it: you could not bear the thought that the Head would be lost altogether, and so you insisted that it be known that it had been in your possession. You would not allow Deals to make it vanish from the face of the earth. This was because you refused to believe what Susannah had told you and you wanted the site further explored. Mr Deals's joke had been altogether too convincing, and this must have become very inconvenient for him over the years. That night, though, everything was decided in the unconscionable time it took the police to come, and, once it had been, there was no going back. Besides, you did not really want to. In fact, the murder probably reinforced the idea of Dionysos's savage power. You were being led, you felt, to his greatest sanctuary, almost by the trail of your daughter's blood. Horrible as it was to you, her death, in some respects, justified the spiritual reality of your god.'

The silence that followed this disquisition was profound. Catherine did not dare move. The unveiling had been so awful, so clearly accurate, that it even made her feel as if she herself had been caught out in a lie, as if she, poor sinner, had reached the Judgement Throne where every casual word she had spoken had been recorded, where every fib, each backbiting remark, was being weighed before her eyes against the flimsy stuff of her virtues.

Edward leaned towards the old man and held out his hand in an odd gesture of reprieve. 'What you must realize now is that you were not in any way responsible for her death.'

He turned to Phil, almost pleading, Catherine thought. 'And of course you weren't either, Mr Deals. You say that you loved her. I am sure you did love her, but I know there are good reasons why you did not want to move to England and be under her thumb.'

Phil sighed and cast his eyes to heaven, like an angry, disturbed child. He was almost pitiful in his hostility. 'Gee! So *Dionysos* did it after all! I knew it!'

There was an odd and dangerous little silence.

'Do you think so?' Edward asked, retracting slightly. 'I thought so myself for a while – not that Dionysos actually killed her, but that she had her life taken from her because of some large inadequacy. It may make it easier for us all to think that about her, but I'm afraid it isn't true.

'Neither God nor Dionysos murdered Susannah. He, or whatever He stands for in your minds, could not have exacted such vengeance. What, after all, is Dionysos? An archetype? I have heard it said by some that he was in some respects an archaic prototype of Christ. Whatever he is, he is the god above all who represents self-abandonment. I have argued long and hard with myself before I became convinced of it, but Susannah both could and did abandon herself . . . to God. In fact, because of this, not despite it, she was never sacrificed. Susannah's body and spirit were one in a curious way. She neither courted the disaster, nor avoided it. She had given herself, quite simply, and well in advance of her murder – rather like Martin Luther King or Gandhi, don't you know? not really counting the cost.

'It has taken me a long time to accept this, but I feel certain now that she was incapable of being satisfied with anything less than God. It is terrifying, isn't it? But in her case it was true, and she died preserving something that represented integrity to her, her virginity. Not everybody's idea of it, but *hers*. If you think she haunts this house, maybe it is because you sense her grief that you have made her death into a vehicle for mistrust and self-loathing. I know this because I knew her. And there I must rest my case.'

'You will absolve me, then?' said the old man after a long silence. He looked up into Edward's eyes like a trusting child.

'Of course!' said Edward tenderly.

'What for? Chickening out?' Phil's voice cut the air. It was indeed, as Catherine saw it later, like a sudden wind bearing winter or the smell of death. He looked at Vaughan with contempt, Rumpelstiltskin unmasked and in a cruel rage, splitting himself in half with fury.

'And will you absolve me of this too?' Vaughan asked.

Before anyone knew what was happening, the gun exploded. James Vaughan had taken his revolver from under the dirty rug in which he had been wrapped and had shot Phil Deals through the heart.

'Susannah kissed me,' Vaughan said quite simply to their astonishment. 'Before she went downstairs to let the murderer in, she kissed me and I pushed her away. She clung to me and begged me to give the Head

218

back. She told me she loved me. She had never told me that before, and I pushed her away.

'But,' he said, indicating the body of Deals on the floor, 'I was never a coward. You see, I'm a Sandhurst man.'

XIX

IT WAS a crisp November day, almost perfect weather for a funeral, or so Catherine Phocas thought as she slipped away from the little knot of mourners. The wintry sun had burnt off all but a decent shroud of English mist, which clung to the autumn trees, veiling the final red and umber of the leaves in white.

It was remarkable to her that James Vaughan had not been cremated, much less buried according to the Latin rite, but in the end it appeared that he had left instructions for the funeral, the ripeness of long association having persuaded him, she supposed. A surprising number of family had come and two of his ancient colleagues. They stood in ruminative attitudes after the first and formal clod had hit the coffin. Catherine imagined none of them had attended the funeral of a murderer before, and perhaps this was why they studied the newly dug grave a little self-consciously. The only people who might have grieved for her uncle were dead, one significantly by his hand. Oddly enough, however, she had the sense that he was generally missed, the relic of a communal past and, until lately, a survivor. Heaven alone knew how he had weathered the shooting of Phil Deals, but he had quite simply risen above it.

Theo had already stolen away to the car and was quietly revving it at the cemetery gates. Wherever they were going, he always planned a full-scale tactical battle with the traffic, and although caterers, she hoped, were busy back at the Bayswater flat, he did not like leaving things to chance. Some things never changed. She sighed. It had been her idea to provide a proper lunch. Somehow it seemed to make up for the mean funeral Theresa had given her mother, a funeral Theo had not attended. And, after all, some of the mourners had come a very long way, most strikingly Geoff Deals, Phil's brother, and his wife Sandra.

'Are you all right, Cat?' Theo asked as she slid into the car beside him. He gave her hand a worried little pat.

'Me? Oh, yes. I'm only fussing. I keep thinking it is we who should be looking after Father Edward.' She glanced at the chill green lawn beyond and a troupe of mourners as they moved slowly in the distance down the hill towards waiting limousines. Was that their funeral or someone else's?

'Well, Xenia made it hard for him to refuse. He'll be all right. She has rather a crush on him.' Theo laughed and nosed the Saab forward; coming to the Chiswick roundabout, he lunged into the hippodrome situation he had predicted.

'Xenia's *driving* . . .'

'Don't!' He smiled and shook his head. 'They'll be all right,' he added, 'maybe through the power of prayer.'

'Well, at least Marina and Paul are dealing with the Dealses. What do you make of them, Theo? I still can't get over it.'

Now on track, he shot up the A4 past the lumbering traffic, Ben Hur. Over the past eighteen months, they had cautiously got back together, taking sips at a time rather than whole gulps of each other, but now it seemed a different marriage. It was as if the old one, too rigid and fragile to survive, had been put out for collection by the dustmen. If the new model was not exactly rapturous, it was serene. Now and then, there passed between them flashes of understanding which seemed to illuminate the whole with a painful kind of happiness.

'I suppose,' he said, 'they have the honesty to be grateful to your uncle.'

'For shooting Phil?' She had met the sober, well-mannered Geoff in Thessaloniki, where he had come in order to arrange the shipment of his brother's corpse back to America. Curiously, Phil had left minute directions in his will about the disposal of his body. A poem by Ferlinghetti was to be read and his ashes were to be scattered over the grass tennis courts at his childhood home – to give nutrients to the soil. It had been very embarrassing. At that time, her uncle had been in a Greek gaol, and Theo had arrived, a welcome Fortinbras, who had restored a semblance of order to the Jacobean conditions at hand.

Even now, a small reminder of this time left Catherine enervated. No blame had attached to her. The brother had bent over backwards to be nice. All the same, she could not erase the memory of Phil being shot dead point-blank two yards away from her. Apart from her feeling she could have somehow prevented it, the murder seemed grubby *News of the World* stuff. They had all been plastered over the papers for a while. The truth was that it rattled Catherine to have to cope with Geoff and his wife this day, and Theo knew it.

The American's grand gesture of forgiving Uncle James by coming to his funeral did seem a lot to impose on Edward too. He had taken the murder very hard, blaming himself for not foreseeing it. His guilt was 'the arrogance of *not* being Father Brown', he said, though no one else agreed with him. The shocking episode had left him changed, sadder.

Every time Catherine saw him, he seemed to become meeker, more spare. He had retired now and lived in a cottage on the Norfolk coast. It always reminded Catherine of a seashell. In the right light, the water made clear, bright patterns on the white sitting-room walls. There was something about him too which seemed to be attentive to a private sense of sound, as if he were living on an ocean and heard a larger rhythmic ebb and flow than a mere inlet from the North Sea could muster. Still, he had been willing to say the Requiem Mass, at her uncle's somewhat odd last request, and had seemed to think it splendid of the Dealses to attend the funeral.

'Oh, the shooting was awful,' Theo said, 'but I do think everyone sees now what your uncle was up against in Phil.' The Greek trial had brought out a wealth of mitigating circumstances, making a strong argument for diminished responsibility. In the end, it had been Theo who had managed to get Vaughan extradited, his sentence commuted. He had spent the last year of his life in a pleasant and needlessly secure hospital where Catherine had dutifully visited him.

She did not like to remember the trial, where she had been a key witness. 'I didn't think the new Lord Aubin – "Hugh", I expect we should call him – would come,' she said, changing the subject. 'Sad he didn't make it to Mummy's funeral, because she did so value the connection. I'm sure you didn't recognize him. He was a page at our awful wedding and only four when you last saw him.'

'Oh, I knew who he was, all right! And so did Mrs Deals. I get the impression that she "values the connection" too. She edged nearer and nearer to him at the graveside. Maybe he will ask them to stay and make their trip to England worthwhile.'

'Did you see the way she narrowed her eyes at Marina?' Out of sheer hysteria over the impending lunch, Catherine was beginning to enjoy creating an enemy out of Sandra Deals. 'Marina used to go to dances with Geoff in New York.' Maybe Marina did look a little too dashing in charcoal grey; she had tackled the Dealses with outstanding charm the moment they had walked into the church. Paul, himself the picture of probity, had taken their left flank.

'I did not tell you that you look very nice today, Catherine,' Theo said awkwardly.

It unnerved but touched her that these days he made a point of paying her little compliments, making himself remember to do so. 'Thank you,' she said and glanced at her new felt hat in the driving mirror. It was smart, she had to admit, and subdued enough, she hoped. The cortège was nowhere to be seen behind them. Theo had gained the Hammersmith flyover and they were sure to hit a bottleneck on Talgarth Road. He had been right about the traffic, she told him.

Quite suddenly, a memory of her uncle's house came back to her, his bijou drawing room perched atop a dreadful squalor they had discovered while everything was being sorted out. Amazingly, they had found a buyer for 'The House of Death', as one paper had called it . . . some ghoul, she thought, or a hardened rationalist. She had crated up the good furniture, the paintings. It had taken her days to sort out her uncle's books and papers, and more days still to convince him that the police were not interested in the contents of his safe. That had seemed the saddest thing of all: Deals had fed him with a constant drip of lies about the Church of the Transfiguration and the site near it. From this 'evidence' her enfeebled uncle had plotted a literally mythical sanctuary of Dionysos on sheet after sheet of graph paper. What he had so fiercely hoarded against Susannah's searching gaze had been a fiction.

In fact, if Catherine were honest about it, she had become cautiously fond of her uncle. On the whole, however, she had managed to accept him as a monster, a freak who was slightly puzzled at the real world where love and affection changed hands. She had found his family stories interesting. Once back in England, his health had improved; he had even gained a little weight. Catherine had taken to bringing him chocolate, of which he was very fond. In fact, he had eaten voraciously, almost as if he had been starved.

About Phil Deals, he had been completely reticent. He had pleaded guilty to the shooting and expected no quarter from anyone. Things emerged, however, which made Catherine wonder at the sheer scale of Deals's bizarre maltreatment of her uncle.

Above all, it had upset her when she discovered that Phil had withheld letters to her uncle from her mother. In fact, Lady Simon, perhaps responding to pressure from Susannah, had sought a reconciliation with her brother. It had given Catherine a jolt to read her mother's apologies, especially for making moral judgements. To her surprise, she discovered that Lady Simon had been extremely fond of Nancy Schuyler; it had been sad, but not as astonishing, to learn that Susannah's mother had killed herself after discovering her husband in bed with an adolescent boy. Lady Simon had made a touching reminder of their childhood days together, and finally a little stab at understanding. Even given no reply to this ameliorating letter, Catherine's mother had pressed on, writing again to ask about her brother's health. Again, this might have been at the instigation of Susannah. Worst of all, however, was the letter she had written directly after Susannah's death. Although it had been laced with the silly little pieties which had always characterized Lady Simon, it still conveyed genuine feeling.

Catherine supposed she would never know if her uncle had eventually read the letters she had bundled up for him, because he never talked directly about them, but in the end she thought he probably had. In the few months before he died, he had become voluble first about 'Isabelle', then about 'darling Isabelle', snatching memories of her almost from the air. 'Isabelle' had loved her Shetland pony; 'Isabelle' had hated their German governess. And Catherine had privately sucked these stories dry of the small nourishment they contained.

By the time Edward arrived at the Phocases' Bayswater flat, the other guests had assembled and the party, as it were, was in full swing. He supposed it was not too unkind to think that Xenia, for all her glamour as a budding *mezzo*, was the worst driver he had ever had the good fortune to survive. She had taken a wrong turning at the cemetery and as a result they suffered a wild and perilous tour of west London in her sporty little MG. He was fond of her, though, and happy to hear her news. She was in love. Strapped into the bucket seat, he been subjected to a litany of her boy-friend's almost infinite virtues. Underlying everything, he felt, the reconciliation of Theo and Catherine had done her good. Indeed, she had said so. She was living in Fulham now, and when they arrived in Bayswater she made a flourished entrance into her parents' flat, an independent woman, a woman of the world.

Edward did not like even the most sedate kind of party and, although he would have done much for Catherine's sake, he plotted his escape route on arrival. He took a glass of wine from a sort of butler, and hoped there wasn't going to be a long sit-down lunch. Perhaps it had already begun. Xenia had deserted him and the guests were all crowded at the far end of the well-appointed drawing room. Through the misty refraction on his spectacles, he searched for Catherine.

He was sure she would be pleased about the news he had received about Susannah's Cause, and he had saved it up to tell her; the Bishop had written to him informing him that it was to be put forward after all. The last concern, Susannah's possible collusion with a thief, was cleared up now all the evidence had been assembled.

Her letters to Lady Simon from Thessaloniki had shown growing alarm about her father, and Edward could see why the old lady had sup-pressed them, for they had put her brother in a compromising light. Just before Susannah died, she wrote that she would go to any length 'to get rid of' the Head of Dionysos, which she believed to be stolen property, but the sad outcome of Edward's investigations had shown that his summary of the situation was right on all counts that mattered.

When the written statement of the old market-stall holder in Thessaloniki had arrived in Susannah's favour, the Bishop had been thrilled. Apart from this, there had been a new 'miracle'. Shortly before he died, James Vaughan (the hardened sinner) had been shriven. If that was not enough, he had written a full account to the Bishop of his daughter's extraordinary goodness to him, especially during the last years of her life. She had tried, he said, to save him from his folly and from the 'wretch' who had made his life miserable. Edward had misgivings about contrition that took this form, but it seemed tendentious to argue with it.

He knew the Bishop and rather liked him, but he had squirmed when congratulated on the exemplary guidance he had given Susannah, advice which she had recorded in her diaries. Not only had he dreaded the idea of strangers combing through her journals, it drained him to think she had boiled their conversations down to a collection of pious aphorisms.

Edward had been relieved to find that Catherine's sister, the Mother Prioress, was not at Vaughan's funeral. He had spoken to her on his return from Greece, and she too had congratulated him from behind her impenetrable bars. He had left, however, with the strong intuition that he was going to be kept in the dark about the original text of Susannah's journals. They were preparing her arduous history for presentation at Court, as if she were a débutante, and it was not inconceivable to him that the Mother Prioress had already applied a blue pencil to the writings, lopping off awkward bits which did not conform precisely to the image she might wish to create. Of course, he was sure she would never conceal anything terrible; nevertheless he imagined that anything too human might go. Edward was only glad he did not have to live to see the day when, glossed and prinked, her shortcomings airbrushed from her portrait, he would have to venerate the pious extraction of Susannah's life, a life, he now realized, she had lived truthfully. Oh well, he expected her relations would be pleased, and so, of course, was he in his own way. Saint Susannah.

With his glass of white wine firmly clutched, he peered down the long drawing room where the rest of the company were clustered. As he approached, he realized they were intent upon a small crate that lay upon the table. In the midst of the blurred circle of friends and relations, most of whom he did not recognize, stood Geoffrey Deals, attended by his wife, who stood, all lipstick and button earrings, like Nancy Reagan at the President's elbow.

Xenia turned and saw him coming. 'Father Edward!' she cried. 'Can you imagine! The Head of Dionysos has been found.'

'I'm sorry?'

'Oh, Edward!' Catherine sobbed, from what emotion he could not tell. She grasped his elbow and led him into the circle. He peered at Geoffrey Deals.

Not without his brother's sense of drama, the tall, solemn American raised his hand for silence. He was middle-aged, but he still had the dazzling good looks of a well-preserved movie star. This had explained something to Edward when he met Geoff in Thessaloniki. There could have been no measuring up to that rugged brow, that splendid physique, the careless ooze of an unassuming animal confidence in Phil's younger brother.

'Father Knight . . . Good to see you again,' Geoff said in a rich, cultivated baritone. His funeral clothes exuded an American equivalent of Savile Row. This was the man who Phil was not. 'You're just in time for the unveiling.'

Like a magician's assistant, Sandra Deals stepped forward. Her black suit was so smart it resembled a polished shell. 'It has taken Geoff and me nearly fifteen years,' she said in an equally cultivated alto, 'but we finally tracked it down. We wanted you to see it before we returned it to the Greek government.' Slowly, she eased the lid from the slatted box; then her hands dived through the protective nest of wood shavings and she carefully removed it, elevating it for everyone to see.

It had not been, Catherine later thought, too theatrical a gesture for the occasion, nor for the beauty of the piece itself. The Head was nearly life-sized, of almost flawless marble except for a faint chip from the lower lip of the discreetly smiling god. Its lucidly carved hair streamed back on to its shoulders, and just below the elegant locks it was possible to see the verifying iconic insignia: the faint outline of a leopard's pad and claws. But for that, it might have been a goddess; the beardless marble cheek almost seemed to blush. Theo gave a gasp, and as for the two venerable archaeologists, old colleagues of James Vaughan, they came to life as one, muttering and questioning . . . awed.

Geoffrey Deals held up his hand again. 'Please, please. Let me explain.' But he already had the complete attention of his audience. 'What you see before you is indeed remarkable. It is, as James Vaughan always said it was, a marble from the early fifth century BC, but, as for its provenance, we really cannot tell.'

He cleared his throat. 'I know it is hard to understand why I have come across the Atlantic to attend the funeral of the man who shot my brother, but I hope you will see why I want to say a few words on behalf of James Vaughan.' As no one did see why, the group shuffled back and fanned out slightly, as though anxious to give him room for explanation.

'I'm afraid it is no secret that my brother Phil was a skeleton in our closet,' he continued. 'His death brought out some embarrassing disclosures, but they were nothing new to us. By the time Phil came to live in Greece, he had exhausted the wits of the family . . . my parents and my sisters had disowned him. Doctors, clinics, we tried them all on Phil. Switzerland! Nothing seemed to work. When finally he settled down as James Vaughan's companion, we all breathed a sigh of relief. Here at last was a man of character and distinction who cared for Phil and didn't mind keeping an eye on him. I don't know whether any of you know this, but James really did try to help him – and Phil loved it for a time. The problem came, of course, when James needed help himself. I am afraid that Phil simply could not cope with that. In an odd way, though, I think the bust of Dionysos here was a misguided gift of gratitude.'

Catherine gazed at the Head, which, mounted on a plinth, stood on her coffee table. It had been cleaned and was as eerily white as bone. 'Where did you find it?'

Geoffrey Deals, who clearly had a funeral oration in mind, seemed taken aback at the interruption. 'I was coming to that,' he said.

'You'll never guess . . . at a *major* auction house.' His wife was evidently pleased to get a word in edgeways.

'All right, you tell them, Sandra,' Geoff said with the practised tolerance of a man who has had to learn not to put down women.

She shot him a quick, meaningful glance. 'We happened to be in Salonika the night Susannah Vaughan died. Phil was bragging at the top of his voice about this head, which he claimed he found in a ditch—'

'You see,' Geoff interrupted, 'he was very proud of being a "trainee archaeologist". Although I am not sure James Vaughan did try to teach him, it is how Phil thought of himself, and so it didn't really matter.'

'Well, it did in a way, Geoff,' Sandra said.

'OK, it did.'

'What I am trying to say is,' she continued, 'Phil was on an allowance and Geoff administered his trust. That night, he told us he was broke. Phil never needed to be broke.'

'You mean you can prove he really had *bought* the Head?' Edward asked softly.

'There is no way of being sure, but I know now that he sold it,' Geoff said, regaining at last the dramatic centre of the group. 'You'll remember there was a lot of stuff in the press after Susie's death about a possible stolen artefact?'

'Phil told us he had dumped the Head in the sea the night she died,' said Catherine.

'Phil said one thing and then he said another,' Sandra replied shortly. 'It didn't take us very long to realize that he'd been up to something . . .'

' . . . and so we started the long series of inquiries that led to—'

'—finding it!' She was triumphant.

'I think the family and friends of James Vaughan have the right to know because it played a great part in their lives together. Who knows if it led to the shooting? Now, I don't want to be disloyal to Phil's memory, but he did enjoy—'

'Torture!' said his wife succinctly. There was an embarrassed silence.

Geoff coughed into his hand. 'Thank you, Sandra, I think the word is a little extreme, but he did like to wind people up, there was no getting away from it.' Perhaps sensing the social horror of his audience, he continued in a lighter vein. 'It seems that Phil found a dealer for the Head, maybe the very one he had bought it from, although there is no proof. Antiquities of this kind are regularly "laundered" through Geneva, and we think it went there, where the dealer sat on it until it was safe to sell. My agent bought it here in London a few weeks ago. Phil was dead, James was in a home . . . Well . . . who would care any more?'

'Are you sure it's the same one?' Theo asked, scrutinizing it.

'It is identical with the slides they found at the time of Susannah's death. I took the precaution of getting copies made. Now, I'm convinced that the vendor was in on it from the beginning, but it's hard to prove.'

'He isn't a Russian, is he, Geoff?' Marina asked this from the somewhat jealous shelter of Paul's arm.

'Why, yes!'

'Gregory Lipitsin?'

The Dealses were collectively astonished. 'How in the world did you know that?'

She leaned forward as if she were about to lay her hand on the beautiful marble, her lips curled in a smile as enigmatic as the god's. 'It's a long story,' she said, 'but it was an educated guess.'

'Poor Uncle James. He died before he saw it again, then?' Somehow Catherine couldn't bear it. 'Did you let him know you had found it?'

'We thought it best not to,' Geoff Deals said primly. 'The shock might have killed him.'

'At ninety, he was going to die anyway,' Catherine whispered, 'and now he's dead.' Then, looking into the blank eyes of the ghostly, telluric deity, she turned away. 'Lunch!' she said.

They trooped after Theo into the dining room where the baked meats awaited them, Marina and Paul Mason, Xenia, Charles and Rosamund Simon, who had unexpectedly made an appearance, the Dealses, the new Lord Aubin, and the excited brace of elderly, hungry and slightly drunk archaeologists who set upon the Dealses like terriers.

But Edward lingered, his dim eyes focused on the spectral marble. Who had carved such a thing? Each stroke of the chisel seemed to have been made as an act of worship. The beautiful object emerged into the Classical era almost shyly. Delicate fronds of hair seemed to escape the rigours of an archaic style, and the modelling of the jaw gave the piece a tentative sensuality. It was like looking down a long tunnel into some profound Arcadian mystery just to see it. The cracked lower lip pouted slightly as if it had been stung or kissed, but in the brow there was an almost unseemly power, and for a moment the blank eyes assumed a leonine ferocity, as if, animated, the god could leave the stone and tear him to pieces.

With one part of him, Edward longed to run his fingers over the Head, letting its curious ambiguities travel into him like long-forgotten vibrations of music danced at ancient festivals. With another part of him, he had a sudden, violent will to smash it. This shocked him and he withdrew. A whole Renaissance stood between him and such iconoclasm, a whole gentleness of spirit which was too much his own to traduce. Beautiful as the Head was, it seemed to hold in its thoughts the fearful polarities of nature: life, death; male and female; Olympus and the dark underworld where the primitive consciousness had been free to voyage without reference to Christian eschatology. Like Shiva, it held within its temples the potential for creation and destruction. What it built up in joy, it tore down in madness; what it gave in wine, it took away in drunkenness.

For a moment, he became absorbed in a glimpse of Susannah's struggle against the Head, its terrors . . . no, her terror at her own ambiguity, perhaps. A painful but oddly peaceful memory came to him of Susannah curled over herself in an almost foetal ball, tearing away at her wretchedness, her faults both true and imagined, and he wondered how

229

deeply her father might have undermined her with his Dionysiac obsession, especially if he misunderstood what the true, oracular power of the Head had been. Edward glanced again at its remote, curved smile. The frightful test it set was surely to discriminate between ecstasy and ecstasy. What had Phil Deals called Susannah? 'A sex-starved weirdo', that was it.

Edward felt a gentle touch on his shoulder and gave a start, but it was only Catherine.

'We hadn't seen it, had we?' she said.

He shook his head.

'Poor Uncle James . . .'

'They're putting forward Susannah's Cause after all. I meant to tell you,' he said.

'Then she triumphed.'

'To her credit, I'm not so sure she would have thought that way. Your uncle lost everything.'

'That is because he didn't see!' Catherine said passionately, herself a little triumphant. 'He didn't know how to look.'

'What do you mean?'

'His eye never went beyond beauty, whereas she . . .'

Catherine floundered.

'I wonder if she possessed the essence of the very thing he wanted,' Edward said at last.

'No, she at last embodied it,' Catherine said. 'And he never knew.'